THE
CUBAN GAMBIT

BOOK 3 OF THE ONE HUNDRED YEARS OF WAR SERIES

JAY PERIN

Publisher's Cataloging-In-Publication Data
(Prepared by The Donohue Group, Inc.)

Names: Perin, Jay, author.
Title: The Cuban gambit / Jay Perin.
Description: [Middletown, Delaware] : East River Books, [2022] | Series: One hundred years of war series ; book 3
Identifiers: ISBN 9781736468050 (paperback) | ISBN 9781736468043 (ebook)
Subjects: LCSH: Presidents--United States--History--20th century--Fiction. | United States--Politics and government--1945-1989--Fiction. | Petroleum industry and trade--History--20th century--Fiction. | Nineteen eighties--Fiction. | Man-woman relationships--Fiction. | Conspiracies--Fiction. | LCGFT: Political fiction. | Thrillers (Fiction)
Classification: LCC PS3616.E7443 C83 2022 (print) | LCC PS3616.E7443 (ebook) | DDC 813/.6--dc23

Editors:
Chase Nottingham
Elizabeth Roderick http://talesfrompurgatory.com/

Cover: www.ebookorprint.com
Maps and illustrations: Murat Bayazit
Video (book trailer): Nauman Gandhi
Special mention: Marcus Jordan https://www.marcusjordanart.com/

www.EastRiverBooks.com

To the One They Called God;
To the Best of Men;
To That Goddess of Knowledge;
To the Chronicler.

Table of Contents

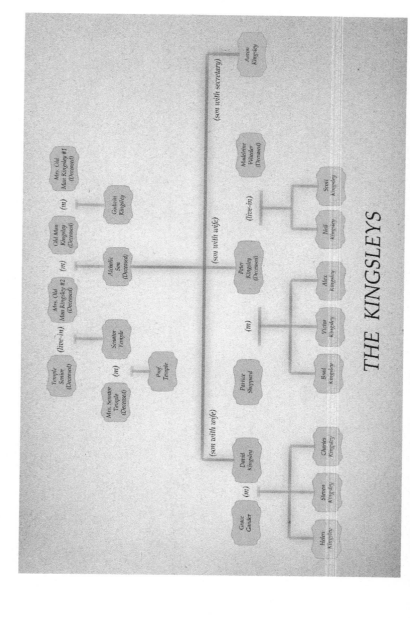

THE KINGSLEYS

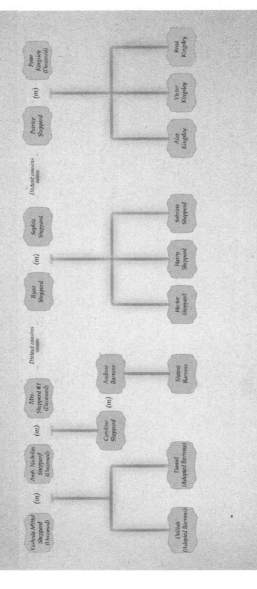

THE SHEPPARDS

Yoshuda Miittal Sheppard (Deceased) (m) Amb. Nicholas Sheppard (Deceased) (m) Mrs. Sheppard #1 (Deceased)

Delilah (Adopted Barrons) — Daniel (Adopted Barrons)

Caroline Sheppard (m) Andrew Barrons

Shawn Barrons

Distant cousins

Ryan Sheppard (m) Sophia Sheppard

Hector Sheppard — Harry Sheppard — Sabrina Sheppard

Distant cousins

Patrice Sheppard (m) Peter Kingsley (Deceased)

Alex Kingsley — Victor Kingsley — Brad Kingsley

Part I

Chapter 1

April 1986

The White House Situation Room

Only a few bulbs were lit, leaving part of the conference table in shadows. Waving the defense secretary—a retired four-star general—back to his chair, President Temple strode over, followed by the chief of staff.

"Did we get him?" asked Temple, already knowing the answer. If Gaddafi, the Libyan dictator, had been killed, the message would have reached the White House long before the messenger.

"Sorry, sir," the general said. "Malta appears to have warned him."

Unperturbed, Temple nodded and took his seat. Taking Gaddafi's life was not the objective of the operation, after all.

Three senior military officers marched in through the door, their footsteps muffled by the deep carpet. Unlike the others in the room who were dressed casually in sweats and tees, the new arrivals were in service uniforms. Manacled to the wrist of the one in the middle was a titanium case, which he laid in front of the president. One of his mates uncuffed him, and the other unlocked the case to take a videotape out.

"Thank you, gentlemen," said the general.

There were a few more hours until dawn. Temple sipped sweet, creamy coffee and settled back in his chair to watch F-111 bombers dropping laser-guided devices on the Tripoli airfield, blowing apart the planes on the tarmac. Grainy images from the gun cameras flickered on the screen. Deadly flashes lit up dark-blue sky, and deafening sound waves blasted through the air, leaving the buildings in the vicinity shaking. Libyan gunmen scrambled to respond with surface-to-air missiles, but most of their shots went wildly off the mark.

The general reported, "One bomber has not made it back to the base. And we won't get another chance at taking out Gaddafi anytime soon. Once the news breaks, the press will be all over it. There will be questions on whether the killing of two American tourists by Gaddafi's men was worth all the casualties from the bombing."

The chief of staff argued, "Getting Gaddafi would have been the icing on the cake, but we didn't go there to kill him. Our only purpose was to punish him for the mistake of taking *American* lives. The *American* president has that responsibility. Also, the deaths of those two tourists were hardly the sole reason. The Gaddafi government has been accused of many crimes."

There was another objective to the mission, one neither the general nor the chief knew, a secret Temple never jotted down in his journal. By the time he started in the Oval Office at the age of seventy-four, he'd already collected many such secrets. In only a few months, he'd complete his two terms as president, leaving the White House as an eighty-two-year-old man with even more stories which could never be revealed to another person. They'd go with him to his grave, including this last-ditch attempt at avoiding what he knew he must eventually do.

Shrugging, the general said to the chief of staff, "Unfortunately, the global media will feel no urge to inform the public about the rest of the crimes committed by Gaddafi's supporters. It's significantly more sensational to create a David and Goliath story where the evil Americans attack a smaller nation over oil."

"Set up a press conference," Temple spoke. "I want the public to hear directly from me."

The three military officers reversed procedure and left with the tape. Excusing himself to the president, the general followed them into the hallway, as did the chief of staff. The door closed, leaving silence in the situation room. Temple stood, hand in his pocket, and flipped through the papers on the table.

From the shadows in the back, a familiar voice asked, "The crew of the missing aircraft?"

Temple responded, "The pilot and the weapons officer."

"Two good men sacrificed." Harry moved to the pool of light.

The president studied his former protégé. The seventeen-year-old boy who'd jumped off a cliff to escape Gaddafi's border patrol had grown into a man, well-muscled to suit his tall stature, his dark hair now cut short. The intensity of his dark gaze remained the same. With an inward smile, Temple admitted though his own blue irises and average height hadn't changed, his hair was for a long while almost completely salt with very little pepper. Time... it decayed appearances, equations. Years ago, Petty Officer Harry Sheppard would've saluted and nodded an affirmative to Temple's plans. Now, the SEAL-turned-commodities broker looked the commander in chief in the eye and challenged his decisions.

Keeping his voice mild, the president asked, "You don't believe the bombing was for a worthy cause? Seems you have forgotten there were people in the Libyan government who worked with Sanders." The oil tycoon who arranged multiple attacks on a teenaged Harry might have been hauled off to prison months ago, but his former friends still clung to their own fiefdoms. Gaddafi, the Libyan strongman, was one such old pal.

"I've forgotten nothing," Harry said. "But if we were planning to punish Gaddafi, why inform Malta beforehand?"

Temple blinked. Harry recognized what the general didn't, what the Maltese government didn't. The leak of the plan's details came from the Oval Office. The American president allowed Gaddafi to escape. The protégé understood his mentor as well as the other way around. It was another of Temple's miscalculations in a long line of similar errors where Harry Sheppard was concerned.

In measured tones, Harry continued, "Somehow forcing the criminal who holds power in Libya to see the error of his ways would have been a meaningful endeavor. Failing that, to kill him. What was the objective of *tonight's* mission? A warning to stay clear of American interests followed by a promise to turn a blind eye to his systematic elimination of political enemies? All to keep in place a thug you believe you can control."

Go on, Harry, urged Temple. *Let's see if you manage to get to the bottom of why I called you here.* The blatant hostility in Harry's eyes didn't suggest he'd recognized the air raid on their common enemy as a peacemaking attempt. The president sighed. "Those are the words of an idealist." He waved away Harry's sudden objection. "You're familiar enough with global politics to know we can't always pick our partners."

"I agree with you to some extent. What I don't understand is the kind of game we're playing. What is your intention, Mr. President?"

"Stability, peace, prosperity. Aren't these good enough goals?"

"Do you honestly believe keeping Gaddafi in place will help the world get there?" asked Harry. "He will continue his crimes toward his own people, *and* he will eventually turn on us."

"Perhaps," admitted Temple. "Or perhaps this will buy us time to devise another plan for Libya. A better ruler."

"Better ruler?" Harry asked, a note of mockery in his tone. "Or someone you imagine you can control better?"

Like Lilah... Harry didn't say it, didn't need to say it. Sanders was gone, replaced by Lilah. The replacement possessed every quality Temple looked for in a future leader. Only, she refused to be guided by the elders who got her where she was. Harry's support let her stay in the position. Two idealists—neither yet thirty—were now more or less in charge of the oil sector. In their hands was the power to ruin entire economies. One thoughtless decision, one offhand remark, could lead to wars, to utter chaos. Temple briefly closed his eyes. He didn't dare sleep at night, pondering all the calamities which could result, knowing he set them in motion.

When Temple didn't respond, Harry continued, "You know Gaddafi will get your threat... if he doesn't do what he's told, he'll be replaced. There's a good chance he'll choose to cooperate. That would make the sacrifice of the troops' lives worthwhile to you... not to mention the casualties on the Libyan side. The American public doesn't know any of it yet, but someone will inevitably blab. The public might not condone what you did. Hence, the attempt to preempt unwanted interpretations of your motives by speaking directly to the nation. Who will call you out on it? Who will dare confront the commander in chief about the deaths of two young people who signed up to serve their country?"

"Harry, you of all people should know authority confers responsibilities on an individual, on institutions." The White House symbolized the pinnacle of might, but the real struggle for its occupant began when he accepted the mantle of command. He became a willing prisoner to the oath he swore, his entire existence chained to the weighty words. No matter how long the war, how brutal the battle, how painful the loss of life, a principled leader could not quit. "You were a Navy SEAL... decorated veteran. You're a business leader whose actions can make or break the lives of millions. You used to understand the idea of sacrifice, the cost of the blood shed on your orders. You should know the real meaning of power lies in the burden it brings."

"I didn't begin life with power, Mr. President," reminded Harry. "I had no control over things happening to me, let alone to others. The nation chose to bestow me with extraordinary training and incredible trust. The trident was an honor granted me by the American people. I needed... will always need to work to make myself worthy of it. My mission is to serve the citizens of this country and humanity at large. I will follow the same principles I swore to defend. I've made my share of mistakes, been knocked down on my backside here and there, but the navy expects me to haul myself up. I will do my duty toward my fellow man or die trying. *That* is the true meaning of power to me."

Temple contemplated his former protégé. No... whatever the overtures of peace offered, Harry would not relent. Nor would Lilah. *Pity,* the president thought. There was so much they could've done together.

It was time... there was a weapon Temple had hoped he would never have to use, a lethal chess piece he kept waiting in the wings for years. The pawn would soon find himself the most important piece of the game. He would take out Harry Sheppard.

"The navy would expect you to know this as well," Temple said, keeping his tone smooth. "From the day mankind started forming military orders, knights have been required to follow the directives of their superiors in battle. Anyone who serves in the armed forces accepts the possibility he might one day be called upon to willingly sacrifice his life. The commander in chief has the right and the obligation to order any of his men to death for the good of the nation. Remember it well, Petty Officer Sheppard."

Chapter 2

Later in the week

New York, New York

The doors of the metro train swished open, and Harry joined the crowd in a rush to get to their destinations... other men and women in suits on their way to work, noisy teenagers in oversized tees with bookbags on their shoulders, a couple of Asian women, one of them heavily pregnant. Puddles of slush dotted the platform and the stairs as commuters hurried in from the outside, carrying the unseasonal snow flurries which hit the city in the early hours of the morning. Paying little heed to any of it, Harry strode along and mulled the reason behind Temple's invitation to listen in on the Libya debriefing.

The timing was all wrong for the president to attempt another assassination. He and his stepbrother—Godwin Kingsley—were surely aware Harry and Lilah had cottoned on to their plans. The president and former justice would worry she'd blame them even if Harry died of a random flu. Lilah would retaliate by walking out of the alliance. The fledgling network would thus be destroyed, something Temple wouldn't want. It was the reason Harry could go around *sans* security for the moment, enjoying the freedom of being one of the crowd. So why—

Setting the walls and pillars of the platform vibrating, the train rumbled out before Harry was halfway up the stairs. "Excuse me," said a thickly accented female voice from behind, the annoyed tone yanking him out of his thoughts. When he halted and turned, he found one of the Asian women glaring at a *burka*-clad figure stomping her way up. "Be careful, please," the Asian lady snapped at the rude commuter and extended a protective arm across her pregnant companion. "You almost knocked my sister down."

The woman in the all-enveloping burka didn't offer apologies, but she did slow by the time she got to Harry. The lady was clearly tall and hefty. Still, *he* wouldn't have been as easy to shove aside.

At the top of the stairs, Harry stopped for a few minutes to buy coffee and a sugared donut from the vending cart, exchanging pleasantries in Arabic with the Iraqi owner who'd occupied the spot for years now. Rain and flurries splattered on Harry's hair and business suit, but he declined the use of the vendor's umbrella. The walk to work was short, and a little water wasn't going to hurt. Chattering masses continued to flow in all directions. By the time lights changed at the intersection, and buses and cars vroomed down the street, Harry was again on his way to the Gateway office in World Trade Center.

Keeping to the outer edge of the sidewalk to avoid the throng, he took a bite of the warm pastry. With the chatter and honks and rumbles all around, one shouted "Hey, mister!" shouldn't have been audible, but there was an urgency in the words which made him whirl.

A heavy form rammed into him, black cotton flying all around. Harry's unexpected one-eighty changing the trajectory of the collision, he didn't immediately lose balance as he should've. His arms flailed. The coffee cup slipped from his grasp. An unsteady step backward on the wet pavement... a second step... honks, shouts, screams. Harry careened off the sidewalk, stumbling in an awkward dance on the road. A checker cab roared down in his direction, its fender zooming larger every nanosecond. Tires screeched. Barely a foot from his torso, the cab jerked to a stop.

"What the hell?" The cabbie poked his head out of the window. "I'm gonna call the cops on you, damn fool. Drunk and disorderly in the morning!"

Heart pounding with unpleasant speed, Harry held up a conciliatory hand. "Sorry. It was an—"

"He got pushed," spat the same voice which called out the warning. The Asian woman from the train station shook her fist in the direction of the sidewalk. "Hurry, hurry, hurry... so careless... what if you got killed? Stupid person."

When Harry peered to check who she was talking about, the rude burka-clad woman from the subway was disappearing down the street. There were a few curses and exclamations from the other pedestrians, but for the most part, the world hustled on without a second glance at the near accident. The cabbie, too, didn't waste more time and drove off.

"Are you all right?" asked the pregnant sister.

"Yeah, thanks." It took Harry another half hour to thank the ladies with donuts.

When he finally walked into his office, his secretary was ready with the pile of messages she wanted him to go over right away. Work kept coming. Contracts, irate partners who needed soothing, a minister who wanted a deal on oil supply to his small island nation... lunch was takeout Chinese at his desk. Through it all, the morning's incident hovered around his mind's edges.

"Harry," called his father, tone concerned. Ryan Sheppard stood at the office door, hands tucked into his pockets. Behind him was Hector, the oldest of the Sheppard children. One glance was enough for most people to tell Ryan and Harry were father and son. Except of course for Ryan's beard and the signs of aging. Blond and blue-eyed Hector took after their mother. Sophia Sheppard used to be an integral part of the company when it was first set up, cutting down on work only over the last couple of years. "Did you run into a problem this morning?" Ryan asked. "Some fellow is waiting for you with baklava. He wants to know if you're okay after the near miss."

In the lobby, Harry thanked the Iraqi vendor in effusive Arabic for sharing his personal stash of the sweet only because Harry once mentioned it was his favorite snack. Red-faced, the vendor admitted he'd never been inside the World Trade Center despite working a block away for many years. Harry took the man around, showing him the view from every window in the place.

"*The* best donuts in the city," Harry proclaimed to his staff. Natasha, his secretary, swore she'd buy breakfast pastry from the Iraqi man's cart every day.

Finally, after escorting the unexpected guest to the elevators, Harry returned to his office, only to find his father and brother still there.

"Done?" Ryan asked wryly before his expression turned grave. Hector was in the next chair. "About what happened... I thought we'd have room to breathe now that Sanders is out of the picture."

Shutting the door, Harry shrugged. "It can't be Sanders. What's he going to do from prison?" He had no money, and none of his old friends even dared talk to him for fear of the authorities suspecting them of involvement in his criminal acts.

"True." Ryan nodded. "Nothing else going on?"

"Like what?" Harry asked, noting the studiedly casual cadence of questioning.

"We want to make sure you're not off on things we don't know about," Hector stated. "Some new shenanigans with Lilah and the Kingsleys."

Harry blinked once and took another look at his brother's face. Did Hector's drinking problem now extend to work hours? But there was no flushing, no clumsiness. "Only the same old 'shenanigans' we all agreed to," Harry said. "The business alliance." Drunk or not, Hector hadn't exactly cooperated with the plans thus far.

Ryan held up a pacifying hand. "We're simply worried about your safety."

Harry stared hard at his brother for a few more moments. "I'm fine. People don't always look where they're going is all."

It took another couple of minutes for Ryan and Hector to leave. Harry swiveled his chair and stared out through the windows at the skyscrapers looming against blue-gray sky. Hector's attitude... no, it wasn't merely the brusque manner which kept Harry thinking about the close call the rest of the afternoon.

The force of the shove... the size of the woman... a lot could be hidden by a burka, including the gender of the person.

Shaking his head, Harry told himself to stop being paranoid. Rude people who happened to be in a hurry were not exactly unusual in New York City. Nor were plus-sized women who could deliver masculine-level shoves. Accident... that was it. Not a clumsy attempt at assassination, ordered by Temple.

Chapter 3

Later the same day

Elsewhere in the World Trade Center

The privacy shades were down, blocking anyone walking by the glass door to Lilah's office from spotting her.

In the hallway, her brother-in-law—Victor Kingsley—was belting out Barry Manilow's hit, "Copacabana." A second later, the smoky baritone voice belonging to Alex—the third of the five Kingsley men—joined Victor's.

Go, go, go, Lilah mentally urged. *The night club awaits.* She needed all of them out before phoning Harry. He'd returned intact from the White House visit, and she took her first relieved breath in two days. She knew the president wasn't going to try anything just yet. Even so...

"Hey," Victor called from the hallway. A moment later, a firm knock landed on Lilah's door.

She bit back a huff and glanced at the clock. Like her, Harry had developed the habit of working late before heading to the gym. He'd still be in his office in five minutes, no family or staff around to overhear what was said on either end of the line. "Come on in," Lilah said. The sooner she talked to the Kingsley brothers, the faster she could kick them out.

The door flung open, and Victor danced his way in, swinging his blazer around on a finger. Despite his giant form, the boxer/chef/company troubleshooter moved with grace. Behind him was Alex. Whether in jeans or in business clothes as right now, the thirty-two-year-old former sniper cut a striking figure. The Kingsley combo of light-brown curls and blue irises had given him a miss. Instead, genes from his mother's side bestowed cognac eyes and dark hair. He was at least half a foot taller than Lilah's five-eight.

"You haven't changed," Alex complained, his glance taking in the reddish-black skirt suit she'd worn all day. "Sabrina's not gonna be happy if you don't show up for the party." The employees of Peter Kingsley Company were given juicy bonuses to celebrate the financial success of the last quarter. The New York staff and their significant others also got this night out at the club.

Lilah laughed. "Tell your wife *you'll* be the one working late if I don't have the numbers ready before you fly to Russia."

It took her more than five minutes to shove the two men out and shut the door. Thank God her husband was spending the evening with his grandfather. Forget the fact she didn't need him overhearing what she was about to say. The little interaction between her and his brothers could trigger—

The phone rang—her personal line. Grabbing the receiver, Lilah plonked herself into the leather chair. Before she could utter a greeting, Harry said, "Turn on CNN."

Receiver cradled on her shoulder, she took her glasses from the desk drawer and picked up the remote. Across the room from her was a row of windows, privacy screens already drawn. The television sat to the far-right corner. The program opened with the president's address to the nation on the events in Tripoli. Temple was of average height, not an imposing figure, but he was a presence when he so chose. The gravity in his eyes was reassuring to the world which had been gnawing its nails about the shelling of the Libyan capital by U.S. bombers. The image on the screen changed to damaged city streets, to destroyed buildings and burning vehicles and military patrols.

A few seconds later, Lilah murmured, "Tripoli..." The camera focused on a couple of structures which appeared intact. "I think I've been to that neighborhood." Before the deaths of her parents on their way to the Paris vacation, she traveled frequently to Libya to visit the Sheppards. Dangling a glossy black pump on her toe, she asked, "Isn't that the French embassy?"

"Yeah," Harry said, his rich, deep tones low as though his mind was drifting through his memories of the town.

Lilah said with a watery laugh, "I hardly noticed anything the last time I came... too busy daydreaming." About him—her best friend and childhood sweetheart.

Harry admitted, "So was I. Had the weekend all planned out, too."

Both were blissfully ignorant of the destiny awaiting them. Neither knew Sanders's mercenaries were plotting an abduction in retaliation for Harry's father's failure to sell his oil drilling company. They didn't realize a retired American soldier lived in the mountains of Libya, a criminal who would brutally assault a sixteen-year-old girl while her friend was away.

Lilah bit her lip hard, yanking her thoughts out of dark recollections. "Which of our plans worked?" she asked. "All this... I'll be thirty soon. So will you. Are you where you imagined you'd be by now? I thought I'd be working my way to being an appeals court judge in a few years. Instead..."

Delilah Sheppard was adopted by Andrew Barrons. Giving up her dreams of love and a legal career, she married Brad Kingsley, great-nephew to the American president. Thus, a coalition of businesses was formed, one big enough to bring down Sanders.

"Where would the world have been without those sacrifices?" Harry countered. "This alliance was our only option."

"I suppose," said Lilah, not bothering to conceal the thread of doubt in her husky voice. Almost seven years passed since Harry first told her about the scheme to dethrone Sanders. The frenetic campaign against their enemy, the constant presence of bodyguards, the media frenzy... it was over only a month ago. "Sanders *is* now under lock and key."

"Moving on," Harry said. "We're also in a better position than before *vis-à-vis* the law." The U.S. government had decided to stop prosecuting vertical integration—the same company owning A to Z of its own production process rather than relying on external partners. The proposed network would involve quite a bit of horizontal integration which *was* still illegal, so they would have to keep stock purchases low enough to stay out of trouble.

Barrons O & G would buy shares in other oil businesses all the way down the stream while the Peter Kingsley Company purchased stock in oil services outfits. The Sheppards' company—Gateway—would focus on traders. Then, Delilah Sheppard Barrons Kingsley would direct each parent company involved to sell more stock to the Peter Kingsley *Network*, again keeping the sale just low enough to avoid governmental scrutiny. The small companies within the network would also integrate vertically within it. The alliance would work hard to persuade other businesses to cooperate, but they expected little resistance. Everyone knew the network was needed.

Everyone knew the three companies in the core alliance were the best positioned to create such a network.

Harry wanted to look into renewable fuels as well... costs were prohibitive at the moment, but eventually, mankind's ingenuity would make alternative sources of power workable. Humanity needed energy to survive, and the world wasn't gonna stop using oil simply because of fear it might run out, but diversification of sources was important. Harry was talking to a couple of engineers about it. They were all hopeful renewables would lead to a cleaner environment *and* prove to be the key to the network's plans to force peace between warring groups.

Whatever the kinds of fuels the businesses concerned themselves with, the end result would be a vast alliance of such companies, integrated horizontally and vertically. A web spanning the world. It would function as a quasi-democratic setup, with complaints about management evaluated by an elected board.

"Three phases," Harry mused, "and we should be done."

Victor Kingsley would kick off phase one, negotiating with companies based in the Americas and the Arctic. Once he was done, Lilah's twin and Harry would turn their attention to Western Europe, Africa, and the Middle East. The third and final phase would be Alex's—Russia and the Soviet bloc, Asia, and Australia. Only then would they be big enough that governments around the world wouldn't dare do anything for fear of tanking the global economy. Only then could the alliance sign the charter making the network official.

"Thus, our cartel will be formed," said Lilah.

"Stop calling it a cartel," Harry chided. "The tabloids do it to make us sound like mobsters."

"Okay, what would *you* call it?"

"An extrajudicial regulatory authority intended to ensure peaceful coexistence of businesses and uninterrupted supply of energy to the world," Harry said loftily.

She laughed outright. "In other words, a cartel."

"All right, call it what you want. Are you telling me it would have been better to leave Sanders as the *de facto* emperor of the sector?"

"No, of course not," Lilah admitted, turning off the TV. "But what if Temple and Godwin's plans worked? Remember Argentina."

"I do," Harry murmured. "I can't let myself forget their faces." The faces of the tribespeople who perished in the president's attempt to eliminate the man standing in his way. The smoke, the fire, the screams... "If I'm not careful, if I don't watch myself every moment..." Harry Sheppard would become another Jared Sanders, a brutal tyrant who stopped at nothing.

"It won't happen again," said Lilah. "You won't let it. But Temple and Godwin knew how you would react to any mention of Sanders, and they played you." After the failure of the attempt, the fire was blamed on Sanders. His protests to the contrary were dismissed as attempted revenge, and the innocents involved were given incentives to stay silent. None of the rest dared blurt the truth. The day the world realized what happened, they would all go down... Temple, Godwin, Harry, the Kingsleys... "Uh-huh... do you see why I call it a cartel? A bunch of people willing to kill, maim, and rob only for the sake of the imperial throne. The president and a former supreme court justice! And Brad—"

At the abrupt stop after the mention of her husband's name, Harry asked, "Brad? What are you talking about?"

"I meant Brad is the CEO," Lilah said smoothly. "But Mr. Temple wants Godwin to run things from behind the scenes."

Unfortunately for the two old men, Harry's clout with Lilah's husband and his brothers meant her recommendations usually carried the day. "So now, you're in danger."

"Lilah?" Harry called, the concern in his voice quite clear.

"What?"

There was a pause as though he was searching for the right words. "Things going all right with you and Brad?"

"I... of course," said Lilah. Harry would know—or at least suspect—it was a lie. The snappishness in Brad's tone at meetings... his sneers... her coolness toward him wouldn't have been missed, either. It didn't mean she wanted anyone asking about it. Especially not Harry. Anyway, things *were* looking up for her on the personal front. Earlier in the year, a conversation between her and Brad somehow drifted to where they saw themselves in the future. Babies... both were ready for kids. With the obstetrician giving the all-clear, they'd already started trying. Brad would know it meant sorting out the problems in their marriage. "We're busy... so home life sometimes takes a back seat. But we're making it work."

"Glad to hear it," Harry said. A beep interrupted their conversation. "Hold on a second. Another call... it's probably Verity... I forgot about her message. Gimme a couple of minutes, and I'll call you right back. We need to go over the Russian project."

Lilah bit back a wince. "We'll talk tomorrow. I want my dinner."

"You're welcome to pop by and share leftover Chinese." The Sheppards' family business, Gateway, Incorporated, and the Peter Kingsley Company both had offices in the South Tower of the World Trade Center as did Barrons O & G, owned by Andrew Barrons, Lilah's brother-in-law. It would only take Lilah a couple of minutes to ride the elevator to Harry's office. "I'll have it heated up by the time you get here. It's diced chicken with cashews."

She said in a sing-song voice, "I have samosas waiting for me at home."

"Your cook?"

"No, I found a new Indian restaurant."

"You didn't get me any?" he complained.

She snickered. "I'll bring you some for lunch tomorrow if you promise me a chess game. I swear I'll be gentle when I beat you."

"Ha, ha," Harry grumbled. "At least I'm not a sore loser like you."

"*Sore loser?* You cheat! No one gets a royal flush every round in poker. It's a statistical impossibility!"

"See what I mean?" Harry teased. "You simply don't like admitting defeat. Sore, sore, sore."

After almost a minute of laughing on the phone, she called, "Umm... Harry?"

"Yeah?"

"*Temple's* not going to admit defeat," Lilah said.

"No," Harry agreed. "There will be another attack."

Before the Argentina episode, Temple made the mistake of simply trying to sideline Harry. This time, there would be no attempted sidelining. The president would make sure the obstacle in his way was one hundred percent dead, leaving Godwin Kingsley running the network from the shadows. The two men would not risk Harry making a comeback somehow.

"But it's not the same as before when we didn't know what he was up to," continued Harry. "Temple knows by now we figured out his game. I'm sure he's praying you don't decide to walk out of the alliance." She'd stuck around to get rid of Sanders. If she left now, there would be no way of circumventing the legal hurdles to integration on such a large scale. "You *won't* walk out because we all know the alliance is needed. But if I were to die..."

Lilah would be out in a heartbeat. No way would she let the two criminals build the network through her.

"Temple will wait until after the network is official," Harry concluded. At that point, Lilah quitting wouldn't make a difference as no government could go after the structure without risking global economic collapse. Harry's life would soon be forfeited, and Lilah would be left with an empty title.

"It's hard for me to accept..." Lilah mused. "...I mean, if I were in Temple's place... he'll be eighty-two this year. *Eighty-two!* The same as Godwin. Temple has achieved so much. He has his legacy already. So does Godwin. Why would they then..."

"Power is hard to give up," said Harry. "World history is dotted with such leaders. They do know they'll die sooner rather than later, but they still cling to power. And they make sure it transfers to their progeny. In this case, to the parent company... Kingsley Corp."

"I wish we could go to the FBI, the Interpol, *some*one... but who'll believe us?" Lilah muttered grimly. They possessed no proof, merely a series of convenient coincidences. In fact, they were quite certain Temple wouldn't order any eavesdropping on his enemies' phones precisely because leaks from such snooping would carry more credibility than direct accusations from Harry and Lilah. All their lines were anyhow supposed to be secure, but the American president would make sure their conversations remained a secret.

She and Harry had also considered the idea of updating his family and talking to her twin brother about Temple. If one of them threatened to withdraw from the network, Temple would have to back off. Andrew Barrons—adoptive father to Lilah and her brother—was another possible ally in this fight against Temple and Godwin, but Andrew couldn't be trusted not to be in cahoots with the president.

Harry argued against the idea of informing any of them. There was the fact anything Lilah said to Dan—her twin—would potentially endanger *his* life, too. The same went for the Sheppards. Besides, Dan and the Sheppards were not as invested in the alliance... they could follow through on their threat to destroy it.

"Our outlook hasn't improved any," brooded Harry. "The people who can both keep the network intact *and* stop Temple and Godwin won't hear a word against them."

With a sigh of frustration, she muttered, "The Kingsley grandsons themselves. Brad, Victor, and Alex." Even the Argentina episode was assigned by the three men as betrayal exclusively by the oil scout who took Harry and Alex there. For the Kingsley brothers, their grandfather and his stepbrother remained blameless. The moment Harry or Lilah voiced any of their suspicions to the brothers, their alliance would be over. Harry wouldn't let it happen.

"Then there's our investigation," Harry said. The one potential weapon was their covert probe into the peculiar chapter in Godwin Kingsley's otherwise unblemished judicial career—the apparent cover-up of the untimely death of the girl his half-brother was dating.

"Still nothing from your detective?" she asked. No evidence of wrongdoing was found at all in a case which smelled rotten to the core. "How about picking the third option? We can simply stop the expansion. After all, we do have an alliance with a decent amount of say in the oil sector. If there is no network to fight over—just the three companies—Temple won't have much reason to kill you."

"I agree with you in principle. But once again... what happens when another tyrant pops up? What happens to the common man then? There will be no protection left."

"Trust me... if it weren't for the very question you just asked, I would've quit the minute Sanders got arrested. I've been so conflicted about it all. Here's a question for *you*. What happens fifty or a hundred years from now? Will history call *us* tyrants, too?"

"Pompous princess," he teased. "We'll be lucky to get a footnote in some book no one will ever read. We'll be forgotten within weeks of our deaths."

"If Temple could possibly manage it, you would be dead within weeks," Lilah snapped. "And you... you won't let him win, either. Even if it costs you your life."

"We have time until the network is complete," Harry said.

"Time to do *what?*" she asked, desperately hoping he wouldn't confirm her fears.

Harry sighed. "There's this old quote about Abraham Lincoln. 'Nearly all men can stand adversity, but if you want to test a man's character, give him power.' You already saw what Temple and Godwin did with the power they have. I don't particularly care about winning, *per se*. We simply cannot afford to lose. The world cannot afford for us to lose. Time to do *whatever* it takes to keep you in charge, Lilah. It's my duty. I will carry it out or die trying."

The countdown began the day Sanders was hauled off to prison. Every paper signed by the alliance, every deal concluded, every hour which passed took them closer to the moment the network would be finalized. Each territory conquered by the new overlords dragged them to the moment Temple and Godwin would go on the attack. Harry Sheppard would launch his kamikaze strike against Lilah's enemies. All of them would die, and she would be left alone, ruling an empire she didn't want.

Part II

Chapter 4

A few days later, mid April 1986

Upper East Side, New York City

From the plush couch, Alex looked around the living room of what used to be Peter and Patrice Kingsley's apartment at the family mansion, listening to Harry talk about the Russian phase of their expansion plan.

They were there for Justice Godwin Kingsley's eighty-first birthday. Grandfather claimed not to want a celebration, but Alex was in town and couldn't let the day pass without commemorating it with at least a visit. He'd invited Harry along, hoping Grandfather would enjoy the company. After Sanders was defeated, the patriarch commented often enough on Harry's role in the episode, about his shrewdness, his political savvy. Coming from anyone else, Alex would've labeled it flattery, but Justice Kingsley did nothing, said nothing he didn't mean.

He was currently at the Knickerbocker Club, meeting some of his contemporaries. When the butler called the club, the justice asked Alex and Harry to stick around until he returned. With the butler's permission, Alex chose to take a trip down memory lane instead of waiting in his grandfather's office.

"Siberia has huge reserves," Harry said, following Alex as he wandered around. "We *need* to get a foot in. Venezuela is another must-win sector. We hope every American company will agree to be part of the network, but nothing can be taken for granted. Most of the Middle East will not join... we'll try, but we need to make sure the network has enough members to be an effective counterweight to OPEC. They're all for the idea of a second, American-led alliance *now*. I mean, chaos affects them as much as it does us, but you can bet they're preparing for the day things are not chummy between the two groups."

Alex heard every word of what his brother-in-law was saying, but his heart was caught in the snares of the past.

The shouts and laughter of three little boys echoed in his mind, their hapless nanny chasing after them. Well, chasing after Alex and Victor. Brad was usually the nanny's helper. The marble staircase leading down from the bedrooms... if Alex looked carefully, he might see the scuff marks left on the banister by the thick-soled leather shoes of the little monsters determined to turn their mother's hair gray by sliding down every chance they got. He smiled at the gilded skylight under which they would lie, waiting to spot Santa, only to fall asleep on the carpet. Victor once convinced Alex the figures in the frescoes on the ceiling came alive every night. Experts called the style French classic, but to Alex and his brothers, it had been home. Until Peter Kingsley, their father, decided to take off.

"Russia has oil," Harry conceded. "Israel is ready to provide them technical know-how in return for guaranteed annual supply. What *we* can contribute is capital... the weapon you'll need to use."

Alex looked to his right where the large saltwater tank still lined the wall, exotic fish flitting about inside. Next to the aquarium was the door leading to the dining room. Directly across were the large windows looking out to the gardens and the garage, velvet drapes pulled aside to let sunlight pour in. Mother's favorite spot in the house had been the chair by the window. She used to sit there for hours, sometimes watching her sons play, sometimes simply enjoying the view.

For all the magnificence of the home and the sepia-toned memories of his early childhood, it now reminded Alex of the indifference from the man who'd given him life. "Harry, do you know what's the most powerful weapon in the world?"

"Information," Harry said immediately. "And a good sense of how your adversary is likely to react."

Alex laughed. "No, dude. It's not information; it's not money. It's indifference."

Harry shook his head. "Detachment works only to an extent, yet you're right in a way. Very few nations trust the Soviet Union. No one cares what happens to... we're not talking about the Russians, are we?"

"No." Alex gestured with his hands, unsure how to elaborate.

"Indifference," Harry murmured, brows drawn in contemplation. "When you don't care what happens, your disinterest makes your blade sharper... it's easier to gut your opponents when you don't give a damn."

"A blade would only kill a man. What indifference does is destroy his identity. I remember..." Alex stood, walking to the arched doors leading into the dining room. He pointed toward the large table, the twelve chairs around it, only five of them usually occupied.

#

Twenty-eight years ago, August 1958

New York, New York

"I'm trying," Father said from across the dining table. He dabbed his lips with the white napkin.

Dinner was at five when Father returned from his long trips because he always left to meet his friend right after. Three-year-old Alex held up his glass of lemonade, peering at his parents through the liquid, hoping Father would tell Mother to let them forget about the veggies. He did that sort of thing when he was home... allowing them to eat candy when they were not supposed to, watch scary movies, things Mother never let them do.

Alex craned his neck to see Brad on Victor's other side. Brad was squinting across the table. He'd broken his glasses the week before, throwing around a football with their cousins. The chauffeur was supposed to pick up the new pair in the morning, something which matched Father's. Even without the glasses, Brad looked like Father. The same curly, brown hair, the same blue eyes. Except everyone said Father's size went only to Victor. At five, Victor looked like he was already ten or something. Alex resembled Mother with her brown eyes and hair. He fervently hoped he wouldn't grow up small and thin like her.

Between Alex and Brad, Victor mumbled, shoveling all the Brussels sprouts on his plate into his giant mouth. But his eyes were now on their parents, not the food. Alex knew what his brother was thinking. They all knew Father's work took him all over the world, and they all missed him. But Mother's smiles completely vanished whenever he returned. Her face sometimes went all funny as though she'd cry any moment.

"I really am trying... but I need... you don't understand," Father said.

Alex saw Brad stare holes into his plate. Brad was sure Mother got sad because Father hardly spent time with them even when he was home, and Brad came up with an idea he hoped would fix the problem. They'd talked it over a million times, with Brad coaching Victor and Alex exactly when to add their voices. "Father," Brad said, bravely interrupting the conversation of the grown-ups. "I have a baseball game tomorrow." He played shortstop.

"Huh?" said Father. "Oh, okay... very good."

"Can you..." Brad took a deep breath. "Will you come to watch? It's Saturday. You don't have work. And you like baseball." Father once played for the West Point team, and there was a picture of him on his desk, holding a gloved hand high in the air. The Yankees were his favorite... cards and autographs and everything. Naturally, his sons were Yankees fans, too.

"Ah, I don't know, buddy..." Father took a big gulp from the wine glass.

"He is your son," Mother interjected, her voice low. "She can spare you for one day."

Alex knew who "she" was. Father's friend. That pretty lady with yellow hair they met in Father's office when Grandfather took them for a visit. Seeing them at the door, she'd said, "Your boys," which made Father look up from the papers on the desk. She'd given them candy and asked them to call her "Maddy."

"I'm aware of my responsibilities," Father said to Mother, his tone abrupt. Brad jerked his head to the side, signaling Alex and Victor to pipe up. Before they could, their father took a quick glance across the table at Brad and said, "You need to take him to an optometrist, Patrice. Get his eyes checked. See how he's squinting."

Now Brad looked as though he were about to cry.

"Brad's been wearing glasses for three years," Mother said. "If you boys are done, why don't you watch some television? *Mickey Mouse Club* is on."

As they were filing out, Brad turned at the door. "Please," he said, almost whining.

Father was already pushing back his chair, eager to be gone, and didn't hear his son's appeal.

Watching the Mouseketeers dance on the TV in the playroom, Alex asked, "Can we still go to the game, Brad?"

Brad shrugged. "I'm quitting. I wasn't very good at it, anyway."

"Hey, if you're quitting, can I have your cards?" Victor asked.

Eyes on the television, Brad said, "Shh!"

Engrossed as Alex and Victor were in the show, they were only vaguely aware of Brad leaving the room. When the nanny exclaimed, "Brad!" they looked up. He was crouched next to the fireplace, throwing pieces of paper in. His baseball cards. Running to the hearth, Alex and Victor watched Yogi Berra's smiling face curl, then crumble into ash.

"I wanted them," Victor howled.

"No," said Brad, voice taut, and tossed another one into the flames.

1958 was already a bad year for three young baseball fans in New York, what with the Dodgers and the Giants moving to California. Fall wasn't any better, either.

Four months later, November 1958

Mother's face looked strange as though the smile were painted on. "No," she said to Uncle Aaron, Father's younger brother. "I'm *not* canceling Alex's birthday party."

Uncle David—Father's other brother—was also there. Three boys, with Father in the middle. Just like Brad, Victor, and Alex. Uncle David had two sons and a daughter, but Uncle Aaron didn't have any children yet. He didn't even have a wife.

Grandfather walked into the banquet hall in the family home and strode to the boys, muttering something about life going on.

It was only recently Alex learned Grandfather was not really their grandfather. There was a brother—a half-brother—who died a long time ago. Alex's father and uncles were this half-brother's sons. Uncle Aaron was also a half-brother of Peter Kingsley, Alex's father. After hearing this news, Alex approached Grandfather in tears, but the old man merely laughed, saying fatherhood meant a lot more than donating sp—he stopped there and coughed. Uncle Aaron guffawed until tears came into his eyes and told Alex to forget about who was real and who was not, who was half and who was full. They were a family.

The Kingsleys were one *big* family, with Grandfather as the petri dish. Alex frowned. No, it wasn't the word Uncle Aaron used. Alex would have to ask later. They all lived in the same mansion with separate apartments assigned to each Kingsley son. Family or not, Alex was mad at his uncles. How could either of them even dream of canceling the party?

Mother continued, "Alex is turning four, and he's going to get his celebration."

The men exchanged glances, then turned as one to look at where Alex stood, his head forty-two inches above the ground.

Ignoring them, he hopped from foot to foot and looked around the room. The banquet hall had been rearranged to accommodate the puppet show. Sad-face, the boy clown, was chatting with his sister, Happy-face, as they twisted balloons into interesting shapes. There was a huge... something... behind black curtains, occupying almost a third of the hall—the surprise promised by Grandfather. Alex couldn't wait to see what it was.

On the buffet table, there were ice creams and sorbets and sherbets, and Alex planned to sample everything. He hadn't seen it yet, but the Kingsley chef did promise a magnificent cake with layers of fudge and chocolate, jelly in the middle, just the way Alex liked it.

The list of invitees had been pre-approved by Grandfather, and most of the kids would be from the Kingsleys' social circle. Cousin Steven and Cousin Charles—Uncle David's sons—were already present. They had the same Kingsley brown hair as Brad and Victor, but while Alex's brothers got their blue eyes from their father, the cousins got the gray of the family ancestors. Steven was five, same as Victor, and Charles was four, same as Alex. Helen—Uncle David's daughter—was only a few months older than Brad but never wanted to hang out with the rest of them. The chauffeur's son was also invited to the party at Mother's insistence, but he sat in a corner and glared at his hosts. Steven was the only one tolerated by the brooding big kid.

"Here's your first guest, Alex," Mother said as a little girl walked in, holding her nanny's hand.

More guests trickled in, bearing packages Alex longed to tear apart. At his side were Brad and Victor, their suits just as crisp as Alex's, their shoes just as gleamingly polished. They were equally impatient to see the goodies. Unfortunately, their nanny was in charge of the gifts and firmly said they'd have to wait until after the party.

Finally, they were allowed to join the rest of the guests in enjoying the food and the entertainment. Pizza was devoured, ice cream slurped, lemonade spilled. They crowded around the clowns and the puppets, laughing without restraint. Balloons popped unexpectedly; accusations of perfidy abounded.

Through a bullhorn, Uncle Aaron yelled, "Boys and girls!" When he gained everyone's attention, he slapped on a large tricorn. "Time for the surprise." The staff pulled on ropes, drawing the curtains back.

Open-mouthed, Alex stared at the huge replicas of ships. On one side was a vessel sporting a black flag with skull and crossbones. There was a crow's nest, gray sails, and a rope ladder hanging off the edge. Facing it was another large vessel, flying the Stars-and-Stripes on top. Its sails were bulky and white, the oars wooden. Scary-real cannons pointed outward. Some adult reassuringly murmured, "Only toys," but none of the kid brigade paid any mind.

With a roar, the guests rushed forward. Captain/Justice Godwin Kingsley commanded the USS Kingsley, ordering his men to attack Atlantic Aaron and his dastardly crew. Stiff and steady, Brad stood at the captain's side, ready to assist. The decks swarmed with sailors and pirates, shooting with pretend guns, dueling with wooden swords.

Fighting off a mean-faced buccaneer with brown ringlets and blue eyes, Alex looked back at the door for the hundredth time. Father knew the party was tonight. Alex loved playing with Grandfather, but he wanted Father as the captain of the naval vessel.

Not far from the door, Mother was talking to the chauffeur's boy, kneeling by the side of his chair. She was gesturing at the ships, probably trying to cajole him into joining the rest in play. The boy scowled in Alex's direction. Since grouchy was the only expression the boy seemed capable of, it didn't bother Alex, but Mother was acting pathetic, fond hand on the blond head and all. More so when the boy shook away her affectionate gesture.

A blunt object landed on Alex's belly. The pizza almost came back out. With an embarrassing thump, he landed on his bottom, watching balefully as the pirate waved her wooden cutlass in victory. "I killed you," she shrieked.

"Cease-fire," Uncle Aaron yelled. "Time for the birthday cake. It will be delicious, I promise you. Nothing but the best for my men."

Sweaty and laughing, both crews abandoned ship to fidget on the small chairs while the accompanying adults milled about. At the front of the hall, Alex stood with his brothers, one eye still on the door, hoping Father would make it in on time.

"You're such a cutie, Alex," said a neighbor, bending almost double to meet his face, her bony fingers playfully pinching his cheek. "Tell me, where's your daddy? Is he with his friend?" Alex was used to the hushed whispers about Father's friend though they'd left him puzzled in the beginning. He, too, played with his buddies, but no one ever laughed at him for it. It was only recently he figured out fathers weren't supposed to have lady friends other than mothers. But no one ever directly asked Alex or his brothers about it until tonight. Until this woman with the mean glint in her eyes. The question left Alex with a fluttery feeling in his tummy.

There was a giggle at the woman's side. The newcomer's chins—all three of them—quivered in mirth. Her large bottom stuck high in the air as she also bent down to talk to the brothers. "What do you boys want? Another brother or a sister?"

There was an audible gulp from Victor, but he looked confused. So did Brad.

"They don't care," said the first woman. "It's not like they're ever going to see the new baby."

"What baby?" Brad asked, pushing his glasses up his nose with a finger.

A tall shadow fell over them as Grandfather materialized at Alex's side. "Madam, I meant to ask you," he said conversationally. "Your brother—has he been having financial troubles? Something came across my desk last week, and I thought I recognized your family name."

With speed Alex wouldn't have believed possible, the first woman straightened. "You're mistaken, Godwin," she snapped.

Her friend—eyes rounded and mouth open—was creeping backward. The stealth was impressive, given her girth.

Grandfather inclined his head, the captain's hat still on his long, white hair. "I'm sure I was. The old families in this area have had their share of problems, but we've never resorted to embezzlement. The Kingsleys certainly have not, whatever else we've been guilty of."

The first woman's jaw dropped. She resembled one of the groupers in the living room tank, leaving Alex fighting an incredible urge to stuff her large mouth full of fish food. Unfortunately, before he could fulfill his fantasy, she excused herself and beat a hasty retreat.

When she left, Brad repeated, his voice timid, "What baby?"

Uncle Aaron joined Grandfather, but before he could speak, another voice interrupted. "Your daddy's gonna have a baby with his gurrrlfriend," crooned Cousin Charles, his words ringing through the hall. "He's gonna live with her now."

"Charlie!" cried his nanny. As usual, Charles's father said nothing. The servants sometimes commented he was blind to his sons' mischiefs. Uncle David *was* nearly blind from some childhood illness, and his wife—Aunt Grace—always wore dark glasses for her headaches.

Grandfather wheeled around, piercing the poor nanny with his stony gray eyes. "Get Charles back to his room."

Alex's mother was hurrying forward through the crowd, finally leaving the chauffeur's son alone. Her face was pale. "Babies are for mothers and fathers," Alex whispered, not understanding. "Father cannot have a baby with his... his..."

"Gurrlfriend," sang Charles, unrepentant as he was hauled away to his parents' wing in the family mansion. His brother, Steven, and their friend—the chauffeur's son—followed. Steven's face was dark red with embarrassment.

"Alex," sighed Uncle Aaron, squatting on the floor. "Oh, God."

"Are they going to be father and mother now?" Alex asked, pressure building in his chest.

Mother dropped to her knees and wrapped her arms around Alex. "I... yes, they are, but..."

"He won't be our father no more?" His voice rose. Everything blurred. Tears spilled down his cheeks. "Is it why he's not at the party?"

"Alex," snapped Grandfather. "Don't make a scene. You're four."

Charles's taunts had drawn attention, and every eye in the hall seemed to be on the Kingsley boys, waiting, watching.

A shout went up from the back corner. The kids stood to greet the chef rolling in the giant cake made of chocolate and fudge and caramel, thick syrup drizzled on the top. Grandfather tucked Alex's small hand into his own much larger one and strode forward, head held high. Brad and Victor followed. Sandwiched between his mother and brothers on one side and Grandfather and Uncle Aaron on the other, Alex blew out the candles.

The fork in his hand trembled and clattered against the thin white plate. Alex ate the large piece, thinking it tasted like sand. He posed dutifully for the photographer, taking pictures with his brothers, his mother, then Grandfather. They heard the hushed conversations, saw the curiosity in the glances thrown at their mother, but there were no further comments directed at the frightened boys. Grandfather remained with them the entire evening, his tall presence enough to deter questions. He continued at their side in the rest of the party games, teaching Alex how to aim the dart to pop the most number of balloons. Grandfather was there until the last guest straggled out.

When the event was done, the boys huddled together on Brad's bed, scared of what the next day would bring. The room was dark, light from the hallway filtering in under the door. They'd left the unopened gifts in the playroom. Downstairs, Grandfather was talking to Mother, his deep voice raised in annoyance and frustration. Grandfather's brother—*step*brother—arrived, asked there by Uncle Aaron to lend a hand in solving the family crisis. Mr. Temple was the senator from New Jersey.

"No," said Mother. "If Peter wants a relationship with his sons, he will have it. Besides, I think you're going to find he won't let you blackmail him with family. Not again."

"Patrice," said Grandfather. "I know my son better than you know your husband."

"Godwin," admonished Mr. Temple.

"It's fine," said Mother. "Godwin's probably correct, but I won't allow my children to be used as pawns against their father. Enough is enough. Peter found happiness, and I won't force him to give it up."

The three boys listened to it all. There was a muffled sob from Victor. "Father's not coming back, is he?"

Brad shushed him, continuing to listen to the conversation of the adults.

"How could you let him do this?" Grandfather thundered.

"*Let* him?" asked Mother. "You were the first person I approached when I found out about Peter and Maddy. Whatever the circumstances of our marriage, I was too naïve to expect anything less than complete loyalty. Do I have to remind you of what you told me, Godwin?"

"Patrice—" Grandfather's angry voice broke off. "I asked you to empathize with his weaknesses, not let him walk away from his birthright."

"I was pregn... by God, *seven months* pregnant with Alex, and I was told to put up with it!"

Alex cringed. Mother was shouting, and she never shouted.

"My dear," said Mr. Temple, his tone soothing.

She ignored the efforts to pacify her. "I did! I tolerated it all. I stayed in this heartless place because of—" Something squeezing painfully within his chest, Alex wondered what she meant. This was their home. How could they not stay? "Then, something happened," Mother continued. "The more I saw them together, the more I realized... he's not weak, Godwin. He's with Maddy because she makes him happy. Now, their happiness involves a baby."

Grandfather huffed. "It's not unusual for men in Peter's position—"

"Peter doesn't care for what is usual," Mother said. "He doesn't want to keep Maddy as his mistress and me as his wife. He doesn't want to hang on to the business when marrying me was what got him promoted over his brothers. Accept his decision."

"His decision is going to impact his children—your sons!" Grandfather roared.

Uncle Aaron interceded, trying to mollify Grandfather.

Godwin Kingsley would not be placated. "But you're right. Let Peter pursue happiness. If he didn't bother to attend his own son's birthday party, why would he worry about the rest of the Kingsley family, least of all a father like me who's not even his real father?"

Something slammed, telling the boys their grandfather had departed. Alex followed Victor and Brad to the door of the bedroom. Through the crack, they watched Uncle Aaron jog after Grandfather. Mr. Temple stayed, talking to Mother. "Don't make any hasty decisions," the senator warned, a hand in his pocket.

"I won't," Mother promised, her voice now more tired than angry. She collapsed onto the couch. "I won't let Godwin use my boys as weapons, either."

"Think hard before you do anything, Patrice," said the senator, sitting next to her. "You have to be there for all your sons."

She laughed. The sad sound tied Alex's tummy into tight little knots. "I tried. God knows I tried. You know what? Shame on me that I did. For my own selfish reasons, I put Brad, Victor, and Alex through four years of their father's indifference."

"What about—" The senator glanced at the window overlooking the gardens and the garage, then turned toward the stairs leading to the bedrooms.

The boys withdrew in a hurry.

Mother said, "I'm the only remaining parent for the three of them. Their well-being has to be my priority."

"Give it a week or two is all I'm saying. Let tempers cool."

The senator bid Mother good night, saying he was expected in DC in the morning. Their voices receded as she escorted him out.

"Did Father give you a gift before he left?" Brad asked Alex.

Alex shrugged, wanting to tell his brothers he didn't care.

Digging into his pocket, Brad came up with a quarter. "Here," he said. "Happy birthday."

"What will you do for cookie money?" Alex asked, slightly anxious. The elementary school allowed them to purchase snacks, and Patrice gave both Brad and Victor twenty-five cents a week. Alex was waiting to turn five to be eligible for an allowance.

"I stopped liking cookies," Brad said, pushing his glasses up his nose.

In the morning, Patrice found all three on Brad's bed, Victor occupying most of the space. Alex's cheek was on Brad's chest, and tucked under his arm was Victor's humongous head.

#

Back in the present, April 1986

Upper East Side, New York City

From the arched doorway, Alex surveyed the dining room. The polished wood floor gleamed under the discreet lighting exactly as it had in his childhood. The red velvet upholstery on the chairs was the same, matching the drapery at the large windows. Even the deep crystal dish in the center of the table looked familiar. It seemed to him the ghosts of the three boys were still sitting around, waiting for their father's answer.

"Why *did* your mother put up with the behavior for so long?" Harry asked from the living room couch.

"I've never understood," said Alex. "The first time I heard her express some anger about... you know... the affair... was when Father left. Even then, it was more to blame Grandfather than Father... after which she walked out, us in tow." Patrice Kingsley claimed Godwin was treating them as second-class citizens, trying to pressure her into using her children as weapons to force Peter's return. It may have been her hurt pride talking, but she believed what she believed.

Pulling out one of the velvet-covered chairs, Alex collapsed into it. What the hell did he label memories of pain and happiness all mixed up together?

Following him in, Harry ran a finger over the smooth surface of the table. "Your grandfather did ask her to tolerate the affair, and he *was* using you."

"I'm not blaming her or Grandfather," Alex said instantly. "They were both... we all do what we think is right, I suppose."

"How can you possibly excuse Godwin?" Harry exclaimed. "Imagine what she went through as a wife and mother, Alex."

"Dude, I..." Alex sighed. "Those were different times. Grandfather did what he thought was best for the family. It didn't work is all."

Harry stared hard at Alex for a few seconds as though considering saying something. Then, he shrugged. "Yeah, different times... go on... what happened after you left this place?"

"It was rough. Mother refused to take a penny from the Kingsleys or the Sheppards." She loathed her own kin, the Sheppards. The only explanation she ever gave was they were a mercenary lot and pushed her into marriage with the Kingsley heir to further their business interests.

"How did you manage?"

"Mother did some typing work. Father was working in an office someplace. He sent her a little bit of cash every month. She was too proud to take help from either family... but no problems accepting a check from the same man who left her in such dire straits."

"He was your father. It was his responsibility, the least he could do. Actually, Godwin also could've tried to help. If he stopped the pressure tactics..."

"No, dude," insisted Alex. "Grandfather made a couple of mistakes, but it was Mother's decision to stay away. The reason for all of it was my father. Forget taking responsibility for his sons... the least he could do was remember we, too, were his sons. He didn't. Oh, he apologized for missing my party. Came by for other birthdays and Christmas and such. But we decided we would never again cry over someone who didn't cry over us. In a few months, whatever little we once felt for the man was gone. When he saw we weren't willing to give an inch, he stopped visiting."

"Your mother didn't have anything to say?"

"Not really. Maybe she saw our reaction and thought it better. She remained friendly with Father. Even with the girlfriend. Mother wouldn't let us say a word against either. She was the one who insisted we name the company after Father."

There was complete silence from Harry.

Alex laughed. "First time I've seen you speechless. Brad hated it the most, but then, he hated *them*—Father and his girlfriend—for doing what they did. So did Victor and I, but Brad was really cut up.

At the time, he understood more than us what it meant for Mother. Brad used to swear he'd never let anyone do anything similar to him. Not only the infidelity. Father's selfishness tore apart the life she'd built for herself. Brad tried hard to make up for our father's absence where Victor and I were concerned. The steady one, the big brother we could always count on."

"At six?" Harry marveled. "Good God! A child shouldn't have been put in the position, but he stepped up, didn't he?"

"He's still the same," said Alex.

With a thoughtful nod, Harry asked, "So from the time you moved out, you lived in Brooklyn?"

"In Park Slope. Mother rented a two-bedroom unit in one of the buildings." All three boys slept in one room. There was no nanny, not many toys, no more birthday parties, no television. Radio delivered the news—first man in space, Berlin Wall, MLK's dream, the assassination of JFK, the Civil Rights Act. Rips in the boys' clothes were carefully sewn by Patrice. She made sure the front door was locked every night, but the brothers needed to band together against street gangs and schoolyard bullies. Broken bones, black eyes... hours in the waiting room at the local clinic, only half listening to their mother's anxious scolding... walking back just to save the fifty cents it would cost each of them to use the bus. "It wasn't all bad." Alex shrugged. "There was more freedom." There was warmth when they gathered for dinner at the old, scratched countertop, Patrice serving hot food straight from the stove. "In a while, we started forgetting the life we left behind."

"Doesn't seem like you've forgotten anything."

"What I mean is we started to look ahead. It wasn't as if we forgave. We didn't. We couldn't. Until I was four, I used to think of myself as Peter and Patrice Kingsley's son, Justice Godwin Kingsley's grandson." Alex gestured at what used to be their living room in the Kingsley mansion. "This was our home. We had our grandfather, uncles, even those bastard cousins. Thanks to our father, we lost all of it. There was no one we could call our own. We didn't know who we were any longer."

"You ended up paying for your father's mistakes. At least you weren't alone. You had each other."

"Plus, our grandfather. Mother cut off contact, but he kept asking her to bring us back. Not our father. He had kids with his girlfriend by then."

"Twin boys, right?"

"Right. Father died when I was ten, and we returned to the family home. The girlfriend died a couple of months after. Mother wanted to adopt the boys, but Grandfather decided it would be better for them to stay with their uncle. To avoid gossip, I think. Without Grandfather's support, she didn't have any legal claims on them."

Harry shook his head. "Your mother is an extraordinarily strong, extraordinarily *strange* woman."

"Tell me about it," Alex muttered. "There are times I feel she made a huge mistake in returning us here."

"Why? I would've thought you'd be excited to get back home."

Alex glanced around the large hall. "The cliché about never being able to go home again is true. It's weird... there were problems with our cousins, but Grandfather loved us. Hell, *he* was our father in every way which counted. Still..."

"Right," Harry said almost tonelessly.

"Mister Alex," interrupted a nasal voice. The butler was at the door. The old fellow had to be pushing eighty, but he still maintained his erect posture. Unfortunately, the gliding gait which once allowed him to move silently was gone, courtesy of his creaking joints. "Justice Kingsley is back from the club and will meet you and Mr. Sheppard in his home office."

#

Five minutes later

Through elegant hallways, the butler led the two guests until they were at the door to the *sanctum sanctorum*—the patriarch's office. Nothing ever changed in this room, Alex thought with fondness. The antique globe in one corner, the turn-of-the-century photographs on damask-covered walls, the large desk with the chessboard on top... seated majestically in the leather chair behind the desk was Godwin. Quirkiness of the silvery mane tied in a low ponytail notwithstanding, his gray eyes and rigid carriage conveyed gravitas and rock-hard integrity.

"Alex," exclaimed Godwin, his voice weighty. He stood as if to go around the desk, but Alex got to him first and greeted him with a hug. "Thank you for remembering this old man today," said Godwin. He nodded in the direction of the guest. "And Harry... what a surprise to see you here! Your brother calls on us often, but I believe this is only your... second time?"

Grinning easily, Harry said, "I find surprising people to be a great deal of fun, sir. If certain men had their way, I would've met my maker after my first visit to this place. Yet here I am."

Alex bit back a grimace, hoping Harry wouldn't say anything else about the meeting which led to the Argentina episode. The Kingsley patriarch blamed the double-dealing oil scout for the horror, not Harry and Alex. Still, none of them wanted to be reminded of it, Godwin included.

Strangely, Godwin merely laughed. "Perhaps I should've said what a *pleasure* it is to have you as a guest in my home. Brad speaks very highly of you. Medal of Honor winner, brilliant tactician, negotiator, genuine hero."

"The pleasure is entirely mine," said Harry. "I get to talk to a principled statesman such as you, an authority on law and justice and ethics. An unblemished career all the way to the Supreme Court. Plus, as Alex's grandfather, you're family."

As soon as they were out of the house, Alex would let Harry know he needed to dial down the sweet-talking. Grandfather wasn't the sort to appreciate—

"My grandsons are fortunate you consider them family," continued Godwin. "Brad got where he is because of you. Sanders could not have been defeated without your help."

"Never," Alex agreed in mild bemusement. "The network, Brad as CEO... wouldn't have happened without you, Harry. My brother appreciates the goodwill from everyone. We all do. Dunno if I told you before... Brad's pretty tickled by what you said at the press conference. You know, when we were dealing with Sanders."

Whenever the press wrote about Brad, the statement was quoted. "...*good businessman... effective* and *ethical... a great partner... excellent boss...*"

"Grandfather has made it clear how proud he is of Brad." Laughing, Alex continued, "But we *expect* family to be encouraging. You, on the other hand... another businessman and a military hero... Brad trusts you mean what you say. He trusts *you*."

"I'm honored," Harry said.

"Brad's what they call a standup guy... always has been," Alex mused. "On a personal level, Victor and I couldn't ask for a better brother."

"Steady and reliable even as a boy," Harry murmured. "Family man."

"Absolutely," said Alex. "Don't get me wrong. We have our disagreements, but at the end of the day, we also have each other's backs. And that includes our mother, my wife, and Lilah."

"Good," said Harry. With a barely audible sigh, he repeated, "Good."

Chapter 5

A week later

Brooklyn, New York

Lilah leaned against the wall next to the bedroom window and prayed for patience as she glanced at the magazine in her husband's hands.

The slats of the Venetian blinds were open, letting in the rays of the morning sun. Cars already honked outside the brownstone residence she inherited from her parents. As soon as she could scrape up the money, she'd bought out her siblings' share in the property. This weekend, it would be Lilah alone in her beloved home as Brad was on his way to Panama where the headquarters of the Peter Kingsley Company was located. She was staying back to fine-tune the Russian project, but today was supposed to be a day of peace and quiet. The plan was to lounge on the couch in old jeans and a favorite tee, the latest Stephen King bestseller in her hands. A brief reprieve so she could tackle her problems with a rested brain.

Instead... was a little peace too much to ask? But then, she did need to prioritize her marriage alongside Temple and Godwin's plans for Harry and not simply for her and Brad's sake. Almost three months had gone by since they started trying, and she harbored a suspicion... Brad would be a wonderful father when the time came, but how could she bring a child into a home where the parents were constantly quarreling over imagined infidelities and professional insecurities? God... she needed to find a way... some way... if only she could get through to him, make him understand there was nothing going on between her and his brother. Or between her and anyone else!

"This is pornography," Brad insisted in his usual refined tones, his mouth twisted in revulsion as he shook the magazine in her face. He was already dressed in pants and an Oxford shirt for the flight to Panama. His brown curls were arranged elegantly on his scalp, blue eyes flashing behind round glasses.

"It is only a *pencil sketch*." The female figure wore a robe which hid the naughty parts, and her face carried a vague resemblance to Lilah's.

"I'm not talking only about the drawing," Brad snapped, tossing the periodical onto the bed. He wiped his hands on his pants as though worried germs populated the pages in the guise of words. "The whole thing is full of filth about you." She'd already skimmed through. The author of the serialized story left plenty of hints in the media to suggest the tale was an accounting of Lilah's life, but he kept his claims vague enough to escape having his socks sued off. The fictional Lilah was a *femme fatale*, seducing men into doing her bidding. Her bedroom antics were described in great detail. And—surprise, surprise—she possessed blue-black hair and hazel eyes, the same as her template. She, too, used blue lotus oil for perfume. "All I needed to see before my flight," said Brad.

"Gimme a break," Lilah muttered. As her husband's eyes widened, she held up both hands. "All right, all right... I understand your irritation. Trust me, I do. Don't you think I wish I could stop all the stupidity? But fighting it in court would only invite more publicity, and we'd lose, anyway... these publishers leave themselves enough wiggle room to claim it was never about me. And really... it's come to the point I don't much care. *I* know what I am."

"It's not about you knowing... the whole world thinks... the rest of us somehow manage to avoid such publicity altogether. Why can't you? Have you heard the kind of questions I—and the rest of the Kingsleys—get from the press because of you?" He glared at the magazine lying face down on the mattress. "Grandfather called me last night about this great literary work. Someone mentioned it at his club."

"You tell Godwin I didn't *ask* to be—" Lilah stopped and took a deep breath, reminding herself Brad was the one person who could put a stop to Godwin and Temple's machinations.

Lilah wished like crazy she could rewind the last couple of years and put more effort into her equation with her husband. Perhaps then, she would've had a prayer of getting him to believe the fantastic tale she wanted to tell. But how could she have done anything differently when she still couldn't bring herself to talk to him about her past? About the assault she survived, the throat-closing fears she needed to overcome.

"When you return," Lilah started, "I want us to go somewhere. There's a therapist—"

"What?" Face darkening, Brad said, "Think about what you're saying. The minute the media figures out we're in counseling, there will be problems."

Marital troubles between the CEO and CFO of the biggest oil alliance in the world? Of course the markets would react.

"My wife, the financial wizard," jeered Brad. "Remember this stupidity the next time you act like you run the show."

"I mean we could see a counselor quietly—"

"I can't even fire you because of the damn pre-nup. The company is *mine... my* business which I run the way a business should be run... ethically. And you... but everyone understands my situation. The men who ask to meet you... you think it's because of your financial genius? How come none of the articles talk about your work? It's always about Alex. You and him, the star-crossed lovers."

"Stop, Brad," she warned, anger making her husky voice raspier than usual. "Don't start again. We can't continue this way... not when we work together and not when... my God! Imagine our child listening to all this! And to hear it from his or her own father?! Imagine the hurt!"

Immediate chagrin struck his features. For a moment or two, Brad stared at her. "I would never hurt..." The angry flush slowly left his cheeks, and he took a deep breath. "I'd rather die than cause pain to my own son... or daughter."

Lilah closed her eyes for a moment. "I know," she whispered. "Our baby will be a lucky child. I just want us to—" She made a helpless gesture with her hands. "You and I need to sort ourselves out."

"I'm sorry," Brad said abruptly. "I know half the things the press says about you are lies."

"Almost everything they say about me," she interjected.

He nodded. "Yeah... but it gets difficult for *me*. I wish you could see it from where I stand. Maybe a therapist *can* help."

Biting back the retort springing to her tongue, Lilah inclined her head. A loving son and brother, she reminded herself. A decent boss to his staff and competent enough steward to the business alliance. If only he'd show a little bit of faith in her. If only she could trust him with her secrets.

Part III

Chapter 6

A week later, May 1986

Prudhoe Bay Oil Field, Alaska

"Phase one begins," Harry murmured to himself. Hands tucked into the pockets of his ski jacket, he trudged alongside Alex and Victor as they made their way to the waiting bus.

Flat tundra dotted with lakes and rivers stretched into eternity. In the distance, a herd of oxen clustered around a small water body, and gulls flew above, emitting piercing calls. The rig workers paid no mind to any of this as they stomped about between the wells, flow stations, and the miles of pipelines and cables. The rumble of motors, trucks honking, shouts from the tough men who refused to let nature defeat them... this bitingly cold spring morning in Alaska's North Shore was different yet damned similar to the sweltering days Harry spent as a teenager, working at his father's wells in Libya.

The shuttle carrying Harry and the Kingsley brothers and the rest of the group to the Arctic Ocean soon bumped across the ground. From the seat next to Harry, Alex said, "Dude, imagine back in the day... coming to this place... frontier town to beat all frontier towns."

"We should've come later in the year," Victor grumbled from behind.

"Your engineers in Venezuela will continue their assessments without you hovering over them," Harry said. He did not want to listen to any more of Victor Kingsley's weird griping, which started on their flight. Victor kept going on and on during the team's weeklong inspection tour of the area and this sightseeing trip to finish off the expedition. "The local manager in Caracas should be able to handle things for a few weeks until you return."

"At least there's no snow," commented Alex. The entire team was dressed in thick jackets and scarfs, though—the three executives, the engineers, and Gateway's Alaska manager. They were all chattering, clicking pictures. "And the sun doesn't set until after eleven."

"I'm not concerned about the weather," said Victor. "I wanted to finish my work in Venezuela before taking off to Alaska."

Alex huffed in irritation and twisted around. "What's up with you?" he asked his brother. "You were there when we agreed on the schedule." Victor would kick off the expansion plans. Most of the oil sector in the Americas had already worked with one or the other of the three companies in the alliance, so it made sense to start in the region. The rest of the executives could take their time, studying business setups across the world and starting negotiations.

"Aren't you supposed to fly back and forth between Caracas and Anchorage?" Harry asked. "If the local manager there is not competent, then the answer should be to replace the fellow—pronto."

"She," muttered Victor. "The local manager... Luisa... and yeah, she's competent. Very much so."

Something in his voice... Harry finally turned from the window and raised an eyebrow at Alex. Before any questions could be asked, the shuttle came to a jolting stop.

The sea was still frozen over, with a polar bear lumbering across the blocks of ice. Forgetting for a moment whatever was vexing him, Victor bragged about jumping in for a swim if only it were water. Alex snickered.

"Harry," called a voice. Gateway's Alaska manager came marching to them. "We're cutting it close. The press conference in Anchorage is scheduled for tomorrow morning, and your return flight to New York is in the afternoon. You *are* flying back right after?"

"It's the plan," Harry said. "This is Victor's show." It was the Peter Kingsley Company's first foray into Alaska and the Arctic region, so Gateway would introduce the Kingsley brothers to local media and politicians. Harry would then return to his own business, while Alex stayed for a few weeks. For one, he was somewhat at loose ends with the Russian bureaucrats involved in negotiations rushing back to Moscow to deal with the fallout from the nuclear explosion at Chernobyl. For another, Alex's presence might help Victor set up his team in Alaska while still shuttling to other regions without things falling apart anywhere. "Do you need me to stick around?" Harry asked the manager.

"No, the shuttle driver got a radio message," said the manager. "Someone was trying to reach you at the hotel in Anchorage. Something about your bike. The chap said he'll contact you when you get back to the city."

"The Harley?" Harry asked, straightening. "What happened to it?"

"Shit," said Alex. "You left it in the garage, right? I hope it didn't get scratched. Maybe you can use the radio to find out."

"I think it was the garage operator who called," offered the manager.

Victor snorted. "It's a *bike*. You can call the garage after you return."

"It's my *Harley*," Harry corrected, the devout tone making the others laugh.

The sixty-minute press conference the next morning went smoothly, and Harry was on his way out. Alex left Victor talking to the manager and followed Harry to the street. Tourists were walking up and down, enjoying afternoon in downtown Anchorage.

Flinging his overcoat to the back seat of the taxi waiting at the hotel entrance, Harry called, "Alex... uhh... we're not anticipating problems, but be on the lookout. Tell Victor, too."

"Heh?" Alex stared. "What do you mean?"

"Argentina," Harry explained. "It's unlikely anyone else will try the same thing... not now... but we need to stay alert."

Alex raked his fingers through his hair. "I have also been looking over my shoulder since then. We're bigger now, and success does make us more vulnerable."

Harry nodded. "There will be others who don't want us to win for whatever reason."

"Any specific threats?"

"None I know of. I doubt anyone will try physically attacking you... it would be risky." Harm to an executive of a leading business would cause trouble in the markets. If it happened within the borders of the United States, the feds would make an example out of whomever came up with the damned fool idea. It was the reason most senior businessmen—including Alex and Victor and Harry— were able to go out and about without personal security when in America. When they were battling Sanders, it was a different story. Brad and Lilah still used bodyguards but only when they were outside the country. "Regardless, we should watch out for traps of other kinds. I've left word with a couple of my contacts to alert Victor if they hear something. Remind your brother not to take anything at face value."

Later, Harry declined the offer of a drink from the flight attendant and snapped open his briefcase. Everyone involved in the campaign carried copies of an atlas specially printed for the network. There was an overview of the world with its current political borders, followed by detailed regional maps. Critical locations were highlighted, and technical notes abounded. He stared at the first page for long moments before taking out his Sharpie and putting simple markings on the paper. *Three phases,* Harry told himself. They were only at the beginning of phase one. Time was on his side.

Harry's markings on the world map.

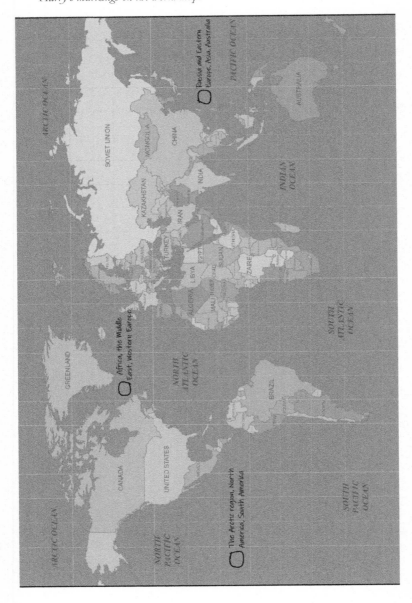

Chapter 7

Walking back to the hotel suite with Victor, Alex was still mulling Harry's warning. There was a youngish man waiting at the door—preppy type from his perfectly done brown hair and bowtie to the navy blazer. "Mr. Kingsley?" he asked, moving the dark brown leather bag to his other hand. The hallway was empty except for a hotel employee pushing a cart along. "Victor Kingsley?"

An hour later, Mr. Harvard Lawyer was gone, leaving Alex and Victor to consider the offer shoved under their noses.

"Who the hell calls themselves something like Scoundrel Society?" Alex marveled.

"Arrogant S.O.B.s," agreed Victor, forking pasta into his mouth at the dining table in the suite. From what the lawyer chap said, the Kingsley brothers would find it much easier to get permits and the like if they made certain political contributions. The movers and shakers of Alaskan politics behind the deal weren't even worried about getting caught, let alone being kicked out at the ballot box.

"So what's our next step?" asked Alex. "You've spent time studying this region."

"We..." said Victor, gulping red wine. "...are going to accept their offer."

"Dude—"

"Nothing illegal about campaign contributions," Victor insisted.

Early the next morning, Victor got an invitation to a meeting. The conference room was full of names and faces Alex was familiar with from newspapers and TV.

"All the senior executives of the company will donate," Victor assured the scoundrels of the... well... Scoundrel Society. "We're also willing to bundle contributions from our partners. It's important to support politicians who do good work." Like getting the coastal plains of the Arctic Refuge opened for exploration.

Alex massaged the back of his neck, thankful Victor was the main man to deal with the bastards. Not as if Alex didn't realize corruption went on, but these were American politicians. The same people he and other soldiers like him used to trust when they went off to battle the enemy.

"You will also need to keep the environmental groups happy," advised Mr. Harvard Lawyer.

Both Victor and Alex nodded in comprehension. They walked out of the room with their lead engineer, fairly certain things were in hand. As they were waiting for the elevator, Alex glanced back and frowned. Was it all so simple—an ethically reprehensible but legally acceptable transfer of money in return for politicians not making life difficult for the company? Harry's warning kept echoing in his mind.

The next afternoon, Alex was standing in front of the phone in the living area of the suite, his hand hovering over the receiver. Dammit, he badly wanted to talk to his wife, reassure himself this wasn't bribery. The Peter Kingsley Company wasn't asking for any special favors. They simply wanted to avoid getting caught in red tape. Alex cursed. He couldn't talk about the deal with Sabrina, not over unsecure lines.

Victor walked out, a white towel wrapped around his waist, drying his hair with a smaller piece of terry cloth. A knock sounded at the door. When Victor jerked it open, a tall man stood there, smiling ingratiatingly. "I am Jones. Remember? We met yesterday at the meeting."

"The congressman's campaign manager," said Victor, nodding. "Is there something we missed discussing?"

"Not here," said Jones.

The playground at the park was packed with kids and accompanying adults, teenagers rollerblading around the edges of the clearing. The empty bench facing the play area was deemed public enough to prevent an eavesdropper from getting close without being spotted.

"Let's cut to the chase, shall we?" the manager said to the two Kingsley men, handing a card to Victor. "Campaign contributions are taxable at our end. We don't want you to record this as one. Instead, we want you to deposit the money at this place. Under your own name."

Victor looked at the name and address and said mildly, "If the Peter Kingsley Company does not record this transaction officially and we transfer the amount offshore with intent to give to you, it *can* be considered a bribe by the authorities. How will we justify the transfer of such a large sum to a bank known to help its customers with tax evasion?"

"File it under miscellaneous expenses and transfer it to yourselves," the manager said impatiently. "These are after-tax dollars for your business, and the bank is not under American jurisdiction. The feds ain't gonna track the money. You can then take all of it out in cash and bring it to us. The local government won't ask questions. *I'll* take care of moving it to the proper accounts without the taxman's involvement." Tone persuasive, Jones added, "This is pocket change when you stand to make billions out of the area you want opened up."

"Lemme think about it," said Victor, tucking the card into his pocket.

Back in the hotel room, Alex and Victor eyed the phone. Alex picked it up and unscrewed the caps at both ends of the receiver. Nothing strange, nothing to suggest an electronic bug. "Still can't take the risk, dude," he said.

In complete silence, they walked to the lobby. As they strode to the street, Alex glanced at the glass doors. There was the reflection of a man setting a cup on the table and hurrying outside.

Victor asked the doorman for the schedule of the People Mover, the public transportation system in Anchorage. As they got on the bus, the man from the hotel lobby boarded right behind.

Whistling softly, Victor beckoned to Alex and got off at one of the stops. There was a sports bar on the block. The boxing match between Sugar Ray Leonard and Marvin Hagler was being retelecast. Alex relaxed on the barstool with a beer in his hands, but Victor's eyes practically bored into the television screen as he followed the punches, the scores.

The crowd roared as Leonard attacked with a flurry of blows. Victor asked the bartender for directions to the closest payphone. Alex inclined his head in a tiny nod.

A minute... two... if there was someone following the Kingsley brothers, they would be trying to listen in on Victor's phone conversation now.

Alex waved to the bartender. "Boss, I need to call a cab." Two rings on the establishment's phone, and someone picked up in New York City. "Alex here... Victor Kingsley's brother. Wait on the line; don't hang up."

A few seconds of acting as though he were on hold, and Alex got his chance. On television, Leonard threw more rapid punches. The crowd roared yet again.

Alex said urgently into the phone, "I think I'm being watched. We need to talk. How do we do it?"

"Go to a public phone next to a neon sign." Listening to the hurried instructions, Alex grinned.

The sun took a while to set, this being Alaska in May, but lights went on in the city streets long before. There was a payphone—not the one Victor went to—at the end of the block. As neon signs flashed on and off, blocking potential eavesdroppers, Alex once again called the number Victor gave him. "Shawn, I think Victor and I are being set up." The surprised squawks from Lilah's brother—the adopted one, not her twin—took a few moments to die down. "Never mind how and why," said Alex. "We can get into it later. For now, we need your help."

#

Tucking his hands into the pockets of his coat, Alex trudged alongside Victor on the trail leading to the park bench. No kids or rollerblading grownups yet. Early mornings were still bitingly cold in this region.

"So what did you decide?" asked the campaign manager.

"I will do what the big man wants," Victor said.

The staffer tried again, "How about some details?"

"It isn't something I do on a daily basis," Victor said, glancing away. "I'm gonna need instructions, and they will need to come from your boss's mouth. I want to be certain you're acting on his direction."

Alex bit back a smile. Not a word, not a phrase any enemy could use against Victor. If there was indeed someone taping them, they wouldn't get anything incriminating.

In another week, Victor got further instructions and called Shawn. "I need the money wired to this place. No questions, bro. Trust me on this. I wouldn't let you get into trouble for me and my brothers."

Two more weeks later, Alex and Victor again sat on the park bench, a briefcase at their feet. The campaign manager—Jones—marched to the bench and sat next to Victor, breathing in deep huffs. Alex continued to watch the kids at the playground. One particular skater—an adult—was having a lot of difficulty. Her left leg flew out from under her, and she sat down heavily. There was someone jeering loudly at her.

"So what do you have here?" the manager asked.

"Exactly what the congressman asked for," Victor said. Opening the briefcase slightly, he showed Jones the contents. The campaign manager's eyes widened a tad. Victor snapped the briefcase shut. "Take it and count the cash in your room."

"Heeelllppp!" the luckless skater shrieked.

She floundered, bending forward to regain balance. Unfortunately for her, she overshot her mark, and her feet flew back. She went careening into a man who'd been ambling along, carrying his travel backpack. The skater knocked down the unlucky tourist. The pair of them tumbled onto Victor and the manager. Alex scooted to the end of the bench to avoid the melee.

The skater's arms went around Victor's neck while the tourist grabbed Jones for balance. Jones landed on the ground with the tourist sitting on top of him. The contents of the backpack spilled out... clothes, shampoo bottles, a wallet, a briefcase, a map...

The woman kept screeching in shrill tones.

Wincing, Alex put his fingers to his ears and stood. He picked up the backpack and started shoving the scattered stuff back in.

"Sorry," the tourist said to Jones, scrambling up. "And thanks, man." Grabbing his backpack from Alex, the tourist hefted it onto his shoulders.

The woman was still on Victor's lap, screaming her head off.

"You're fine, miss," the tourist said, tone excessively soothing. "I'm fine, too. See? No harm done."

The screaming subsided into soft sniffles, and she finally stood. Shaking his head, the tourist left.

Victor picked up his briefcase. Dusting off mud, he handed it to the manager.

Leaving the manager there, Alex and Victor returned to the entrance of the park. Black cars raced from the back to where the brothers were, engines vrooming and tires squealing.

"Two of them," Alex said. "Keep moving."

With a small nod, Victor whistled as he walked.

Two more cars sped directly toward them and spun to a stop barely inches from where they stood. Coming to a halt, Alex grinned. Black-clad men jumped out, pointing guns.

One of them bellowed, "Freeze! FBI."

"Put your hands up," another one shouted.

One of the agents came forward with a pair of handcuffs. "Victor Kingsley, Alex Kingsley... you are under arrest."

"On what charges, may I ask?" queried Victor.

"For attempted bribery of a congressman," said the agent.

"Before you make fools out of yourselves, gentlemen," a female voice said, "why don't you check exactly what the bribe my colleague is accused of attempting."

The agents turned and saw the skater and the tourist. Both were walking to the scene. Somehow the woman seemed to have acquired quite a bit of grace in the ten minutes since her ignominious fall.

An officer was dragging the campaign manager to the group, briefcase still held in his hand. The agent grabbed the case and snapped it open. Bundles fell out... old magazines and newspapers, even some toilet paper. There was a disbelieving gasp from the campaign manager.

A click came from somewhere, followed by many others. "Hold it right there," shouted someone, shoving a microphone toward an agent. "Our audience would like a comment."

#

Question after question after question from the federal agents, threats to throw all of them in jail... "Yeah, Victor transferred money offshore... funds for which he *already* paid taxes," Alex admitted for the thousandth time. "It's really none of the FBI's business. Point is he didn't give any of it to your corrupt politician."

Records from the offshore bank would show there was a transfer of money from Shawn to Victor as payment for the sale of his shares in some internet company. This money was then transferred to a charitable foundation also with an account at the same bank. The foundation was supposed to be donating the entire funds minus expenses of handling it to an orphanage in the Cayman Islands. Roundabout way of donating, but there was nothing illegal about it.

"But the Jones fellow claims you did give him the cash from the Cayman bank," said the agent.

Alex pointed to the pictures of the slim form in a baseball cap leaving the bank building. The face wasn't visible, but it was clearly a woman—Victor's very competent manager from Caracas. "Luisa went to the bank as Victor's representative and got money out. She brought a very small part of it back to the States. Except for the top layer in the briefcase, the rest was fake." Printing fake money was not illegal as long as it was clear to most people the notes weren't real. With Victor's face on them instead of dead presidents... yeah, fake.

Victor, too, had not forgotten what happened in Argentina. Local officials there were in cahoots with the oil scout who tricked Alex and Harry. Victor mulled informing Temple about the bribe request before proceeding with a counterattack, but if there was a trap being laid, the enemies most surely also accounted for the president. And who knew if any potential fallout was intended to bring down Temple through his relatives?

So a tip was called into the FBI about the trouble in Anchorage. A few friendly reporters were alerted something major was going down at the park. A very public confrontation, from which no corrupt cop could extricate the Scoundrel Society. No way could the Kingsleys be framed.

Victor didn't want to take the chance of the few hundred dollars in the briefcase being branded a kickback, so he arranged for a little switching with help from Shawn and Luisa—the clumsy skater and the backpacking tourist.

Elsewhere in the federal building, Victor, Shawn, and Luisa would be saying the same thing to the officers. Gateway's lawyers were around to make sure no one got into legal trouble... except perhaps for confronting the FBI with the press at the scene of the arrest.

"Are we done here?" Gateway's lawyer asked the officers. "Yes? So let my client go. Let all of them go."

And yeah... they learned later there had been no setup, no attempt to trap the Kingsley brothers. The politicians merely wanted to get their accounts padded.

"The sons of bitches belong in prison in any case," Victor said to Brad over the speakerphone. "But it does mean Alaska is likely a loss."

"A big loss," agreed Lilah. She was listening in from Brad's office. "Not many government types are going to cooperate with us. They might kick up trouble at the very idea of a network."

Victor chuckled. "Lilah, I wouldn't have expected you of all people to suddenly start expecting the worst. Yeah, the plan will be a harder sell in Alaska because of community sentiment. Local leaders versus outsiders and that sort of bullshit, but a little media play here and there... we're gonna look like heroes, and no politician in the U.S. will dare oppose us by the time I'm done. The absence of Alaska won't leave too big a hole in our network... I'll make sure of it. You will be able to check off my part of the expansion much sooner than we imagined. Phase one, complete."

Tone strangely uneasy, Lilah muttered, "So fast?"

Harry's markings on the world map at the end of phase one.

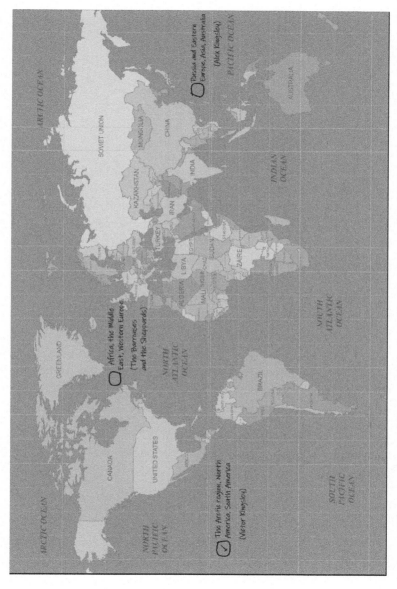

Part IV

Chapter 8

A week later, May 1986

Executive Residence, The White House

Temple stood from the couch as a lean man with age-incongruous black hair and bright-green eyes was being shown in by the staff. Following Noah Andersen, former attorney general, was a diminutive woman with plump cheeks and stone-gray hair, her eyes twinkling behind thick-rimmed spectacles. Wilma, secretary to the president, declined the offer of a seat as the two men settled into the comfortable furniture arranged around the television set. The living room was small enough to fit into your average American townhouse. Except, the home belonged to the people of the United States, every grain of dust in it a witness to momentous decisions. Grimly, Temple hoped the building was not about to witness the abject failure of his latest plan. The many assumptions he made, the countless calculations... success was in no way guaranteed.

"I gave the tapes to the butler," said Wilma. "Wish I could stay and watch with you but got a big date tonight with the grandchildren!"

"Enjoy," said Temple, smiling. As the secretary left, he explained to Noah, "My mother's movies."

Film from the turn of the century couldn't have been easy to find, but Wilma apparently managed it. Temple wasn't quite sure why he wanted them. He didn't know what new insight he was hoping to get from watching his mother enacting Galatea, the mythological statue which came to life. Temple was into his teens when he first met the woman who gave birth to him, and to her credit, she never presumed any standing to dispense maternal advice. When she needed something from him, she simply stated her case. Still, Temple couldn't remember a time when he refused.

His father... Temple already knew what the gentleman would've said. Only a select few were privileged to serve in the U.S. Congress, and even fewer were called upon to be the nation's chief executive. With such power came the soul-crushing weight of dark responsibilities. If Temple weren't prepared for the responsibilities, he shouldn't have run for the office. Since he was already there, he needed to carry out his duties.

As commander in chief, Temple mourned every life taken under his watch, some despite his best efforts, some he arranged. But he couldn't allow grief to stop him from doing what he must. A good president could not afford to be a good man.

A good man would never dream of putting his child through the trauma Temple was about to. His only offspring—the classics professor—rarely called, let alone visited. The president tried to remember how long it had been since they talked. Months, definitely. Lilah had touched a paternal core in Temple he didn't know existed. What he was about to do to her in the effort to get rid of Harry... there was no forgiveness for such deeds.

"Don't you have to use the theater?" Noah asked, breaking Temple's train of thoughts.

"Heh... yeah." The White House Family Theater would have the equipment so Sylvia Kingsley, *née* Fontaine, could once again come alive on screen. "Later, maybe." Temple nodded in the direction of the scene unfolding on the television. "Watch this now."

A few familiar faces were present—Brad, Victor, Alex, and Harry. The press was peppering the men with questions about the news from Alaska.

"As the kingmaker of the oil sector..." one of the reporters started.

"I detest the term," Harry interjected, the friendliness of his grin not changing an iota. *"But yes, the sector needs someone like Brad, and I appreciate the opportunity to work with him."*

Seated next to Harry, Brad pushed his glasses up his nose and gave the crowd a pleased smile. He'd opted for a business suit while the rest of the group was dressed casually in cargo pants and light-colored shirts. With brown curly hair and blue eyes, Brad's appearance was acceptable enough, but he became practically invisible when one of his brothers was around. Unfortunate... especially where his wife was concerned.

"No Lilah," Noah remarked.

"As usual," said Temple. If she deigned to attend a couple of such events and show the public what she did in the business... but no. "What do you think of this Alaska incident?"

Noah shrugged. "They exposed political corruption... *of course* the public is eating it up. Still, Victor's stunt didn't make the business any new friends in places where it counts."

"But nothing we can use against Harry," the president brooded.

"Clearly not. Temple... what *is* your plan against Harry? Why the hell are you so reluctant to discuss it even with me?"

"Because I've been hoping for an alternative," Temple admitted. For Harry to relent or something else which might force Lilah to back down.

"So was I," Noah said quietly. "It's a pity. He's an interesting young man... a sharp mind."

"Unfortunately, we need to start preparing now." Switching topics, Temple asked, "The latest update on Brad?"

Noah blinked. After contemplating his old friend for a moment or two, the former attorney general said, "Off and on quarrels. The same stuff... gossip about Lilah, the yellow press. Office staff is whispering. So are the people at home. All are under nondisclosure agreements, but it's usually not enough to stop chatter."

Temple inclined his head, partly in agreement, partly in relief. Thus far, his calculations proved to be on the mark. Thus far... with some more time to go during which Brad needed to be kept in the dark about his wife's past. Some more time during which the couple could not be allowed to reconcile. Some more time of keeping a monster on a leash. Some more time... at the end of which Lilah would become the cause of Harry Sheppard's destruction.

Chapter 9

A day later, May 1986

World Trade Center, New York City

"Is Mr. Kingsley expecting you?" asked Brad's secretary, voice hesitant. "He said he's going to be busy with calls." She was always very protective of her boss and his schedule, even from his own family.

"I'm his..." Lilah gritted her teeth so hard her jaw hurt. Snapping at the staff was completely unfair. "I apologize. I should have given you time to rearrange his schedule before walking over, but something important came up with reference to the meeting next week with the Soviet ministers." A bald-faced lie of course.

In a couple of minutes, she strode in, barely glancing around the office. Not that there was much to notice. Brad preferred simplicity in décor, and other than the sturdy oak table and the leather chair, the room held only a display case with industry awards and trophies sorted in order of importance. Oh, and there were three photographs—one of him with his mother and brothers, the second with his grandfather, then a formal picture taken of him and Lilah soon after their wedding.

"I thought you had the Russian pipeline project under control?" Brad asked, closing the folder on the desk before standing. "*You* talked to Moscow and the Israeli government. *You* decided the amount of capital we're willing to invest. I was asked not to hang over your shoulder, checking on your work."

"What is *wrong* with you?" Lilah snarled, beyond caring the secretary could hear every word. "Why are you bothering my staff?"

"What's wrong with *me*?" Brad exclaimed. "You refuse to answer when I ask about your plans, and I'm the one with the problem?"

There was an audible gulp from the secretary as she closed the door and left.

Lilah threw her hands up. "You didn't just 'ask about my plans.' You wanted to know my schedule for the whole day, down to the minute!" After the quarrel last month, there was peace in their home for a while. They worked together in the office, discussed baby plans at night. Then, a new episode of the fictional Lilah saga appeared in the magazine, featuring her *and* Alex this time. Yet another argument later, she declined to detail for her husband how she was about to spend her workday. "When I wouldn't play along, you called my assistant," Lilah accused. "Behind my back!"

Face set in stubborn lines, Brad said, "After you spent two hours at lunch."

"Do you have any idea how embarrassed I was?"

Brad stated, "I was worried about you."

"Ha! Why did you ask her who I was with?"

"She told you? That's it. The woman is fired."

Lilah massaged her pounding temples. "For doing her job? She's my assistant, not your spy."

Nostrils flaring, Brad said, "I'm the CEO of the company, *darling*. You—and your assistant—work for me. In fact, the only reason *you're* still in the position is the damn pre-nup. Crunching numbers is not a unique skill. I could find another CFO with no trouble—better qualified, too, and easier to deal with."

Lilah shook her head in incredulity. "You believe that's all I do? From the day we got engaged, I've been working just as hard as you. Look around, Brad. We went from underdog to the premier oil services business in the world in a few years. You think I had nothing to do with it? What about Alex? And Victor?"

Brad ground out, "Alex doesn't run this company. My brothers follow *my* instructions, and I make sure we do everything correctly, ethically. They have no problem giving me credit for their success. Harry does, too. You're the only one with trouble remembering who the boss is." He jerked open a drawer and tossed the folder inside. "If it hadn't been for the shape we were in, I would never have agreed to the contract your family forced on us. Now, I'm stuck with a CFO who tries to act as if she runs my business."

"I wasn't..." she shouted, pounding a fist on the papers piled on his desk. "You know something? I sacrificed my life, the career I had in mind, to marry you. This business was built on my blood, sweat, and tears as much as yours. My ethics and my values matter in this company just as much as yours."

"You should hear yourself," Brad interjected, snarling. "No one else but me would put up with it."

Lilah's fingers clenched around the papers. Struggling with the urge to rip the documents into pieces, she glanced at the sheets.

"The Peter Kingsley Network," said the header on the cover. Those four words chained her to this man and this office.

The girl she used to be recoiled at the idea of such immense authority in one person's hands. She didn't realize at the time authority shackled the one unfortunate enough to wield it. The door was unlocked, but Lilah couldn't leave. She'd made certain promises to the many victims of Sanders's tyranny and the world at large. Those vows kept her prisoner to her own power.

If she could abdicate in favor of someone she trusted... if she could leave all her personal messes behind... if she could return to the legal career she imagined so long ago...

The vast organization planned by the alliance would eventually have a board and a chairman. The board would be elected at the network's first official meeting. The chairman—whomever it was—would be in an extremely powerful position. He or she would be as powerful as Brad Kingsley, the chief executive officer of the network. A chairman could even have authority over the CEO. *If* they made it so in the charter. Once the network was finalized... once she managed to hand control to a trustworthy chairman...

Lilah shook her head. After the confirmation she got from her doctor an hour ago, she *couldn't* cut Brad out of her life even if everything else aligned perfectly.

Taking a deep breath, she smoothed out the papers. "How did we get from the topic of you tracing my movements to this? It always ends up being the same fight! We need to sort ourselves out, Brad. There are commitments we took on when we got married—"

Brad sneered. "The only reason behind our marriage is corporate politics, right? If it hadn't been for the network, you would have married someone else. My brother, maybe? Alex?"

"Alex has nothing to do with our problem."

"If he has nothing to do with our *marriage,* why was he bringing flowers on your birthday?"

"Oh, Lord! That was in *January*—Brad, he considers me a friend! Besides, you filled our home with roses."

"Yeah," he said bitterly. "And you helpfully informed me lotuses were your favorite."

"For crying out loud, how many times do I have to apologize? Yes, it was insensitive; but no, I didn't do it on purpose. It was a stupid mistake."

"*Alex* somehow already knew what you liked."

"I grew up with Sabrina. She probably told him." Sabrina even knew the florist who made Lilah's favorite perfume, blue lotus oil. "And *you* should've—" Lilah bit back the rest. Anyone with eyes should've seen the lotus pond she got the landscapers to put in outside her office windows in Panama.

The intercom buzzed, and Brad's secretary stuttered, reminding him he needed to leave for his meeting with the Chinese ambassador. "I'll see you later," he said tersely to Lilah.

She'd started the morning with so much hope, and now... Brad was at the door when Lilah blurted, "I was at the doctor's." Brad stopped, his hand on the knob. She clarified, "At lunch, I mean. I did one of those home pregnancy tests. It was—" She smiled, unable to help herself. "—positive. I wanted to have the doctor confirm before saying anything to you."

Brad wheeled around, his eyes wide. "B-but," he stuttered. "We just started trying..."

"I *know.*" Lilah nodded, another smile breaking through. "What can I say? I have Sheppard blood, and we happen to be a fertile lot."

Breathing hitching, Brad smoothed back his hair. "Are you sure?" Before she could respond, he continued, "Of course you are.

You went to the doctor. My God." He glanced toward the window for a second before bringing his eyes back to her. "We're going to have a baby. I'm going to be a father!"

With a soft laugh, Lilah inclined her head.

In a couple of strides, he was next to her, his hands cupping her face. The leathery fragrance he favored floated to her nostrils. "I'm so sorry," he murmured. "I was a complete jerk."

"Yes, you were," she returned pertly.

His thumbs rubbed circles on her cheeks. "Only because I can't stand seeing those stories. Lilah, you're my wife... the mother of my child... I'll make it up to you, I swear."

The intercom buzzed a second time. "You'd better leave," Lilah said. "Don't make the ambassador wait."

Glancing at the door, he swore. "We'll celebrate at home... actually, why don't we take a break and go somewhere?"

"We can't both be off at the same time. I was planning to work from home when you leave for Panama next week... just to relax for a bit." The moment the words were out of her mouth, she wished she could take them back.

Thank God, Brad didn't seem to read any nefarious meanings into what she said... for once. "Yeah," he said. "You should. Pregnant women are supposed to get rest and relaxation. It won't be good for the child if you don't."

As she returned to her office, Lilah swore they were going to fix whatever it was. Somehow, she was going to get through to him. If she didn't, none of them would get their happy ending, and Harry would forfeit his life.

Part V

Chapter 10

A week later, June 1986

World Trade Center, New York City

"Electric shock?" Harry said into the phone, puzzled. "From *my* bike?" The words caused the tall, lanky African-American in the leather chair across the desk to look up in concern—Dante, Harry's boss and COO of the business. They were discussing a couple of projects in Harry's office when the phone call came through. Harry held up a hand, requesting silence while he talked to the son of the retired mechanic who ran the garage where the Harley was kept.

"Yeah," said the son, continuing with the update. Harry now used the Harley only for pleasure rides and parked it in the garage not far from work to avoid vandalism and theft. The elderly mechanic was trying to move the bike to make space for a luxury car. The second he turned it on, current shot up from the handlebar. He screamed in pain but was unable to let go. Luckily, one of the attendants slammed the hand away with a plastic traffic cone, saving the mechanic's life. "Dad says there were a couple of kids hanging out in the street, smoking crack. Could've been them."

"Maybe," said Harry.

Only a month ago, the mechanic reported an attempted theft of the bike. The would-be robber was spotted by another vehicle owner. Before he could be apprehended, the man escaped. The mechanic had tried to contact Harry in Alaska about the incident. Since then, the bike was kept parked in full view of the garage office. Now, this electric shock.

Crackheads trying to steal the bike made sense. Rigging it to deliver a shock? If the mechanic didn't need to move it, *Harry* would've been at the receiving end of the shock the next time he decided on a drive.

"I'm glad your father's all right," he finally said.

When he hung up, Dante quirked his eyebrow in a silent question.

Harry gave a quick explanation while punching in a number on the keypad, letting the speakerphone ring. "I'm calling Lilah. This bike thing... could be idiot kids on a high, but remember all the attacks Sanders tried in Libya. We can't take a chance."

Dante groaned. "How many times are you going to do this? You've called twice just tonight. She's either not home or doesn't want to talk to anyone. Besides, Brad already told you she wanted time to relax before starting full steam on the expansion plans. This bike thing is only an excuse for your paranoia."

The shrill tone gave way to the answering machine. "Report back as soon as you get this message," Harry barked. "Going AWOL is *not* okay."

"Rude," reproved Dante. "Lilah does not have to check in with you before every move."

Collapsing into his own swivel chair, Harry picked up the paperweight and played with it. The heavy crystal with the embedded peacock feather was a gift from his sister Sabrina. The feather Lilah once gave him had been tucked inside his desk drawer for a long time. Sabrina's son spotted it when she brought him to visit his uncle, and shortly after, she got the paperweight made. "The Russian project is critical to the network, and Lilah is supposed to be personally handling the finances."

"Give it a rest, will ya?" snapped Dante. "She deserves a break. The moment you spout your nonsense about the bike, she'll come running back. Don't do it."

Not only would she hotfoot it to New York, she'd insist they put their plans for the network on hold... on account of a random occurrence which didn't have anything to do with their enemies. With a sigh, Harry picked up the list of proposed investments for the Peter Kingsley Network.

The sky outside was already turning purple in preparation for the night. Chatter had long died away in the office, and even Harry's secretary left, stating she needed her sleep unlike "certain people" she knew. Only he and Dante remained. While Dante's main role in Gateway was as COO, he worked with Harry in his extended role as liaison with the Peter Kingsley Company, and they were both heavily involved in the expansion plans.

Someone sneezed outside.

"Who's still here?" asked Dante.

Harry glanced at the small digital clock on the desk. "Cleaning crew, probably. They should be locking up and leaving soon."

Between the custodians and Harry's secretary, his office stayed tidy enough for a naval inspection. Papers were arranged in neat stacks in order of importance, maps hung on the wall, the television set was tucked into one corner, and the latest in communication technology was arrayed on the ebony desk. The blue-gray carpet saw much traffic on a daily basis but was kept meticulously clean even around the potted plant next to the desk. Unlike the rest of Gateway's rooms, the walls in Harry's office were painted creamy-yellow, the color reminding him of bright-sunny days, and the row of windows behind the desk overlooked downtown Manhattan. The mild smell of a floral room freshener clung to the air. Within minutes, the three remaining custodians poked their heads in, calling goodbyes to Dante and Harry.

As the footsteps of the departing men faded, Dante turned his attention back to the documents. "Some of these fellows run their businesses like little dictatorships." The report from a small African company was flung straight to the trash can.

Harry grinned to himself and retrieved the papers. "If I work with only those who get the Dante seal of good behavior, even Gateway might not qualify."

"Don't start again with your insane schemes," Dante said, eyes narrowed.

Harry settled back into his chair. "Results, old man. Even you can't argue with the numbers, and I make you look good."

"Just don't get yourself killed; I hate breaking in new brokers. Should've fired you the first day I started as your father's secretary. Lots of people have prematurely gray hair, but this smart aleck calls me an old man. You were only fourteen, and I thought I'd give you a chance to grow out of it."

The gray hair had thinned considerably, Harry noted. Dante was not yet forty-five, but there were wrinkles on his dark skin. Harry grinned. "Who else would've put up with your nagging for minimum wage?"

"You were a gofer." Besides assisting Dante in secretarial duties, there was Harry's part-time job at the rigs. "What did you expect?"

The phone rang, and Harry leaped. The chair rolled backward and was brought to an abrupt halt by the potted plant. "Hello—"

Before he could tack Lilah's name to the greeting, another female voice asked, "What, Harry?" Sabrina... trust siblings to be rudely matter of fact never mind how many years separated them. She was twenty-three to Harry's almost-thirty. Hector, the oldest of the three Sheppard children, was thirty-seven.

"Uhh... what are you doing in Lilah's home? And where is she?"

"C'mon, Harry, I don't report to you. Neither does Lilah."

Dante, clearly having heard Sabrina's reprimand, wore a smug I-told-you-so expression.

Harry wasn't going to win this bout. "I apologize, Runt. Just tell me Lilah's all right."

'She's fine... playing with Mikey. I'm keeping her company while Brad's away."

So Lilah was still in the city. "Okay, please let her know—"

Something crashed outside. Harry jolted.

Dante sprang from his chair, and the papers in his hand fell, scattering on blue carpet. "What the hell!"

"Call you back, Runt," muttered Harry. Dante was already running out, prepared to confront the trespasser. Harry hissed, "Wait for backup, old man." Dialing the downstairs lobby, he asked them to get security.

He slid the desk drawer open and took out his Colt. Gesturing at Dante to stay behind, Harry padded toward the door, ready to intercept the intruder if he tried to escape.

Through the crack, he watched. Shadows shrouded the empty cubicles, the faint recess lighting leaving only a dim glow. Something moved in the periphery of his visual field. Head jerking to the side, Harry took aim. A paper, blown about by the breeze from the air conditioner, fluttered to the floor. He growled under his breath. Somewhere to the left, a clock ticked in rhythm with the pounding in his chest.

The air in the office shifted. Harry sensed enemy presence in the territory, the stench of danger sharpening every sense. Hackles rose; nostrils flared.

A large form lumbered out from the gloomy corridor, cursing when his limb collided with something. There was a rustling sound, and the burglar bent. Whoever he was, stealth didn't seem to be a concern. But then, he wouldn't have expected anyone else to still be around.

Corporate espionage? Or perhaps a killer sent by the enemy. Muscles coiling, Harry listened intently for the sounds of building security.

The bulky figure kneeling on the carpet grunted and heaved himself up. The predator in Harry smelled escaping prey. Vision narrowed to his target, the whisper of every breath reaching his ears. He trained the gun on his quarry.

"Security," a voice thundered outside. The front door vibrated from pounding fists.

The burglar yelped, pivoting to run back inside.

Weapon covering the thief, Harry slipped out, hand groping along the wall for the light switch. The front door exploded open, and at the same moment, white brightness flooded the office.

Dropping the folders to the floor, the intruder raised his arms. Rotund form, blond comb-over, blue eyes. Will Luce, Sr., Harry's father-in-law.

#

Half hour later

"Do you believe him?" Dante asked once all parties removed themselves from the office. Luce claimed he was merely catching up on work assigned by Hector, Harry's brother. "The fellow does only the minimum necessary to keep his job."

"Don't know, old man," said Harry. "But the folders he had *were* from the accounts he handles."

"Luce is not used to any sort of work," Dante stated. "He inherited money and invested in Gateway. It was a mistake to hire him. If he weren't Verity's father..."

...he'd have been fired a long time back, Harry finished. "He *was* our biggest shareholder outside of immediate family." Until Luce lost his stock in a game of cards with Harry who then put it in a trust for the man's children, operated by Gateway's board. "Hector was only making sure there was enough cash for Will to live on. Verity has been asking me to release the stock from the board's control."

"Don't do it," Dante counseled. "Who knows what he'll do if it's returned?"

"Even if the board releases it, nothing can go to Will without my say-so," said Harry. His consent and a majority vote by the board were required for the shares to return to the original owner. "I'm not about to let him have it." Liam, Verity's brother, was in fervent agreement.

Dante yawned. "Let's talk about it tomorrow. You should be heading home, too. Your wife must be getting worried, especially if Luce has called with his version of the story."

Another evening at home with Verity seething with resentment at any mention of the network or the Kingsleys. Harry mostly managed to ignore the sulks, but since the topic came up... "May I ask you a question, Dante? About... uhh... the ladies."

The look on Dante's face was priceless. In the week after his wife was killed by a drunk driver, Dante made the grief-fueled confession she'd been the only woman in his life. As far as Harry knew, Dante was still mourning her. Harry, on the other hand, was the darling of the tabloids for his rumored girlfriends.

Damned awkward thing to bring up, but Harry wasn't comfortable discussing this with his parents or brother. "Verity's been talking about starting a family."

After a few seconds, Dante prompted, "And?"

Harry gestured restlessly. "She's young... and bored, I think. Not a good reason to have children."

"You do spend a lot of time in the office. She wants your attention and thinks a child will do the trick. It's not difficult to figure out."

"There are other things she can do. I asked her to join us; she seemed interested in the work before we—"

"—before you got married," finished Dante. "She was getting to know you. It does not mean she wants to make your obsession her life's goal."

"My obsession?" Harry laughed. "You must admit, though, it is a magnificent passion, worth all the blood and sweat and tears. Verity cannot see it. She likes the trappings of power and fame but not the hard work going into it."

Huffing out a breath, Dante said, "C'mon, Harry, don't compare her to Lilah. It's not fair."

"Who said anything about Lilah?"

With a speaking look, Dante insisted, "Oh, yeah, you're comparing them. They're very different women. Verity was brought up in the lap of luxury, and her father might be an idiot, but he adores her. Lilah might behave like royalty, but her parents were middle class, and they died when she was young. She knew she was expected to make her own way in the world."

"A middle-class princess?" Harry smiled and reminded Dante, "Barrons is one of the wealthiest men in America."

Dante shrugged. "When have Lilah's half-sister and brother-in-law ever considered her family? Even if they did, it makes no difference at this time. You had your chance with her and chose not to take it. Verity is a pretty girl, a nice young woman, and she loves you. You knew the deal when you asked her to marry you. Don't change the rules of the game after the fact."

"If she doesn't want to be a part of my dream, she can at least understand I have other responsibilities. I don't have time for a child."

Dante's eyelids flickered. "Most women—wives, especially—don't appreciate being told they come second to the rest of the universe. Show her how much you value her presence in your life, and she'll be willing to wait until you're also ready for children. Now, go home before she reports you missing. It's late."

"G'night, Dante," Harry said.

Dante sighed. "You're not leaving, are you?"

"The Russians await," Harry said. "I'll make sure Verity gets all the attention she could possibly want after."

Groaning, Dante said, "I need to get some sleep. See you tomorrow." Pivoting, he bumped into a rolling chair, toppling it. It collided with the wall of a cubicle which shuddered in response, but there was barely a muffled thump to be heard.

The gun was still in Harry's right hand. With the other, he helped Dante straighten the chair. The suite which overflowed with humanity during the workday was deserted and seemed cavernous. The only sounds were the voices of the two men. Restlessly, Harry surveyed the brightly lit office space.

The crash they attributed to Verity's father... the loud sound was surely caused by something heavy. Harry did a slow three-sixty, studying the hall, the upright and intact furniture. Fax machines, copiers... all equipment seemed in place. "Stay in my office for a few minutes, Dante," Harry instructed. "I need to check the accounting division. Any sign of trouble, call security back."

Shoes sinking into the thick carpet, Harry strode to where his brother's staff did their work. The air conditioner continued to run, its subdued hum the only sound. He scanned the room. All the tables were in their place, with chairs behind. Papers were piled tidily on desks. Walking to a file cabinet, Harry tugged experimentally. An overweight man like Will Luce, unaccustomed to exercise, toppled one of the heavy pieces of furniture or equipment, causing the loud crash? He'd then managed to set it back up within seconds, cleaning the mess before walking out to be confronted by building security?

Whistling softly, Harry withdrew. At the entrance to his office, he beckoned Dante and reached for the switch. The hall plunged into sudden darkness. In silence, they crept along the wall, scrutinizing the gloom. Only a thin line of light leached below a door.

As they watched, the door swung open. In the brightness spilling into the hallway, the figure slipping out was easily recognizable. Graying hair, short beard, features very similar to Harry's. The CEO, Ryan Sheppard. Harry's father.

#

Ten minutes later

"Are you done interrogating me?" Ryan asked through clenched teeth.

Leaning his hip against a desk, Harry sighed. "It's no interrogation, Father. Only trying to understand... why couldn't you simply walk out there and let us know you were still around? Why all the deception?"

"Deception? *I* run this business. Why should I explain my presence to building security or even *you*?"

Dante interceded. "Got to admit, Harry, it would've been a damned farce—you confronting your father *and* father-in-law with armed guards, all in the space of one hour."

Harry pinched the bridge of his nose. "I suppose you're right."

But Ryan's aggression, the jitteriness... the Sheppards used to be close, leaning on each other through the last couple of years in

Libya. There were bad months when money was tight, and they counted pennies to make payroll. Now, they were worth billions, but the ties of love and loyalty and trust binding them together seemed to have vanished.

Harry yawned. Perhaps a good night's sleep would clear the cobwebs in his brain. The morning might tell him there were no grounds for suspicion.

Together, the three men cleaned up the mess on the floor, the fax machine and associated paraphernalia which lay broken on blue carpet.

"Thank God, no papers," muttered Dante. "It would've been a pain in the backside to sort through orders and vendors."

Harry stilled. "Where *are* the papers?" he asked. Gateway's business was spread across the globe, and constant communication was maintained with buyers and sellers. It would not be merely unusual for nothing to have come through in the hours between the end of the workday and now. It would have been impossible, short of technical malfunction.

"I took care of it," growled Ryan.

They closed the door behind them, heading home. Before he turned the lights off, Harry noted that the shredder was nearly full. *What didn't you want me to see, Father?* Harry asked silently.

Chapter 11

Two days later, June 1986

Dresden, East Germany

The Soviet diplomat leaned to the side and whispered something to his compatriot, the minister for gas industries. The statesmen, as befitted their status, were seated at the head of the table with Alex and Harry not too far down. The Americans had been granted an exclusive audience outside of the prying eyes of the press. East German officials, eager for their piece of the pie, listened in on the conversation. The minister spoke in rapid Russian, the slightly bald man at his side translating. "Our scientists say Siberia is..." The interpreter swallowed before continuing. "...full of it."

Alex stared at the Russians, trying to maintain a fixed expression. Harry coughed. He spoke a number of languages, but Russian was not one of them. Alex threw a questioning glance at his brother-in-law's secretary, a trim, blonde fifty-year-old with snapping blue eyes. Over copious amounts of vodka one evening, Natasha had told Alex her grandparents fled the Soviet Union with their teenaged children after the Bolshevik revolution. They passed on the traditional practices and language to their progeny. Natasha was born in Brooklyn, but she, her children, *and* her grandchildren spoke fluent Russian.

She muttered, "That's what he said."

The diplomat interrupted, explaining haltingly, "Much petroleum."

Ah. Alex bit back a smile. Across the table, Harry casually covered his mouth with his fingers.

The minister proceeded to elaborate through his interpreter. "Petroleum everywhere, but not the money. We need assistance; you want our oil. Can we scratch each other?"

Natasha said, "I think he means 'you scratch my back, I scratch yours.'"

"Da," nodded the minister. *"Russkiy?"*

"No," she said shortly. "I just know the language."

Scanning the conference room in the newly built Hotel Bellevue, Alex noticed Harry's eyes on the Soviet interpreter, who in turn was contemplating Natasha. The man was in his thirties.

Thumbing his nose, the official sniffed, dismissing Harry's secretary before continuing translating between three languages.

Eyes partly shut, Alex studied the Soviet interpreter. Erect posture, minimum required movements, alert. Alex took a closer look at the interpreter's ID, wondering what it was about Tash that caught his attention. What's more, why Harry was keeping the carefully bland look on his face?

The negotiating teams came to a tentative agreement soon after and arranged to have Alex accompany the Soviet officials to Siberia for a first look around. Israel would send a couple of government representatives along to sign a deal with the Russians as part of the larger contract with the Kingsleys.

Later, walking briskly across the courtyard in front, Natasha snapped, "What? I'm American."

Harry raised his hands in surrender. "Didn't say a word."

"I have nothing to do with the Soviet Union," she said. "Never set foot in the place, never wanted to." She climbed into the back of the Trabant with Alex. "Who volunteers to travel to Siberia?" she asked him. "There's nothing there."

Harry sat in the front passenger seat. The driver assigned to them drummed his fingers on the steering wheel.

"Only billions of dollars in petroleum," remarked Alex. "Plus, the pictures look beautiful."

"Better you than me," she shuddered. "Make sure you get another Russian interpreter for the trip."

Alex coaxed, "C'mon, Tash, you and I can paint the place red."

"Russia is *already* red," said Harry.

The other two groaned, Alex thwacking him with a rolled-up newspaper.

"Take that beautiful wife of yours," suggested Natasha. "You don't need a *babushka* spoiling your fun."

"Tash, you're the prettiest grandmother I've seen," Alex said.

"Flirt," Natasha accused, amused indulgence in her tone. She peered through the car window. "How long from here to West Berlin? I can't wait to get back to—" Alex tapped her on the knee before she said something which might be carried back by the driver to the East German authorities. Plus, there was the danger of electronic bugs. "—the hotel," she finished.

Harry twisted around in his seat. "Feel like a couple of rounds of poker when we get back? I have a deck on me."

"Of course you do," grumbled Alex. "But what's the damned point when you count cards or whatever?"

"I swear there won't be any 'whatever,'" Harry said, laughing.

"Like I'm fool enough to... oh, why the hell not?" Alex scratched the back of his neck. "It might be my last chance to have fun before I get back from Russia."

In a couple of hours, they were at Checkpoint Charlie, and Natasha was visibly jittery as they dismissed the driver and walked toward the Allied side.

"Breathe," Harry suggested, grinning at Natasha. "Only a few more steps—"

A high-pitched shriek drowned out the rest of his words, followed by the loud rumble of an engine. Alex was about to turn and check what the hell was causing the racket when Harry tackled him without warning, both hurtling into a parked motorbike. The world titled. Something sharp dug into Alex's hip. A crash... the vehicle toppled, and his feet slipped out from under him. When he scrambled up, a van was vrooming away, its metallic brown sheen barely visible through the cloud of dust and thick, black fumes.

Natasha was still on the ground next to the men, Harry's arm wrapped protectively around her shoulders.

Shouts of alarm, thundering feet... "Are you all right?" asked an East German border official. A few others hurried toward the Americans.

Coughing into his elbow, Alex extended a hand to Natasha. "I'm good. Tash? Harry?"

Natasha nodded.

"Me, too," Harry said, heaving himself up from the ground to peer intently in the direction of the main road into which the van had already disappeared. Blood beaded along a line on the back of his hand. "Near miss number two... maybe three."

"Huh?" Alex asked.

Harry shook his head. "Something similar happened on the way to work a few weeks ago."

"Idiot drivers," Alex agreed. They were everywhere.

It took a couple of minutes to disperse the small crowd, but Harry detained the border officer for some more time, asking questions about the ownership of the van. The fellow denied all knowledge, adding it was not a government vehicle. And no, he didn't think any of his colleagues would have the license number of a random automobile parked on the street. Most likely, it was some kid in an unauthorized bid to cross to the other side who eventually decided not to risk it and was careless in his hurry to escape. Such desperate attempts to defect were not uncommon. The officer personally escorted the Americans to West Germany.

"See what happened?" Natasha asked, climbing into the waiting car. "You don't get how lucky you are to be born in a free country." She threw a quick glance at the infamous wall which divided the city in two before her eyes darted away.

Alex refrained from pointing out Natasha was also born in the States.

Before their cab turned into the side street where the Savoy Berlin was, an elegant stone building came into view. The same as he did the last couple of days, Alex spotted the equally tasteful plate by the door which announced the identity of the establishment—Eden, Gentlemen's Club. Also as he had the last couple of days, he caught Harry's speculative look in the direction of the club when they exited the car at Savoy's doorstep.

With a raised hand, Harry asked Alex to wait while Natasha disappeared inside the hotel. A few guests and hotel employees were walking around, but no one was close enough to overhear the Americans talk. "The Soviet government is working on converting the ministry of gas into a corporation," said Harry. "A state-private partnership called Gazprom. Also, there's chatter about a pipeline from Russia to Germany. Get the Kingsleys and Gateway a foot in the door, Alex, and make certain the deal includes Israel."

Alex nodded. Lilah once struck up a friendship with a former Israeli first lady who passed a few years ago. When the woman was still alive, she'd made it a point to introduce the then-law student to the academic and political elite in her country. One of the outcomes was the close collaboration between the engineers of the Peter Kingsley Company and researchers in Israel. The Kingsleys already sold oil to the Jewish nation as part of the arrangement, but it was important to Tel Aviv to have multiple sources of energy supply. The Kingsleys and Harry were in agreement over the need to keep reliable partners happy which meant ensuring Russia guaranteed a certain number of barrels every year. Business ties aside, both Harry and Lilah were emotionally attached to the country, having spent the first few years of their lives there.

Harry straightened the lapels of his blazer. "Also, we should go over to your old girlfriend's place for a visit."

Alex was confused for a moment. "My old girl—" He nearly choked on his own tongue. *"What?"* In a quieter tone, he asked again, "What?" Lupe Valdez, the owner of Eden, had been a one-night stand when he visited her original establishment in DC. A few months later, Alex met Sabrina. One drunken evening, he and Harry traded stories, and the tale of Alex's tryst with Lupe tumbled out. He heard from Harry at the time there was a second Eden in Las Vegas and a third one in LA. In the years since, Lupe Valdez expanded her chain to European cities, but the presence of an Eden in Berlin was nothing of interest to Alex Kingsley. "I'm a married man." Alex rolled his eyes. "So are you, dude."

Harry ptchaaed. "I don't mean for us to ogle strippers. Remember what I said about Ms. Valdez before. She's powerful... perhaps more so than Lilah." At Alex's disbelieving snort, Harry elaborated, "Power is not always about the cash in your pocket. Eden in DC is a gathering place for rich and well-connected men. I assume it's the same here. Try to imagine the kind of information Ms. Valdez has access to."

"Ahh... what's wrong with you? Can't you stop thinking about the network at least when sexy women are involved?"

Laughing, Harry said, "She'd be a good contact to have. Plus, she already knows you."

"No," Alex said immediately. "I don't care what info you think you can pick up. Sabrina would pickle my balls and feed them to me if she found out."

Harry winced. "I really didn't need the visual."

"Well... she would." After a second, Alex asked, "Anything specific you're looking for?"

"Hmm? No... and yes. My bet is Ms. Valdez knows many, many secrets... all the people who went through her club in DC... former and current politicians, lawyers and judges, businessmen, military leaders. Dirty deals... skeletons in the cupboard... those sorts of things. She could be of huge help to us if she so chooses. She might even be aware of things about our old pal, Sanders, which *we* never heard of. Who knows? Maybe even about your cousins and other relatives. Plus, I'm sure some of the Russian friends we met in Dresden pay an occasional visit to Eden. Or at least, Ms. Valdez might know *of* them, especially a certain interpreter."

"The fellow at the meeting?"

"He caught Tash in her lie about not being Russian."

Alex shrugged. "Not a lie. Tash *is* American, not Russian."

"Regardless, he picked up on it. If you don't want to go to Ms. Valdez for info, I'll have someone else run a check on the interpreter. Will let you know if and when I get something. I'm sure *he* means to keep an eye on you in Siberia."

"What makes you think he'll show up there?"

Harry turned back to the road and stared hard for a moment or two. "The van at the checkpoint."

A lightbulb clicked on in Alex's brain. He cursed. "KGB? You think the van was them... the interpreter, too? Damn. I wonder if they know I was in Afghanistan." Alex's five years of active duty had officially been in *Pakistan,* but he'd spent a large chunk of it battling Russians in the Hindu Kush mountains on orders from the CIA. Outside the chain of command, Harry was the only one who'd been told this part of Alex's life. No one else in his circle of acquaintances could even begin to understand what it was like.

"You bet they know. The interpreter... something in the way he was acting... he's good, though; I didn't even notice him until he made the mistake of reacting to Tash. Maybe I should cancel the West Point event next week and go with you. Between the two of us, we should be able to tackle any unexpected complications."

Alex shook his head. "Not necessary. Come to think about it, what would the KGB gain from running me down? I mean, the Russian deal is to our mutual benefit."

"The dots don't connect," Harry agreed, frowning. "Perhaps it was for me... but the timing simply doesn't fit. Or it could be some rogue terrorist, someone I dealt with before who figured out my identity."

"Makes no sense," Alex said. "Your work was mostly in the Middle East, not Soviet territory. I'm sure the commies have friends who'd like to see you dead, but why would they attack you after so many years—or allow any of your old enemies to launch an attack on *their* territory—right when we're about to work together? They have plenty to lose by pissing us off. The border patrol is probably right... it was a defector who got careless."

"There's always our old buddy, Sanders," Harry muttered.

"You're kidding, right?" Alex asked, laughing. "Sanders is not getting out of prison any time soon. Even if he does, how's he going to pay for a hit job on you? The man doesn't have a dime to his name now. Arranging a kill on the other side of the world would take serious cash, I imagine."

A flicker of something passed across Harry's face. "True." Once again, he looked toward the road as though reconnoitering the perimeter for reappearance of the vehicle. "I should talk to Lilah."

"Talk to—for God's sake, don't. She's going to have nightmares every time you step out of the country. She might even call a halt to the whole network business and order us all to stay home. And for what?! Some desperate fellow who was only trying to get to freedom? Stop being paranoid, dude. Like I said... there's no one with motive *and* the money to plan an attack on you right now."

After a few moments of silence, Harry nodded. "Yeah... we don't want to risk Lilah pulling the plug on the network when there's no reason to."

Chapter 12

Next week

United States Military Academy

West Point, New York

At the special banquet, the young men and women in military formals were thoroughly enjoying the speech by celebrated former SEAL and Medal of Honor recipient, Petty Officer First Class Harry Sheppard. So was President Temple.

Recounting experiences, Harry told the audience about the good their country could do in the world, his anecdotes sometimes roaringly funny, sometimes poignant, always compelling. Finally, he switched to a discourse on relativism. "...understand how reality is subjective. The limitations you place on yourself prevent you from appreciating others' perceptions. Break through those constraints; empathize with those realities. And you will find the divine spark within you, that which we call the soul. Your collective fire is what makes our nation truly a bright light in the darkness. Congratulations, graduates, and God bless America."

As the audience stood to applaud, Temple clapped along, thinking back to the info he'd been given. The hidden weapon against Harry was getting increasingly desperate. A little desperation was good for motivation, but there could be no more unauthorized moves. Three times, Harry escaped death. Three times, the network dodged inadvertent destruction. Temple needed to tighten his control over the situation.

The president cast a quick glance around the crowd, looking for his friends and coconspirators. Amid the graying heads of the military's top brass, Noah Andersen's jet-black hair was not difficult to spot. The former attorney general rejected the suggestion that dye-induced youth looked ridiculous on a man in his late seventies. He was standing at the back of the hall, watching Harry with a bemused smile on his face while Godwin Kingsley, Temple's stepbrother, renewed his acquaintance with some of the bigwigs attending the event. Godwin had his own eccentricities, but no one ever dared confront him on it.

Unconventional appearances notwithstanding, Temple was glad to have their company. The president had invited the other two along when he was requested to give the commencement speech at the graduation ceremony. Godwin didn't have previous commitments for the week, but Noah needed to cancel travel plans. Even as a young securities lawyer, Noah had made time to roam the planet. He claimed it helped him keep his finger on the pulse of global politics.

The three men talked long into the night after the banquet was done. The little group would disperse only after the ceremony the next day. Plans needed to be discussed, their strategy to put an end to the problem of Harry Sheppard confirmed.

The morning which followed was beautiful, with sunlight drenching Michie Stadium as the cadets stood at attention. Harry and Verity Sheppard sat among the guests. She was attired in a pale-yellow dress which tied in a floppy bow at the neck. Very much young and with it... like Mrs. Temple used to be, God rest her soul.

Noah declined the president's offer to introduce him to Harry and stood to the side, chatting with a former associate from the justice department, keeping an eye on the goings-on just the same.

"Class of 1986, dismissed," announced the first captain. With wild cheers, the newly commissioned second lieutenants tossed their hats into the air.

The sun glinted off the five-pointed bronze star on Harry's chest as he saluted the valedictorian. Following the tradition at the military academy of honoring the first enlisted man to acknowledge you as an officer, the graduate handed Harry a newly minted silver coin.

"Thank you, sir," Harry said to the young officer.

Temple returned Harry's polite nod and watched as he went his own way.

"Shall we?" asked General Potts, the dean of the academy, appearing at Temple's elbow.

Once inside the dean's office, the president dismissed his protective detail and relaxed into the leather chair. "Noah, Brigadier General Potts has been of great help to me over my career. He's been the dean here for many years, and all the Kingsley grandsons had the privilege of being taught by him."

Potts waited until Andersen and Godwin sat before seating himself. "Yes. Alex was one of the best to come through here. It's a pity he decided to leave the service."

"Family obligations," grunted Godwin.

"So I heard from Phillip," said the general, referring to his son who remained a good friend of Steven Kingsley, one of Godwin's other grandchildren. Steven once attempted to murder Brad and his brothers, but the Kingsley name and wealth erased a lot of sins in the eyes of his acquaintances.

The president accepted Potts's offer of iced tea. "How come you didn't want to meet Harry?" Temple asked Noah. "I mean, you keep saying he's an interesting character. It *would* be fascinating to analyze him. The metamorphosis from the uncontrolled emotion of a teenager to his unnatural objectivity as an adult... his dispassion, if you will."

"On the contrary, my friend." Noah shook his head. "The extreme feeling you mentioned is what drives Harry. He's just better than most people at hiding emotions. From the public and perhaps from himself." The lawyer took a sip of the sweetened drink. "Harry's true talent is his understanding of psychology—individual *and* collective—and his ability to communicate." Noah twisted to face Temple. "The news conference at the Plaza during the Sanders project was a virtuoso performance in mass manipulation... propaganda. The press knew it, and they still ate it up!"

"Thank you," said Temple, chuckling. "I like to think he learned it from me."

"He never showed any interest in politics?" Noah asked.

"Not the electoral kind," said Temple.

"Pity," said Noah. "Under different circumstances, you might've been grooming Harry Sheppard to follow you to the White House someday. You and he are very alike, Temple."

"Don't forget you're talking about our enemy," Godwin said, tone amused.

"I don't know, Godwin," Noah pondered. Clearing his throat, he turned back to the president. "Temple, the strategy with Sanders was... Harry and Lilah achieved what the justice department couldn't in my years as attorney general. They put Jared Sanders in prison."

"They did it with the silent backing of a sitting president," reminded Godwin.

"Regardless," said Noah, "They have proven themselves quite capable. Plus, once the network is formalized, Gateway will only be one among many companies. Yes, Harry might continue to have personal influence over Brad and the rest, but it won't be as bad as it is now. I'm sure we can make our voices heard. Are our reasons to remove Harry still valid?"

"What?" Godwin sat up. "The Kingsleys will *not* play puppets for Harry Sheppard or Lilah."

"Who's asking you to?" inquired Noah. "If Harry continues to shut you out, all you have to do is advise your grandsons to cool things with him for a bit. They will listen to you... they would *now* no matter how highly they think of him." The need for cooperation from Lilah and the Sheppards kept Godwin from issuing that command. But once the network was set in stone...

"We already tried to sideline Harry once," Godwin said, gaze turning flinty. "It didn't work. This time, we need to make sure he has no way of returning. The Kingsley family has put in a lot of effort toward this network, Andersen. I'm not giving it up without a fight."

"Forgive me, Godwin," Noah murmured, eyes narrowed. "I fully acknowledge your capability, but the idea behind the network was to form a strong collective. Let's not forget that."

Prudent public servant General Potts was, he stayed silent.

"Perhaps," said Godwin. "But let's also not forget the promises made to Kingsley Corp. Barring evidence of incompetence on our part, I expect both you and Temple to keep your word. If I could find a way around the death beneficiary clause in the pre-nup Brad signed, I'd want Lilah out, too."

The marriage contract between Lilah and Brad not only kept her in place as CFO, it contained clauses on who could inherit her stock in the three companies. The person or persons named in her will needed to be someone other than her husband and his immediate family. Once she had children, she could name them beneficiaries, but the shares would be held in trust by an external executor in the event of Lilah's death. The control of the network would thus pass to an outsider, something Godwin would not want.

Mentally thanking his former protégé for his insistence on the clause in the pre-nup, Temple set his drink on the coaster. "You are right, Noah, but so is Godwin. Lilah is capable... extremely so... but she needs to operate in the world as it is and not as she imagines it should be. She simply will not take advice from those of us with experience. As long as Harry is around to make things happen her way, Lilah will not negotiate with us or anyone else who disagrees with her perspective. It is a critical lesson for a future leader. If we decide to merely squeeze Harry out, you can bet he will still pull every trick in the book to get Lilah what she wants. There's no other option... he needs to go."

"Exactly," Godwin grunted.

"Hmm," Noah said. "It *is* a pity, though."

Temple mused, "In any case, Harry and Lilah have figured out what's going on, so a direct attack is no longer possible. He will have his own plans for us, but we will change his mind. He'll be given a new target, one he won't be able to ignore."

"What do you mean?" Noah asked.

"Noah, you see Harry's eloquence," the president murmured. "I have heard his silence."

#

Two weeks later

The White House

The personal secretary to the president opened the door, letting in the brigadier general. "Thank you, Wilma," Temple said as her eyes went to the turntable. Sinatra's "Nancy" was coming to an end. Wilma claimed Temple played Sinatra when he was perturbed about something. Her left brow rose almost indecipherably before she excused herself and closed the door behind her.

The other two guests were already seated across the desk from Temple. General Potts moved with the swift efficiency of a lifelong military man and placed the black bag he carried on the tabletop. Taking several folders out, he said, "It's been so many years I'd almost forgotten about it. This is the copy of Harry Sheppard's report of his escape from Libya, and these are the military records you asked me to bury."

Noah and Godwin read through the documents, occasionally pausing to ask questions or make notes. The folder on Harry had some markings and comments in Temple's writing. In one spot was a note in thick red ink, questioning the absence of pertinent details.

The president went about the nation's business, walking in and out of the Oval Office while his comrades reviewed the records. *All attachment is illusion,* Temple kept reminding himself, but memories of the chaotic weeks following Harry and Lilah's escape from Libya refused to go away.

The girl Temple eventually came to see as a daughter had been fighting for her life, her unconscious form kept breathing by a ventilator. Chemical pneumonia... doctors weren't sure she'd make it. Harry was the only one available for the authorities to interview. He claimed he'd been attacked by a former colonel in the U.S. Army who stole everything the teens carried on them. They took refuge in a church while Harry recovered from the assault. There was little detail in the part about the robbery as compared to the rest of the document. Yet Harry was insistent the U.S. government find the colonel and punish him for his crime. When Lilah woke, she corroborated the story.

There was something about it all... Temple carried enough gray on his head to spot a lie when he saw it. The then-senator did his own investigation, and the conclusions were horrifying.

He approached the one man who should've demanded justice for Lilah. But there wouldn't be any. The man made a deal with Temple. Harry's safety was important to the man. So was Gateway's future. The lad was to be kept out of everything. In return...

Glancing through a window at the White House grounds, Temple shook his head. There was no force in the world which could've stopped Harry from searching for the colonel—not the military, not even his own family. Quietly enough that no one would ferret out details Lilah clearly wanted to keep private, Harry had continued his quest to find the rapist. All these years of searching with no success whatsoever, and Harry never quit.

When Temple returned to the Oval Office toward noon, Godwin glanced up. "Sheffield Parker, the colonel who received an other-than-honorable discharge from the army after multiple accusations of rape. Harry and Lilah ran across this same colonel during their escape from Libya. So Parker is your weapon against Harry."

Part VI

Chapter 13

A week later, July 1986

Midtown Manhattan

"America's first supermodel," the tour guide in the Yankees cap said to the group of Japanese tourists clicking pictures of the marble statue in front of New York Public Library.

At the closest intersection, a three-girl guitar band dressed in stars-and-stripes swimsuits and cowboy hats started up their rendition of Bruce Springsteen's "Dancing in the Dark."

The tourists turned to peer.

Gamely, the guide raised his voice and continued, "The same lady posed for many of the sculptures you see around the city."

Lilah kept striding toward the front steps of the library building before she realized Sabrina had stopped to dance. Laughing, Lilah retraced her path. "You look like you want to run away and join them," she teased.

"I might," said Sabrina. "If Alex agrees to go with me." Tendrils of blonde hair were plastered to her cheeks and forehead. Her cool grass perfume had worn off, leaving her smelling of warm sun and crazy excitement. "Let's get you out of the heat. You are *pregnant!*"

"Shh!" said Lilah. Other than her and Brad—and the doctor— the only one who knew was Sabrina. Brad wanted to keep it quiet until they could throw a party and announce it to the rest of the family, but Lilah couldn't resist sharing her delicious little secret with at least Sabrina.

"Oh, all right," grumbled Sabrina, making a zipping motion across her mouth. "You and your weird mysteries." Green eyes widening, she gestured at the magnificent edifice in front. "The other big mystery in your life... skulking about the public library. What if some reporter spots you?"

"I'm not worried." Lilah often ran into many recognizable faces on the streets of New York City, where celeb spotting was rather a mundane event. Besides, journalists' interest in her was limited to the next salacious story they could cook up with her as either the temptress or Alex Kingsley's discarded lover.

No one would ask why Lilah couldn't use the microfilm projector at work... what she was researching... and if the question were actually raised, the trip was a fun outing with Harry's sister. Sabrina already agreed to be cover without even asking why Lilah needed one. Sabrina understood secrets very well.

In a couple of hours, Lilah massaged her brow and sighed. Neither Harry nor his detective missed anything when they checked. None of the newspaper reports or genealogy documents offered anything more than what they already knew.

Seventeen-year-old Ambrosia "Amber" Barrons—the girl Godwin's alcoholic half-brother used to date—died many years ago from an apparent suicide. The drunk was the son of Godwin's father and President Temple's mother. Amber was Andrew Barrons's cousin. Chances were the alliance was also based on business just like the Peter Kingsley-Patrice Sheppard marriage, but there was no actual evidence of a relationship—real or manufactured—between Amber and the Kingsley drunk. Except of course for Godwin's word after her death.

Following Amber's purported suicide, Godwin claimed she played a former boyfriend against the half-brother until he refused to have anything more to do with her. This then caused her to kill herself.

Amber's spiritual advisor accused Godwin and his stepmother—Temple's mother—of hounding the girl to death. The priest was transferred to a mission home in Colombia and was killed within a week of reaching his new church. The civil war in the country claimed another innocent victim, stated the official report. Then, there was the cash settlement Godwin made with Amber's parents which was the only break in pattern in the life and career of the retired supreme court justice.

Turning off the projector, Lilah returned the microfilm and hunted down Sabrina on the third floor. She was gawking at the magnificent paintings in the Rotunda.

As they were walking out into the warm sunshine, Sabrina asked in her strong, clear voice, "You sure I can't help you with whatever? I could hack into—"

"Shh!" said Lilah, nervously glancing at passersby in the street. "I get nightmares thinking about your hacking tricks. Sabrina, you swore you wouldn't tell anyone."

The younger woman put a hand to her heart. "I won't. And *you* swore there's no danger to you."

"There isn't." Not yet, anyway.

"And you'll tell me if there is." When there was no response, Sabrina warned, "Lilah..."

"Okay, I promise."

Climbing into a cab, Lilah squinted at the majestic building they just left. She'd found records of the Barronses and the Kingsleys going back to the time before the discovery of America. She also found a mention of Amber in the Barrons lineage, even though Lilah never heard the name uttered in the household. Why, when the death involved the heir to one of the other old-money families in New York?

Too many unanswered questions, and the media never showed much interest in the story even when the concerned parties were alive and kicking. Then, the drunk died very painfully from liver failure, and the whole episode was forgotten by the world.

Harry's detective had said he'd try to locate people who'd been around the two clans at the time. Somehow, they needed to get something on Godwin and Temple. Something that would force them to back off. Something that would save Harry's life. Lilah simply couldn't let him—

"Look..." Sabrina said as the taxi crawled down Corporate Row. She pointed toward a shiny, concrete-and-glass building. "Steven."

Lilah peered. "Kingsley Corp office is in there. Not surprising."

"What's surprising to me is why he couldn't get along with Alex and the rest in the first place," Sabrina murmured. "I mean, Alex has told me stories..."

Chapter 14

Twenty-one years ago, January 1965

Upper East Side, New York City

"Was this house always this big?" Alex asked his mother, his voice echoing in the large hall.

Plush furniture set around the large fireplace, velvet drapes at the French windows, sun pouring in through the gilded skylight... unlike the two-bedroom in Brooklyn, the sounds of the streets hardly filtered in here. The fragrance of fresh roses clung to the air.

Mother teased, "I thought you'd find it smaller. Didn't you just tell me you're now a big boy of ten?"

"He spent six years in the dump you called a home," Grandfather said from the door to their apartment in the mansion. "No wonder he's feeling overwhelmed by all this."

Uncle Aaron chided, "C'mon, Father. They just returned." Hands linked behind his back, he smiled at Alex's mother. "Welcome back, Patrice."

Mother was having none of it. She strode forward to respond to Aaron with a hug, giving an astounded Justice Kingsley the same affectionate greeting. Awkwardly patting her shoulder, he said, "Well, at least Peter's boys are back with their own family."

The smile vanished from Mother's face; her arms dropped to her side.

"Father!" exclaimed Uncle Aaron. "We didn't come here to rehash old quarrels."

Mother raised a hand. "It's all right, Aaron. Godwin obviously still blam—"

"They're my grandsons!" Grandfather bit out. "I haven't seen them in... all right, all right. Aaron says this is our chance for a fresh start."

It took Mother a few seconds to speak. "Fresh start," she agreed, her hard eyes holding Grandfather's.

Uncle Aaron rubbed his hands together. "In the spirit of new beginnings, we're here to take the boys out for a special treat. An afternoon at the range. Where are Victor and Brad?"

A nasal voice spoke from behind Alex, making him jump. He hadn't even heard the butler glide close. "Mr. Brad and Mr. Victor are already waiting by the garage. Does Mr. Alex require to use the lavatory before he leaves?"

Alex pivoted to stare up at the old fellow. First, Mother found the toy soldiers he used to play with when he was four—*four*—and left them on his bed. Okay, so they were kinda awesome. Still... now, this! "I'm ten, not two," he exclaimed.

Grandfather laughed. "So you are. Let's go shoot some targets, son."

In less than an hour, Alex and his brothers were at the Westside Range. Cousins Steven and Charles were also brought along. Waiting for their earmuffs and protective glasses, the boys stared open-mouthed at the men casually carrying their guns around.

"Justice Kingsley," a voice thundered. A man—gray-haired and brown-eyed—marched toward them. "The senator told me you'd be here. I need a favor."

Steven and Charles wandered off, completely uninterested in the recently returned cousins. Alex continued looking around while the men talked. Thinking he'd glimpsed someone familiar, he craned his neck around Grandfather's friend. There. A tall, blond man. No, a boy. Steven and Charles were talking to him.

When they were moving back to the Kingsley mansion, Alex had seen the same boy by the garage. Vague memories surfaced. "The chauffeur's son?" Alex murmured, trying to remember the name.

"Who?" Brad asked, peering toward the reception desk. "Oh, him? Yes. We met his father when you were looking around the house. Met him again, I mean."

"The chauffeur's son?" Victor echoed Alex, his tone carrying across the room. "What's he doing here?"

The blond boy swung in their direction, eyes narrowing when he recognized them. In a couple of quick strides, he closed the distance. "What do people usually do at a shooting range?" he asked, a sneer on his face. "The name's Armor. Richard Armor. Not 'chauffeur's son.'"

Before any of them could respond, it was time to go in. Heart pumping hard, Alex waited his turn. A few feet from them, Richard Armor was systematically destroying the targets, satisfaction on his face at the applause of those around him.

"He's good," remarked Grandfather's friend. "Competitive. Keeps an eye on everyone else's scores."

Indifferent to the marksmanship of his servant's child, Grandfather grunted.

An employee brought them a pistol. Grandfather's friend said, "Good gun for the boys to learn on. Brad, you first."

Steven growled.

"You wanna go before me?" Brad asked.

Without answering, Steven took the gun and positioned himself.

"Eyes on the target," the man said.

"Okay," Steven responded, but his face was turned in Armor's direction, his stance mimicking the older boy's.

"Step back, Steven," the man said, voice firm.

"Why?" Steven asked, attention jerking back to the man.

"I'll explain once the first round is done. Who's next?"

Blinking owlishly, Brad stepped up.

"Eyes on the target," said the man.

Which of course had Brad looking up at him.

"Eyes on the target," the man repeated, "not on me."

Tone high-pitched, Brad explained, "I was only trying to see what you were saying."

The man sighed. "Step back for now. Victor, your turn."

Victor elbowed his way forward, his heavy form nearly knocking Grandfather off his feet, and took the gun from Brad.

"Eyes on th—"

One report. Victor had the gun cocked and trigger pulled before being given a single order. The BB didn't go anywhere near the target, ending up in the large pile of chopped rubber at the back which—as Grandfather explained—functioned as a bullet trap.

"All right," the man said, exasperation in his voice. "You've had your turn. We'll review the rules one more time before the next round. Charles, let's go."

Giggling in excitement, Charles took the gun, turning it around in his hands. He pulled on something.

"No!" snapped the man. "Step back. Alex, your turn."

Smile fading, Charlie offered Alex the gun.

"You ready?" asked the man.

One final rub on his pants, Alex's palms were dry. "Yes, sir." He took the gun. Beautiful, shiny black. It was heavier than he expected. Colder. A drumming started within his chest. Power surged through his veins.

"Eyes on the target," the man said.

Alex's gaze narrowed. There were concentric circles on the tan-colored paper, numbered inward, ending in eight at the edge of the black middle. Two more circles showed within the black, the center-most one about an inch across. Everything faded until only the center existed in his field of vision. Sounds receded.

"What do you see?" the man asked, the words echoing as though coming from a distance.

"Black," Alex replied.

"Black what?" asked the confused voice.

"The center... it's black."

"The dark circle is all you can see?"

"Yeah."

Alex felt a form drop down next to his right shoulder, a hiss sounding close to his ear. "The hammer," the man explained, helping Alex pull it back. Alex complied when he was asked to place his finger on the trigger.

"Fire," said the man, tone low.

Alex pulled the trigger. The pistol made a short puffing noise with hardly any recoil. The black circle tore. He blinked.

"Incredible," the man murmured. "His first time."

Slowly, Alex became aware of a rising wave of applause. He handed the gun to the man and tore off his glasses. "Did I do good?"

The thundering ovation got even louder, accompanied by shouts and hoots. Feeling dazed, Alex looked around the cheering crowd, spotting a scowling Richard Armor at the periphery. Brad and Victor were open-mouthed, and Steven was sneering. Charles was looking someplace else.

Alex didn't care about any of it. The huge grin on Grandfather's face told Alex he had indeed done "good."

Someone thumped him on the back. "I have a feeling we're going to meet again, Alex Kingsley," said the man who'd instructed him. "I'm General Potts, dean of the U.S. Military Academy at West Point."

Over the next few months, Grandfather took Alex almost every week to the range. They invariably spotted Richard Armor there. He was already very, very good, but he kept working on his skills. There were a couple of times Alex was tempted to clap hard, but he was always stopped by Grandfather's hand on his arm. "I expect you to be even better, Alex," Grandfather would say.

General Potts said Alex possessed a keen eye and steady hands. *Both* his hands since he was ambidextrous. When he took the gun, people gathered around to watch, indulgent looks on their faces until they realized the ten-year-old could outshoot most of them. Even Armor watched, except the perpetual scowl on his face got worse when he saw Alex's scores.

Patrice, on her part, insisted on all her sons attending a dance studio. Brad merely tolerated the lessons until he could return to his job sorting papers in Grandfather's office. While Victor did enjoy his time in the studio, the kitchen was his favorite place. Alex... he *loved* dancing. The music teacher at school said he possessed a good singing voice, too. All of it meant sniggering and derisive questions from Cousin Charles whenever their paths crossed. Charles even asked who was paying for the lessons before he was hushed by Steven.

Alex did his best to ignore the taunts. At least when he walked through the doors of the shooting range, he felt he was home.

Which was good since he felt like an interloper in the Kingsley mansion. His brothers, too. The long oak table and the twelve velvet-covered chairs in the dining room should've felt familiar and comfortable to Alex. Instead, he felt small, nearly invisible.

At dinner, Victor agreed emphatically. "The house didn't change... we did." Fork clattering against thin china, he shoveled spaghetti into his mouth.

Mother took a sip of red wine and stayed silent, but Alex knew she was listening to every word.

Not taking his eyes from his plate, Brad declared, "You don't know what you're talking about. We belong here."

"Bro," exploded Victor. "Are you trying to tell me you don't find all of this strange? This big house, the staff calling us 'Mister'... do you really feel like you belong?"

"So what do you want us to do?" Brad asked, voice low. "Walk out? Prove to Grandfather we're just like Father?" His eyes darted to their mother.

"No!" said Victor. "We won't. Point is we don't know how to act rich."

"Why do you feel the need to 'act rich'?" Mother interrupted. "In fact, I don't want any of you even thinking you're rich. We're here only because our absence made it easier for the Kingsleys to ignore our claims to the business. After your father's death, they never even consulted me on how to vote his shares. Officially, I was his wife until the moment he died. Your grandfather and uncles should've talked to me, and they didn't. But returning here doesn't make us any richer than we used to be in Brooklyn. Always remember that. Spend as little as possible until you start earning on your own."

"I don't want a penny from the family," Victor replied. "Steven and Charlie already act like we're charity cases or something. It's been a year since we moved in, and they've talked to us... what... five, six times?"

"Really?" Mother asked, her eyes flashing. "Let me have a chat with your Uncle Aaron."

Afterward, playing cards in Brad's room, Victor mumbled, "I wish I never said anything in front of Mother. If Steven and Charlie don't want to talk to us because we used to be poor..."

Alex commented, "They hang out with Armor, and it's not like he's got money." The chauffeur's wife and son lived with him in the apartment over the garage. Grandfather never encouraged fraternization between the family and household staff, but short of locking Steven up, there was no way of putting a stop to his friendship with the older boy. No one could find an excuse to split them up. Armor was an arrogant S.O.B., but he also excelled at everything he put his mind to... school, sports, girls, you name it.

The maids in the household gossiped left and right about Armor, drooling over "the widest shoulders" and "the bluest eyes" they'd ever seen. Since he'd graced most of their beds and according to rumors, those of all the heiresses in their zip code, Alex could only conclude ladies found petulance easy to tolerate when it came with muscles.

Armor was also ambitious as hell and competitive. Even though he was only sixteen, everyone around already knew he was going places.

"We weren't here for six years; Armor was," Brad said, tone calm. "He and Steven are almost like brothers. Let's see what happens after Mother talks to Uncle Aaron."

It would have been better if she hadn't. Better if the cousins forgot each other's existence.

A few months later, January 1966

Alex clenched his hands into fists. Snow from the nor'easter was still piled high on either side of the gravel path running all around the mansion, and the pond on his right was frozen solid, but the anger roiling his insides was enough to keep him warm. Inside the house, someone was playing a halting version of "Greensleeves" on the violin. Unfortunately for the musician, Cousin Charles's hyena screeches were loud enough to drown out the song. The other two sons of bitches—Steven and Armor—looked on. "Who's your daddy, Alex?" Charles asked. "The same as Victor's? Or a different one?"

Both Steven and Charles inherited Kingsley brown hair, just like Victor and Brad. While Alex's brothers had blue eyes, their cousins sported gray irises like all the Kingsley ancestors. Alex looked like his mother, which was what triggered Charles's taunt.

"Stop, Charlie," Steven muttered, his face red. "Mothers are off-limits."

The violin-playing came to a halt mid-note. Not looking up to see why, Alex wiped his runny nose with the back of his gloved hand. The biting wind got his eyes watering, too.

"Yeah, Charlie, stop," said the blond bastard, Richard Armor, a smirk on his mug. "Can't you see little Alex is crying?" Rich—as Steven called him—was getting ready to go away to college. West Point, no less! All the Kingsley men were expected to go there.

Armor was the one Charles depended on to save him from the consequences of bad behavior. After all, what was one eleven-year-old like Alex to do against a teenager who'd been training for the military?

"Hey," Victor shouted from behind. He ran to them, stepping in a puddle and splashing dirty water. "What's going on?"

Alex straightened and watched his foes do the same. Victor might only be twelve, but he already matched Armor in height. Victor could easily sit on stupid Charles while he broke a limb or two on the others. "Charlie wants to know if our father left us because we are not his," informed Alex. "He says our mother—"

Victor snarled and leaped toward their cousins, his heavy fist landing on Charles's cheek with a satisfying crunch. Within seconds, Victor got Charles in a headlock, kicking out at Steven's gut. "I'm taking you to Grandfather," Victor grunted and grabbed Charles's hair, hauling him in the direction of the mansion. Charles slipped on the ice-slick stones and screamed, but Victor wouldn't let go. Charles's knees dragged on the gravel as he was lugged along.

Armor roared, diving onto Victor's back. Victor stumbled, and all three of them fell. Steven jumped in, trying to break Victor's headlock on Charles.

Alex joined the melee, stomping and kicking Armor. But one out-flung forearm, and Alex fell, the back of his head hitting the bricks edging the path. Pain zig-zagged all the way to his eyeballs.

"Stop," shouted a voice.

Alex sat up, rubbing the sore lump on his head. Uncle Aaron huffed toward them, Brad and Mother not too far behind.

"Victor, Steven, Charlie," yelled Aaron. "Stop! Richard, what the hell are you doing?"

The combatants disentangled themselves, getting to their feet. Wet patches decorated their clothes, dirt and gravel sticking all over.

"Victor punched me," Charles sobbed, a gloved hand held to his face. "And he dragged me by my hair. I think my cheek's broken."

"Enough," Uncle Aaron snapped at Charles. "I heard what you said." He glanced up at the second floor, where the dining-room window in Peter Kingsley's wing looked out on to the pond and the path by it. Helen—Steven and Charles's older sister—stood there, a violin in her hands, her music teacher right behind. "So did everyone else... including your Aunt Patrice."

Steven groaned. "Charlie, I told you—"

Before he could complete his reprimand, Patrice Kingsley reached them. "Stop fighting," she said, frantic eyes darting between Armor and Victor. "You're family."

Alex started, "But the sonuva—"

"Alex!" she snapped.

"Okaaay," said Victor. Turning to a furious Armor, Victor continued, "Our dear cousins and this bastard son of a chauffeur—"

"Mother," Brad shouted.

Alex jerked around toward their mother and saw her arm raised, ready to strike Victor. Her whole body was shaking. "B-but..." Alex stammered. Victor was trying to defend *her*.

Everyone was staring at the tableau. Charles had his shoulders hunched, giggling behind the hand held to his bruised cheek. His mirth ended in a hiss of pain. Steven was merely open-mouthed in surprise and confusion. Armor—the anger in his eyes was replaced by a gleeful look, the smirk back on his face.

Victor shrank into his clothes. In no more than a whisper, he asked, "Mother?"

Slowly, her arm dropped. Her breathing was harsh. Strange tears on her lashes and in her voice, she said, "I thought I raised you better."

Admonishing Victor, Brad said, "Behave yourself. They're our cousins. Mother, they—"

She'd already pivoted, striding back to the mansion, crossing paths with Grandfather on her way in.

With measured treads, Grandfather reached the little group by the pond, nodding in approval at Brad and his little speech.

"Father," started Uncle Aaron. Briefly, he gave an update on the latest fight.

"I need to go to the hospital," whined Charles, his hand cradling the spreading bruise on his cheek.

Alex mumbled under his breath, hoping the justice would take circumstances into consideration. Victor was staring firmly at his feet.

"Consider yourself lucky," Grandfather said to Steven, "Victor didn't beat you black and blue."

Steven jerked back in shock. "But... look, I know what Charlie said was stupid, but..."

"Oh, it was stupid," Grandfather agreed. "The Kingsleys were cursed the minute you idiots were born."

Victor straightened with a disbelieving glance at their grandfather. Steven's eyes suddenly seemed to glisten.

"Father," said Uncle Aaron, shifting on his feet. "It was Charles. Steven didn't—"

"I don't care which of them said what," Grandfather stated. "With all the advantages this family has to offer, these two are growing up to be such pathetic excuses for men. Whereas..." He gestured toward Brad. "...look at your cousin. Learn a thing or two from him."

Brad flushed, his chin held high.

"You will treat them with respect," Grandfather thundered at Steven. "Do you hear me?"

Gaze fixed on the ground, Steven said, "Yes, sir." Charles muttered something which could have been agreement. Armor didn't say a word, but nor did Grandfather bother to acknowledge the presence of his servant's son.

Having delivered judgment, the justice left, his fingers curled around the lapels of his thick jacket.

"I'll call the doctor," Uncle Aaron said to Charles. "Brad, make sure your mother's all right."

Nodding, Brad jogged back to the mansion. Halfway there, he wheeled around to admonish his brothers. "No more fighting, okay?"

Charles snickered, then groaned in pain.

"Stop," Uncle Aaron ordered. "Brad's right. No more fighting."

The fighting never stopped.

Charles's cheek was definitely broken. Barely able to open his left eye because of the puffiness, he still glared at Victor. "You wait," Charles mumbled. "I'll break *your* cheek and drag you by your hair."

"You should thank me," Victor retorted. "Now you have an excuse for being ugly."

Steven snapped, "Charlie, I don't want any more lectures from Grandfather. We will treat them with respect as he said."

Sure enough, the very next week, Steven and Charles respectfully presented Victor with a peace offering. Victor had eaten every one of the raspberry tarts before he started puking his guts out. Mother didn't need convincing to summon the family physician, and the vomiting soon stopped.

The next day, Alex snuck into Steven's room and found a bottle of the emetic, ipecac. Alex marched to Grandfather's home office where Brad was helping Uncle Aaron with reports to the company's partners.

"Enough with this silliness," Brad said, glancing at Grandfather's bland face. "Ipecac is not poison, and anyway, Steven wouldn't have done it. He's a Kingsley, not a criminal. Victor ate something bad is all." But Brad's eyes were uncertain.

Walking back to their wing, Alex said to Brad, "You *know* it was the ipecac. I bet the whole thing was Armor's idea. No way a pharmacist sold it to Steven. He's only thirteen!"

"Maybe," said Brad. "Try not to do anything stupid until I talk to Mother."

But she refused to hear a word against Armor, telling them there were plenty of ways for a rich kid like Steven to get something as simple as ipecac.

"I could've been killed!" Victor sat up in his bed, face pale and drawn. "Mother won't believe Armor did anything wrong even if we catch him red-handed, pouring antifreeze into my drink."

Alex snorted. "Why don't you stop eating everything you see? Then, we won't need to worry about making Mother believe whatever."

Brad ordered his brothers not to report Armor to the family elders. Their mother would be incredibly hurt if her sons went over her head. Plus, there was the matter of Armor's dad... Brad didn't want to do anything which might cost the man his job. It didn't matter. Brad overhead Uncle Aaron and Uncle David argue about Armor's role in Steven's misdeeds.

Uncle David firmly declined to address it, dismissing everything as "silly pranks which hardly require adult intervention."

Aunt Grace murmured, "Plus, Victor attacked my sons, and Godwin refused to do a single thing. I'm glad Richard is around to help Steven and Charlie."

Attacked, my— Alex ground his teeth when he learned of the conversation.

Uncle Aaron chalked up Grandfather's inclination to be more forgiving toward Alex and his brothers to the absence of a father figure in their lives. Alex was glad for it, but he didn't get why Grandfather didn't simply toss out *Armor*. Justice Kingsley was not blind or deaf or dumb not to see what was happening. Yeah, yeah... the chauffeur was a loyal employee. Still...

"We'll get our own back," Victor swore. He was in the kitchen, learning how to prepare ice cream from scratch, but the employees were not close enough to hear his whispers. "Any ideas how?"

Alex sneaked a slab of chocolate from the glass dish on the counter. "Yeah, but we need to wait a few days, or our cousins won't buy it."

A month later, Charles conveniently overheard Victor and Alex discussing nudist movies, a.k.a. porn. Tempted by the prospect of naked women—if only on film—Charles followed Alex and Victor to the soundproof entertainment room in the basement. Unfortunately for the would-be connoisseur of erotica, they slipped behind him and shoved him into a closet, locking him in.

It took the household most of the day to find Charles there, curled up in a corner, his pants soaked in urine. Having been updated by Charles as to the identity of the perpetrators, Armor informed Patrice Kingsley. She believed *him*, of course.

Forced to apologize to the hated cousins and grounded indefinitely, Alex and Victor hung out in Brad's room.

"You have only yourselves to blame," Brad said hardheartedly as he sorted old clothes for donation.

Victor snickered. "Bro, it was worth it. Charlie was stupid enough to admit to the ipecac, and Grandfather grounded him and Steven. On top of the time Charlie spent in the closet!"

"We'd have been all right if Mother didn't interfere," Alex complained. "Grandfather didn't say a word to us, so why did she have to believe Armor?"

"I don't understand why she's so damn fond of the bastard," Victor groused. "He's only the chauffeur's son, for God's sake! Not even his real son! Only adopted."

Brad raised a hand. "Don't you understand it's precisely why Mother stands up for him? How do you think he feels hearing you call him a bastard when he probably is one? She's sorry for him is all. As for his little tricks against us... we'll just have to keep our eyes open."

#

Back in the present, July 1986

World Trade Center, New York City

Sweaty in his workout clothes, Harry collapsed into the leather chair across Alex's desk and guffawed until tears sprouted in his eyes. "Porn? How old did you say you were? Eleven?"

Tossing him a can, Alex grinned evilly and settled into his own seat. His smirk turned into a grimace.

Gym routine had gone on longer than usual today... weights, pull-ups, push-ups, sit-ups, runs. On evenings when Alex went to the range, Harry sparred at the boxing ring. Then, there was weekly swimming in the Atlantic until hard winter set in, and he was forced to use the indoor pool at the club.

Beer afterward had become a ritual, but tonight, there was another reason for returning to the office. Scattered on the tabletop were toys from the 1950s—soldiers, tanks, artillery. Alex's old stuff he asked the Kingsley butler to send finally arrived, and he invited Harry to admire the collection.

"We didn't actually have any porn," said Alex, arranging the soldiers in battle formation. "But don't tell me you've never sneaked a *Playboy.*"

"Buddy, I lived in *Libya,*" Harry said. "At eleven, I hadn't seen a single skin magazine."

Chagrin on his face, Alex fell silent.

Harry added, "We made do with the *National Geographic.*"

Alex cursed a blue streak, leaving Harry roaring with laughter.

"What is *up* with Charlie?" Harry asked after a minute. "You make him sound slow, but he did get into West Point."

Alex snorted. "I have my doubts who actually showed up at the testing center as Charlie. Anyway, he ain't slow... simply a drunk and a bully. Maybe a power thing. The servants used to stay far away from him, but I've never heard of Charlie doing anything to anyone who could punch back. At least not anything his parents and brother couldn't help cover up. Steven's main problem was with *us,* specifically Brad. They both wanted to be the man in charge."

"And Armor didn't appreciate being outshone," stated Harry.

"I suppose," said Alex. "Even if it was only with a BB pistol." He sighed blissfully. "A beautiful Daisy, their Model 179. What did you learn on?"

"Colt Frontier Scout."

"A real revolver! Cool."

Harry echoed Alex's sigh. "Hell, *yeah.*"

"How old were you?" asked Alex.

"Same as you. Ten. Lilah's papa took me to the range. All three of us... Lilah, Dan, and I... her papa insisted we learn how to shoot. She wasn't all that interested, but her father wouldn't budge. He said she needed to know at least the basics."

Sabrina was taught the basics, too. Back when she still lived with their parents, Harry was adamant she learn how to defend herself. New York City wasn't exactly free of crime. In fact, one of the perks Gateway offered its employees—and their families—was free self-defense coaching at Hector's gym. Sabrina grumbled about overprotective older brothers and advised Harry to tell men not to attack.

After a few moments of silence, Alex said, "I never thanked you, dude."

"For?"

Alex flushed. "You know... the whole mess with Lilah... you helped me sort it through. Then, introducing me to Sabrina."

"Glad everything worked out," Harry said, ignoring the twinge of discomfort in his chest at the memory of his role in the episode.

"It really did," agreed Alex. "And not just in my life. Brad's a great guy... kind, considerate, loving... damn glad I didn't end up hurting him. We're a family, but I forgot it for a while."

Harry nodded. Yes, kind and considerate Brad Kingsley was the right man for the network and for Lilah. She was safe and secure amid people who loved her, her future filled with joy.

Chapter 15

Later the same month, July 1986

Midtown Manhattan

The movie theater erupted into laughter as the three high schoolers from *Ferris Bueller's Day Off* got into their next ridiculous fix. Slurping lemony soda, Lilah sputtered helplessly around the straw.

"Memories," exclaimed the blonde with the Diana bob and a pair of large glasses perched on her nose. Vivian was forced to holler to be heard over the cheering audience.

Both Lilah and the third member of the trio from their own school days turned to stare at Vivian. "You stole your father's car and totaled it?" asked Ginger. Her once-long strawberry blonde tresses were now cut in spikes.

Vivian pouted. "You know what I mean."

Lilah grinned and nodded. Life back then was a lot simpler... at least until the deaths of her parents.

The entire tub of popcorn was gone by the time the movie was done. Stepping out to the muggy heat and the relentless traffic of the streets, Lilah said, "Oh, I needed this so badly!" An evening with pals who knew the person she used to be.

"Me, too," echoed the other two.

It was a rare occasion when all three were in New York at the same time. Careers, family, so many things to occupy every minute of the day. None of them had kids yet. Lilah would be the first among the trio to become a mom.

They didn't know it yet, but she'd invite them to the announcement party. There was a strange sensation in Lilah's chest when their cab pulled up to the World Trade Center. Happiness... it felt really, really good.

"Are you sure you don't want to go drinking with us?" Ginger asked.

Yeah, and when Lilah didn't take a single sip, her news would be out before the official proclamation of the impending arrival of the newest Kingsley. Smiling widely, she lied, "I have an early meeting tomorrow. Got to prepare."

The janitor was vacuuming Lilah's office when she walked in. One phone call to the company chauffeur service, and she could nap in the car all the way to Brooklyn, but there was nothing particular she needed to do at home. Brad had again left for Panama. He'd decided to alternate between the headquarters and New York, wanting to keep a personal eye on their two main offices. Well... base of operations had been moved to Manhattan some time ago, but maintaining a strong presence in Panama was critical because of various legal reasons.

Walking to the row of windows lining the wall, Lilah stared down. The deep red of the evening sky had turned into a shimmery black. Lights from the vehicles lining up along the streets of Manhattan turned the island into an iridescent concrete jungle, teeming with life. In the middle of these dark woods, she was alone in her tower of mortar and steel.

Alone, but not really. Lilah ran gentle fingertips across her belly. The baby would be here in February. Alex and Sabrina's son, Michael, would finally have a cousin to play with. There was Gabriel, Victor's son with the girlfriend who'd died, but as nice a guy as Victor was, he seemed disinclined to take any physical responsibility for his child. Gabriel still lived with his foster parents. Any children Harry had would be Michael's cousins, too.

A sudden spasm zipped across Lilah's lower abdomen, gone within seconds. She frowned. Pregnant women were supposed to eat healthy, and she'd filled her belly with popcorn and soda. Perhaps a salad... funny how lethargic she felt even in the first trimester of pregnancy. Briefly, Lilah eyed the phone... the chauffeur service... no, it was late, but traffic would still be horrendous. Unlike the packed streets, the crush in the subway would be tolerable by now.

An hour later

Brooklyn, New York

The steps swam in front of her eyes, and Lilah clung to the rail, praying she wouldn't fall. She should've pulled the emergency cord in the train, but the pain hadn't been this bad seconds ago. Another cramp hit her in the lower abdomen. Chin to her chest, she puffed, trying to breathe through it. *Oh, God,* she prayed. If she could make it all the way up, the station agent would be able to call for help.

Late as it was, the crowds on Fifty-Ninth Street station had thinned, and there was no one to notice her predicament except a group of teenagers with a boom box. Fast rhythms in high volumes sent sonic waves slamming against her eardrums. The throbbing in her belly kept pace when the cadence picked up.

Nauseous, she blinked hard and extended a foot, carefully locating the next step. Sweat-slick fingers slid from the banister. Lilah teetered. The floor rushed up to meet her.

She didn't know if she fainted from the pain or if she hit her head and passed out. She didn't remember much of the next few minutes except that the kids were crowded around, their frantic voices shouting for help. There were a few coherent memories of emergency personnel strapping her to a stretcher.

"I'm pregnant," she tried to say, wincing when a sharp pain went up her arm.

"Turn off the damn thing," shouted the technician, a short and buxom black woman with a warm touch. The music stopped, and the chastised teenagers slunk away.

"They helped," Lilah whispered, but no one heard her.

"Hold on, hon," said the technician, her voice now kindly. "We're giving you fluids. You seem to be losing blood a little too quickly."

Sometime that night

The Brooklyn Hospital Center

White-coated men and women glided like ghosts, their voices echoing around Lilah. Something beeped to the side. Images faded in and out, but the tearing pain in her belly was a constant. She cried, begging for help, but her lips wouldn't move. She was aware of signing something, the lights on the ceiling zooming past when she was wheeled to the O.R. The pain soon stopped. She was so relieved. There was something she needed to ask, but she was so sleepy.

In her dreams, she was jumping up and down on a trampoline. Breath whooshed out of her when she fell. Somewhere in the distance, a baby cried. Whose child was it? Impatiently, she brushed the hair from her eyes to check.

A playground. There were kids all around, but they were laughing and screaming in childish joy. Where was the wailing noise coming from? It bothered her.

"Ms. Kingsley," said a voice, startling her awake. "Your brother's here."

Dan? She opened her eyes, squinting against the harsh light in the room. A blurry form stood at the foot of the bed. She blinked away the haziness.

"Can't turn my back on you for a second," her twin joked, his dark eyes shadowed by concern. Dan was dressed in a suit, his jaw clean-shaven. As always, he looked perfect, like he'd just stepped off the cover of *GQ*.

Where *were* they? Lilah tried to check, but her head pounded when she shifted. Making soothing noises, a woman in white shirt and pants moved into Lilah's visual field. A nurse. There was a steady beep punctuating the low hum of the air conditioner. Lilah tried to speak, but her mouth was dry. The nurse offered her some ice chips. Sucking on it soothed Lilah's raw throat. "What happened?" she croaked.

"You don't remember?" asked Dan, resting his hip on the bed and ignoring the nurse's frown.

Lilah tried to shake her head, but that made the pounding worse. "I was... bleeding; what happened to..."

Dan looked puzzled.

It was the nurse who told her, brown eyes sympathetic, "I'm sorry, Ms. Kingsley. You'd already ruptured, so they did laparoscopy and repaired the tube." She added cautiously, "You did give consent, but it was an emergency, anyway—an ectopic. The embryo was not in the uterus. It was implanted in the Fallopian tube... I suppose it was too early for you to have had a sonogram, or your own doctor would've told you the pregnancy needed to be terminated. If we didn't operate fast, you could've died."

"You were pregnant?" her brother asked.

The nurse explained to him it wasn't merely a fall from the subway steps as he'd been told over the phone. Brad was already notified by the hospital. He was upset but understood the necessity of speedy decision-making. Everything had been taken care of, and Lilah could return home in a day or two. She'd need someone to help her, though, preferably female. A home nurse, maybe.

There was intense sorrow within Lilah's rib cage, but only the tiniest whimper escaped her lips. Tears welled, but none dropped from her lashes. The comforting warmth of Dan's hug enveloped her. She nodded when asked if she were all right.

The ruptured Fallopian tube was repaired, the nurse said again. Plus, the second tube was intact. "Such a lot of scarring," she clucked, tone sympathetic and concerned at the same time. Still, Lilah was not yet thirty; she could try again for a baby.

Through the haze of her pain, Lilah heard the words. She knew she should ask questions, but she couldn't think.

Part VII

Chapter 16

A week later, late July 1986

New York, New York

Verity surveyed the reflection in the silver-framed, rectangular mirror hanging on the living room wall. The tie-dye bikini was worth every penny of its high price tag, hugging her rounded bottom and plump breasts while managing to draw eyes to her tiny waist. The design's magic worked well on her. Verity was five-foot-five—the perfect height for a woman—and curvy in all the right places.

She turned half a circle, inspecting her smoothly waxed legs and perfectly pedicured toes. Wrapping the matching sarong at her hips, Verity exhaled in satisfaction. She was twenty-five, she was rich, she was pretty.

With a sudden frown, she peered into the glass. Platinum-blonde locks, gray-blue eyes... she *could* use a bit more tan. Her hair... the Farrah Fawcett 'do was still popular, but it was so *seventies*. Madonna, the singer, styled hers into ringlets, but Verity didn't think she'd look good with curls. Maybe she could simply let it grow out. That woman, Lilah, had hair hanging to her mid-back. Fashion magazines went crazy over the kind of styles she showed up in!

Verity growled. Lilah was a nobody who used her looks to climb the corporate ladder and thought she had the right to tell a man like Harry what to do. Unfortunately, Harry *let* her boss him around, taking seriously every one of her commands. All last week, Verity heard him on the phone a million times, almost begging the woman to call him back. Anyway, that seemed to be done, thank God, with whatshername finally deigning to show up to work.

The stupidity did give Verity a better idea of how she could sort out her marriage. A change of tactics was called for. Something more subtle...

Easy enough to say, but Alex Kingsley was expected at the apartment. Harry and Alex had plans as usual. Really, the two men were spotted together so often that the stupid tabloid—*The Big Apple Reporter*—insisted Sabrina was Alex's beard. He, of course, was also supposed to be cheating on his wife with Lilah. At least it meant the social climber was never linked with Alex's best friend/gay lover.

The idea! Verity shrugged it off. Today, *she* would be the one photographed with Harry.

When Harry sauntered out from the bedroom in jeans and a Polo tee, Verity cast an appreciative glance at his tall and muscled form. First, a couple of sprays of Chanel Nº 5 into her cleavage. Drawing her locks high, she called, "Harry, I need a hand, please." Obediently, he ambled to her and held her hair to the side as requested. She yanked the elastic band of the strapless top side to side, pulling it higher. Bountiful breasts threatened to spill over the cup, her creamy skin just a few shades lighter than the yellow-orange fabric. Their gazes met in the mirror, and she pouted. "Go with me, Harry; my friends are dying to see you again." She could already see them on the boat, sailing the Hudson, surrounded by envious companions.

He laughed softly, his breath moist on her cheek. "What am I going to tell Alex?"

"That you prefer your wife's company. Harry, we haven't had any fun together in a long time. Just us, I mean." Behind her, his chest moved in deep, steady breaths, and the warmth of his body penetrated the scraps of nylon covering her curves. Verity shifted, glorying in the sudden arousal pressing into her lower back.

"Have I been ignoring you?" he asked, arms sliding around her waist. Her waves tumbled down her back. The reflection in the glass was perfect.

"Of course you have," she said pertly. "You can make it up to me, though."

"How?" he inquired, nuzzling her neck.

Verity giggled. "That's a good start."

He traced her shoulder with hot kisses, hands cupping her breasts. "Are you sure you want to go sailing?" he asked, lips tickling her ear.

"My friends..." she murmured, gasping when he tugged the top down. *"You* have this baseball thing with Alex."

Harry turned her in his arms, letting his cotton shirt graze her soft skin. Pleasure shooting through her nerve endings, Verity sank into his embrace.

"Meeting the coach," he breathed into her ear. "Alex and I sponsor the team."

Verity pulled back an inch. "Yankees?" Alex was a huge fan. Harry was more interested in boxing, but he enjoyed most sports as did Verity. She could go along, perhaps.

"Huh?" Harry's chest shook with laughter. "Alex's old elementary school."

A kids' team? Some kind of PR plan, no doubt. Disappointed, Verity puckered her lips. "Go with me," she beseeched, peeping through her lashes.

Harry drew her back against him. "Better idea. Stay home, and don't answer the door. Alex will leave. I'll call the coach later and write a check." The sarong slithered to the floor, his fingers grazing the top of her bikini bottoms.

Verity trembled. "What's gotten into you?" she whimpered, feeling dizzy.

She'd been hoping for baby steps... it wouldn't be long before she got him completely housebroken. Here he was, offering to set aside work!

"I'm married to a sweet, beautiful girl who loves me," he said, peeling the last piece of fabric from her body. "Reason enough."

He led her into the bedroom, his gaze roaming all over her naked form as she settled herself on the sheets. Leaning back on her elbows, she watched as he drew the blinds and switched on the lights. "That's the only thing about you which hasn't changed after we got married," she commented.

Stripping off his shirt, he asked, "What?" The bed dipped when he sat, running fingers through her blonde locks.

"The lights stay on when we make love," she teased. "You *have* to see me." The hands in her hair clenched for a second. "Oww," she complained.

"Sorry, didn't mean to hurt you."

Verity didn't have time to wonder about the fleeting wariness in his eyes. With frenzied hands and feverish mouth, he launched an attack, touching and tasting every part of her body. Limbs slick with perspiration slid against each other. She moaned in pleasure when he told her in excruciating detail what he planned to do. His skin smelled of sex, musky and dark. Salty on her tongue.

She had just registered the loss of his warmth when she heard the drawer slide open and the telltale rip of a foil packet. Flipping to lie on her back, she panted, "No need, Harry."

"Too risky," he said and rose over her, adequately protected.

"No," she repeated.

"What do you mean?" he asked, supporting himself on his forearms. His voice was thick with unspent lust.

"You said we could try for a baby." Asking her to wait until they finished dealing with Sanders was almost the same, wasn't it?

"Later." Harry bent to take her mouth with his.

Pushing away the fingers on her inner thigh, Verity shifted to her side. "Listen to me, Harry; this is the perfect time. Also, your parents would love to have a grandchild." There was Sabrina's boy, but he was a Kingsley, and Hector didn't have any children.

Harry stilled. Body hovering over hers, he dropped a soft, affectionate peck on her cheek. "In a year or two. You're young."

"Sabrina was only twenty when Mikey was born," Verity said, pushing against his chest.

"You *know* it was an accident," Harry said, moving aside. The haze of desire in his eyes dissipated, replaced by cold clarity. "What's the goddamned hurry, anyway?"

"Accident or not, see what happened to Alex and Sabrina. My God, he's even staying with his in-laws for his wife and son. Alex Kingsley, well-known playboy!"

Harry growled. "You believe having a family will tame me. Verity, bringing a child into the world has to involve a lot more thought. How are you going to take care of a baby when *you're* clearly still a child?"

Verity sat up, shoving hair out of her face. "I'm too stupid to have a baby?" she snarled.

"I said you're childish, not stupid," Harry corrected, blocking the small pillow she flung at him.

Looking wildly around, she grabbed the box of condoms and hurled it at his chest.

"Verity, stop... it came out the wrong way," he said, sweeping the small silver packets to one side. "I only meant you need to mature a little, enough to care for someone besides yourself."

Wiping angry tears with the back of her hand, she shouted, "Great! I'm self-centered, too? Let me tell you something; most people think I'm all right. I have *lots* of friends. Just because I'm not bossy like your precious Lilah doesn't mean I'm not smart."

"Lilah?" Harry asked, voice taut. "Why are you bringing her into this?"

A loud jangling sound rang through the apartment. Verity jerked her head toward the living room.

"Alex is here," said Harry, bounding from the mattress. He dressed himself—quickly and efficiently—and closed the door behind him.

In the middle of the large bed, Verity gathered the cotton sheets around her and listened to the muffled voices of the two men on the other side of the wall. With an angry growl, she threw a pillow at the door, sobbing when it fell to the floor without a sound.

In two minutes, she pulled on a pair of slacks and a peasant blouse, no longer in the mood for anything fun. When she joined the men outside, she wondered if Alex would notice her red-rimmed eyes, but beyond flicking a glance in her direction, he did not react to her unhappy appearance.

Harry was talking to Alex about his new gun. "SIG-Sauer P226. It's the new official sidearm for the SEALs. Thought I'd try one out."

"Looks badass," Alex commented, turning it over in his hands.

"Love at first sight," Harry proclaimed.

Alex laughed. "What happened to your Colt? I'll take it if you want to sell."

"Nope. Keeping it at the office."

Verity grabbed a can of soda from the refrigerator and slammed the door.

"Give me a minute to get my stuff," Harry said to Alex.

"Are you going with us?" Alex asked Verity, waiting for Harry to retrieve his wallet and keys.

She shrugged a shoulder at Alex, deliberately keeping her gaze averted from her husband.

"Harry, if it's only two of us, let's take the Harley," Alex suggested. "I've been waiting to get that bad boy out on the road."

"Sure," said Harry. "I drive; you sit behind. Them's the rules."

"Come on, dude, you have to let me drive the bike someday."

"Get your own," Harry responded, bringing out the extra helmet from the hall closet.

"He doesn't even park it here, you know." Verity plunked herself into a chair at the small dining table. "In a vault!"

"Vault?!" Alex laughed.

"Close, but not exactly," Harry explained, no trace of his recent annoyance remaining in his eyes. "I told you about the attempted theft. Then, some crackheads got to it. The old fellow who runs the garage said he could keep it in a locked section—people rent space there for antique cars and such. Expensive shit... high insurance. Whoever wants to take out a vehicle will need to inform the manager in advance because there are only two keys. The manager then gets the key from the owner to open the section. So yeah, sort of like a bank locker. I've been thinking of buying the place."

"The garage?" Alex asked.

"Good investment," Harry said. "I'll keep one set of keys. Maybe you can keep the other... safer to split up."

The corner of Verity's mouth twisted up. "You should be flattered, Alex; those keys are gonna be the most important thing in his life. He trusts you enough to take care of *his* baby."

Glancing between her and Harry, Alex asked, "Why so grumpy? You're not allowed to ride it, either?" He turned to Harry. "She rides well, dude. I taught her myself. Taught her how to shoot, too." Verity's brother and Alex became friends long before any of them met Harry.

"He knows," said Verity. "Only, more impressed by other things." Like insignificant little nobodies who thought they could boss around the rest of the world.

Harry didn't pay any mind to her frustration, but Alex's eyes were on Verity, his brows furrowed in puzzlement. She didn't think even Alex would understand her intense loathing for Lilah. He was almost as enthralled by the woman as Harry.

Verity didn't get it. Lilah's parents left her only a teeny tiny bit of money. Everything else there was to her name was charity from Ryan Sheppard and Andrew Barrons. In fact, Verity heard gossip about Lilah donating most of it to some Native American tribe in Argentina. Anyone else in her position would have been grateful to the Kingsleys and the Sheppards, but *nooo...* Lilah bossed them around. They *let* her.

Maybe the tabloids were right. Was Lilah sleeping with Alex Kingsley? With all five brothers? Was that the hold the woman had over them?

Harry opened the front door. He'd already dismissed his angry wife from his mind and was ready to tackle his next adventure with Alex.

"Gimme a minute," Alex said and walked to the table. Spinning a chair around on one leg, he straddled it, eyeing her. "I hope you're planning to attend the party at Brad and Lilah's this afternoon. He wants to celebrate before we start the next phase of the expansion. Who knows when we'll all be together again under the same roof?"

If she didn't see Lilah for another three-thousand years, it wouldn't be long enough, Verity decided. Wildly, she wondered how Alex's wife managed to tolerate the other woman. "Is Sabrina going to be there?" Verity asked.

"Obviously... and Mike, too," Alex said. "It's a family gathering."

"I want to talk to her," Verity said. "Where's she now?"

"Plans with Lilah."

Chapter 17

That morning

Elsewhere in New York

Babies. Newborns with their eyes scrunched and hands clenched into little fists. Infants staring into the camera with toothless grins. Twin toddlers on trikes. Pictures of children delivered by the good doctor adorned the walls. The sounds of the television filtered in from the waiting room. There were none of the sterile smells usually associated with medical offices. Instead, a faint floral fragrance clung to the air.

The exam table was small with stirrups at the bottom. Arranged neatly on a tray were steel specula of various sizes. Clutching together the ends of the patterned gown, Lilah waited in the chair across the doctor's desk, unwilling to climb on the table until she absolutely needed to. Positioning herself for a pelvic exam left her feeling defenseless and humiliated.

With a mild squeak, the door opened to let in the gynecologist. She was a diminutive woman with short black curls bouncing all around her lively face. Her brown eyes were grave, though. To Lilah's relieved surprise, the doctor did not urge her to the table. Waving away the nurse who followed in, she drew up the chair next to Lilah's and sat, a folder open in her lap. "Lilah," said the doctor. "The surgeon sent me reports from your admission. He's concerned about the amount of scarring they found in the tubes. Frankly, so am I. Anything you'd like to tell me?"

"Scarring?" asked Lilah. "How?"

The doctor closed the chart and put it on the table. "I won't document anything without your permission," she promised. "Have you had any procedures done?"

Lilah was confused. "Not unless you count the ectopic."

"Abortion?" the doctor asked bluntly.

"No," Lilah said. "This was my first pregnancy."

With unblinking eyes, the doctor studied Lilah. "Infections?"

"None," Lilah said. She'd heard about sexually transmitted diseases, but how could... she'd never...

Darkness rushed in.

"No!" said Lilah.

"What?" asked Sabrina, turning in the driver's seat. Traffic on the Brooklyn Bridge was stalled. Music streamed from the CD player in the car. Sabrina's brows drew together. "Are you okay?"

"I'm..." Lilah sat up. The air-conditioning was on full blast, but she was drenched in sweat. "I'm all right," she lied. "Fell asleep for a minute. Bad dream."

Sabrina's expression turned severe a moment before she reached to the side to turn off the audio. "You haven't been sleeping regularly, have you?"

Lilah shook her head. "I'm fine... will be, anyway."

Green eyes warm, Sabrina said, "I know you'll be. Just wait and see. This fertility specialist is supposed to be absolutely the best." She threw her braid over a shoulder, and her gaze darted to the clock radio. "I hope we get there on time." One of the many advantages money brought was that people, including the world's most sought-after doctors, cleared schedules for you, but it still was not easy to get the consultant to agree to this weekend appointment. If they missed it, God only knew when they'd get another one.

"Still early," Lilah said, relaxing into the seat.

"True." Sabrina tapped the steering of the brand-new Aston Martin convertible—a gift from her husband—with her fingers. "Who knows when traffic will get moving, but this baby is fast, zero to sixty in five seconds."

Lilah smiled. "Does Alex know you or what?" Even the metallic blue color was his choice, the color which not-so-coincidentally happened to be his wife's favorite.

"A new car is no evidence of true love," Sabrina proclaimed.

Lilah threw her hands up. "What does the poor man have to do to prove himself to you?"

Face mutinous, Sabrina said, "If only *he'd* asked me the question..."

"How can he ask if he doesn't know what kind of crazy thoughts you've been thinking?" Sabrina worried she was more a tie between the Sheppards and the Kingsleys than wife and mother of his son for Alex, but she refused to tell him what was on her mind.

"I shouldn't have to say anything," Sabrina argued. "If he loved me and not just Harry's sister, he would figure it out."

"Your logic..." exclaimed Lilah. "I don't know what to call it."

Sabrina stuck her tongue out. "Anyway, Alex and I get along just fine." Her eyes crinkled in mischief. "He does know what I prefer in bed. Hits all the right spots... what's Brad like?"

Lilah nearly choked on her own tongue. Thankfully, she was saved from having to answer by a loud argument between two drivers. A shrieky siren cut through the noise on the bridge. Snaking his way around the traffic jam, a motorcycle cop brought the altercation to a halt. It was another thirty minutes before Lilah and Sabrina got to FDR Drive.

Checker cabs on Brooklyn Bridge and the water taxis below were carrying sightseers into Manhattan to enjoy summer in the city. Watching the boats bobbing on East River, guilt and melancholy intruded on Lilah's thoughts. Dull was the first word which occurred to her in response to Sabrina's question. And outside the bedroom, it was either the same wretched arguments or total boredom. Lilah hadn't wanted Brad with her even on her doctor's visits. Nor did he wish to be there.

Lilah saw a hazy form, shrouded in white, standing over her. Shrieking without stop, she scooted back on the carpet. Her leg hit something. A chair toppled.

The form moved, its arms outstretched.

"Stay away," Lilah screamed, one hand clutching the robe closed. "I'll kill you." Her other hand scrambled on the carpet to find something, anything, to use as a weapon. Terror, rage, the need to escape.

"Lilah," shouted a female voice. The shrouded monster flickered off, morphing into the doctor. Her lips were moving, saying something, but her voice echoed, the words incomprehensible. The door opened, a nurse peeking in, her eyes widening in surprise at finding the patient on the floor. The doctor told her to come in and close the door.

Lilah's back hit the wall. She tried to stand, but her legs were too weak to hold her up. Snarling and sobbing, she curled into a ball when the doctor approached. The nurse thrust a glass under Lilah's nose.

She gulped the water, some of it dribbling down her chin. In another couple of minutes, she hobbled back to the chair with the doctor and the nurse assisting her.

"Do you need us to call your husband?" asked the doctor, straightening the toppled chair and settling herself in it. The nurse hovered behind.

"No," exploded Lilah.

Alarmed, the doctor sat back. "Does he... Lilah, we can help."

She was confused. Does Brad... *what? The haziness in her brain dissipated. Heavy despair took its place. "I thought I was over it," she whispered.*

"Over what?" the doctor asked. "Lilah, I cannot, in good conscience, let you drive back home on your own. I don't dare call your husband without making sure he had nothing to do with your episode."

"Please, don't call Brad," Lilah said, voice trembling. "He doesn't know anything about it." Then, it tumbled out. The dark memories she'd worked so hard to suppress.

The sixteen-year-old girl. Mind full of plans, heart bursting with dreams of her best friend. Her virginal body changing, drawing eyes.

The shock of a heavy hand on her shoulder, her terrified scream smothered by the palm over her mouth. The obscene name, the order to shut up, or else. The teeth on her lip, biting down. The taste of blood in her mouth. Her tears of pain. More screams. The hard slap on her cheek. Her clothes torn away. Her limbs flailing, unable to put up a fight. The fall to the carpet.

The terror. Her futile struggle to push away the monster astride her. The pain when her weak arms were wrenched apart.

A woman's shadow at the door, the kitchen maid. Hope. Lilah's cries for help. The shouted order at the woman to leave. Blinding panic when the maid turned to run.

The attempt to slip out from under the monster's heavy form. Thunderbolts of pain radiating from the back of her skull when her head was slammed into the floor.

Masticated food regurgitating into her mouth. The world turning a thick gray. The dark fog in her brain. Her feeble cries for Harry, begging him for help.

The incessant pain. The unrelenting cruelty. The tight grip around her windpipe. The cries of terror, trapped in her throat. The choked prayers for Harry to return. The fear that death was near.

When she paused, the doctor took her hand.

"No!"

Wheels squealing, the car swerved. Sabrina cursed at the loud honks and got back in lane. "Okay, you have *got* to stop doing that," she complained, her eyes on the road. "Scared the bejesus out of me."

"Sorry," Lilah mumbled. "I'm nervous about the appointment, that's all."

Speeding along, Sabrina said, "I bet you just need to take some pills. You'd better be careful. I've heard some of those things can cause multiples, and you already have twins on your side. Who knows, you may end up with three or four, maybe five. Boys run in the Kingsley family, so..."

Lilah sputtered. Suddenly, incredibly, the sputtering turned into hysterical laughter. Hooting, she doubled over. "What do you think I am? A cat or something? Five boys!"

"Why not?" Sabrina asked, looking mildly amused at Lilah's overreaction. "It would be fun."

"Oh, really? In that case, *you* do it."

"*Moi?*" Sabrina breathed in horror. "I'm too busy."

Lilah pinned the younger woman with a glance. "Yes, you are. With your crazy computer pranks. I have nightmares of the feds invading the Kingsley mansion, looking for you."

"Pooh," said Sabrina, parking the car on Fifth Avenue. "If the FBI can't secure its own systems, they deserve every bit of what they get. And I never accessed important stuff, only left little gifts for them to find. Plus, I haven't done anything after they passed the silly law against hackers. All I can do now is mess around with the stuff we have in the Panama office and send my ideas to the magazine." Sabrina was a regular—and anonymous—contributor to a new periodical called *2600: The Hacker Quarterly*. She snickered. "FBI has an entire team devoted to locating 'Knight-errant.' All those geniuses, and they haven't been able to figure out it was little ol' me sending the silly messages."

"The world doesn't know what it escaped when Sabrina Sheppard decided to avoid a life of crime."

"That's true," Sabrina preened. "I could've been the greatest bank robber who ever lived. Or a spy."

Lilah arched an eyebrow. "Or a crazy hacker?" They laughed. "Why can't you go legit? Someone with *your* talent? Companies will line up."

Eyes glinting with mischief, Sabrina said, "I'd be telling them how to run their business. They'd fire me within a week *and* sue you for that glowing recommendation."

"Open your own business!"

"Nah. I don't have the discipline."

"*I* offered you a paycheck several times. You're doing quite a bit of work for me; make money out of it."

"Then, the rest of your staff will expect me to show up every morning, show up at meetings, etcetera, etcetera. Give it up, Lilah. I'm rich; I can afford to be eccentric."

"At least let me tell Alex how good you are with electronics. He's been bugging me to let my 'secret weapon' digitize his records. Imagine how pleasantly surprised he'll be to know it's his wife."

"He'll be *surprised* for sure. I told you. To him, I'm just his wife and Harry's baby sister." Turning off the engine, Sabrina appeared to ponder coming clean. "Nah. He'd march me to the FBI office to confess. Alex is way too law-abiding. He'd even think of it as rescuing me from myself. I'd like to ride to his rescue, for once. Knight-errant to his damsel-in-distress."

The ridiculous image of Alex Kingsley in a medieval gown popped into Lilah's head, batting his eyelashes at an armor-clad Sabrina. Lilah snickered, climbing out of the car. "I hope I get to witness the scene."

Lilah had once been a damsel-in-distress. Only she hadn't been grateful. In the back room of the Libyan church where they took refuge, she cursed Harry for leaving her alone, accused him of being in cahoots with the monster. She raged at him for not helping her leave town right away.

"You didn't go to a hospital, I take it?" the doctor asked.

"The bastard had friends on the council," Lilah tried to explain. *"We needed to hide."* The people's council controlled everything. If she and Harry got caught, the rapist would've assured they were killed. Or Sanders would have. Or Gaddafi's men. There were many enemies, and she'd been too badly injured to outrun them. Harry and Lilah hid in the church until she recovered.

"So we'll never know if you caught an infection," the doctor said.

"If I did, there would've been pain and fever, right?" Lilah argued.

"Most of the time," the doctor conceded. *"It sounds like you were already in considerable pain. You might not have noticed."*

"What about after?" Lilah asked. *"Shouldn't there have been some kind of symptom?"*

"Not always. You didn't notice anything at all?"

"Noth—" There was never anything, except... Lilah murmured, half to herself, *"Periods have been more painful since then."*

"That could be it," the doctor agreed.

"No," Lilah said, gripping the armrest. *"Lots of women have painful periods. It doesn't mean anything. Does it?"*

The doctor sighed. *"Tell you what... let me put in a referral to a fertility specialist. I'll send him your records, and you can have a conversation with him."*

Lilah and Sabrina made their way up the stoop of the three-storied limestone building on Museum Mile. With rich reds and dark woodwork, the waiting area resembled a Victorian living room, the arrival of the world-renowned doctor in his pristine white lab coat an unwelcome reminder of their reason for being there. Lilah trembled, worried what he might say in her sister-in-law's hearing. Beyond the news of the ectopic, Lilah never divulged anything to anyone besides the gynecologist. Brad didn't even know she'd been kidnapped alongside Harry.

"Please, don't say anything about this to Brad," Lilah said, dressed and waiting for her husband in the doctor's office. *"Tell him you gave me something, and I can't drive."*

Sipping coffee from her cup, the doctor walked around the room. "I could say you needed a sedative for the exam."

"Thank you."

"Did you ever talk to a psychiatrist about things?"

"Not for a long—" Biting her lip, Lilah admitted, "Actually, I've never talked about it to anyone other than Harry, but I did other things. Self-defense classes, weapons training, kickboxing."

Back in her chair, the doctor stated, "You never saw a doctor."

"I did," Lilah corrected. "Kind of. I needed help with... physical intimacy. Only, I told him it was because of the abduction. He gave me something."

"Oh, my dear," said the doctor, patting Lilah's knee.

"I have a right to privacy."

"You do," agreed the doctor. "And you dealt with it the way you found most comfortable. But seems to me you were... still are content treating your symptoms. You won't get closure without tackling the actual issue."

"I will," Lilah insisted. "Once I stop being so... once I know I can handle it without breaking down, I'm going to hunt down the bastard. I swear I am." She *needed to be in control when she finally confronted the criminal. She needed to know she'd be strong enough to pulverize the monster.*

Thirty minutes later, Lilah didn't know if she possessed the strength to deal with the reality the fertility specialist was forcing her to confront. She'd been worried about what Sabrina might hear, but now, Lilah could only be grateful for her sister-in-law's presence.

The specialist's words ricocheted around the room. "...untreated infection... you're lucky nothing life-threatening... pregnancy would not be advisable."

Lips cold and stiff, Lilah tried to respond, but no sounds came out. There was an ache in her throat, a pressure in her eyes.

"Medications..." Sabrina asked, voice unsteady.

"...high chance of another ectopic, even uterine rupture," the specialist explained. "Too risky."

Sabrina mewled in distress. "Please," she begged. "There must be something."

"Surgery, but success rates are not encouraging with the amount of scarring your sister-in-law has."

Lilah felt Sabrina take her ice-cold fingers, rubbing them between warm hands.

"There's surrogacy," the doctor said. "Legally, it would be murky. Adoption is also an option." He looked at Lilah as though expecting her to embark immediately on a plan of action.

The breeze from the air conditioner dried the sweat on her skin. She shivered. "This room is too cold," Lilah complained.

Slipping off her chair, Sabrina knelt and wrapped her arms around Lilah's shoulders.

The doctor's eyelids flickered. "Whatever you decide, I'm here to help." When he handed over papers, he gave them to Sabrina. "I can talk to your husband if you want."

Brad. Oh, God, Brad. Lilah whispered, "Thank you. I'll take care of it."

Walking back into sunshine and warmth, she wondered why there had been no evidence in the universe of the catastrophe to come. How did this disaster sneak up without warning? She'd have to break the bad news to her unsuspecting husband, devastating his dreams of fatherhood.

His entire family would be at their home in the afternoon. How could she possibly... "Don't tell anyone," Lilah said abruptly, belting herself into the seat.

Swinging back onto the highway, Sabrina assured her, "Of course I won't, but it's nothing shameful." She didn't ask how the scarring happened, what kind of infection it had been.

Whispering a prayer of gratitude to whatever power sent this friend into her life, Lilah said, "I know. I just don't want this to be discussed at the get-together today. All the questions... everyone feeling sorry for me... I can't take it. Please?"

Chapter 18

A few hours later

Brooklyn, New York

The entire Peter Kingsley clan was expected at the brownstone Lilah once lived in with her brother and their parents. She was glad she'd offered to have the gathering here instead of at the 21 Club as Brad originally suggested. Any other place, and she wouldn't have been able to handle an evening of socializing. Not tonight.

Vehicles honked in the street below. A weird combination of odors permeated the air, that of charred pretzels and takeout food and rotting garbage. Buildings were packed in tight rows in this part of the borough, but this particular one was on higher ground, and on clear days, Lilah could see all the way to the gray-blue waters of the Hudson from her rooftop. A brick chimney, unused for decades, projected up on one side of the roof, purple clematis twining around it. Flowerpots were lined up neatly against two sides of the half-wall bordering the concrete floor, roses of different colors waving gently in the breeze. There was even a ceramic birdbath at one end with smooth pebbles at the bottom of clear water.

The garden had been Brad's idea, and to Lilah's relief, it didn't leave him much time to frequent the casinos when he was in New York. He nurtured the plants himself, perhaps the only times Lilah saw him visibly relaxing other than when he believed he was alone with his brothers. Someone from the local nursery was arranged to take over care of the flowers when Brad was out of town. He'd also called in a contractor to increase the height of the rooftop wall. Lately, he'd been muttering about getting a dog, a gentle breed good with kids.

Ignoring the heaviness in her chest, Lilah dismissed the catering staff, telling them she could take care of the rest. One evening of peace... she needed it before talking to Brad.

A pair of seagulls, mates, cawed raucously and flew over the roof as Patrice Kingsley strolled in with Neil and Scott, the twin sons of her husband's mistress. The iron door to the roof swung open a second time, and Victor walked through, carrying folding chairs. Harry, Alex, and Brad were right behind.

Leaving Brad doing introductions, Patrice joined Lilah. "I love that young man," said Patrice. "I love all of them, but there's something special about Scott."

Tilting her head, Lilah studied Patrice. She'd passed on her dark coloring to Alex, but unlike him, she was small and skinny. "You're an amazing woman," Lilah said. "How *can* you?"

"How can I love Maddy's children, you mean?"

Lilah nodded. This was the first she heard the other woman's name. For Brad, Victor, and Alex, their father's mistress was "she," never to be referred to by name, and Lilah assumed Maddy/she did not come up in their conversations with Neil and Scott. "How could you *possibly* ask your sons to name the business after the man who walked out on you?"

"The company belongs to all five sons of Peter Kingsley. The name reminds them they're brothers, not just business partners." After a few beats of silence, Patrice added, "I lost a child once. When something like that happens, you find it easier to see that baby in every other child. You always wonder what your own baby would've been like at that age, at every age."

For a fleeting second, Lilah wondered what it had been, abortion or miscarriage. Would *she* do the same? See the baby she lost in every child? Patrice went on to have other children while Lilah would never have even one. Blinking hard, she said, "I'm sorry."

The door swung open again, letting through Verity, Sabrina following with a wriggling toddler. They spoke to Victor for a few seconds before joining Lilah. "Who's the Golden God?" Verity asked, awe in her lilting voice.

Lilah threw a glance at the twins. "Neil, one of the half-brothers. Didn't Victor introduce you?"

When Verity and Patrice headed in Victor's direction, Sabrina snatched a can of beer from the icebox, wiping it off on her jeans. "God, I need this." Between gulps, she said, "I've had a difficult ten minutes."

She declined to elaborate, but the fire shooting from her green eyes toward Verity's back made Lilah very glad to be on Sabrina's good side.

"Your brothers?" asked Sabrina.

"Walking in." Lilah smiled at her twin and at Shawn, Andrew Barrons's son with his never-mentioned first wife.

Dan was meticulously dressed, as always... well-cut sports coat and open collar. His shoes gleamed so bright he could probably use them as mirrors. Lilah asked him to bring his secretary along, but the red-haired cutie was not with him. They'd been making silent eyes at each other for years. Unfortunately, it was not a match the Barronses would approve of.

After greeting Lilah and Sabrina with hugs, Dan sauntered to Alex.

Shawn stayed, closely eyeing Sabrina for reasons Lilah couldn't fathom. If she didn't know he was gay, she'd have thought there was attraction in the brown eyes.

"You change your mind about the ladies or what?" Sabrina asked, grinning at Shawn.

Lilah's hand flew to her mouth, muffling laughter.

Shawn turned a sickly shade of green. "Behave yourself, little punk," he finally admonished Sabrina, shaking a finger in her face.

At thirty-seven, he was the same age as Sabrina and Harry's much older brother, Hector.

"You're the one wearing beads, and *I'm* the punk?" Sabrina asked, her eyes on the amber beads around Shawn's neck.

Of course the beads. Shawn was dressed dapper, his sandy hair stylishly cut to brush against the collar of his printed shirt. But he never took off the beads, no matter the occasion, no matter his clothes. Unfortunately, he refused to satisfy Lilah's curiosity about them.

"Forget my necklace," said Shawn. "I recently realized you were studying electronics before you quit college. Have you considered completing your degree at some point?" He was something of a name in information technology circles, having invested heavily in the sector when the market was only beginning to wake up to the possibilities. Then there was his consulting company which was already a multi-million-dollar enterprise.

Sabrina's smile dimmed. "I might," she said and left it at that.

Shawn soon wandered off to talk to Victor, his best buddy. A little later, Lilah and Neil leaned against the half-wall, chatting about something or other. The breeze made a long, dark tendril fly loose from her braid. As she tried to get it off her face, Alex approached, followed by Verity.

"You look good together," Verity told Lilah. "His coloring is golden, and you're sort of exotic... do you dye your hair?"

Lilah blinked. "Umm... no."

Dr. Neil Kingsley was handsome, charming, educated, articulate, and nice. "Why aren't you married already?" Verity quizzed.

His piercing blue eyes glinted with sudden humor. "Haven't found the right girl yet," Neil replied with the ease of someone who'd fielded the same question a million times.

Brad and Harry approached just then, and Lilah stiffened, waiting for the familiar displeasure to cross her husband's face at Alex's presence near her. Thankfully, Brad simply flung an arm around her waist. Forcing herself to smile at their guests, Lilah wished for the interminable evening to end.

When Brad left to get a drink, Harry asked, "Everything all right, Lilah?"

"Of course," she tossed off easily enough.

"I was about to ask, too," said Alex. "Are you coming down with something?"

The simple cotton frock and flats should've passed muster with everyone else dressed in garden party casual. She forced a grin to her face. "Oh, thank you so much, both of you. Just the compliment to make me feel great." She turned to Verity, inviting her to commiserate on the insensitivity of the two men but got only a thin-lipped smile in return. The men laughed, but Harry continued watching her through narrowed eyes.

Scott was in the chair next to Sabrina's, holding Alex's son, Michael, in his lap and looking thoroughly uncomfortable. Of the brothers, he resembled Brad the most, down to the glasses. The three-year-old was squirming to get away from this newfound uncle to explore the roof with its interesting nooks and crannies.

As the evening went on, Lilah was seated beside Scott. Taking advantage of his reticence, she contemplated the stars in blessed silence.

Scott fidgeted, looking sideways as he spoke. "You're very symmetrical." Immediately, he flushed.

"Huh? Thank you." *I think.* When he squirmed again, she asked, "Are you okay? If the chair's uncomfortable—"

"Not the chair." He looked around, then up. "It's me... I can't stop moving."

"Why?"

"Because I'm nervous. I move when I'm nervous. Actually, we're all moving. Very fast. We just don't notice it. It's because the stars keep moving."

"Tell me about the stars, then."

Scott knew stars. He studied them. He talked to her about galaxies and black holes and dark matter. His jerky movements subsided, and he spoke fluently, eloquently even. Just for a few moments, Lilah's thoughts were yanked from the doctor's office.

As he wound down, she said, "You make me want to go there and see for myself."

"I do?"

"Truly. I want to see this fascinating world you've described for me."

He looked at her directly for the first time. "It's just matter and energy."

"You make it sound like a painting... God's painting."

Scott smiled, the tension draining out of his face. "Astrophysics *is* art... like violin and math."

"Violin? Do you play?"

"Yes." With no trace of self-deprecation, he added, "I'm very good."

Lilah bit back a smile and revised her initial impression, comprehending what her mother-in-law said. There was a lack of artifice in Scott that was very endearing.

Before she could respond, Alex joined them. Chatting easily over cans of beer, the rest pulled up chairs—Dan, Shawn, all the Kingsley brothers, Patrice, Sabrina, Michael, Harry, and Verity.

"So what did you decide?" Brad asked his half-brothers. "Feel like joining the family business?"

Neil and Scott exchanged glances. "I'm a surgeon, Brad," Neil said. "Scott's degree is in astrophysics. What are we going to do there? Not as if we wouldn't like to work with you, but—"

Victor interjected, "And I used to be a chef. We could teach you."

"Try it out for a while," Patrice suggested. "You two should have *some* involvement in the company."

"Our jobs," Neil demurred.

"Get a leave of absence," Dan said. "Everyone in the sector needs to know you and Scott are part of the family business. What if someday you're left with no choice but to take up active roles? Employees need to accept you as executives. If you agree, you'll be working with me on the expansion plan, and Harry can focus on the big picture."

Reaching sideways, Harry snatched baklava from Lilah's plate and added his two cents. The entire group was intent on convincing Neil and Scott to join the business. Only Verity and Lilah were silent. Harry's wife was studying the gathering with her eyes slightly narrowed and her mouth turned down. Lilah was more interested in the dynamic between Neil and Scott. The brothers were communicating in glances the way twins could. They were clearly tempted, hesitating only from fear of having to leave the comfortable futures they'd envisioned for themselves.

Finally, Neil said, "I guess we could give it a shot for a year or two."

A whoop went around the group. Slapping Scott's back, Victor hollered, "All right!"

That called for another round of drinks. When Alex offered Lilah a can of beer, she declined. "C'mon, Lilah, what's with the brooding?" he asked.

"I'm not brooding," she denied automatically and pasted a smile on her lips.

"Oh, yeah, you are." Victor examined his nails. "Nobody mopes when I'm around—Victor Kingsley, father confessor."

Alex snorted. "Since when?"

"Since before you figured out girls were different," Victor retorted. "I can turn any woman's tears into smiles," he said, waggling his eyebrows.

Alex groaned. The duo started regaling Lilah with stories from their misspent youth, sending the rest of the audience into peals of laughter.

Harry interjected with anecdotes from their quest to take down Sanders, including the time the three men were ejected ignominiously from the Plaza. "Lilah, you should have seen Victor arguing with the chef," said Harry, eyes brimming with laughter. "Alex and I thought they were going to brawl."

"The *imbécile* wouldn't admit his omelet could have used help— lots of help," Victor said. "It takes an *artiste* to cook an egg the right way." His voice throbbed, giant frame quivering like an outraged rooster's. "Ask the two philistines," he said to Lilah. "I invited them home after the conference."

"He means he dragged us to his apartment, kicking and screaming, and force-fed us eggs," Harry corrected.

Alex flopped in his chair, making choking sounds.

"The Three Stooges," teased Sabrina, sputtering with mirth.

Scott hummed the theme song from the comedy show, stopping when the others exploded in hilarity. "What?" he asked, glancing from face to laughing face for a couple of seconds before seemingly reaching the conclusion the group wasn't laughing *at* him. He chuckled at Victor's comical glare.

Lilah was hardly in the mood for revelry, but she joined in, hoping to avoid further scrutiny of her blue mood.

Plopping a drowsy Michael into Lilah's lap, Sabrina asked in a whisper, "You okay?"

Lilah nodded, feeling grateful.

As the laughter died down, Verity asked Lilah, "I want to know how you do it." When Lilah raised a confused eyebrow, Verity added, "I mean, look at all these men making fools of themselves trying to get a smile out of you. What kind of magic is this? Do you drug them or something?"

Startled, Lilah stared. An awkward silence descended on the group. Sabrina and Patrice stiffened. There was restrained anger on Dan's face, watchful concern on Shawn's. The shock and dismay in Harry's eyes were quickly masked, but not before Lilah spotted it.

No, she didn't imagine the malice. *Tonight, of all nights.* With a forced laugh, Lilah responded, "You're good for my ego, Verity. I'm as involved in the business as they are. That's the only magic."

"Well, whatever it is, I wish you'd share.," grumbled Harry's wife. "You have even the married men dancing to your tunes, for God's sake. Look at Alex, playing the clown. *I* would settle for my husband's attention."

A chair clattered. Standing, Neil announced, "I'd better get going. I'm gonna have to meet the chief of surgery tomorrow morning about the leave of absence."

Within the next few minutes, the party broke up.

Chapter 19

An hour later

Through the slats of the wooden blinds on the bedroom window, Lilah watched the street. Her throat tightened at the sight of the woman pushing a double stroller along the brightly lit sidewalk. The barefooted infants in the baby carriage stared at the crowd with wide eyes and open mouths.

Behind her, Brad sat on the bed, digesting what he'd just heard. "Infection?" he asked. "What do you mean?"

"I was ill... in a manner of speaking." Lilah turned from the window and took a couple of shaky steps toward him. "We didn't know each other when we got engaged. I would've told you about this a long time ago if we met and fell in love the usual way." Kneeling next to the bed, she took his hand in both of hers. "Some years ago, when I was hardly more than a child, I... had a problem."

"What problem?"

"I... umm... I..." She closed her eyes. "I was attacked. That may be why."

"Atta... *attacked?* You mean like rape?"

The word... the very sound of it... she didn't realize it until this very second, but the word itself was terrifying. She hated it. Absolutely hated it. "Yes," Lilah whispered. Bending her forehead to their linked hands, she let the tears fall. In the moments which followed, there was no noise in the room other than her shuddering breaths.

Shaking her hold loose, Brad asked, "How come none of the doctors told you fertility might be an issue?"

"I didn't see a doctor," she said.

"Your family didn't take you to one?" His voice was as refined as always despite the increasing edge to the tone.

"They didn't know. They still don't know." With a tentative touch to his knee, she explained, "I couldn't *get* to a doctor for weeks, and by then, I'd healed, so there didn't seem to be any point."

"Sure. It's easy enough to figure out. What was it? An illegal abortion? It would explain the scarring."

"Abor—" Lilah shook her head violently. "*No,* that's not what happened. Why would I lie to you? Hear me out, please."

"Did you know you couldn't have children when we got married?"

"*What?* My God, Brad! How could you think... I would never do that to... please, just let me tell you the whole thing."

He slashed the air with his hand. "What whole thing? This unbelievable story about rape? You'd have never said *any*thing if it weren't for your problem."

"Brad, please... I was waiting until we got comfortable with each other. I never dreamed this would be how I finally—"

"Of course! Women like you always have an excuse."

"Women like me?"

"Didn't you hear Harry's wife? She was too well brought up to come out and say it, but there's a dirty word used to describe women like you."

Still on her knees by the side of the bed, Lilah froze in shock.

"Unfortunately for me, I'm stuck with you." Punching the mattress, he continued, "What did *I* do to deserve... this is not right."

Lilah whimpered. Brad stared stone-faced into the room, not responding to the tiny sob from his wife.

Her chest... it hurt so badly. Taking in a deep breath, she tried to stand but stumbled back to the carpet. There was no assistance offered, no hand extended to help her up. Hauling herself to her feet, she walked out of the room, out of the house.

She wandered aimlessly along the sidewalks. Lilah didn't know how far she went nor how late it was. Finally, she came to a stop outside a glass door, the board above proclaiming it to be a restaurant. Without knowing quite why, she walked in.

"Miss?" asked the kindly proprietor. "Are you all right?"

Lilah took the offered table and sat until late, doodling with her fingertip on the red-and-white tablecloth, ordering dishes which she barely tasted, drinking Lebanese coffee. The reflection on the windowpane showed dark lashes standing out against the stark pallor of her face. She asked the waiter, "May I use your phone, please?" Lilah looked at the time displayed on the machine. Too late to call anyone. "I changed my mind," she told the waiter. "I don't need it."

When she left the place, the crowded street seemed to fade away, leaving her alone on a deserted path. Completely, eternally alone. Her parents, her twin, her friends, her sweetheart... the baby she'd already imagined... there was no one. In her mind, she wandered a silent, icy realm, her solitude, her own personal hell.

Thoughts foggy, she walked up the steps to her room. Brad was still sitting on the bed and stood as she entered.

Gruffly, he offered, "I'm sorry. I was just upset there won't be any children."

Wasn't she supposed to feel angry? Or sad or confused or *some*thing? Why was there this chilly vacuum inside her? Where were all the words she was supposed to know, words which could pay him back in kind for his cruelty?

Brad appeared relieved at her silence. "We don't have to tell anyone there's a problem with you. There will be too many people wanting to know why. The truth could be embarrassing to explain."

Lilah lay awake through the night, curled into a tight ball on one side of the bed. Somewhere toward dawn, she fell into a dreamless sleep.

Chapter 20

The next morning

Brooklyn, New York

Sunday in their home was silent as always with both Brad and Lilah involved in their respective routines. When he took himself off to Atlantic City, she was thankful. Lilah usually worried about his gambling habit, but today, she couldn't care less. Her clothes were already in a separate walk-in closet, so it took only a couple of hours to move her things from the master bedroom to the room she'd used as a child.

She longed to call the mountain club. Rappelling the Adirondack cliffs would clear the cobwebs in her mind. Or a kickboxing session. Or *some*thing.

But there was Sabrina. She was not an insecure mess like Brad, but Lilah refused to lose the friendship because of Verity's innuendos about Alex. Almost fearfully, Lilah drove to City Island to visit Sabrina at her parents' home.

Sabrina was in a mood to run in the park. Jogging with a three-year-old in tow meant pausing by every funny stone and pursuing every colorful bird. Lilah was wondering how to bring up the topic of the night before when Sabrina fumed, "If she weren't my brother's wife, I would've pulled her hair out."

One hand on the rough trunk of a tree, Lilah stopped. For a second, she merely stared at Sabrina. The baby was again off, chasing a squirrel across the grass.

"'What kind of magic is this?'" Sabrina perfectly mimicked Verity's childlike voice. "'Do you drug them or something?'"

An unexpected tickle started in Lilah's chest. Laughter bubbled up, spilling through her lips. "Oh, God, the melodrama!"

The women howled. When mirth tapered off, Sabrina's face tightened. "Get this. She asked me how I managed to become pregnant without Alex knowing. As though I did it on purpose!"

An image of Verity holding a baby popped into Lilah's mind. Harry's baby. Acute resentment rolled into a tight, hot ball in the middle of her chest.

"Verity turned out to be exactly as I thought," Sabrina raged. "A spoilt brat who will stop at nothing... it's always 'I want, I want, I want,' with her. Now, it appears she wants a child no matter what my brother thinks of the idea. Of all the women... why *her*? I wish somebody knocked some sense into Harry before he—"

Harry might mock Lilah by calling her "Princess," but he'd married the real-life article. A demanding princess who wanted a child with him. Everything simply fell into Verity's lap. The man, the baby, *everything*.

"I have to let him know what she's planning," Sabrina muttered.

"C'mon, Mikey," Lilah shouted, not wanting to hear any more. "Let's play catch."

When they returned to the Sheppard home, Harry and Alex were there with the younger two Kingsley brothers. Verity was with them.

Thankful that playtime with Sabrina's son returned some measure of composure to her mind, Lilah greeted the group. Harry, too, kept his expression carefully casual.

"Naptime, Mikey," Sabrina said, holding out a hand to the toddler.

"I'm going with you." Lilah also needed to rest for a few minutes. The leftover cramps from her miscarriage were excruciating.

Verity accompanied the women to the bedroom. When Lilah asked for a painkiller, Sabrina said she'd fetch something better. Admonishing her son to stay put, she left the other two watching him.

Curtains were drawn in the sunny room, the sounds of the sea beating on the rocky shore a soothing lullaby to the occupant of the queen-sized four-poster bed. The toddler stayed awake, counting his fingers and toes with great interest and announcing triumphantly he possessed twenty. Lilah acknowledged his discovery with a high-five and returned to the leather chair by the fireplace. Verity took the second chair, broodingly studying Sabrina and Alex's wedding pictures on the side table.

There was a photograph of the couple in their formals, sharing a sweet kiss. The second one showed them with her parents and brothers. Hector had his wife, a gym instructor, with him, but Harry was alone.

"Were you at the wedding?" Lilah asked, trying to tamp down the bitterness. Harry's wife would always be part of the same social circle as the Kingsleys, and it would be better for Lilah's peace of mind if they could at least be cordial.

"Yes," came the clipped response. Then, knuckles to her teeth, Verity burst out, "I came here to talk to you. Alex said you were visiting."

A vicious cramp hit Lilah's lower abdomen. She curled deeper into the leather chair, wincing. "All right," she managed to hiss out. An apology from Verity would make life easier for all of them.

"I want you to stay away from Harry."

Huh? Lilah squinted. Perhaps she misheard. "Sorry? I didn't get what you said."

"No matter what *I* want to do, Harry is always too busy with you Kingsleys. I'm tired of this network or whatever."

"What?" Lilah shook her head.

Voice hard, Sabrina said from the door, "Do you understand how many commitments Harry has?"

"You don't have to lecture me on commitments," Verity snarled. "Just because I'm not an oil engineer doesn't mean I'm stupid and irresponsible."

Sabrina strode in and handed a hot-water bottle to Lilah, her face red and tense.

Uncaring of the anger from Harry's sister, Verity continued raging at Lilah. "I could be a CFO, too, if I put it in a pre-nup. It's not like you earned the stock or got it from your parents. Sabrina at least got her money from her family. *You* have no right to lecture anyone."

Furious, Lilah opened her mouth to snap at the offensive little twit, but Michael was staring at them. She threw a pointed glance at the toddler, but Verity was beyond noticing.

Harry's wife scrambled out of her chair, shaking a finger at Lilah. "If the Kingsleys were smart, they would stop letting you ruin everything, and Harry would have time to spend with *me* instead of chasing around after you and your family. I'm tired of waiting for him to come home. I deserve a life, too. Enough with you."

Another cramp struck, making it doubly difficult for Lilah to keep her wrath in check, Michael's presence notwithstanding. *My God! Harry's married to this... this* brat?

Green eyes stony, Sabrina ground out, "Enough with *you*." She took two steps toward Verity. "Insulting Lilah at the party in front of everyone!"

Suddenly, every ounce of good sense flew out of Lilah's mind. She stood, leaving the hot-water bottle on the chair, and neatly shoved the combatants apart. "All right," she said. "What do you want to know?"

"What?" snapped Verity.

"You asked me yesterday why the men were trying to please me, right?" Lilah nearly shook with the need to teach the thoughtless twit a lesson in decent behavior, but she kept her husky voice as smooth as she possibly could. "You asked if I drugged them."

"Heh?" said Verity, face now confused.

"I don't drug anyone, but you've seen what the tabloids say," Lilah murmured, eyes boring into Verity's. Tone lowering forebodingly, Lilah hissed, "About black magic."

"What?" Verity repeated, rearing in shock.

On her other side, Lilah saw Sabrina's open mouth and the utter bafflement on her face.

"It's not magic as most people understand it," Lilah said. "My mother... she taught me the ancient ways."

"Ancient ways?" Verity parroted.

"Yes," Lilah said, steepling her fingers. "The secrets to keeping men obedient and eager to please. Passed down from mother to daughter since the creation of the world. When men see me, they don't see the real me. They see... perfection. Everything they ever desired. A woman who works dawn to dusk and in the evening greets her husband at the door with a glass of wine in her hand."

Sabrina made a strangled sound.

"Wearing black satin lingerie," Lilah said, malice oozing through every word. "My tricks make them believe I'm not normal. They think I don't sleep, I don't eat. They don't ever notice me shower or use perfume, but I still smell sweet. They never see me use the bathroom."

"She doesn't even pass gas," Sabrina contributed, her words ending in a peal of laughter.

At the same second, both Verity and Lilah pivoted to stare at Sabrina. Her face was nearly purple from uncontrolled mirth. Lilah lost it. For the second time that day, she howled, holding on to Sabrina.

Voice shrill, Verity accused, "You're mocking me." She glared at the other two.

"Took you this long to figure it out?" Sabrina sputtered.

Lilah was still guffawing, much to the confusion of Michael staring goggle-eyed from the bed.

"Stop," Verity shrieked, hands fisted at her side, stomping a foot.

Sabrina halted, tears of mirth on her lashes. "You're right," she spat. "I should have put a stop to *you* yesterday."

"You little—" Verity said, nearly sobbing in anger.

"Look, Verity," Lilah said, suddenly drained. "You're upset with the Kingsleys and me because Harry spends a lot of time with us. Try to remember what he's doing is just as important to the Sheppards. Gateway does a significant amount of business with the Kingsleys, and Sabrina is Harry's sister."

Alex called down the hallway just then, letting them know Neil and Scott were leaving soon. Verity glanced between the door and the women facing her, the incoherent anger slowly leaving her face, replaced by wariness. "I didn't mean to... I was upset."

Lilah released her breath. "We'll deal with this some other time. You two go ahead and talk to the guests. I can wait with Mikey until he falls asleep."

Letting Verity walk on ahead, Sabrina turned back at the door and bowed low. Hand to her chest and eyes widened in *faux* awe, she said, "I am—officially—impressed."

"*I'm* exhausted," Lilah said. "Also, we shouldn't have... it was two against one."

"Oh, for... *she* started it."

"Are we in grade school now? Both of us should've known better."

"No way. I refuse to put up with that sort of bratty behavior. *You* wouldn't put up with it from *anyone* else. Only reason you're feeling guilty is she's Harry's wife. You're afraid you retaliated because—" Sabrina went into a coughing fit. Glancing toward the toddler on the bed, she muttered, "Oh, crap. He heard everything."

"*Now* you remember your son?" Lilah asked, her heart thudding in thankfulness Sabrina had abandoned her attempt at psychoanalysis.

Sabrina made a face. "If anyone asks, we were teaching Mikey to stand up for what's right." Eyeing the hallway outside, she added, "I really, really hope my brother isn't crazy enough to talk about crucial business stuff in front of Verity. What if she blurts out things she shouldn't?"

Harry had never divulged any of Lilah's secrets without first checking with her, but the business... spouses saw and heard things even when they weren't meant to.

Alex called again, and Sabrina mouthed "later" before skipping off to the living room. Sophia—Harry and Sabrina's mother—was talking animatedly about something, her voice traveling upstairs.

Funny... the senior Sheppards hardly ever acknowledged Lilah's existence. Except for her green irises, Sabrina was a younger version of her blonde and blue-eyed mother. But Sabrina Sheppard was the most incredibly loyal of friends, a fiercely protective sister.

A small sound from the bed drew Lilah's attention. The baby... she scooted onto the mattress and cuddled next to him. Michael's jaw was still agape. Hoping he would somehow forget the scene he witnessed, she dropped a feather-light kiss on the top of his head. He looked up and pulled a thick lock of hair. "Ouch," she said and pretended to bite his pudgy fingers. She ran her fingertips across his tummy, tickling him and making him laugh. "Shh," she said. "Mama thinks you're sleeping." He covered his mouth with his hand, and they giggled together in delicious mischief.

Breath stopped in her chest for a few seconds as she looked down and saw the dark-haired child she'd never have. In his face, she saw the father of her own son, a son who would never be. Incredible pain weakened her limbs at the thought of the years ahead. A sharp sob escaped her lips.

"Lilah?" asked the baby, worry on his innocent face.

She smiled at him, eyes blurry from unshed tears. Lilah nose-kissed him, and all was once again right in his world.

"Story?" he requested, climbing onto her lap.

While he rested his sturdy little body against her torso, she started, "Once upon a time, there was a brave and handsome prince who lived in a country far, far away..." She told him tales from a wonderful land of sun and color and laughter where all things were possible, and everything was magic. Slowly, his eyes drifted shut, and he fell asleep, nestled in her arms.

Holding the baby close, Lilah dreamed an impossible dream that he was hers, theirs. The father of her child would come in any moment and smile at his family with tender love. She closed her eyes tight and shook her head, trying vainly to stop the voices of reality from intruding. Then, the sound of that beloved laughter echoed up the stairs, reminding her of how foolish she was being. Like the baby, he wasn't hers, would never be hers. Lilah wanted to beat her fists on him, to rage at the fate which brought them to this moment. She wanted to collapse in his arms and let his tears mingle with her own. She wanted to kiss him through salty tears and make love with a desperation that would consume them both. But he wasn't hers, would never be hers.

Finally, silently, she allowed her heart to shatter into a million pieces.

Chapter 21

A week later, August 1986

World Trade Center, New York City

Lilah looked at the report in front of her, numbers blurring together. Voices echoed around the conference room. The Kingsleys were going over the remaining phases of the expansion plans with Harry, and Lilah was supposed to present the financial forecast, but she couldn't focus.

Brad had been relentless in his verbal abuse since she changed the sleeping arrangements at home. Sneering dismissals of her right to be angry, rage over her imagined flirtations... even Lilah's lack of response couldn't stop him. He changed tactics after the first week, telling her how sorry he was. There were flowers every day, sometimes jewelry from Tiffany's. Lilah thanked him for his apology and left the gifts on the dining room table. She needed to keep up civility, enough to maintain their business relationship until she decided what to do.

"Bombay High Field..." started Victor, commenting on the offshore operations in the Gulf of Cambay.

For the hundredth time, Lilah went over options. Telling Harry what was going on was out of the question. If he understood the extent of Brad's cruelty toward her, one more name would be added to the list of enemies intended for elimination. Harry would see it as a guaranteed way to protect her personally and to get rid of another threat to her control over the network. Lilah didn't know if she were willing to take such drastic measures against a man simply for his insecurities and his pettiness.

Maybe I should simply quit...

She could concoct some story about wanting to return to her legal career. Harry would fuss to no end, but she'd be firm. The network could continue to grow with her as paper wife and paper CFO. Separate apartments for her and Brad in the same house? Separate lives?

No, in her absence, Harry *might* still be able to get the Kingsleys to do as they were told, but officially, he didn't carry the same authority as Lilah to object to dubious business plans. If it weren't for the need to keep her around until the network was final, Godwin would've asked his grandsons to show Harry the door a long time ago, perhaps in favor of Hector. The Kingsley brothers would not say no to a direct order from their precious grandfather no matter how much in awe of Harry they were. The other reason Harry was part of the power circle was the clout the Sheppards carried in the alliance. Gateway wouldn't have the same influence once the network got bigger. If Brad were to be persuaded Harry's word didn't matter even before the network was a done deal, Lilah's absence would make it easier to break the stalemate.

Also, the media could somehow get to know about the living arrangements. ...*the potential for trouble in the market*...

"Lilah," someone called.

If Harry were to be elected chairman... she shook herself mentally. It would take a miracle to get them there. First, he'd need to stay alive and out of prison after dealing with their enemies. Only then could she hand over control and walk out of the nightmare her life had become.

"Lilah?" Alex barked.

She looked at him in confusion. "I'm sorry. Were you talking to me?"

Alex tapped at the open schedule in front of him with the tip of his pen. "Last year's report from the Indian company?"

As she handed him the neatly arranged pile of papers, she saw Harry give her a thoughtful look from across the table.

Oh, Harry. Whichever way I turn, I can see only trouble ahead for both of us. Through her lashes, she watched him scribble on a piece of paper.

"Has Sabrina decided what she's going to do while you're away, Alex?" asked Brad. "I hope she spends some time in Panama. The idea of not being able to see Michael is tough."

Laughing, Victor said, "You should be working on your own brood."

Brad cleared his throat. "Well... about that... it's not happening."

Lilah sat up. He was not going to announce it here, was he?

"Shooting blanks, bro?" Pen in his left hand, Neil was checking off agenda items and didn't see his brother's face cloud at the crudity. Then, registering Brad's silence, Neil sat up, offering embarrassed apologies which were waved away.

Waves of fatigue washed over Lilah. Even if Brad were genuinely trying to save her from painful questions, there was no going back for either of them. Unfortunately, they were both stuck in this empty shell of a marriage, caged by their political commitments.

The Kingsley men and Harry continued their work, and if Lilah's hand shook a little when she poured coffee into her mug, no one noticed.

When they finally called it a day, Harry asked, "How about coming over for dinner tonight?"

Gathering papers together, she shook her head. "Can't. Brad is visiting his grandfather, and I have plans to go to Green-Wood."

"I'll go with you," Harry said.

Lilah glanced at Brad. He didn't seem to have heard Harry. It might not have mattered, anyway. Her husband's jealousies were centered mainly on Alex.

There was one journalist waiting in the parking lot. Seeing her with Harry, the reporter turned away in obvious disappointment. Lilah nearly laughed. For the media, she was mainly Alex Kingsley's rejected lover, which meant his supposed best pal never starred in the stories about her. She could shout the truths of her past from the top of the World Trade Center, but no one would believe any of it.

#

An hour later

Brooklyn, New York

Since it was summer, they had a few hours before the cemetery gates closed for the night. Leaving Harry to follow, Lilah walked ahead. The space near the pond was surprisingly empty for the time

169

of the year. Small green monk parakeets flitted around, chattering raspily.

When Lilah got to the glade with the graves side-by-side, she dropped to the ground, her back to a tree. As always, there was a strong smell of root beer coming from the bark. *Say a prayer for me, Mama,* she whispered. *Make my miracle happen.* Temple and Godwin needed to be defeated, and Harry needed to stay alive to be chairman. Lilah couldn't go on in a reality without him.

Harry knelt by the markers and brushed off the fallen twigs and blossoms. Watching him trace the names of her parents on the granite tombstone, Lilah said, "They've been gone fourteen years."

He stripped off his blazer and tossed it to the ground before heaving himself to her side. Wrapping an arm around her, he asked, "Do you want to talk?"

The tenderness in his voice somehow caused her throat muscles to tighten. "The doctor says there's a lot of scarring. The chances are low, almost non-existent."

His fingers clenched on her shoulder. "Brad said—"

"He didn't want to go into details, that's all."

Harry stared at the graves, still holding her close. Almost inaudibly, he asked, "The scarring, is it from..."

"Yes."

There was a muted grunt from him, a sound of acute pain.

Turning her face into his chest, she closed her eyes and fought the longing to sink into his warmth. The faint whiff of his sandalwood cologne somehow caused moisture to sprout behind her lashes. "I'm fine, Harry," she lied. "I've had time to process."

He drew her even closer with his other arm, his body trembling in tandem with hers. Under her ear, his heart thudded in a steady rhythm. They stayed that way for hours, his shirt soaking up her tears. Neither noticed the deepening gloom when the sun set, and the other visitors left. Neither said a word. They didn't have the vocabulary to articulate the pain, to soothe the agony. Clinging to each other, they grieved in silence for the children who would never be.

When the security guard walking by said the gates would soon close, they finally left, Lilah declining Harry's offer to see her home. Brad would have returned by the time they got to the brownstone, and she didn't want Harry picking up on the vibes in the house. He insisted on walking with her to the subway station, a tall and quiet presence at her side all the way to the corner of Fourth Avenue and 25th Street.

The narrow platform was brightly lit and packed with commuters and noisy tourists. Waves of muggy heat flowed around them. Watching the R train chugging in, Lilah said, "I'll see you tomorrow."

In a fierce whisper, he swore, "I *will* find the bastard. Colonel Parker will pay for what he did before I deal with Temple and Godwin." Before Harry went on his suicide mission.

Lilah started. She'd vowed to put down the monster herself, but she always knew Harry was also searching for him, and she always knew the rapist would die when he came face-to-face with her best friend. She never once imagined what would happen after. When Harry found the criminal who assaulted her, Temple and Godwin would no longer need to attack the man standing in their way. They could easily use the authority of the state to hunt Harry down for murder.

Part VIII

Chapter 22

Same time, August 1986

Lorton, Virginia

The black car sped along the George Washington Memorial Parkway. There were none of the usual traffic restrictions attending a presidential trip. No one would know Temple was in the unmarked vehicle, accompanied by his security detail.

The lights on the road seemed to merge, creating a multichromatic tunnel against the backdrop of the dark night. There might have been noises, but Temple hardly heard any of it. He simply wanted out of his prison for some time. The news he heard from Godwin... even Noah wasn't around for Temple to unburden himself.

The former attorney general was busy with the plans for Colonel Parker. The business of luring the criminal into cooperating was a complicated one. Several anonymous contacts had been made, enough for him to realize he was dealing with people who knew quite a lot about his activities. But until they got him on tape, confessing to his various crimes, Noah wouldn't reveal his identity. Once it was done, Temple and Godwin would—

Temple sat up, causing one of the secret service officers to glance toward him. With a reassuring nod, Temple turned to stare unseeingly at the road. The former justice's first reaction to the revelation of Lilah's past was annoyance at Temple. There had been no thankfulness in Godwin that a bright young life didn't perish in the assault. No worry about infections. The new virus called HIV...

it wasn't known to the world at the time, but who could tell how long it had been circulating? Godwin Kingsley ground out his displeasure at the info not being disclosed when the alliance was being discussed. Only when Noah asked why the horrifying incident would have any bearing on the initial negotiations did Godwin stop complaining. He still raised one critical question: was there a pregnancy test done on the girl at the time?

Temple explained it took him weeks after Harry and Lilah's escape to connect their silence with the colonel's history and deduce what might've happened. By then, she was off the ventilator and coherent enough to be asked for consent before a detailed examination. But yeah, the one thing Temple got the medics to confirm was that she was not pregnant. Godwin was mollified, knowing there was no child of Lilah's not fathered by Brad to eventually claim rights to her property.

Now... when there would be no children at all... Godwin had been persuaded to leave her alone due to the network and the pre-nup and because he knew her stock would eventually go to the next generation of Kingsleys. Lilah would've realized she needed to designate someone acceptable to the family as beneficiary while including a clause which would guarantee her continued life. But would she actually take the step? Harry would surely prod her into it no matter what her feelings about her husband's family.

"We're here, sir," murmured a secret service officer.

Already? Temple peered through the tinted window at the Pohick Church, once parish to George Washington. Only a single bulb burned at the door, revealing the shadowed form of the rector. Calling at this late hour with a request to visit the place would've inconvenienced the clergyman, but Temple needed to make sure he was doing the right thing.

A few minutes later, he was sitting in one of the box pews, staring at the shadowed pulpit. Was Lilah's infertility a result of the assault? Nothing of the sort was said by Brad in his conversation with his grandfather, but Temple couldn't help worrying. His hand curled into a fist. At eighty-two, his punch wouldn't carry enough force, but the criminal who assaulted Lilah couldn't go unpunished.

Except, he would... Temple would help him escape justice, instead condemning to death the very man who never stopped fighting on her behalf. Harry Sheppard's destiny had been written the day Temple figured out what happened, and not even by him. Harry's own family did it to him.

Chapter 23

A few days later, August 1986

World Trade Center, New York City

Verity leaned against the wall next to the office door, waiting for Harry to be done talking to his secretary. Today, he was going to listen to his wife for a change. The envelope Verity picked up at the travel agent's would help her get her marriage back on track.

On the drive home from Brad and Lilah's after the rooftop party, Verity had been prepared to snap off Harry's head if he as much as coughed in disapproval, but he said nothing. Not a word, not even a glance of disappointment. *Good,* Verity told herself. The fiasco came about only because he'd ignored her.

She would've rubbed his nose in it if it weren't for Alex hanging out with Harry every single evening. The only communication between her and Harry was in bed. Even that... something had happened in the last few days. Verity was sure of it.

New shadows lurked in Harry's face, a restlessness in his movements. He barked over the phone in his home office about finding someone, no matter the cost. Half the time, his mind seemed to be someplace else. Even while making love! There was that one night...

"Sorry," he'd mumbled when his watch scratched the delicate skin of her upper arm. He'd forgotten to remove it. Leaning over her, he lost balance and fell on one arm, his elbow pinning her hair.

"Ouch," she said, her scalp burning.

"Sorry," he mumbled again.

Harry touched all the right spots, but Verity couldn't help feeling he was simply following a memorized routine. His kisses tasted the same, but they didn't leave her hungry for more. He tried his best to tease her into the same mindless lust, but all she could do was watch the flatness in his eyes. He couldn't even arouse *himself* enough to reach satisfaction. Sweaty and uncomfortable, Verity wanted it to be over.

Finally, collapsing onto the mattress, Harry murmured, *"Verity, I..."*

She cuddled close. *"It's all right."*

His mouth twisted, the smile mildly bitter. *"Yes, it will be all right. It has to be."*

In the days following, Harry came to bed earlier and put in more effort. But while his body was next to hers, his mind didn't seem to know it. The embarrassing failure was not repeated, but he simply was not the man she married three years ago. It wasn't enough, no matter what Verity told him.

This network business of the Kingsleys was ruining her life, and she needed to do something about it. Paris... the Eiffel Tower... she and Harry would recapture the enchantment of their honeymoon.

Pacing the office, he was busy rattling off instructions to the trim fifty-something woman who'd been working with him for years. "It's better to talk to Scott directly and tell him what to expect instead of merely faxing the list of executives to meet. He is in London for the next ten days, so factor in the time difference when you call. Can you do it from home?"

"Absolutely," said the secretary.

"Thanks," he said. "Tash? Do remind him to keep me updated."

The older lady smiled at Verity as she walked briskly past to leave the room.

Harry shut the door and raised an eyebrow at his wife. "What brings you here?"

"A surprise." Giggling in excitement, she handed him the envelope. "Look what I have."

He pulled out the tickets and frowned. "These are for tonight."

"Yes! We can celebrate your birthday with a kiss on the Eiffel Tower."

Harry pinched the bridge of his nose. "I wish you'd consulted me. I can't get away this weekend."

"It's only for a couple of days!"

"You know I have responsibilities here," said Harry. "I can't fly off at a moment's notice."

Verity couldn't *believe*... all the effort she put into this... "But it's for your birthday."

"Work doesn't stop simply because I was born on a certain day."

When a firm knock sounded at the door, Harry jerked it open, face creasing instantly into a welcoming smile. Alex... and Lilah. Verity nearly screamed at the ceiling in frustration.

"Hey!" greeted Alex, his surprise clear at finding her there.

Before she could respond, Harry started urging the duo into the conference room attached to his office suite. "Why don't you spend the afternoon here?" he suggested, nodding at Verity. "The four of us can have dinner together before heading home."

Dropping a pile of binders onto the conference table, Alex sat. There were a couple of small boxes on top of the files. Another set of folders was already present next to Harry's spot.

Going to the counter, Verity poured herself some iced tea and ignored the few drops she spilled on the marble top. The view from the room was pretty—the tall buildings of downtown Manhattan gleaming against blue sky—but she was beginning to feel like a prisoner on the island. She... *they* needed to get away. If not Paris, someplace else. Harry needed to focus on his own wife for a while.

"Before we start," Alex said, "happy birthday, dude. The big three-oh!"

"Another number is all," said Harry. "Let's get to work."

"Five minutes ain't gonna kill any of us," Alex insisted. "We brought presents."

Curiosity made Verity peer.

"Baklava," said Alex, handing Harry one of the boxes he brought in with the work stuff. "Sabrina bought it from some Middle-Eastern place."

Harry's face brightened. "Does my sister know me or what?" Opening the box, he broke off a chunk and put it into his mouth. "*God,* this is delicious."

Sliding the second box across, Alex said, "This is from me. Muhammad Ali versus Joe Frazier... all three fights, videotaped in full."

"All right!" Tone devout, Harry added, "The greatest of all time. Although the new kid is good... Mike Tyson."

"Your turn," Alex said to Lilah, waving at the small paper bag in her hand.

Still chewing baklava, Harry took the bag from Lilah. Drawing a book out, he smiled, pure pleasure lighting up his eyes. *Zen and the Art of Motorcycle Maintenance.*

"Lilah and I met the author some time ago at an event and got a couple of signed copies," Alex said. "She thought you'd like one."

"Perfect," Harry said.

Of course! Whatever Lilah does is perfect. There were lines on her forehead as though she... why on earth was Perfect Lilah looking so worried?

"I find a lot of what Mr. Robert Pirsig says very relevant," stated the woman. "'The past exists only in our memories, the future only in our plans—'"

"Oh, yeah?" Harry interjected, eyes narrowed.

"'—the present is our only reality,'" Lilah concluded. "Getting stuck in the past is a distraction no one can afford. I'm sure you've heard some such in the SEAL program. We should keep it in mind where the network is concerned. There might be old enemies we run into... I don't want you going off on some tangent without checking with me first."

Alex snorted and sketched Lilah a salute.

Laughing, Harry bopped Lilah on the head with the book. "Yes, Admiral. I *have* heard 'some such.' I never planned to go off after anyone without talking to you. You'll be the first person I call if and when something pops up."

Verity couldn't make heads or tails out of any of it, but the tension in Harry's voice appeared to have dissipated ever so slightly. All it took was a paperback from Lilah? Verity's jaw hurt from gritting her teeth hard.

Alex pulled a folder from the pile. "We'd better get to work. My first stop in India will be Assam. There are some promising fields there and in the other eastern states and perhaps even going upward into the mountains. Then, it will be Bombay High and the offshore outfit. The quality of the crude is even better than Middle-Eastern oil."

"Alex!" Despite her annoyance with the Kingsleys, Verity was awed. "You sound like an expert."

He glanced up. "What do you think I've been doing these last few years?"

A smile playing on her lips, Lilah told Verity, "He holds his own with our engineers now, and that includes yours truly."

The woman was actually acting as though nothing ever happened! Widening her eyes, Verity said, "Everyone knows Alex has already managed to impress *you*."

The warmth on Lilah's face dimmed instantly. Verity would've danced in triumph... except there was Harry's steady regard. His utter lack of expression left her feeling really small... and seething.

Alex apparently didn't notice any of it. "The desert in the west is said to have rich deposits, too... Rajasthan, the abode of kings."

"You're excited," Lilah teased, turning away from Verity.

"Yes, I am," he admitted. "When I was with the army, I spent five years in Pakistan but never got a chance to visit India."

Picking up a slim folder, Harry tossed it to Alex. "Enjoy your visit but figure out which fields are worth our while. The key is to acquire with minimum effort and expenditure. And keep an eye out for any long-term prospects. In fact, I've been going through some renewable fuel proposals... we'll talk more at our next big meeting. Back to India... in the folder are the résumés of the politicians you'll need to know." A second folder slid Alex's way. "The business leaders. Don't make the mistake of underestimating any of them based on credentials. They can be as ruthless as our old friend Sanders, even more in fact, since they can usually get away with more than Sanders ever dreamed of. Some of them were on good terms with him, so watch your back."

Verity rolled her eyes. Sanders—another name she was sick of hearing.

Harry settled deeper into his chair. "The Foreign Exchange Regulation Act is supposed to keep foreign ownership of Indian firms below forty percent, but there's a clause exempting core sectors from this which we can use to our advantage."

Acts... clauses... whatever. Verity supposed knowing such details brought cash into the bank account, but what was the point in being rich if they couldn't pause long enough to enjoy the money?

"Remember, everything's negotiable," Harry said to Alex. "First, see how we stand to benefit, then get a foot in the door. Afterward, we can try for better terms. We took a major loss in Alaska. Can't afford any more setbacks, no matter how small the sector."

"This has to be done the right way," said Lilah, her tone abrupt. "Not by taking advantage of unscrupulous politicians. Or what's the difference between Sanders and us? Don't forget the trouble in Arg—" She threw a glance in Verity's direction which didn't quite reach her.

"We never intended what happened," muttered Alex, a strange guilt in his eyes.

Harry sat up in a jerky move. "No, we didn't, but Lilah... if you find me going down the same path, stop me any which way you can."

The red slashes of anger faded from Lilah's cheeks. Voice almost inaudible, she said, "It would be easier if we could just drop the idea altogether."

"What idea?" asked Harry. "The network?"

She smiled weakly. "Never mind. There are too many people depending on this, depending on me. Plus, we can't turn back the clock, can we?"

Alex added his thoughts. "Harry, she's right about setting some limits on what we are willing to do."

Harry continued to look speculatively at Lilah for a few seconds before turning to Alex. "All right. Let's set down limits... on paper if you want."

Verity set her iced tea aside and crept out to the hallway, mouth tightening as she ran an unseeing eye along the Monet reproductions on the steel gray walls. She didn't know what it was about Lilah that held Harry's attention, while she, his wife...

The door to Verity's left was slightly ajar, and she spotted her brother-in-law on the phone. She smiled. The Sheppards, including Hector, liked her.

Knuckles raised to knock, she heard Hector say to the other person, "...Neil Kingsley. And his brother Scott. Make sure Harry doesn't find out."

Verity lowered her hand and retraced her steps to the conference room in Harry's office. What was she supposed to do... call her husband out and let him know right away what she overheard? Or wait for the other two to leave?

Not even noticing her presence, Harry picked up the book, *Zen* whatever, and placed it among the folders in his briefcase. Lilah's gift... Verity's fingers itched to tear it from his hands and rip it to shreds.

"...there you go... Alex agrees with me," Lilah said to Harry.

Verity laughed, the sound shrill to her own ears. "You always know the right things to say. Especially to Alex. I'm surprised Sabrina doesn't mind."

Lilah chuckled without missing a beat. "Why would she? I'm the CFO of the company."

Harry's face could've been carved from stone for all the reaction he gave. He had the gall to... deliberately ignoring *him*, Verity returned to the spot next to the window.

Later, she went to the closed kitchen at the back of the office suite to get some ice from the refrigerator. A hand grabbed her elbow and jerked her around. "What the hell's the matter with you?" Alex demanded. "You've been taking these digs at Lilah for some time now. Don't think no one has noticed."

She pushed him away with her other hand. "Oh, have you? You know what *I've* noticed? You—all of you, including Harry—acting like idiots over her. A stupid little book, and Harry lights up like... I'm not a fool like Sabrina to put up with it."

"Don't drag my wife into your silliness." Alex added, "She's not a jealous immature child like you. You don't like the fact your husband has a life outside of your charming arms, and you object to Lilah because Harry talks to her. How about you try to understand him and his dreams? Maybe you'll find there's something for the two of *you* to talk about."

Alex, the friend Verity knew for years, didn't understand. *No one* did, least of all her husband. Hot tears ran down her cheeks. "What about *my* dreams? He's not interested in them." Verity wiped the moisture off her face. "I want the man I married back. I want her— all of you—out of our lives."

Alex shook his head. "Did you stop to think who Harry was before you married him? You're not just disinterested in what he does; you want him to give it up altogether for the privilege of being your consort. A few more years for him to get this done... is it too much to ask? Isn't marriage about supporting each other?"

"There were two of us at our wedding. Harry made some vows, too."

"If you think your husband is betraying his vows, talk to *him*. Get your claws out of Lilah. She's someone I care for." Shaking a warning finger, Alex started to leave the room.

"Maybe I should tell Sabrina what you just said," Verity snarled.

He turned back. "Sabrina understands Lilah, and she trusts me. Try it sometime... empathy for another woman and trust in your husband."

As Alex stalked out, Verity hurled a crumpled paper napkin into the trash can. Ignoring the three people in the conference room, she went to visit her father in Hector's accounting division. Resting her chin on the cubicle wall, she poured out her woes as he went over a sheet of numbers.

"I'll be done soon, Princess. Then you and me can have dinner together. Let Harry wait for you for a change. It'll do him good. It's because of him I've got to work even in my old age."

Verity smiled waterily. Papa was only fifty-five, hardly in his dotage. He'd been so happy the stock he lost was kept in trust for the Luce children, and he'd been so sure it would be returned to him once she married into the Sheppard family. It was a shock when Harry refused to let the board sign over as much as a single share. He was right, though... Papa did have a gambling problem.

Hector walked by, raising a hand in greeting when he saw her. "Is everything okay in Gateway, Papa?" she asked.

"What do you mean?"

Doodling with her fingertip on the fabric covering the wall, Verity related what she overheard Hector saying. "What didn't

Hector want Harry to know about Neil and Scott? I don't understand."

"Who knows? Maybe Hector's planning a surprise for Harry."

"Heh? Like a party or something?" What did Scott Kingsley have to do with it? He was weird. But Neil... idly, Verity wondered if there were such things as manly angels.

"Just don't say anything to Harry. You don't want to spoil the surprise."

"Okay, I won't." Engrossed as she was in admiring the lovely pink polish on her long nails, she didn't notice the crafty look in her father's eyes. It never occurred to Verity she was betraying her husband.

Chapter 24

In a few weeks, September 1986

Amsterdam, The Netherlands

In the middle of the cobblestone pedestrian roundabout, the musician in dreadlocks hammered out a lively rhythm on the bongo drums between his knees. All around him, young people danced to the beat. Restaurants set out tables in a large, haphazard circle, and waiters walked between them, serving cold beer and snacks to the diners.

Summer in the Netherlands was beautiful, but Scott Kingsley was too busy frowning at the flowers to enjoy the city. Sunlight bathed the iron table where he was sitting, and in the center was a glass vase with a dozen tulips arranged in charming disorder. Scott didn't enjoy disorder. He occupied himself, setting the flowers in a neat circle against the rim of the vase.

Red, yellow, orange...

"Mr. Kingsley?"

... orange, red, yellow...

"Sir, there is a call for you." The waiter handed Scott the cordless set.

"Scott, Harry here. I got your message."

"Ahh... Harry... thanks for calling back. You wanted updates." Scott was initially supposed to work with Victor and learn the ropes. Then, Harry called Brad and asked for the youngest Kingsley brother to meet the officials in Gateway Europe as the representative of the Peter Kingsley Company. Alone. All by himself. There would be no discussions on the network project, simply meetings to introduce himself to them. He was to make notes after each encounter, detailing his impressions of said executives. "*Now* can you tell me why you wanted me to do this? I mean... you already know all the men I met."

"If I told you before, it would've colored your takes on them." Dan Barrons was supposed to negotiate with the main people in Gateway's European division, but he simply wasn't getting anywhere... lame objections to minor terms in the contracts. Nor were they outright refusing to join the network, resulting in wasted time all around. "Alex said you put a lot of effort into studying social cues. He thought perhaps you could help us zero in on the problem."

Scott nodded his understanding. "People often say something, but their faces say something else."

"As in? Do they look away?"

"Sometimes," agreed Scott. "They sometimes stare without blinking. One of the executives pointed at me. He looked... threatening. His words were okay."

"Threatening? Who?"

Scott gave the name.

"Just him?" Harry queried. "Anyone else you remember?"

Scott sighed. "I always remember everything. It's a blessing... and a curse." He rattled off names.

Satisfaction evident in his voice, Harry said, "Thanks to you, cuz, now I know which of them need watching."

It took Scott a moment to compute what Harry said. "I'm not your cousin, technically. Actually, even Brad, Victor, and Alex are only..." Scott estimated the coefficient of relationship between his half-brothers and Harry... at best one out of five-hundred-and-twelve because of the seven generations or so in between. Which was to say, not related in any meaningful way.

There was surprised laughter from the other end of the phone line, but it didn't seem unkind. "Good to know, but we Sheppards call everyone cousins. There are so many of us it's easier to make sure no one gets offended." Abruptly switching topics, Harry asked, "Are you flying back tonight?"

"In two days. I... I want to visit a couple of museums."

After hanging up, Scott paid his bill and checked the map of the city for the spot he intended to visit. Not as if he needed it, but he'd promised his twin he would carry a map everywhere and tuck money into his socks, and they always kept their promises to each other. A brisk walk of forty minutes later, Scott was there.

De Wallen... the largest of the red-light districts in Amsterdam. He headed straight for Oude Kerk, the city's oldest parish set smack in the middle of the prostitution center. The flame-haired artist was waiting in front as promised.

She was staring up at the roof of the gothic structure and had not noticed him yet. Scott took a leisurely look. White bra-top and baggy denims hanging onto her wide hips revealed an expanse of bare midriff in between. Bright-red curls were held up in a high ponytail. Her face was now partly hidden by dark glasses, but Scott knew exactly what each feature looked like. Thick, slashing brows were the same color as her hair, and light-brown eyes tilted up at the sides. The slightly crooked nose was slated for a plastic surgeon's knife before her wedding to the boyfriend. Her mouth was large and mobile with lush lips. There was a roll held between fingers, the swirling smoke bringing to Scott the cloying smell of high-quality weed.

His heart thumped hard. Mentally, he counted the rate—a hundred and twenty-four beats per minute. There was warmth in his cheeks—vasodilatation—and sweat coated his palms. Scott noted with some surprise he was anxious. He never expected to be anxious.

Treading silently to her, Scott said, "Hi."

#

Three months later, December 1986

Casablanca, Morocco

Dammit all, thought Dr. Neil Kingsley, watching from the back seat of the taxi as the streets sped by. If his awkward and tongue-tied twin could get laid, why couldn't Neil? Perhaps he should've taken up the invitation from the flight attendants. The two ladies had made it clear he didn't even have to pick; they were *both* more than willing to help him relax after the long trip. One was a doe-eyed ballet dancer with glowing ebony skin and toned limbs. Perfect. Except, she spoke with a lisp.

His twin would have called him an idiot. *"Perfection does not exist,"* Scott would've said. *"Except in numbers."* Perfect, imperfect—it didn't make a difference to Scott. Women were always eager to show him the ropes, so to speak.

Neil didn't exactly have time for a social life. Thanks to the groundwork already laid by the three original companies of the network, most of the contracts Neil and Dan Barrons were responsible for were near finalization. The main remaining holdouts were Gateway's regional divisions. In Neil's luggage were the papers faxed by Harry. *"Each of these trading companies is owned at least fifty-one percent by Gateway,"* Harry announced on the phone. *"The rest of the stock in every company is held by the family running it and by the employees. Also..."*

When Neil was in Morocco, he would stay with Gateway's man there. Anything else would be considered discourteous in the part of the world. His host was the same man Scott felt was acting funny. A James McCoy.

As Neil's supervisor on this trip, Dan Barrons would also stay there. One of Harry's friends, Saeed al-Obeidi, would join the meetings. Both men spoke fluent Arabic, which was an advantage. Besides, this McCoy person would know Harry would bring the wrath of God down on him if something happened to the three guests at his home. Still, Harry strongly recommended they trust only each other.

A day later, Neil was strolling the gardens of the McCoy residence. Spotting a little girl skipping to the servants' entrance, he smiled. The awkward angle at which she held her arm... the cherub answered his careful questions, and he accompanied her home, intending to speak to her parents.

From the girl's mother, Neil learned she was married to the driver assigned to him for the duration of his stay at the McCoy residence.

"Are you an angel?" the little girl asked in halting English, touching Neil's hair.

Laughing, he confessed to being a mere mortal before explaining to the mother the child's arm didn't look like it was done by a trained surgeon. It needed to be broken and reset. Neil assured the mom since the child's *abbi*—father—was his driver in the country, the Peter Kingsley Company would pick up the tab.

As he walked out of the ramshackle home, Neil covered the lower half of his face with the *tagelmust*—the indigo-dyed scarf which functioned as both a turban and a veil. It was flimsy protection against the dust and the exhaust fumes. "Insane traffic," Neil muttered, gingerly avoiding the rubbish strewn along the pavement.

When he returned to the McCoy residence, it was almost time for the cocktail party where he was to meet the local dignitaries.

The gathering was pretty much what he could expect from a corporate event in the States. Well-lit hall, officials in suits, food, and drink. "Our income from the last quarter was ninety-five cents a share, up from fifty the year before, an amount close to four hundred million," Neil told the oil executives clustered around, mentally thanking Dan Barrons for the patient coaching he gave on corporate financials over the last few months. "The revenue for the quarter was more than fifteen billion, compared to twelve from the year before. We're growing, and we want you to grow with us."

The wait staff walked around, offering wine. Handing Neil a glass, his host—McCoy—said, "This is a local product. Meknes in Morocco has some excellent wineries."

Neil hid a grimace. He'd sampled it before and found it not to his taste. McCoy was watching expectantly, so Neil took a few sips before excusing himself to join another group. Brushing past a potted plant, he tilted the glass into the roots and left precisely enough wine to avoid offers to refill.

Dan Barrons and Saeed al-Obeidi were also in attendance. All the local businessmen and dignitaries who'd received an invitation had shown up.

Neil was explaining to the Moroccans the structure of the network when his stomach cramped a couple of times, surprising him. Food poisoning? He'd been careful about eating out. Whatever it was, he needed to hold it in until the party was done. A lot of time and energy had gone into setting it up.

"Impressive ideas," murmured one of the politicians. "What are your specific plans for Morocco?"

"Several things," Neil said, swallowing a wave of nausea. "We want to invest in the natural gas pipeline from here to Spain. In turn, this country will reap the benefits of our oil and gas exploration activities and our investment in refineries. If all goes as intended, Casablanca will be our headquarters for the operations in Africa and the Middle East."

Another cramp hit, more intense and sustained. The room swam, and he shook his head, trying to clear his vision. He could see the fuzzy form of Saeed al-Obeidi pushing off from the pillar against which he'd been leaning. Neil's legs wobbled. Dimly, he heard someone calling his name and felt a chair being pushed behind his knees.

Things got blurry afterward. He was aware of a pounding in his head and loud retching. The smell of vomit was all around.

"These foreigners always want to try street food," grumbled the local doctor.

I didn't, Neil tried to say, but the words wouldn't come out. He couldn't even lift his head from the pillow.

As though through a fog, Neil heard a knock at the door. In hushed whispers, someone spoke to Saeed.

Neil was barely conscious when they airlifted both him and Daniel to Spain.

#

Later in the same week, December 1986

The General Hospital of Madrid

"Arsenic," Saeed said to Harry. Fortunately, Neil hadn't drunk the whole glass, and once he started having symptoms, Saeed asked Daniel not to consume any more of the wine. Then, when Dan also started puking, the driver's wife insisted he tell Saeed what he knew, and it saved the two Americans. "McCoy never realized I don't drink alcohol," Saeed finished, his muscles still shaky at the thought of what might have happened.

"He didn't know you are Muslim?" asked Harry, his tone muted. The intro music of *The Oprah Winfrey Show* was playing in the background wherever Harry was.

"Most of McCoy's Moroccan guests were drinking," said Saeed. "My guess is it didn't occur to him I wouldn't, Muslim or not."

"Thank God."

"Yes, otherwise, all you'd have known is we died of a severe infection. I'm betting someone in the Moroccan government was bribed to permanently dispose of our corpses. Perhaps a quick transfer to Spain under some pretext and cremation before anyone could demand autopsies." Saeed glanced back at the private rooms the men were in. Lilah had come running to see Dan, and her guards were outside the door, chatting with the security officials hired by Saeed. The extra protection wouldn't hurt, but no one believed there would be repeat attacks since the poisoning was done with a specific motive. McCoy was cooking the books and wanted to buy time to cover his tracks.

"Three deaths..." Harry's voice was both tired and angry. "I've been contacting the other men on Scott's list. *Of course* every one of them now pretends they never intended to give Dan a hard time over negotiations."

"They've been calling me as soon as you're done talking to them," said Saeed. "Each of them has promised to courier the signed contracts within the week... but I'd put money every single one has been stealing company funds."

"It's not going to end there, Saeed."

"Heh?"

"I mean even if McCoy turns out to be the only one, the discrepancy in his accounts wasn't small. How did he get away with it when the accountants in the parent company were supposed to be looking over everything?"

"What are you saying?"

"That McCoy had help within Gateway."

Chapter 25

Harry's markings on the world map at the end of phase two.

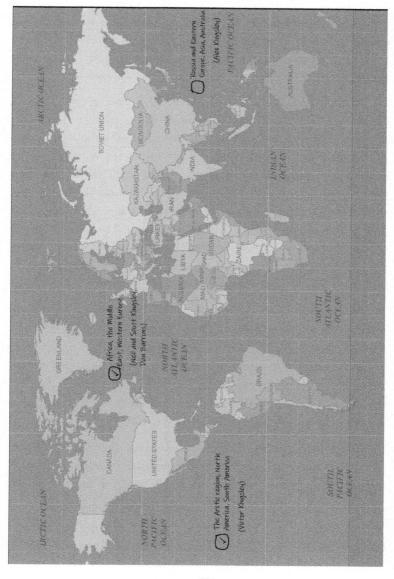

Next month, January 1987

World Trade Center, New York City

"Phase two, complete," Harry muttered.

Outside the office doors, Gateway's employees were streaming toward the exit, chattering about the impending eight inches of snow and ice. The cleaning crew was already about their business and whistling along with the song playing on the radio.

Rubbing knuckles across the five o'clock shadow on his cheeks, Harry stared at the map spread on his desk. The project was moving faster than he anticipated. The metaphorical flag of the alliance now flew over most nations. Only Alex's territories remained to be conquered. Once it, too, was done, the network would truly be a global empire. Monarchs and elected governments alike would need to pay heed to the diktats of the new rulers. No threats of punishment would be required to quell dissent. The other members would ensure compliance. Interconnected as they were, a single thoughtless move could cause economic ripples throughout the planet.

Not simply from the rogue actors... one misstep from the network's leaders and... thank God, Lilah was in charge. If it were someone less ethical... Harry suppressed a curse. No one unethical would be allowed to get near the throne of the business empire. When the time came, the next generation of leaders would be trained to run the world their elders left them. Right now, Harry needed to focus on the problems at hand, not borrow trouble.

There were no helpful breakthroughs on the Amber Barrons story. No chance of convincing the Kingsley brothers of Temple and Godwin's perfidy without risking the network itself. A suicide mission was looking like the only viable option.

Harry knew for a long time the day of reckoning was coming, but how was he supposed to bid goodbye to Lilah without fulfilling his vow to hunt down the monster who hurt her? Where the hell did the rapist go from Libya? How did he manage to vanish this completely?

As though Harry didn't have enough on his plate, there was the issue Alex mentioned. Red-faced and mumbling, the former sniper said something about how while Michael was a blessing, Sabrina intended to be careful—very, very careful—avoiding further surprises. Any future pregnancies would be carefully timed, with both parties fully aware of what they were getting into. Other couples were surely doing the same... you know... like Harry and Verity. The miserable embarrassment on Alex's face was enough to deliver the message.

Harry didn't see the point in confronting Verity about it when he planned on... she would have plenty of support after, financial and emotional. Her father and brother adored her. Harry's family, too.

The Sheppards treated her very differently from Lilah. Over the years, Harry decided it was from the guilt of having bartered her for money. Or perhaps they knew of Temple's plan to have her marry Brad and didn't want Harry hurt. In any case, his decision to put an end to their romantic relationship rendered his family's hostility irrelevant... until today.

"Harry," someone called from the door. Blazer hooked on a finger over his shoulder, Hector poked his head in. "If you stay much longer, you'll be sleeping in the office. It's coming down hard outside."

Ignoring the weather commentary, Harry said, "Hector, good... I need a few minutes of your time. We need to talk."

Hector sauntered in and arranged himself comfortably in the deep leather chair across the desk. "Shoot."

"I have this list of names. Do they mean anything to you?"

Hector took the sheet of paper. "These are some of the senior executives at our European and Middle-Eastern affiliates. What about them?"

"These are also the names of people who got a personal phone call from you sometime over the last few months. Anything you'd like to tell me?"

Hector stood, eyes blazing. "Is there a reason why I shouldn't have talked to them? As far as I know, I'm a big part of Gateway."

"I was wondering if your conversations included suggestions to block the Kingsleys' attempt to acquire stock in the companies."

After all, Hector once wanted Sabrina to marry Steven Kingsley, even knowing the man was at loggerheads with Brad and his brothers. Steven still boxed at the gym started by Hector so long ago.

"Hector did what he did with my approval," their father said from the door. "Harry, I know the network is needed, but the proposed charter says the CEO position of the alliance will go to the CEO of the Peter Kingsley Company." The charter would also include the possibility of future changes to the leadership structure, but Lilah and the Kingsley brothers would remain the senior executives for now. "If we give in to their demands, we'll completely lose control over our own business. This place was built with *our* sweat and blood. I'm not handing it to an outsider."

Keeping his tone soft, Harry said, "Yes, we built it with our sweat and blood... and with the sacrifice of a young girl's hopes and dreams."

"Lilah didn't lack for anything, did she?" Ryan asked. "I strongly recommend you let go of this misguided attachment."

"Materially, she did all right," acknowledged Harry. "But remember this... if her papa hadn't offered to help, the family business would've gone under before Sanders ever came into the picture. If *she* didn't offer to help when you were arrested, you might have been dead today."

Hector growled.

Barely acknowledging him, Harry said to his father, "Don't repay the kindness Lilah and her family did us with betrayal."

"They're asking for forty percent of other companies, and I'm certainly not going to let it happen to Gateway," said Ryan. "Tell the Kingsleys to come up with a more reasonable number, and we can discuss it. The only reason I'm agreeing to even this much is we do need a network."

"See if you can understand where we're coming from," Hector ground out. "I'm going home."

"Not yet," said Harry. "Please sit... both of you." He slid a folder across the desk. "An update on the McCoy situation."

Harry kept an eye on his brother while he and their father studied the numbers.

"Embezzlement?" Ryan asked after long moments. Money was being siphoned off in small amounts from different offices of Gateway. "All of them? When they all own a percentage of their own operations? We set up the outfits as partnerships precisely to avoid these kinds of problems."

"The usual reason, I suppose," Harry said. "Greed. We need to get rid of the whole lot."

"A purge won't buy us any friends," Hector stated.

"There's more." Harry sat up. He'd pored over the documents, hoping to find evidence to prove himself wrong. Each review brought only more certainty Gateway's rot started from its core—from Ryan Sheppard's family. "Something strange... Hector, McCoy was one of the people you called. Most of these thieves were on your list."

A shocked second later, Hector leaped to his feet, snarling.

Ryan held up a hand, asking his elder son to remain calm. Eyes cold, he turned to Harry. "Careful... don't forget I'm Hector's father. He's your brother."

"We both know any embezzlement couldn't have happened without inside help from this office," Harry stated. Everything pointed to Hector. The friendship with Steven, Hector's vacations with the other side of the Kingsley family, his drinking problem...

"Do you seriously expect me to believe Hector is stealing from the company?" asked Ryan. "From me? There's already talk in the extended family *you* framed McCoy because he refused to cooperate with the Kingsleys."

Flinching, Harry asked, "The attempted murder on Neil, Dan, and Saeed?"

Ryan didn't even blink. "Perhaps you found them expendable."

Harry closed his eyes, battling the overwhelming sense of isolation. "So it's come to this. Out of greed, part of my family is robbing the rest. The ones who're being robbed would rather accuse me of murder than give up a percentage to the Kingsleys to form the network."

"No one's accusing you of anything," said Ryan. "I was simply pointing out the idiocy of what you suggested. Dan is Andrew Barrons's son. Don't you think Andrew would've moved heaven and earth to find out how his boy died? There would've been no hiding the embezzlement then. Hector would know this. Gateway is big now, but neither you nor Hector is crazy enough to make an enemy out of Andrew Barrons."

After a moment, Harry nodded. "True enough."

"Coincidence," said Ryan. "It's all I see."

#

An hour later

When Harry got home, his wife was on the couch, waiting for him. "You didn't call me back." Her tone was woebegone.

Right. She'd left a message. Collapsing next to her, Harry rubbed his eyes. "Sorry... busy day."

Taking his hand in hers, she smiled in conciliation. "You're always busy. With the network, the Kingsleys... will *I* ever get a turn?"

"Verity." He sighed. "At least *try* to understand why this is an important project."

"Do what I want for once, Harry. Let's take a break from this and focus on our own lives." As he started to speak, she said, "No. I'm tired of being the one who always has to sacrifice. Let the others do some sacrificing for a change."

Something snapped loose within Harry's brain. "*Sacrifice?* Will you give up your dreams so someone else has a chance at a better life? Will you smile at me even when I have cost you every goddamn thing you ever wanted? Will you put someone else's needs above yours every single time? *That,* my dear, is sacrifice."

Verity sat back, her eyes wide. "Oh, yeah? What have *you* sacrificed?"

Nothing... nothing at all. Harry didn't get to go to college, but his military career and his work in Gateway were exactly what he dreamed of as a young man. As selfish as his family was, he still had them. He lost Lilah but still got to marry the woman he chose, and if he did have a future, it could well include children.

Lilah had nothing *left*. Her parents, her career, the baby she wanted... even the worthless label of Harry's best friend was given to Alex by the media, reducing Lilah's value to vague family ties. All the sacrifice, every bit of it, was Lilah's alone. Not Harry's.

Stricken, Harry stood. He couldn't speak. He needed to leave before.... he needed to get out. Harry heard Verity's agitated calls, heard her steps behind him in the stairwell, but the pressure in his head wouldn't let him answer.

Harry didn't recall plodding through the snow, he didn't remember hailing a cab, but when they got to Bond Street, he asked the driver to stop. Shovels clanged against metal as a couple of figures dressed in parkas dug their vehicles out. Except for them, the block was empty, street lamps casting yellow pools of light over cars buried under snow. Icy moisture trickled down the back of Harry's neck as he rang the bell. When the door opened, Dante took one look at Harry's shivering form and hustled him in without questions.

Dante listened, not commenting, not judging. Over an untouched bowl of chicken noodle soup, Harry talked about his painful epiphany. He related his worries over Lilah's infertility, leaving out the reason for it. He asked the one question he never dared ask until now. Was there another way he could've done this? Some scenario in which she wouldn't have been left all alone?

"I don't have an answer for you," Dante admitted.

"You always said—"

"Yes," Dante acknowledged. "I always thought this marriage merger was a bad idea. But what other way, exactly? And what would have happened if you'd simply said no to the president?"

What would Lilah have done? Would she have run away with Harry? Would they have been content in their own lives, blissfully uncaring of the world suffering under a tyrant like Sanders? Or would the guilt have eventually killed their love, leached their sense of self, until they were reduced to merely the shells of the vibrant beings they used to be?

"One more thing to remember," said Dante. "Brad Kingsley... by your own account... is a good man. Lilah may not have children, but she is not alone."

Chapter 26

A week later, January 1987

The West Wing

Tucking hands into the pockets of his pants, Temple watched his staff move around, sorting papers and packing them, making room for the incoming administration. Godwin was also present, taking one last look at the executive offices at the White House. Even as a retired supreme court justice and a former president, they would no longer have the freedom to walk in and out of these rooms as they pleased.

"I'm concerned about what's going on at Gateway," said Godwin. "Now since Sanders is out, did they decide to stop working with us?"

"Harry will make sure they do," said Temple. "What I don't understand is this attack on Neil and Dan. I have a hard time buying Hector Sheppard orchestrated it." The quarrel between Ryan Sheppard's sons was not public knowledge. Only thanks to Hector's griping to Steven did Godwin learn of it.

The chief of staff walked in just then and greeted Temple. It took a good ten minutes for the man to go over details of the swearing-in ceremony for the new president. Finally, finding a quiet alcove, the stepbrothers sat.

Godwin ran an appreciative finger along the rim of the Ming vase on the end table. "Not Hector... he's not dumb or insane. Although he is now mad enough to clock Harry."

Temple leaned back in the plush chair. "So there's a third party fishing in troubled waters."

"Exactly. Temple, you said Noah's in Texas to make the arrangements with Colonel Parker."

At the abrupt shift in topic to the rapist army officer, Temple turned his head to glance at his stepbrother. "Yeah?"

"It's going to be impossible to keep Parker's presence quiet from Lilah and Harry."

"And they're going to realize we're behind it," Temple said. "But I know Harry. No matter what, he's going after Parker. We'll be prepared when it happens."

Lilah could potentially stop things if she clued Brad into what was going on. General Potts already confirmed there were never any searches for Colonel Sheffield Parker from Brad or his brothers. Moreover, if she talked to Brad about it, Godwin would've heard, which meant Brad didn't know... thus far.

"You told me before someone in Gateway helped you with the Sheffield Parker situation," Godwin ruminated. "Could it be the same man who's playing games with Harry and Hector?"

"Impossible," said Temple.

"Why not? A man who can be bribed into helping a criminal like Parker is without doubt capable of stealing from the company."

"Godwin, first of all, Parker hid himself with no persuasion from me or anybody in Gateway." After Lilah and Harry escaped Libya, stories circulated about the young man's enemies always coming to a bad end. Plus, he was backed by allies in the U.S. "I was merely keeping an eye on the situation and making sure Harry didn't get wind of it. Secondly, you're assuming this person in Gateway helped *me*... and the price of his betrayal was money. What if it happened the other way around? What if the person in question asked me for help protecting Harry from one more enemy?"

After a few seconds of silence, Godwin mused, "There's only one man who has both the inclination to protect Harry and the clout in Gateway to keep things from him all this while. His father, Ryan Sheppard."

Part IX

Chapter 27

Two weeks later, January 1987

Cerro Azul, Panama

Screaming in excitement, Michael splashed after his miniature motorboat, yellow floaties around his upper arms. Water spilled over the edges of the infinity pool, draining into the hidden catch basin. A swim-up bar and the deck in dramatic purple slate completed the picture of casual luxury in Alex and Sabrina's wing of the family mansion.

On the lounger, Lilah slid down the straps of her dusty-red one piece and rubbed sunblock over her arms and face. Her session at the gym got done only minutes ago, and she didn't really feel like sunbathing, but there was something she needed to discuss with Sabrina.

"Eighteen," huffed Sabrina, doing sit-ups on the mat. She'd barely been outside for ten minutes, but perspiration had already left dark patches on her aqua bathing suit. "Lilah, we *have* to tell Hector and my father what's going on. The later we leave it, the less the control Gateway will have in the network."

"The moment you say something to Uncle Ryan and Hector, they'll have the perfect excuse to withdraw," said Lilah.

"*Let* them withdraw," Sabrina said, tone wild. "My brother's *life* is at risk!"

"Shh!" Alex was in Russia, and there was no one around to overhear, but Lilah couldn't help feeling jittery. "Remember what happened to Danny. I desperately need your help, or I wouldn't have put you at risk by telling you."

"I *am* thinking of what happened to Dan," grunted Sabrina, falling back onto the mat with a thump. "Twenty-four... what if Harry's not as lucky? My father can withdraw Gateway and—"

"You think Harry will just let it slide?" asked Lilah. "What happens if the trouble ends up splitting the company? Harry will still be with the network, *and* he won't have the backing of the rest of the Sheppards if and when something goes wrong." Not that she was sure he had it even now. There was a whiff of guardedness in Harry's voice when he talked about Gateway's reluctance to commit more than ten to fifteen percent of their stock to the network. Lilah would have to puzzle it out later.

"Somebody else, then," said Sabrina, doing more sit-ups. "Thirty-two."

"Like who? Brad?" For the eldest Kingsley grandson, Godwin and Temple were well-wishers. Correctly so in a way... Brad was their hand-picked heir, the one who would continue to carry out their grandiose plans for the family long after their deaths. Lilah was simply the means to get the Kingsleys there, Harry the obstacle. "Would Alex take your word on this?"

"No." Sabrina groaned. "What are we going to *do?*" Once again, she collapsed onto the mat, panting.

Picking up a bottle of water from the ice bucket on the side table, Lilah held it out. "Another thing... I haven't said anything to Harry about talking to you. He wouldn't like it for a very good reason. As far as those other than you and me are concerned, you have zero knowledge of the situation, okay? Better that way for your safety. If Godwin or Temple figure out you know..."

Sabrina hauled herself up, taking the offering. "They know *you* know, don't they? God!"

"The pre-nup will keep me safe," Lilah lied. Once Godwin and Temple realized she and Brad would have no children to inherit her shares...

Rounded green eyes on Lilah, Sabrina gulped water from the bottle. "All right," she finally said. "What do you want me to do?"

"You once told me you wanted to be a spy. Here's your chance."

Sabrina returned to her exercise routine, listening to Lilah elaborate. At the end of five minutes, she counted, "Fifty! I'm done. Mikey, pool time's over."

As they walked into the house through the open glass doors, Lilah pointed out, "You didn't do fifty."

Sabrina didn't break stride. "Yes, I did." She threw the towel around her neck onto a chair. "A quick shower, and I'll be back down. Keep an eye on Mikey, will ya?"

"Yes, I will, and no, you didn't do fifty."

"Mikey, behave until Mommy's back, okay? Yes, I did, too." Sabrina disappeared into the next room.

Michael was on the small couch, remote to the television in hand. Exchanging glances with him, Lilah insisted, "She didn't."

A wary eye on the door through which his mother vanished, Michael whispered, "Maybe she doesn't know how to count."

Solemnly, Lilah considered the possibility. "That could be it," she acknowledged.

#

A day later

"Hatchoo," sneezed Lilah. "Sorry," she said, taking the handkerchief offered by Sabrina.

Eyes watering, Sabrina complained, "This house is only a few years old. How did it get so dusty up here?"

Patrice waved a hand. "Attics! No matter how many times I have it cleaned, within a week, we're back to the same. You did say you wanted to see all the Kingsley stuff I got from the old home."

"So I did," admitted Sabrina. "A little dust ain't gonna stop me."

Some attic, Lilah thought. The room was cavernous with large windows looking out to the crumbling ruins of the fortress the home was attached to. If she peered at a certain angle, the moat which surrounded the castle would become visible. Their architect, Maya, had decided to leave a part of the original structure as such, claiming the "atmosphere" would create the "illusion of royalty." Whatever that meant.

"Whoa," Sabrina said, her glance going to the labeled steel trunks lined up along the walls. "You have it all categorized."

Each of Patrice's sons had trinkets and yearbooks and newspaper clippings to remind them of important moments in their life. There was even a half-full bottle of cologne in Alex's trunk— the woodsy kind he apparently favored from adolescence. Kneeling next to a box, Lilah eyed a broken baseball glove labeled "Brad" and wondered when her husband ever showed an interest in the sport.

Sabrina sat cross-legged on the floor and started going through a bunch of black-and-white pictures. Waving an old photograph, she asked, "Wowee, who was *she*?"

Lilah was digging through the pile of mementos in one of the trunks and looked up.

Dropping to her knees next to her younger daughter-in-law, Patrice said, "You don't know? Your husband's great-grandmother."

"Holy guacamole, Batman," Sabrina said.

Lilah discarded the sports memorabilia on the floor and took the glasses from her pocket. "May I see?"

The sex appeal was obvious even in the faded photograph. Curls tumbling down a nearly bare shoulder, skinny straps holding up a skimpy gown, and filmy skirt hardly concealing long and shapely legs, the lady perched on a velvet chair. She was leaning forward, a blonde lock teasing her ample cleavage, a cigarette holder between her fingers. There was an arrogant curve to the full mouth. The middle-aged man next to her stared adoringly.

"Wow," Lilah parroted Sabrina.

"Wasn't she?" murmured Patrice.

"No wonder Godwin never married," Sabrina commented. "He never found anyone who could match up to his mother."

"Heh?" Patrice laughed. "Not *Godwin's* mother. Mr. Temple's." She nearly doubled over at the comical expressions of shock on her daughters-in-law.

"I'd heard his mom was an actress, but..." Sabrina fluttered a hand.

Patrice's whoops got louder. "You didn't imagine quite so much... er... oomph?" At that, Lilah and Sabrina also started giggling. Wiping tears of mirth from her eyes, Patrice continued, "Sylvia Fontaine... she was one of the original blonde bombshells of American movies. When Peter and I got married, Sylvia was already sixty, but the glamor was still there. She died in a couple of years from lung cancer."

"Mr. Temple looks nothing like her," said Sabrina, sputtering.

"Yeah," said Patrice. "Hard to believe, isn't it? The former president of the United States was the love child of a silent movie star and the senator from New Jersey. She had humble beginnings, though. Her family was from Maine. Fishermen, I think."

"How did she end up marrying Godwin's father?" Lilah asked.

Patrice shrugged. "Everyone knew she was never married to Temple's father, and Old Man Kingsley's first wife was institutionalized by the time he met Miss Bombshell."

"Institutionalized?" asked Lilah.

"She jumped into the pool with Godwin when he was a baby, claiming she was cursed, and as her son, so was Godwin."

"Good Lord," muttered Sabrina.

"Poor woman, she was sick," said Patrice. "At least, that's what the servants said. Apparently, she had six miscarriages and stillbirths before Godwin was born. How do you go through so much and not turn insane?" Eyes on the picture of the actress, Patrice seemed to ponder the sorrows of the first Mrs. Old Man Kingsley.

Lilah inclined her head ever so slightly at her sister-in-law. Sabrina slipped out a photograph from under her shirt, the only picture of Amber Barrons the investigator hired by Harry was able to locate. With a tiny nod at Lilah, Sabrina surreptitiously tucked the picture into the pile of photographs on the carpet. They waited for Patrice to return to the here and now.

Their mother-in-law was not yet done with the Kingsley family history. "Old Man Kingsley divorced his sick wife when he met Temple's mother. Sylvia left Baby Temple with her lover and married Godwin's father. They had a son—half-brother to both Godwin and Mr. Temple. Then, the first Mrs. Kingsley died in the asylum."

"What a mess," Lilah remarked.

"Yes, it was," said Patrice. "Our bombshell made it worse. Insisted on her child—the one she had with Old Man Kingsley, not Mr. Temple, obviously—getting the entire inheritance. Godwin would get absolutely nothing."

"Ouch." Sabrina made a face.

"By the time they told Godwin about it, he was already a teenager. Can you imagine growing up believing you were going to inherit all the money, then finding out you're not?"

"He must have hated them both," said Lilah.

Patrice said, "There were a couple of servants in the mansion who used to talk to me. Godwin understandably wasn't pleased at the idea of being disinherited, and he refused to sign any papers relinquishing claim on the ancestral property. So Miss Bombshell threatened to take her child and leave, and her husband went into depression. Wouldn't eat anything, was not sleeping, stopped taking care of the business. Finally, Godwin magnanimously announced he didn't want a single share and vowed to help keep the company in the hands of the rightful heirs. Godwin and his stepmother made a deal. Her son would be CEO, and Godwin would be the president of the family business. Hefty pay... but no stock." Godwin was also chairman of the board of Kingsley Corp.

"Godwin's father was fine with the arrangement?" Lilah asked.

"Guess so." Patrice shrugged. "She was only trying to take care of her children. Mr. Temple was being brought up by his father, the politician. She knew he'd be all right. With the second son, she made sure he got the Kingsley money. She wasn't trying to hurt Godwin with her games. She simply didn't care about him."

"Oh, dear," said Sabrina. "First, his mother tried to kill him. Then, his stepmother got him disinherited, and his old man didn't care enough to fight for him. How could a father be so selfish?"

Patrice sighed, a sentimental tear at the corner of one eye. "He must have loved her very much... Godwin's father and Sylvia, I mean."

Lilah bit the inside of her cheek to stop the laughter from spilling out, but she needn't have bothered.

Sabrina snorted. "I don't think *love* had much to do with it. Look at the picture." The man's face held the expression of a hungry dog, leering at the cleavage of his actress wife.

Frowning at the two young women clutching each and laughing, Patrice said loftily, "I prefer to believe it was true love." She smiled. "Have you two had enough Kingsley family history?"

Lilah coughed.

Sabrina said hurriedly, "No, no. This is important. I'm glad you brought stuff from the Kingsley mansion. Godwin didn't mind?"

Patrice said airily, "Oh, I didn't need his permission to take Peter's things. My husband and I never actually got around to a divorce."

Sabrina chuckled. "Alex doesn't know any of the stories, so someone has to keep track. Mikey needs to know his ancestors." She drew a photograph from the stack, asking, "Who is this?"

Taking the black-and-white snap, Patrice stared in confusion. "I don't remember..." She peered at a corner of the image and exclaimed, "Lilah, look."

Taking half a breath in, Lilah scrambled to her mother-in-law and studied the familiar image of the laughing teenager dressed in a two-piece polka dot swimsuit. Short blonde curls framed her oval face, and there were beads around her neck.

Lilah frowned. Beads? Were they... she'd had the photograph a long time but never looked closely at the beads. Shawn wore similar beads. A Barrons family heirloom? She scrutinized the photograph, hoping to spot other clues.

Barefooted, Amber was leaning back against the railing of a ship and blowing a kiss at the photographer. At the lower right corner of the image, a message was scrawled in flamboyant curves. "Love you always. Amber Barrons."

"Says 'Barrons.'" Patrice said. "Someone you know, Lilah?"

"Huh?" Lilah widened her eyes. "No. I've heard about her, though. She was a cousin of Andrew's. Amber... umm... killed herself in the mansion, so they don't talk much about her."

Patrice grimaced. "Every family has skeletons, I guess. What's her picture doing here? I don't remember seeing it before."

Sabrina asked, voice deliberately vague, "Isn't she the one Godwin's half-brother was rumored to be dating right before he divorced his wife?"

"Really?" Patrice asked.

Lilah scanned her mother-in-law's face for telltale signs of prevarication, but there were none.

"I think so," said Sabrina. "From what I know, he refused to marry her, and she went bonkers. So she hanged herself. You haven't heard the story?"

"No," Patrice said bemusedly. "How did *you* hear about it? This must have been before you were born."

Sabrina waved her hands about. "*Way* before. 1948 or '49, I think."

The pleasant look on Patrice's face faltered. "Yes, well. I was also a teenager at the time. The rest of the Sheppards might have been doing okay, but my father and I lived paycheck to paycheck. Didn't get to run around with the likes of the Kingsleys and the Barronses."

Lilah and Sabrina traded glances, puzzling over the older woman's lightning change of mood.

"How did you meet your husband?" Lilah asked. The Kingsleys wanted a business alliance with the Sheppards' drilling company, but the union between Peter Kingsley—the scion of one of New York's oldest and wealthiest families—and a working-class girl like Patrice wouldn't have been easy to arrange.

Patrice sighed, her eyes pinned on one of the cardboard boxes. She scratched the label with her nail. "Your father introduced us," she said, nodding at Sabrina. "Godwin declared Peter would have to marry me if he wanted to become CEO of the company."

Lilah bit back a grimace, thinking how much the fact had to have hurt Patrice. What was worse... to be rejected in spite of love or to be accepted in spite of indifference?

Patrice tossed Brad's old baseball glove into his box. "Let's take a break."

Mentally sighing, Lilah collected the photographs to put them back in the airtight plastic box. She would have to sneak back to the attic to retrieve the picture of Amber.

One snap in the box caught her attention. Patrice and a vaguely familiar boy were standing side by side, her arm around his stiff shoulders. Something about the pre-teen... he was wearing a football helmet and staring unsmilingly into the camera... there was an itch in Lilah's brain as though she ought to know him. *Alex?* "Sabrina, look what I found," Lilah invited.

Patrice flicked a glance at the picture and snatched it out of Lilah's hands. "The poor boy had no one to go to his game. Godwin kept his father busy, and his mother didn't drive."

"What?" asked Lilah, thoroughly confused.

"Richard," clarified Patrice. "Richard Armor. His father is Godwin's chauffeur. Didn't he attend the shooting party at the Barrons mansion where you met us? Alex said something about it."

There was so much going on that day, but Lilah remembered most of it with sharp clarity. Besides, Brad and his brothers brought up the name whenever they talked about their enmity with Steven. But why had she confused Armor with Alex? With the difference in hair color hidden by football gear, the features... no. Now that Lilah thought about it, the two men didn't look the same. Yet there was something similar, something intangible. "The chauffeur's son?" Lilah asked, trying to process.

Gaze skittering to the side, Patrice made a show of tidying up the mess on the carpet. "Nothing wrong in being nice to the staff."

"Of course not," Lilah answered, directing a quelling glance at Sabrina's arched eyebrows.

Chapter 28

A week later, February 1987

Green-Wood Cemetery

Brooklyn, New York

Sketching a salute, Alex sent the cab along.

"Whyyy New York?" whined Sabrina, wrapping her arms around Alex's waist, her cheek plastered to his back. Her tote bag swung from her shoulder. "You just got back from *Siberia!* Wouldn't you rather be someplace warm?"

"You're a big girl," he said, hardheartedly hauling his shivering wife with him. "You can handle a little cold weather."

"I don't wanna," she said.

Four-year-old Michael chuckled, holding his daddy's hand and blowing puffs of misty breaths from his mouth. They passed under the ornate Victorian gates to the graveyard. There wasn't much snow on the ground, but grass was long gone, and tree branches were bare.

Alex waited for Michael while he examined something at the foot of a bench. Digging through a small pile of dirt, the boy unearthed a short bone.

"Look, Daddy... dinosaur fossil!" said Michael, his gloved fingers holding up his find. His cheeks and nose were red from the wintry air.

Crouching to examine the skeletal remains of a chicken wing, Alex said, "I don't know, Mike. You want to add it to your collection?"

Michael wrapped the bone in a piece of tissue he borrowed from Sabrina and tucked his find into the pocket of his dungarees.

The family continued their way, Michael's hand tucked back into his daddy's. Alex tugged his wife's small form to his other side, the top of her head skimming the middle of his chest. Her hand slipped underneath the lapels of his jacket. "Oooh, you're warm."

Fingers rubbed tempting circles over his belly. Leaning down, he whispered in her ear, "Quit teasing. I can't take you up on it with our son watching."

She whispered back, "You *had* to visit Brooklyn in January. We could have been in our nice, *warm* home in Panama. We could have dropped Mikey with Grandma Patrice and gone to the beach. There's an itsy-bitsy Hawaiian two-piece I've been dying to model for you. Coconut shell bra, and there's a grass mini."

His wife's generous curves in a coconut bikini... blood surged into his groin. "Tell you what... after we get back to Panama, I have two days before I leave for India. Promise to dance the hula for me."

"Only if you return the favor." Sabrina puckered her lips. Alex brushed his mouth over hers, then kissed her again with feverish eagerness.

"Daddy," Michael whined. "Are we there yet?"

Alex looked around the landscape. "Oops." Arguing all the way, they retraced their steps to find Peter Kingsley's grave.

The lake was gray and gloomy under the winter sky. A few visitors were milling about, some snapping pictures. Perhaps out of respect for the dead, there was none of the clamor usually associated with New York City. Tugging a cellophane-wrapped bouquet from her oversized tote, Sabrina said, "We should have waited until summer; could have gotten better flowers. Mikey won't start pre-K until September."

Alex placed the yellow chrysanthemums on the granite and stood. "I don't know if I'll be able to return before then, and my mother really wanted Mike to do this." Patrice wanted the boy to know something about Grandpa Peter. "She used to have me and my brothers visit before every milestone."

Sabrina knelt, cleaning the headstone. She showed Michael the name of his grandfather, helped him spell it. "P- E- T- E- R. Mikey, did you know your daddy's middle name is also Peter?"

Michael pointed to the name beneath. "What does the second one say?"

"Madeleine Wheeler," said Alex.

"Who's she?" asked Michael.

"A friend of your grandfather," Alex said. "She died soon after him."

Leaving Michael tracing the letters, Sabrina stood. "I didn't know they were buried together. How long did he live with his girlfriend before he died?"

"Let me see," Alex calculated, lips twisting into a mirthless smile. "He left on my fourth birthday and died on my tenth, so I would say six years."

Sabrina's head jerked toward the tombstone, her eyes going to the date carved into the slab. Mewling in distress, she wrapped her arms around Alex's waist, offering him her warmth. "I hate him," she muttered into his chest.

"For dying on my birthday?" Alex asked, gathering her closer. "I'm sure he didn't plan to. She died within a couple of months. And Neil and Scott went to live with their uncle." Rubbing his cheek on his wife's golden head, Alex remembered the day he first met his half-brothers.

#

Eighteen years ago, August 1969

New York, New York

The phone was ringing in the hallway outside Brad's room. Resting a hip on the desk, Alex enthused, "Man finally got to the moon. Can you believe it?"

Neither of his brothers responded. It was the day after Brad's eighteenth birthday, and he was packing shirts into his box for his move to college—the United States Military Academy in West Point as per family tradition. Victor, as usual, was in front of the mirror, smoothing his hair. In another year, he would follow Brad to the academy. Alex would have to wait *two* years. While he was counting days, neither Brad nor Victor was terribly enthusiastic at the idea. Just like they weren't too excited by astronauts setting foot on lunar surface.

The damned phone in the hallway wasn't stopping the ruckus. Biting back a sigh of annoyance, Alex took the tape from the cassette player on the desk and slipped it back into its cover for no particular reason. Simon and Garfunkel... Brad's favorite. "Why don't you simply tell Grandfather you don't want to go?" Alex asked.

Without looking up, Brad recited, "I'm lucky to get into West Point. General Potts is a friend of the family."

The ringing stopped. They heard their mother's polite voice repeating the greeting several times, apparently getting no response. The clatter told them she hung up.

Victor checked his long sideburns in the glass, making sure they were neatly brushed. "Bro, you're not the military type."

Brad slammed the box. "Grandfather has done a lot for us, Victor. I'm not going to disappoint him, and I don't want to hear *you* say no when it's your turn."

"I won't," muttered Victor, flicking imaginary lint off his stretchy green pants. "I'll put in my time. Afterward, I'm going to culinary school whether Grandfather likes it or not."

Once more, the phone started ringing. "Who's doing this?" Victor asked irritably. "It's been going on all morning."

"Maybe something wrong at the telephone company." Brad took the cassette and the player from Alex's hands, tucking them into a second box.

"Are you allowed music at West Point?" Alex asked.

"Yeah," Brad said. "It's not prison." Sudden frown on his face, he asked, "They do allow music, right?"

"Dibs on the cassette player if they don't," Alex said.

"Hey," exclaimed Victor, pivoting. "I wanted it."

"Too bad," Alex retorted. "You shoulda stopped staring at the mirror for two seconds."

Brad grinned. "How can he? He's going to the movies with Camilla."

Alex nearly swallowed his tongue. "Camilla from Brooklyn? What the hell is she doing with Victor? He can't even talk to her."

Forget understanding her native Spanish, Victor Kingsley barely scraped through the French classes their mother made them take. Camilla was a new immigrant, barely starting to learn English. Gossip was her uncle worked in some store in the upscale neighborhood and got the owner to help with admission to the local school. *Alex* took Spanish in addition to French, but the lovely Camilla still resisted his attempts to draw her into a conversation about Latin music. "Man, she's..." Alex air-sketched a female figure.

Brad and Alex sighed, lost in contemplation of the absent Camilla's luscious charms. "She's a nice girl," Victor said. Tying a kerchief around his neck, he frowned. "Her family ran into trouble back in Cuba."

"Yeah?" asked Alex.

"Castro and stuff," Victor said vaguely. "Camilla's dad wrote an editorial about Marxism, and... long story short, they were forced to leave everything and take a boat to Florida—at night." The ringing phone interrupted them again. "Enough," Victor exclaimed. "Someone's gonna die." He stalked out.

Sauntering to the mirror, Alex frowned at the pimples scattered across his cheek. He was seriously considering sporting a stubble to cover up the spots.

"Here, you can have it," said Brad, thrusting the cassette player toward Alex.

"Don't you wanna take it with you?" Alex asked.

"No," Brad said, adjusting his glasses. "I think I'm losing interest in music."

"Brad, Alex," Victor boomed from the hallway.

It took the three of them more than an hour to get to Coney Island. Surf Avenue was packed. Cars honked, trying to get through the crowd outside Nathan's Famous restaurant. The divine smell of fish frying in open air was enough to keep the masses waiting patiently. The sun beat down mercilessly, and even in swimming trunks and aloha shirt, Alex was sweltering. Victor had to be roasting, dressed as he was for his date with Camilla.

Blue ocean beckoned at the end of the road. A group of teenage girls in mid-thigh shorts headed down the sidewalk in the direction of the beach, giggling when they passed Alex.

"You know them?" Victor asked.

"Yeah... dance class." Indifferent to female charms at the moment, Alex tried to peer around the clown in front. "How are we supposed to find the hoods?"

"No slurring," Brad admonished. "They're our brothers."

"C'mon," Victor complained, but his voice was weak.

"I bet it's them over there," Alex said, spotting the duo waiting at the far end of the hot-dog stand with several bags of fries clutched in their hands. Huddled together, the ten-year-old boys looked lost. One appeared almost angelic with blond hair. The other bore a startling resemblance to Brad and the late, unlamented Peter Kingsley.

Cutting across the crowd to reach the twins, Victor jostled the clown's elbow. An ice cream cone splattered to the ground, triggering loud curses questioning Victor's relationship with his mother. Alex followed Victor, leaving Brad to mutter apologies and offer a dime as compensation.

Once they were all together, a few moments of uncomfortable silence followed, with the two groups simply staring at each other. The hope in the faces of the younger boys was impossible to miss. Then, Brad smiled. "Let's go to the beach," he said, raising his voice to be heard over the noisy crowd.

The shoreline was even more packed than the street. They all lounged on the sand. Swallowing the last of a salty fry, Alex stripped off his shirt and threw it to the side. "So what's up?" he asked the twins. "You said there's an emergency."

Neil—the blond kid—muttered something about Scott getting into trouble.

"What kind of trouble?" asked Victor.

"It wasn't his fault," Neil insisted, blue eyes flashing. With a tissue dug out of his pocket, he carefully wiped a patch of grease from his cheek. "He doesn't lie is all."

"What do you mean?" Brad asked.

Glumly, Neil said, "He told the math teacher she's wrong."

"She was wrong," Scott maintained, blinking through his glasses.

"You didn't have to prove it to her," Neil snapped, tone wild.

"Oh, man," Victor said.

"The principal was in the room," Neil added. "They're saying Scott needs to go to a special school. You know, for..."

"Got it," Alex said, feeling sorry. "What did your uncle say?"

"He's gonna leave me there and take Scott to this new place," Neil said, voice desperate. "A boarding school. Scott doesn't do well by himself."

Gently, Brad said, "I don't think... I'm sure they have special teachers for kids like Scott. He might do better there."

"He can't go there," Neil shrieked.

"I won't," Scott said, tone unusually firm for a ten-year-old.

The three older boys exchanged glances, surprise and discomfort on all their faces.

"Please," Neil sobbed.

"What's really going on?" Victor asked.

Once Neil finished explaining, Brad stated the best one to approach for help with the situation was Patrice Kingsley.

Wary curiosity was writ large on the faces of the twins when they entered the Kingsley mansion two hours later in the company of their older brothers. At the dining table in their late father's apartment, all five boys faced Patrice. Alex wasn't sure how he expected his mother to react when first meeting her husband's sons with another woman, but the initial surprise was followed only by welcoming warmth. At least until Neil explained what was going on.

"He what?" she exclaimed, her words ringing through the airy hall.

Alex had responded pretty much the same way when he initially heard the story of the twins' encounter with the principal of the special school Scott was supposed to attend.

Eyes fixed on the lemonade glass, Neil mumbled, "He... ahh... ahh... touched me." His face seemed nearly on fire with misery and humiliation. "You know... in the... the... the-nuts." The twins' uncle had taken Neil and Scott along on a tour of the school. The principal, having found himself alone with Neil for a few minutes, placed a casual hand on the boy's thigh, brushing his fingers along the groin seemingly by accident. The ten-year-old sat there, too shocked and frightened to even make a sound.

"Did you two talk to your uncle about this?" Patrice asked.

Scott simply nodded and continued to munch on Danishes, apparently certain he wasn't going to this new school no matter what the authorities had to say about it.

Neil frowned in clear anxiety. "I begged our uncle to... he won't believe me! Says I'm making it up because I don't want Scott to go to a different school."

Bluntly, she asked, "Are you?"

"No! I might have if I thought it would work. I know Scott needs a different school. Only, not this one."

"I'm not going there," Scott assured his twin.

Patrice glanced from Scott to Neil and back. "If I were to suggest a different school—a residential school—you would both agree? You wouldn't be together except on weekends and holidays."

"Scott needs help," Neil conceded. "But you'd have to let me check out the place."

Patrice's lips twitched, but her eyes remained grave. "Goes without saying." She asked Neil not to worry, saying she would have Uncle Aaron make arrangements.

"Wanna stay over tonight?" Victor asked, tone carefully casual.

Looking up from his pastry, Scott simply said, "Yes." Neil nodded, a big smile spreading across his face.

"All right!" Victor slammed a fist on the table. Plates clattered.

Alex asked, "Dude, Camilla?"

"Hmm?" Victor sat back in his chair, hands linked behind his head. "Oh, dammit. Camilla! I need to go to Brooklyn." He stood, nearly flinging the chair to the floor in his haste. His brothers snickered.

"Wait," said Patrice, holding up a hand. "Call Camilla and let her know you won't be making it. You do need to go to Brooklyn, though. Alex, too. Take Neil with you."

Exchanging glances with Victor, Alex asked, "Why?"

"Find this principal," Mother said. "Make sure he never holds even a pencil for the rest of his life with that hand."

It took a second for the command to sink in. *"What?"* asked Alex. "Mother! What the hell—"

"Bro," snapped Victor. "You can't curse at her!"

Opening and closing his mouth a couple of times, Alex tried to respond. Finally, he gave up and confined himself to shoving fingers into his hair.

"You're brothers," said Patrice. "The world should know... touch one, and they'll have to answer to the rest." She turned to Neil. "I'm going to ask you one more time before you and Alex and Victor leave... what you told me was nothing but the truth, right? Because if the principal didn't actually—"

"He did," said Neil. "I swear."

Patrice nodded. "I believe you. I will always believe my sons. Yes, that means you and Scott, as well."

On his way out with Alex and Victor, Neil turned and ran to her. Throwing his arms around her waist, he said, "Thank you. Our ma said... I don't remember her much... she was in the hospital... but she told us if we ever needed something..."

A week after their meeting with the twins, Alex sprawled on a wooden bench in the garden surrounding the family mansion, letting the sun beat down on him. Next to him was Brad, his glasses pushed up into his hair, his eyes closed. This would be the last week before Brad left for college, and he wanted to spend the time with his mother and brothers... all his brothers. Neil was fast asleep on the grass with Scott sitting next to him, engaged in trouncing Victor at Chinese checkers.

"Look at him," Steven's mocking voice floated over. "West Point's standards are going down."

Muttering a curse, Alex sat up and eyed the intruders... Steven and Charles with Armor and a fourth person. Living in the Kingsley residence set smack in the middle of the wealthiest neighborhood in Manhattan was all well and good. Unfortunately, the mansion was big enough to be occupied by all of Old Man Kingsley's progeny.

There was also the domestic staff, one of whom was the chauffeur—Armor's adoptive father.

"Go away," Victor hollered, not taking his gaze from the board game.

"On your feet, Cadet," snapped Armor, looming over the bench.

"Armor," said Victor, abandoning the game on the ground to haul himself up. "Our mother won't let me pound you to pulp. Push me enough, and I might just get temporary dementia."

"Amnesia," Neil corrected, eyes still closed. Scott was looking up at the men towering over them, seemingly putting them under a mental microscope.

"I don't need your mother's charity, *Mister* Victor," Armor said. "You see, as a plebe, your brother will have to follow my orders. I'll have him straightened out by the end of the year."

Guffawing, Alex interjected, "One phone call to General Potts will take care of you. He's still your dean." Alex had learned the first time he met the general at the shooting range he'd come in search of Grandfather on Senator Temple's advice. The general got himself into financial difficulties, and Grandfather helped with a loan. General Potts frequently commented how obliged he was to the entire Kingsley family for getting him out of a tight spot. He'd never let Armor play his nasty little games with Brad.

Armor smiled cruelly. "Think so? Let me introduce you to my friend and colleague, Cadet Captain Phillip Potts."

Potts? Alex took a closer look at the newcomer. Dark-haired and brown-eyed, Captain Potts did resemble the general.

"Phillip," said Armor. "This is the same prick your father was going on about."

Phillip Potts nodded at Alex. "Father claims you can outshoot all of us first classmen put together. Too bad we won't be around when you're ready to join."

Behind Potts, Charles giggled. Steven smiled in satisfaction.

Finally, Brad stood. "What do you want, Armor?"

"It's 'sir' to you," Potts snapped. "Or Captain Armor. You might not be in uniform yet but learn to show respect when you address your superiors."

The twins also stood, flanking Brad, anxiety marking their eyes.

"Oh, yeah?" Victor asked. "Potts, your friend ever tell you I'm gonna be right here in this house for another year? Along with my dear cousins, Steven and Charlie."

The smile on Armor's face vanished.

"We'll have ourselves a party, won't we, Charlie?" Victor asked, voice soft. He threw an arm around Scott's shoulders, sandwiching the boy between himself and Brad. Alex sauntered casually to stand next to Neil.

Eyeing the five, Charles gulped.

With a smile, Brad said, "Captain Armor... sir... I don't plan to show any disrespect. But remember, even if you tie me down, I'll always have Victor and Alex. They're my arms."

Cursing, Steven gestured at the twins. "What are these two? Your legs?"

Brad shrugged. "Mock all you want. We're brothers, the five of us."

"The Kingsley five," said Scott.

#

Back in January 1987

Green-Wood Cemetery

Brooklyn, New York

"Stop laughing," Alex mumbled, watching his wife sitting cross-legged on the ground and rocking back and forth in uncontrolled mirth.

Clutching her tummy, Sabrina howled. "What were you guys doing? *The West Side Story?* No, no, wait. I've got it. The East Side Story!"

Feeling slightly ridiculous, Alex complained, "Oh, c'mon."

"The melodrama! Arms, legs! What was Brad? The head?"

"Maybe," Alex said, lying back.

She hooted again. "'The Kingsley five!'"

Harry didn't think any of it funny when he heard the story. "Girls don't get it."

"Aww," said Sabrina, making a sympathetic moue with her lips. The effect was completely spoiled by her continued sputtering.

"Brothers need to have each other's backs," Alex insisted. "In our case, there was Steven to deal with... and Armor. Steven wouldn't have dared try anything if it weren't for Armor, and *he* knew nothing would happen to him because Steven would go to his father—Uncle David—to make sure of it."

"What *was* Armor's beef with you?" Sabrina asked. "I get he and Steven were already friends by the time you returned to the family home. Still, why would Armor risk pissing off Godwin by playing tricks on you?"

Alex shrugged uncomfortably. "We weren't exactly... Armor didn't like being called the son of the chauffeur. It wasn't meant as a taunt... not in the beginning... except, one thing led to another, and after all the stunts he pulled, it became a weapon for us to get back at him. But he ain't no innocent. I'm sure he saw the advantages in being Steven's friend. The S.O.B. wants recognition. He grew up watching the Kingsleys... he wants the same social importance, same authority, same money."

"So?" Sabrina waved a dismissive hand. "He's ambitious."

"What do you mean 'so?'" Alex snorted. "Armor was ready to kill us over his ambitions. Too bad Mother wouldn't let us do anything about it. She felt sorry for him."

Sabrina laughed out loud. "Sorry? Why? Because he was not a rich prince like you Kingsleys? I'm sure there are many chauffeurs in this world whose sons live perfectly happy lives."

Alex shook his head. "Not the money. Brad used to think it was because Armor is adopted."

With a sharp hiss, Sabrina said, "Adopted? I didn't kn—" She paused. "Godwin *had* to insist on all of you going to the same college."

"The academy wasn't too bad. By the time Victor joined, Armor and his friend were in Vietnam. Once Brad and Steven returned to the family business, the fights restarted."

"Then, you and Victor also returned?"

"You know the rest of the story." The hit job contracted by Steven was followed by the arrangement with the Barronses and the exile Lilah sent Alex on, culminating in his marriage to Sabrina.

Sabrina coughed. "What about Armor? Is he still with the army?"

"Richard Armor," Alex said, "got himself a law degree. He's a major now... reservist. Far ahead of me."

"Only because you left the military," consoled Sabrina. "He's out of your lives, at least."

"Oh, no," Alex said. "I've told you before... Armor and Steven are still good friends." The major even ran Kingsley Corp's Texas office for a while. Steven couldn't see—or simply didn't care—Armor was using him. "Strange thing is Armor's trying to buy his own drilling outfit, but he's been talking to banks instead of asking Steven for a loan. I see opportunity for us in it."

"What d'you—hold it right there, buddy," Sabrina said, eyes sparking. "Remember, you're all grown up now. Time to stop all the vendetta."

"What vendetta? All I plan to do is look out for our company." With his best mobster leer, Alex said, "It's all about the business, Sabrina."

She looked heavenward. "Good God."

Alex laughed. "Like I said... girls don't get it."

Michael came to them, a bunch of twigs in his gloved fist. "For my collection," he said.

After he left to hunt for more, Sabrina grumbled, "Twigs, stones... you name it... he collects it."

"He's a boy." Alex turned toward her, raising himself up on an elbow. "Bet he'd love a brother. He's almost four."

She pursed her lips, eyes glinting in mischief. "Mikey's mom would prefer him to have a sister. I think that was your problem. No girls in the family."

"Steven and Charlie have a sister," Alex pointed out, warmth filling his heart at the thought of a mischievous tyke with his wife's looks, bent on turning her father's hair gray.

"Helen, right?" asked Sabrina. "It doesn't sound like she had anything to do with the rest of you."

"No, she was busy with her own stuff. Got married around seventeen and left the house."

"Probably couldn't tolerate the testosterone exploding all over the place," Sabrina suggested, eyes crinkling. "Where was their mother in the middle of all this?"

"Aunt Grace? She and Uncle David thought Steven was the perfect little prince." Both were blind—figuratively and literally. A childhood illness left David nearly sightless, and Grace needed to wear dark glasses for her headaches.

"What about your grandmother?" Sabrina asked. "I mean, your real grandfather's wife. I know Godwin never got married."

"From what I know, she divorced my *real* grandfather and went her merry way. Died soon after."

"You know," Sabrina said, plucking at a thread on her jeans. "I heard something about your real grandfather. Apparently, he was going around with this girl, Amber Barrons."

"Barrons?" He sat up. "As in Lilah's family Barrons?"

"Yeah. This Amber was a cousin of Andrew's. Sixteen, seventeen maybe. You haven't heard the story?"

"Never."

Something flickered in Sabrina's eyes. "You're not lying to me, are you? To protect some deep, dark family secret?"

Alex had to laugh. "It was no secret he was a drunk and a womanizer. All of New York knows he produced Uncle Aaron with his secretary. If Amber Barrons got involved with the man, all I can say is she should've known better."

The smile on Sabrina's face faded.

"What?" Alex asked, throwing his hands up. "She should've. Did she think he was just some poor misunderstood soul?"

"She hanged herself," Sabrina said. "At seventeen."

Alex grimaced, feeling like an absolute jerk. "I didn't know."

"Obviously." Sabrina patted his knee. "So you have no clue, either."

"I could ask," he offered.

"No!"

Startled by the vehemence in her tone, he stared.

She flushed. "The Kingsleys and the Barronses must have kept it quiet for a reason, right? So why dig it all up and cause trouble? Not like it's going to do Amber any good."

"True," Alex acknowledged. "Let her rest in peace. If my real grandfather had anything to do with her suicide, the universe already meted out justice. He died a very painful death from liver failure."

Looking at the grave, Sabrina murmured, "So many secrets in the Kingsley family. Girls who died young, adopted sons..."

"Armor? He's not a Kingsley."

For a moment, Sabrina stayed silent. Then, she shook herself and stood. "True... we should get going. Hey, if you visit your father's grave before every milestone, how come you didn't bring me before our wedding?"

"I forgot," he admitted sheepishly. There were so many things on his mind at the time. "The last time I was here was before I went to West Point. Brad and Victor were with me."

"Patrice?"

"No, once we were old enough to make the trip alone, she never visited." He turned a slow circle. "There was a funeral going on at the time."

#

Fifteen years ago, March 1972

Green-Wood Cemetery

Brooklyn, New York

Spring was just beginning to hit New York City. Yellow flowers clustered the otherwise bare branches of the trees, and new grass sprouted on the ground, yet the sky was gloomy with sunrays battling the barricade set up by gray clouds. A lone duck squawked raucously in the pond, navigating his way through the drizzle which had not let up since morning.

They'd forgotten to take umbrellas. Squelching mud, Alex and Brad knelt by the grave. Brad dug into his pocket and brought out a candle which he set below the headstone. Dampness trickled down the back of Alex's neck.

"Ahh," groaned Victor, rubbing his back against a tree trunk.

"Dude, what are you doing?" Alex snapped.

"I'm itchy," Victor complained.

Alex snorted. "You look like an idiot. Get down here. I want to be done and out as soon as possible."

"Me, too," said Victor, dropping to his knees on the other side of the grave.

Alex scratched a droplet from his cheek, grimacing at the thought of shaving off the stubble. There was a cute redhead at school who found it sexy, but the military academy did not allow beards on their cadets. He would be the last of this generation of Kingsleys to attend West Point since Neil and Scott declined Grandfather's suggestion. Strangely, the Kingsley patriarch was not too bothered by the twins' refusals.

"Bro," called Victor, drawing Alex's attention. "You're supposed to *light* the candle."

Clicking the lighter, Alex held the flame to the wick. He muttered a curse before closing his eyes in fake meditation.

"Quiet," said Brad, reciting a short prayer.

"Go on," Alex taunted, gesturing at the headstone. "Pretend you're not angry with him."

"We're doing this for Mother, not him," said Brad.

"Thank God she's not making us light one for her," said Alex, referring to the other person buried under the slab.

"Don't give Mother any new ideas," warned Victor.

There was a stifled snort from Brad.

"Go ahead," said Victor. "She's not gonna find out we laughed at the Ones Who Shall Not Be Mocked."

The three young men doubled over, shaking with muffled laughter. Finally, Brad held a hand up. "We have to stop."

"C'mon, Brad," said Victor.

"I don't want to talk about them," Brad said. "This is Alex's big day."

"*My* big day?" Alex asked. "If so, we'd be at the bar, but—"

"Mother insisted," all three chanted together.

Brad shook his head. "I don't know how she can forgive them. I'd never forgive a cheating wife. Wouldn't feel like a man."

"Maybe it's different for women?" Alex speculated.

"Nah," Victor dismissed the idea. "Other women are not like her. My last girlfriend nearly crushed my—" He stopped, clearly having noticed the interested looks on his brothers' faces.

"Now I know why." Alex smacked a hand to his forehead.

"Why what?" asked Victor.

"I thought your voice was higher than usual," Alex explained.

"Soprano," Brad supplied, lips twitching.

It was only a couple of seconds before Brad and Alex exploded into guffaws.

Diving across the grave, Victor's heavy form landed on Alex, squishing the breath out of him. His efforts impeded by the howling he was doing, Alex tried to scramble his way out, fingers closing around wet grass. Victor wrestled both his brothers into the mud and gripped their heads, ready to smash them together. Alex raised his foot in a kick aimed at Victor's 'nads to finish the job started by the former girlfriend.

"Stop," gasped Brad.

"Prepare to die," ordered Victor.

"No, no." Brad twisted his head toward the pond. "Look, there's a funeral going on."

When Victor released his headlock, Alex sat up, spitting out a clump of wet dirt. A sudden gust of chilly wind blew, making him blink. Using a hand to shield his eyes, he glanced across.

There was a clearing by the water, partly hidden by a row of tall trees. Most of the mourners held umbrellas to protect themselves from the light rain. In the pond, the duck continued to squawk, interrupting the barely audible prayers of the minister. Strains of "Nearer, My God, to Thee" drifted to the trio.

"We'd better leave," murmured Victor.

By the time Alex blew out the candle and got to his feet, his brothers were already at a distance. He took another look at the funeral.

Someone was propelling a dark-haired girl forward, but her steps were unsteady. Even from the back, her gait showed the awkwardness of a young kid. Her figure was nicely filled out, though, with rain plastering her black suit to her form.

Alex wondered who was being buried. Was it the girl's father? Was the man like Alex's own parent, someone who discarded his children without a second thought? Shaking off the remnants of past anger, Alex strode forward, trying to catch up with his brothers.

He didn't know what made him look back, but when he did, the girl was sinking to her knees. "Hey," he shouted, stretching an arm out. Of course he couldn't reach her; he was too far away, and he didn't think anyone in the group even heard him holler.

It didn't matter. A boy broke off from the ranks of the mourners, his arm catching her around the shoulders to lead her away from the crowd.

Alex watched, wondering if he should offer help, then discarded the foolish notion. There were, at a minimum, fifty people in the group; the girl didn't need *his* help.

The duo was coming his way. Alex strained to see, but the girl's face was buried in the boy's shoulder, and he had his back to Alex.

Something fell to the grass when they brushed past him. Alex picked it up—a sodden handkerchief with the initials H and S stitched crookedly into one corner.

"Bro," shouted Victor, startling Alex. "Let's go," Victor gestured.

When Alex pivoted to return the handkerchief to its owner, the pair had disappeared. On his way out of the cemetery, he dropped the piece of fabric into the garbage can.

#

Back in January 1987

Green-Wood Cemetery

Brooklyn, New York

"I wonder," Alex mused.

"Wonder what?" Sabrina asked.

"Maybe they could have used my help," Alex said, feeling foolishly sentimental.

Sabrina's green eyes were warm with love. "Perhaps, but they left before you could offer. Such is destiny."

"Do you believe in destiny?" he asked, smiling.

"I believe in making my own," she said, voice firm. "No matter where I find myself, what I do is up to me. Just like what you did after your father left was up to you. You did fine. The girl and boy you saw here... maybe they did fine, too. Even if they lost a parent, they had each other."

"How do you know they were brother and sister?"

Sabrina shrugged. "Maybe yes, maybe not. Maybe friends, maybe boyfriend and girlfriend. Does it matter? She needed him, and he was there."

"I'd like to know what happened to them."

Sabrina rolled her eyes. "You can't let it go, can you? Check the name on the grave, but if you actually show up at their doorstep, they're gonna think you're insane."

Alex scanned the area around him. Tombs littered the landscape, all shapes, all sizes. Trees had been cleared since then, new ones planted, new outdoor furniture installed. "You know, I don't remember exactly where..."

"Okay, what were the initials on the handkerchief? Maybe they match one of the names around here."

Alex thought back. "I forgot," he admitted.

She laughed. "You're out of luck, buddy. Say a prayer for your twosome and leave it at that."

"Daddy." Michael tugged at Alex's jacket. "What's a deadbeat dad? Is it the same as dead?"

"What?" exclaimed Alex.

"Mikey," shrieked Sabrina. "We had a deal."

"What did you do?" Alex asked his wife, eyes narrowed.

Michael said, "I heard Mama say to Lilah that Uncle Victor is deadbeat." The little boy frowned. "He's not dead. I saw him yesterday."

"Sabrina," Alex growled.

"Well, he is," she defended herself. "When was the last time Victor saw his son? I didn't know *your* son was listening." She shook a finger at Michael. "Gimme my dollar back."

"You bribed him?" Alex snapped.

"It was Lilah's money," Michael said.

"What?" Alex asked. "What are you women teaching my son?"

"Teaching *him*?" Sabrina huffed. "The little stinker blackmailed us." Glaring at Michael, she repeated, "Hand over the money."

Face wreathed in an angelic smile, Michael informed his mama, "Spent it. Sorry. Nanny said I could buy crayons."

"We're going to talk about this," Alex said, trying to keep his tone firm. "As soon as I'm back from India."

Walking along the tarred roads leading to the exit, Sabrina said, "Alex, when you're in India, be careful... please."

"Huh?" With a small laugh, he asked, "What do you mean? I'm not going off to war."

The effort it took her to bring the smile back to her face was evident. "Dunno... Argentina... then, Alaska." When he halted, she stopped alongside and raised a hand to preempt his response. "I get it... you learned your lesson. Just be careful, okay?"

"Anything happened since Alaska?" Alex asked. "You weren't this jittery when I went to Russia."

For a few moments, she stared unblinkingly at him, her lips parting open a few times before pursing firmly shut. She glanced restlessly around. "Perhaps this place got to me."

The dead in their tombs... "Yeah," said Alex.

"I almost forgot..." she murmured. "Lilah's parents are buried here."

Alex looked down the path they traversed. "Where are the graves? We could leave a flower or something."

"I don't know. Didn't go to the funeral. I was a kid."

"It was an air crash, right?"

"Yeah, she lost both of them on the same day."

Part X

Chapter 29

A month later, March 1987

Panama

Yes, Lilah crowed to herself. Other members of the rappelling team hollered in delight as they waded to the shallow part of the pool at the bottom of the cascade. Few things could beat the adrenaline rush of descending the Jä Wäkta Waterfall. Few other things brought her the same peace, the strength to continue fighting. Lilah spent a few minutes chatting with the regulars in the group— a couple of retired athletes and an English teacher—about summer climbs before the guard signaled her they needed to leave. There was a curious glance or two thrown her way by the rookies, but most were usually too polite to ask intrusive questions.

She was snoozing in the back seat of the Chevy when the bodyguard pulled next to the mansion in Cerro Azul sometime after dawn. Of course there was work waiting for her, a note on the side table in her secretary's neat writing. Reading it, Lilah sighed. Of course there would be another fight with Brad over this.

Plonking her rear end onto the bed, she made one phone call to Sabrina. In five minutes, Lilah went to the breakfast room in search of Brad, clad in the same soiled jeans and tee and sneakers. When she was at the door, a female voice exclaimed, "There you are, child."

"Patrice," Lilah murmured. At least Brad wasn't likely to start a quarrel in front of his mother. From the way he was eyeing the note in her hands, he already knew what it said.

"...a murder attempt!" Patrice finished. Since she heard about the attack on Neil, she'd been worried for all five brothers.

Brad took a sip of sweetened coffee, leafing through the morning paper. "We're all grown men, Mother," he said mildly. "And we've learned enough to know what to watch for and when to be on guard."

"Patrice," Lilah called. "I might as well tell you now... Harry asked if I could go to Calcutta. I'm flying over tonight." Sabrina wanted Lilah to go as much as Harry did. The setup Alex detailed sounded like another trap.

"Alex is a grown man, as well," Brad said, the edge of mockery evident perhaps only to Lilah's ears. "If he wants to be part of this company, he needs to work for it. He doesn't need you holding his hand."

"*Harry* feels Alex needs help dealing with the unfamiliar business environment," said Lilah, keeping her tone even. "I can make myself understood in Hindi, and I'm sort of familiar with the culture."

"Lilah?" a small voice called. They all looked toward the door.

"Mikey," Lilah exclaimed, "how did you get here?"

"You went away before finishing the story," the four-year-old said, tone accusatory. He toddled into the room, blankie trailing on the floor.

"Oh, my—" She knelt to face him. "Little man, that was two days ago. You could've asked your nanny to... by the way, did you walk here all by yourself?" To reach Lilah from his parents' wing, Michael would have had to go outside the building and walk through the compound or cross the castle with its narrow and steep stairways.

He shook his head, then nodded. At the expression on Lilah's face, he mumbled, "Sorry."

"You know you're not supposed to," she said sternly, then ruined the effect by asking, "How about a visit to the ice cream shop this afternoon?"

As Michael threw his arms around her neck, she hugged him to her heart and inhaled the clean baby smell of him. A pang of yearning went through her. In her mind, she swore to Sabrina that whatever happened, her little family would remain intact. Her child would never be an orphan, reduced to only a bargaining chip for his relatives.

Chapter 30

The week before

Dibrugarh, India

Madonna's "Papa Don't Preach" played in soft tones in the restaurant attached to the hotel. Pushing open the old-fashioned glass panel doors, Alex stepped into the outdoor dining area and halted when cold air blasted his face. The thermometer was registering mid-forties this morning in the small town in northeast India, but combined with wind chill...

Liam sauntered out. "Brr, this is freezing my..." he paused, eyeing the hostess of the restaurant. "...toes off." Verity's brother worked for Gateway as an analyst but on Alex's request, had been assigned to help the Peter Kingsley Company and was now in India with their team.

Directing Liam and Alex to their table, the hostess told them they were to wait there for the union leader. As she walked back into the warmth of the building, Alex said, "Understand the game, Liam. They begin by showing us foreigners our place."

Alex took in the tea gardens sloping away from the back of the restaurant, wispy mist covering the still-green bushes. The palace converted to a hotel was set on a slight elevation. From their table, he could see around the corner of the hotel building to the front and the crowded vehicles on the narrow street curving around a small hill. Shrill whistles from the traffic cop punctuated the sounds of engines.

Liam continued to complain. "So let me get this straight. The unions and the environmental groups are opposing our investment in the company because they think drilling will impact the environment."

"Mmhmm."

"The Indian company will continue drilling even if we're not here. How does any of it make any sense?"

"Everyone knows the issue here isn't the environment. After all their dancing around, we're finally going to hear what they want from us. What *we* want is for them to agree to our plan."

"Gimme the military any day. Much easier than business negotiations."

"Enjoy the experience, Liam."

In concise words, Liam told Alex where he could stick his suggestion.

The door from the hotel swung open again, and a short, hefty man in pristine white pajama pants and long shirt topped with a sweater vest strode out. Black hair framed his clean-shaven face with bright-black eyes. "Hoda," he introduced himself while a hotel employee pulled out a chair. Hoda refused the offer of a drink. "I don't drink or smoke. Or chew tobacco. Filthy habits, all."

His English had miraculously improved overnight. Alex smothered his smirk, remembering the man's thick accent at the rally the night before where he exhorted his followers to fight foreign involvement in local businesses and the destruction of the native flora and fauna the Kingsley dollars were likely to bring. Worldwide, politicians were two-faced.

"I'll come to the point, gentlemen," Hoda said. "I'm the vice president of the Oil Workers Union in our state. Our president has been jailed for links to the mafia here, and they're trying to get me on the same charges."

"Are they true?" asked Liam.

Alex kicked him under the table.

Hoda looked at Alex. "New, is he?"

Murmuring soothing apologies, Alex gestured for the man to continue.

"I need to pay someone a million dollars to get out of this," the union leader said, not a trace of embarrassment in his voice. "You give me the money, and I'll get the union and the environmentalists off your back."

Yeah... Alaska, India... didn't matter. Politics was dirty business. Alex steepled his fingers. "Our laws stop us from directly giving you any money. If your friend is in a position to take political or charitable contributions, we can take care of the problem without involving your name."

Hoda stroked his chin. "Charity may be the better way. It will buy you some good PR as well."

"Why don't you set something up at this end, and I'll make arrangements from the American side."

After a few minutes, they watched Hoda walk away. Liam turned to Alex, fists ready to swing. "Bribery?" Liam snarled. "I didn't sign up for this."

Alex held up a hand. "Not now."

The chair scraped the concrete floor as he stood, beckoning Liam to follow. Nodding politely to the sari-clad hostess, he walked to the elevators, Liam following with a confused expression.

Back in their hotel suite, Alex phoned New York on the specially installed line. "Harry? We need to talk." Relating his encounter with Hoda, Alex asked, "We can walk away from India, but it will be another loss after Alaska. Also, the Russians are watching the developments in Asia."

"They want to see how much clout the network actually has," agreed Harry. "Hoda *could* be another criminal with similar *m.o.* as the crook in Alaska. Another concern is the possibility of this being a setup. Perhaps payback for what happened in Anchorage."

"Regardless, we can't pull the same trick. The Alaska incident was plastered all over the papers. Hoda and his buddies will be on the lookout for double cross. Same result... India will be a loss."

"Tell you what," said Harry. "Let's find out more about this Hoda character. There's a cousin of Lilah... I can get him to make some inquiries. But too much digging from the Indian side will set off alarms, so let's get some of the names mixed up in this business without going through the official channels in the country."

"Since the mafia is involved, Interpol may be keeping track of Hoda and his associates. Any chance you can get the info through the CIA?"

"They won't waste resources on bit players like Hoda. Plus, if we *are* being set up, there may be someone in the CIA feeding them information, and we don't want to tip them off. Lemme contact Lilah's brother. Shawn, I mean. His computer buddies should be able to dig up some dirt."

When Harry called back the next day, it was with surprising information.

"Jùn Wángzǐ?" exclaimed Alex. "He's the drug dealer who works with Noriega's men in Panama!" His real name was something else, but he called himself Jùn Wángzǐ. Apparently, it meant Handsome Prince. The state department called him Opium Prince. "What's he doing with a small-time thug like Hoda?"

"The Thai and Chinese governments have blocked the flow of heroin from Burma into their countries. India is the only land route available to Prince. He has a family connection to the place, too—a cousin in Goa. Alex, these are dangerous men you're dealing with."

"I know." Lilah and Victor had kept Prince and the rest of Noriega's cartel away from the Peter Kingsley Company thus far. "What do we do now?"

"If it's a setup, I doubt any official involvement from the U.S. since Southcom has made it clear they want Noriega out." The United States military's southern command was located in Panama. "I see only two options for us. We can inform the CIA of what's going on and walk away. In isolation, India will not be a substantial loss to the network, but it could snowball. Once word of this second defeat gets around, other companies won't be as ready to associate themselves with us. Imagine if Russia withdraws... the damage will be huge. Or we can cooperate with the gang to get what we want—"

"Harry," Alex warned.

"—*and* get them with an undercover sting."

Chapter 31

Two weeks later, April 1987

Bombay, India

In the presidential suite at The Oberoi, Alex tucked a sharp knife into his boot, telling Liam, "Remember to keep your weapons on you at all times." Hoda and his political bosses were sure to bring muscle to the meeting.

From the messy, king-sized bed, Alex grabbed the Galatz—his sniper rifle—and stored it in the suite's locker. It was not the right weapon in case of an ambush. There was another bad boy in the box delivered the week before—the prototype of a submachine gun a firearms engineer wanted Alex to test. Folded, it fit easily into his backpack. When needed, it could unfold within seconds and spray some serious lead. Alex hoped like hell he wouldn't need it today. The wire was under his shirt, enabling the CIA and Indian military intelligence to listen in on what happened. Harry would also be hearing every word.

Getting Prince would help cut the money supply to Noriega's gang, and India wanted the criminals behind bars, but neither Washington nor New Delhi was willing to risk an international incident by pissing off high-level political leaders without some certainty of proving the corruption of the same politicians. Therefore, if this sting operation failed, most of the blame would fall on Harry and Alex. It was one of the conditions put forward by the CIA to let the alliance continue working with the targeted criminals to expand the network. Still, once there was documented official involvement, it would be harder to point fingers at the network and its member companies.

"You sure you want to go with me?" Alex asked Liam. There would be no participation from any other official or employee of the network. For one, Alex wasn't willing to risk innocent lives. For another, such missions required marrow-level faith between partners. Outside of his family and Harry, Liam was the one man Alex could trust to have his back no matter what.

"Let's go," Liam said.

They were kept cooling their heels in the union office—a nondescript workspace except for the picture of Gandhi alongside those of communists from around the world. It was almost an hour before the leader walked in. "Netaji," Hoda whispered.

The Americans stood politely. Like Hoda, Netaji was dressed in a long, white kurta and matching pajama pants. There the similarity ended. Unlike the bulky Hoda, Netaji was lean with reassuring brown eyes and white hair.

The foreigners were waved back to their chairs. Netaji said something to his assistant who turned to them and translated, "Hoda has explained you'll be giving money to the orphanage?"

Netaji held up a hand. "In dollars. In cash. Okay?"

Alex nodded. "I have half a million here. I want the press conference done before we get you the rest."

Netaji did not like it. He and Hoda argued loudly about getting the entire payment upfront, but Alex would not budge. After they came to an agreement, Netaji departed, leaving his underlings and Hoda arranging the press conference announcing the union's change of heart.

Afterward, Hoda came with them to the hotel room.

Alex called someone in Hong Kong. "Tony?" he queried into the phone. "Yes. We'll take the rest of the money now. Right. I'll wait for her call."

Jotting down a name and number, Alex hung up before turning to Hoda. "The American government would've had questions if I tried to move such large amounts out of the country in one go. Fortunately, my contact keeps loose cash around."

Humming under his breath, Alex went to the minibar to mix himself a drink. He glanced casually at the reflection in the wall mirror. Hoda was looking at the notepad Alex left on the coffee table, memorizing the number on it.

Soon, there was a call for Alex, asking him to meet someone at a railway station. Hoda went with him.

#

In two hours

Victoria Terminus, Bombay, India

"Looks grand," commented Alex, paying the cabbie.

Against the bright-blue sky loomed a huge gothic edifice with multiple wings, the central dome sporting a figure reminiscent of the Statue of Liberty. Ornate carvings and brass railings gave it the appearance of a palace, except masses of humanity moved in out of the building in never-ending waves. Rumbling buses and cars and thick exhaust fumes added to the chaos.

Hoda wiped the sweat from his forehead with a handkerchief. "Where the hell is your cont—"

"Oh, hellooo," crooned a gruff voice.

When Alex pivoted, there was a woman draped in a sari with every color of the rainbow splashed on it. A large part of her midriff was exposed between the cropped shirt and the fabric wrapped around her waist.

"Yes?" Alex greeted, noting she was only a few inches shorter than him. There were also the sinewy arms and the five o'clock shadow.

"Shoo," said Hoda. "Go away." Turning to Alex, the man explained, "She's a *hijra*—a transgender."

Ignoring him, the woman smiled coyly at Alex. "Myself Rekha."

"Did you need something?" Alex asked.

"Go *away*," insisted Hoda, flapping his hands in front of her face.

Rekha turned and spat to the side. The smile returning with lightning speed, she ambulated around Alex and poked him in the tush with a finger. He jumped in surprise.

"Rekha," snapped a voice. The new arrival introduced herself to Alex. "Sheila. I'm Tony's contact here. I have the cash you need. Rekha is my bodyguard."

Alex's heart nearly stopped at the sight of Tony's associate. Tall for an Indian lady, she was wrapped in a blood-red sari. Her eye color was black, and her face strangely devoid of expression, but every feature was otherwise familiar to Alex. *Damn it, Harry! Why her?*

Chapter 32

A month later, May 1987

Back in Dibrugarh, India

The day after Alex and his team signed the deal with the company in Assam, Hoda invited himself to lunch. "Tony says you provide transport to the United States." Hoda arranged himself in one of the chairs at Alex's table. None of the other diners in the crowded restaurant were paying attention to the union leader.

Alex raised an eyebrow. "Tony?"

"So I took that woman Sheila's phone number," said Hoda. "She put me in touch with your cash source... Tony."

"You spied on me?" Alex asked, careful to inject the right amount of anger into his tone. The notion of *Sheila* dealing with these criminal types didn't sit well with him. Harry had listed all the reasons it was a swell idea to involve her—she was a chemical engineer, spoke Hindi, would be trusted by the intelligence agencies *and* the Peter Kingsley Network. Besides, the notice they got was too short to find someone else who fit the criteria. Alex still didn't like it.

"No one spied," Hoda snapped. "You left the phone number lying around. Your mistake." He extended a hand, palm up. "Listen. I came here to ask for some help."

The turban-clad waiter navigated his way around to them and set plates piled high with fragrant food in front of Alex. "What kind of help?" Alex asked, turning his attention to the dish closest to him.

"You didn't tell us you have a sideline in heroin." Hoda smirked.

Alex looked up sharply. "We don't. Tony's important to us, so we do him favors every now and then. He asks for space in our containers, and we don't ask questions."

Hoda laughed. "Sure. Whatever you say." He leaned forward, elbows on the table. "Listen. I have something in mind. I'm going to need your assistance for it."

"Always happy to lend a hand. What do we get in return?"

"Name your price."

"That easy, huh?"

"Tony was getting his stuff from the refineries in Thailand, but with the government crackdown there, he's run out of suppliers. I can get Tony to Prince." At Alex's look of incomprehension, Hoda clarified, "Prince... he rules the opium market in Burma. Rumor has it there's three hundred million worth of stuff under his control. Maybe more... I want in on the American side of the business. The trade in India keeps us comfortable, but this is our chance to get into the big leagues."

"Sounds like you have things all planned out... this prince will supply the stuff, you'll play middleman, and Tony takes care of distribution. What do you need me for?" Spearing one of the dumplings, Alex popped it into his mouth, washing down the spiced meat with ice-cold coconut water.

"For the kind of shipments we're planning, we'll need support from you Kingsleys to get it from Hong Kong to the ports in America—Hawaii, San Francisco, and New York."

Voice tight, Alex said, "The Kingsleys deal in oil, not heroin."

"Oh, come on," Hoda mocked. "You were happy enough to take cash from Tony, and I, too, can make it worth your while."

Alex continued to look at him, angry expression unchanged.

"Look," Hoda said. "You're negotiating with the authorities in Rajasthan and Bombay. Don't you think I can smooth your way there?"

Alex's eyes narrowed. "How? You're a union leader from Assam. Bombay's a big city."

Hoda peered around and leaned forward. The other diners at the restaurant weren't looking their way. None of the staff was close enough to overhear. "Don't think this is just me. Powerful people are involved."

Alex asked, "Like Netaji?"

"Even higher."

Dabbing at his mouth with a cotton napkin, Alex said, "I'll think about it."

Later, back in the hotel suite, Liam and Alex clinked Kingfisher beer bottles.

"Send the team home," Alex said. "I want them kept out of the rest of it."

The next day, Alex contacted Hoda. Sheila and her bodyguard, Rekha, were also at the park for the meeting. "I want to meet your superiors," said Alex. "We gotta know who we're dealing with."

Once they got everyone on tape, the CIA and Indian intelligence would have the evidence they needed.

"All right," Hoda said. "We can arrange it. We'll get everyone together at Pasighat. My bosses, me, you, these ladies."

"No damn way," Alex blurted.

Hoda directed a puzzled look at Alex. "Huh?"

When this was over, Alex was going to deliver a richly deserved butt-kicking to Harry. He claimed Sheila was constantly protected by military security—a hidden sniper, plainclothes officers. A motorcycle and an all-terrain vehicle were kept ready for any vehicular chase. Even the meeting place was carefully checked for hidden traps before she ventured anywhere near the union leader. But joining a gathering of the entire gang of miscreants who'd bring their own protection? Alex wasn't gonna take the risk of her getting caught in a shootout.

Before he could come up with some excuse, Sheila said, "Tony does his own negotiations, so I won't be there."

#

A few weeks later, June 1987

Pasighat, India

The latest military crisis between India and China had just been diffused, but Beijing continued to dispute Indian sovereignty over several territories, including the old British-built town of Pasighat. So the government in New Delhi kept tight control on who could visit the hilltop settlement, and it took the Americans a few days to get a restricted area permit to visit. For the same reason, it was also a good spot for criminals to gather and plot their moves away from the prying eyes of the public and the media.

Jagged mountain peaks towered high on three sides of the place. The Siang River frothed furiously across rocks, sending mist into the crisp, clean air. The guesthouse they were staying in was a little shabby, but Alex was enjoying the colonial-style building which brought to mind the days of small principalities and the rule of royalty.

On the same evening, there was a party organized by Netaji. Wearing tuxes, Alex and Liam went to the ballroom where all concerned were meeting. At the entrance, they were frisked by three groups of security officers—muscle-bound giants working for Hoda and Netaji, their boss, and Tony. Twelve guards altogether.

"You can go in," said one of the giants, the lead guard, presumably.

Alex didn't glance at Liam, but he knew exactly what his friend was thinking. They got a brief reprieve. The thin wire sewn carefully into the collar of Alex's shirt had escaped notice.

Inside, crystal chandeliers lit with real candles hung from the richly patterned ceiling, sweet, waxy fragrance permeating all around. Chairs in neoclassical style lined with red silk upholstery were arranged in clusters throughout the large hall. The wait staff walked around, glasses and cutlery tinkling as they delivered food and drink to the guests.

Alex and Liam walked across the gleaming black and white tiles to the long, arched windows overlooking the river where a man with Chinese features stood talking to Hoda. Alex recognized him from the folder he'd been sent—Tony. Apparently realizing he was under scrutiny, Tony turned. When he saw the Americans, he raised his glass in salute. The union leader also turned and darted to Alex and Liam to hurry them toward the back.

"Sir," Hoda said to someone sitting at one of the tables. "These are the men from the Peter Kingsley Company."

As Hoda moved to the side, Alex came face-to-face with Jùn Wángzǐ—a.k.a. Prince—the drug lord of Burma. The boyishly handsome face sported typical southeast Asian features, but the build was of a pugilist.

Casually, Alex raised a hand to scratch at his jaw, the finger brushing against his collar reassuring him the wire was still present.

"Gentlemen," the drug lord crooned, tilting the wine glass in his hand toward a couple of empty chairs. "I thought the Kingsleys told the Noriega government you didn't want him involved in your business because of his friendship with me."

"I did wonder if you were the same man, Mr. Prince," Alex said, sitting down. Liam was on his right. "Nothing personal against General Noriega, but he's being investigated for his role in drug trafficking, and we have an obligation to obey the laws of the United States. We're in India now. Different place, different rules."

"Just Prince will do. I offered to tell your Drug Enforcement Agency about the opium flow from the Golden Triangle through Hong Kong into the United States. Your government wasn't interested. Probably because some of your top people are involved in this."

"I find the claim hard to believe," Alex said. The drug lord didn't need to know Alex was already aware of the stories. He'd been too young for Vietnam but had met enough vets to hear about the dirty games played by the American intelligence agency.

Prince swirled red wine in the glass. "The CIA gave us arms and money. Then, they took our high-quality number four heroin back to the United States and sold it on the streets."

Ignoring Liam's murmur of angry disbelief, Alex asked, "Why would the CIA work to addict the very people they're sworn to protect?"

"Because they believe the greater threat is the communist ideology. Because the CIA's method of combating communism includes murders and assassinations. Because they needed money to fund these activities, especially during the Vietnam War. Because the average American taxpayer would not have consented to release funds without oversight. Because the CIA does not want the average American taxpayer to know what exactly its agents do. Because the taxpayer would be horrified to know the prostitutes plying their trade along Times Square and the poor teenagers in the ghettos are considered expendable by the government."

What response could Alex give? Things weren't as black and white as the drug lord was making it seem. The millions murdered by communist dictators like Stalin, the moral obligation to stop wholesale slaughter... but a lot of the young people who were sacrificed in the war didn't even know they were in one.

Prince added, "For a former army man, you're certainly very naïve."

"You're telling me the Americans are forcing you to sell drugs?" Alex asked, keeping his tone skeptical.

"Not exactly," Prince admitted. "Since the Vietnam War is over, the CIA has no use for our product, but my people and I still need a means of support. I offered to stop all cultivation if the American government paid us. Unfortunately, they refused."

Out of the corner of his eye, Alex saw Liam opening his mouth to speak. "How absolutely rich," Alex interjected. "First, you accuse the U.S. of drug smuggling and gunrunning. Now, you're blaming our government because they refused to pay a criminal to refrain from criminal activities."

"Oh, I admit I'm a criminal, Mr. Kingsley. Who's the bigger criminal here? Me or the diplomats and intelligence men who addict their own young people to attack an ideology which was obsolete before it began? Or are they lining their own pockets? Who tracks the money they make from the opium trade? And what about the military-industrial complex mentioned by one of your former presidents? What is their role in all this?"

There were always corrupt bastards making money off the blood spilled by American soldiers in foreign lands, and the lives of locals were considered even cheaper. Patriots like Alex who joined the military quickly lost their naïveté. Internal blinkers became a part of the mental gear, helping them keep their eyes fixed on the mission of serving their countrymen. Else they ended up in the psychiatry ward or six feet under by their own hand.

Prince sneered. "Unlike those government officials and businessmen—unlike the *Kingsleys*—I'm not a hypocrite. Your CFO was pleasant on the phone but completely unmoved by my efforts to make her see reason. Beautiful woman, by the way, from her pictures. Pity we never met. Last month, I read the *Time* cover story on your brother's ideas on ethically running a business. Yet, here you are, negotiating with the likes of me just so you can access the Indian oil sector."

"Why are you here at the meeting?" Alex asked. "You don't seem to like us very much."

"Liking is not essential to conducting business," said the drug lord. "I need new customers, and your colleague in Hong Kong, Tony, looks like a promising one. But we'll need help from the Peter Kingsley Company."

At a gesture from Prince, Netaji's assistant spread a map on the table. Burma, Laos, and Thailand—the countries of the Golden Triangle—produced large amounts of opium, which was then shipped to the rest of the world. Thanks to the war on drugs, sea routes along Burma and Thailand were always monitored, and Laos was landlocked.

The markings Harry later makes on his map of the planned drug route.

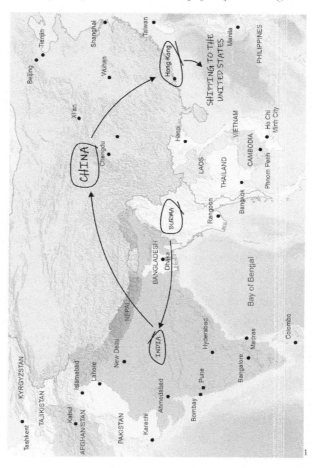

---

[1] *(DATASET CITATION: Tozer, B, Sandwell, D. T., Smith, W. H. F., Olson, C., Beale, J. R., & Wessel, P. (2019). Global bathymetry and topography at 15 arc sec: SRTM15+. Distributed by OpenTopography. https://doi.org/10.5069/G92R3PT9. Accessed: 2022-03-19*
NASA Shuttle Radar Topography Mission (SRTM)(2013). Shuttle Radar Topography Mission (SRTM) Global. Distributed by OpenTopography. https://doi.org/10.5069/G9445JDF. Accessed: 2022-03-19)

China also kept a close eye on its borders with the three countries. In 1986, there was even a high-profile seizure of a heroin shipment. Nevertheless, the land route through Yunnan province to Hong Kong remained a favorite with narco traffickers.

Conveniently for the criminals, India was located between the Golden Triangle and the Golden Crescent—Pakistan, Afghanistan, and Iran. Unfortunately, the American government pressured the Indians into passing something called the Narcotic Drugs and Psychotropic Substances Act, criminalizing even marijuana—until then widely accepted in the country. There was also the problem of terrorist organizations using drug trafficking to fund their activities, which meant intelligence agencies closely monitored the border with Pakistan. Burma was a different story, having maintained good relations with New Delhi for years. With enough political support, eye-popping quantities of heroin could be smuggled into India fairly easily.

While China and India were big markets for the smugglers, the U.S. was considered the prime target. There was always the possibility of using the Bombay port to dispatch the product across the planet, but Prince already had an experienced team in place for transport through China.

What he planned was to move the merchandise to India through Mizoram, then from Sikkim into China. Prince's people would get it to Hong Kong. They needed the Peter Kingsley Company to provide shipping from the Hong Kong port to the United States.

"To New York and San Francisco," Alex murmured. "Plus, Hawaii."

"Yes." Lighting a cigar, the drug lord blew a perfect smoke ring. "In addition, I need you to invest in Burma Oil."

"What?" Alex was genuinely surprised. "I've studied reports from our engineers about your reserves. Sorry to have to tell you this, but they're not worth much."

"I already know it, Mr. Kingsley," Prince said impatiently. "I need you to make a legitimate investment of fifteen million U.S. dollars into Burma Oil, which you'll lose. In return, the opium will be provided to Hoda and Tony's setup. They will ship it via your containers to the United States and profit off American users. You'll get access to all the oil drilling outfits in South and Southeast Asia."

"Money laundering."

"Call it whatever you want. Are you willing to work with us?"

"There's no other option if I want this expansion plan of ours to be successful. So count me in. Since my upfront cost is fifteen million, the drilling deals need to be done before we arrange transport."

"The very reason we have all these politicians here," the drug lord said, his eyes going to the door.

Alex twisted around.

A distinguished-looking older man in a Nehru suit was walking in, gray both in his hair and in his goatee. His arm was around the waist of a girl barely out of her teens.

"Mamma mia," Liam muttered.

Jet-black curls, kohl-lined large eyes, red lips. Thirty-six, twenty-four, thirty-six figure clad in glittering pink Spandex. There was a rhythm to the girl's movements almost as though she were dancing to some internal drumbeat, shaking her hips to a seductive tune only she could hear.

When the gentleman and his companion approached the table, Alex and Liam stood politely. Prince introduced the man as a minister with the central government. Hoda scurried over with chairs for the newcomers and shouted at the wait staff to break out the Scotch. Alex mentally flipped through Harry's folder of Indian politicians and almost exclaimed in surprise as he realized how high up in the hierarchy this person was.

Within an hour, they all shook hands over the agreement. There would be nothing in writing.

Netaji's bespectacled assistant announced, "Hodaji has some entertainment arranged for our foreign guests."

Local culture included tacking on a *ji* at the end of someone's name when you intended to show respect. But otherwise... "Looks like any club back home," Liam muttered a little while later. "Booze and babes."

The politician and his girlfriend sauntered to Alex. "Priya thinks you're very handsome," said the fellow.

With a small smile, Alex inclined his head at the girl.

"She's a movie star, you know. Very popular. Go on, get to know him better." With a pat on her rounded bottom, the man pushed her toward Alex. Sashaying to him, she seated herself on his lap.

Surprise held Alex still.

"Lucky bastard," Liam said under his breath.

Running her fingers through Alex's hair, Priya tilted his face up for a bubblegum-flavored kiss. Alex was too bemused for a few seconds to offer objections. When her other hand wandered over his torso and moved to his groin, he found what was left of his mind and gripped her wrist. "Thank you, but no."

The rest of the men had turned away and were chatting as though this were nothing out of the ordinary. At his reprimand, they turned back.

"What's the matter, Mr. Kingsley?" Prince asked, nodding at Alex's wedding ring. "Worried about the wife?"

Alex stood, easily setting the girl to the side. "I don't share women."

He and Liam soon excused themselves and left town the same night.

#

From the secure line at the Oberoi, Alex made his call. In the background, CNN International played President Reagan's speech at Brandenburg Gate. "...Mr. Gorbachev, open this gate. Mr. Gorbachev, tear down this wall..."

The ring tone broke off. "Alex?" came Harry's voice.

"Yeah. Did you get it?"

"Every word," Harry said. "But—"

"Make sure the CIA and Indian intelligence wait until our contracts are signed before making any arrests," Alex warned. On their part, the Kingsleys would play delaying tactics with money transfers and such to avoid having to actually transport heroin. "We didn't get involved only to do the cops' work for them."

"About the job..." said Harry. "The Indians say they need more evidence. High-level politicians are implicated... an actual exchange needs to be recorded so they don't wiggle out of trouble, either in court or in the eyes of the public."

"Damn." So the smuggling part needed to happen but no sooner than the day Alex got what he wanted. "Recommendations?"

"Sheila," said Harry, explaining what she could do.

Alex huffed. "As long as she limits herself to talking to Hoda. I don't want her anywhere around the rest. Is she in India at the moment?"

"Yeah. There's the peak she's been trying to conquer for a while—Swargarohini—but I don't think she's had time. She's still staying with—" Tone changing, Harry continued, "By the way, the employees at Gateway's Bombay office seem to think I'm a regular at transgender brothels. Care to explain?"

"Heh?" Alex chuckled. "So Rekha did show up."

At the meeting in the park in Dibrugarh, Sheila's bodyguard/friend made a comment about enjoying Alex as a customer if it weren't for prudes like Sheila. He was taken aback but learned later one of Sheila's brothers worked with an international organization. The charity helped the AIDS-afflicted in the gay and transgender communities. This brother suggested she hire Rekha as guard in India. A major rule of the job was Rekha couldn't pursue her other line of work as long as the women stayed together, either in the transgender colony or wherever else they were required to travel. Alex sent word to Rekha she could use Harry's name with Gateway's local manager to find a permanent job if it was what she wanted.

"Oh, yes, she showed up," Harry said darkly. "And claimed to the manager she was an 'intimate' friend of Mr. Harry Sheppard."

Laughing outright, Alex said, "You keep telling me there's no truth without valor and no valor without sacrifice. Time to put money where your mouth is."

Harry spat out a foul curse, questioning the substance of Alex's brain.

In only a few days, Alex got another call. Hoda was furious about the new demand from "that bitch, Sheila." Apparently, Tony's associate was adamant Prince and gang process the heroin according to her specifications. She also expected samples to take to Hong Kong at each stage to run tests. Sheila insisted the lengthy process was necessary to ensure the merchandise she bought for her boss was high quality. "Do you know how long the whole thing could take?" Hoda griped.

Only until the Peter Kingsley Network got its contracts.

Chapter 33

Four months later, October 1987

Bombay, India

Buildings in poor repair crowded the transgender colony all the way down its narrow streets. Shawn had been sure the residents of the locality would protect Lilah if only for his sake as he'd done some work among them. It was his condition for agreeing not to blab to Dan about the "Sheila" thing despite the million guarantees of covert security Harry gave.

The tiny space rented by Rekha featured two bedrooms, one of which now held a single cot for Lilah's use. The equally tiny apartment on the left was converted to an office/gym. In one corner was a small television for Rekha to watch. Thanks to Shawn's worry, there was nowhere Lilah went that Rekha didn't follow, except on bathroom breaks. If she wasn't around, one of her friends would serve in her stead—a 24/7 shadow on top of all the guards and gunmen placed in strategic locations around the chaotic neighborhood.

The CIA stuff filled only a small part of the last seven months. Most of Lilah's routine work was handled via phones and fax, and she managed a few trips to meet partners in Europe and the Middle East. There were no crucial votes during the period which required her personal appearance in the States.

Even if she didn't meet Brad the entire while, the phone conversations were bad enough. He brought up her continued absence each time, accusing her of staying in India only to spend time with Alex, demanding she return home. Lilah usually responded by saying she was hanging up if they were done discussing business.

Then, there was Harry. He flew several times a month to the city, but they weren't supposed to meet in person during the mission and blow her cover. The nightly calls with him were supposedly for mutual updates on various projects. Lilah couldn't avoid talking about Brad, but she kept the mentions mostly work-related. Any comments on her marriage were made in the vaguest terms. On his part, Harry dutifully mentioned Verity a time or two. There would be awkward silence while Lilah remembered the other woman's hateful comments. Of course Harry wouldn't bring up the topic... how could he? What could he say? With a quick chuckle or a silly joke, he'd steer the conversation into a different topic. Lilah would gratefully go along.

Arguments erupted over movies, music, books, the overall state of the world, Harry once giving her a blow-by-blow account of a Mike Tyson match. When Lilah raved about Stephen King's latest novel, *Misery*, Harry annoyed her by making horror film noises, only to later send a collection of the author's works to her address. She demanded to know when he was going to play the sax again, and he retorted by saying when she learned how to be diplomatic. Lilah wasn't kidding. She remembered him playing "Stairway to Heaven" for her, and as far as she knew, Led Zeppelin remained Harry's favorite band. But she laughed along, pretending she'd been teasing.

Harry would keep talking even when her speech slurred with slumber, and her eyes drifted shut. His words melded into one another, a soothing murmur in her ear. The sharp tone of the off-hook signal would startle Lilah awake. She'd laugh to herself, wondering how long poor Harry had stayed on the line that night, listening to her fall asleep.

There was one day when his call came earlier than expected. Words tumbling over each other, he said one of his former colleagues, Eriksson, was killed in a terrorist attack in Spain. Harry was in Gateway's Bombay office... no chance of making it stateside in time for the funeral service. "May I visit you?" he asked. "Just for a bit." With all the festival celebrations currently going on in the streets of Bombay, no one would pay much mind to one of the thousands of foreign tourists in the city. Their mission wouldn't be compromised. Plus, Hoda knew Alex sent Rekha to Gateway, lending at least flimsy cover for Harry's visit.

"Yes," Lilah said, interrupting his stream of unnecessary rationalizations.

In an hour, she was at the barred window of the apartment, peering out. It was only afternoon, but men and women and children were already on the streets with firecrackers and sparklers, ready to celebrate the last night of Diwali, the major religious festival in this part of the country. Garbage was piled high at the end of the block, and next to it was a broken-down car which had been there since Lilah moved into Rekha's rooms. Bollywood songs blasted from a loudspeaker affixed to one of the electric posts, and the humid air reeked of burned fireworks.

"Rekha," Lilah called over her shoulder. "I see Harry... could you go and get him before he gets completely lost, please?"

Five minutes later, Harry walked in with Rekha. Correction: both of them danced in sideways, Harry singing Stevie Wonder's "Part-Time Lover" as Rekha belted out the Hindi song playing on the loudspeakers outside. One quick whirl... Harry was next to Lilah, twirling her into a chair. She laughed helplessly, and he went down on one knee, spreading his arms with exaggerated flourish.

Only those who knew him well would've spotted the glimmer of grief lurking in the coffee-dark eyes. Laughter petered off as she tilted her head in silent concern, but all he did in response was toss her a wink.

Sitting next to each other at the wobbly table in Rekha's room, they ate the spicy vegetable biryani their hostess pilfered from the community potluck. The rice was overdone and oversalted even to Lilah's strictly utilitarian palate, but Harry stuffed his face with it. *"C'est délicieux!"* he complimented in French and blew chef's kisses, sending Rekha into delighted titters. She even brought out for their guest a bottle of the local wine she loved.

"Hey, since you're around," Rekha said to Harry in Hindi. "I can leave Lilah here and help my friend at the theater." Bootlegged movie tickets were apparently a major source of income for said friend, and festival nights meant big business. Rekha would get a cut, and she'd be partying until dawn with the extra cash.

"Just don't tell anyone Harry's here," Lilah warned.

Rekha stuck her lip out in a pout. *Of course* she'd been planning to claim—truthfully this time—that Harry Sheppard spent Diwali night in her room.

Only after Rekha left did Harry talk about his colleague who was killed by terrorists. Apparently, the officer had been a mentor of sorts to Harry when he first joined the navy. Bits and pieces of his time as Eriksson's junior partner, the thorough chewing out they once got from a superior... Harry bragged they'd visited every seedy bar in every country in the Mediterranean region. No concrete details were offered of the jobs they were sent to do in those countries. Given the nature of the problems in the particular area and what little Lilah knew of Harry's prior work... yeah, clandestine business. In fact, she was left with the distinct impression Petty Officer Eriksson died in the line of duty, not as an innocent bystander in the terrorist attack.

There were no tears from Harry, but every now and then, he would pause as though finding it difficult to continue talking.

Her heart aching for him, she leaned closer to envelop him in her embrace, to kiss away his grief. A glint... the wedding ring on his finger... dropping her arms, Lilah almost ran to the little kitchen under the pretext of fetching cold water. Leaning her forehead against the side of the fridge, she berated herself in mutters. "Stupid! Stupid, stupid, stupid."

When she returned to Harry's side, he took the water and downed it in one long gulp. "Thanks... it's like a sauna in here." Leaning back in the cheap plastic chair, Harry stretched his legs out. "America owes men like Eriksson, but no one will ever know what he... the number of lives he saved..."

"Unsung hero," murmured Lilah, grateful her best friend didn't seem to have noticed her momentary foolishness. "Would he have wanted to make any of it public?"

"No way," Harry said. "Secretive S.O.B. Hell, I doubt he even took a piss without first checking the latrine for listening devices." When Lilah snickered, Harry joined in. The bittersweet mirth was followed by a sudden sheen in his eyes. "Eriksson died exactly as he would've wanted... keeping his promises to his countrymen."

"And he left behind at least one person who will always remember him with warmth and gratitude."

Harry smiled. "Thank you," he said, punching her lightly on the shoulder.

Eventually, the fireworks and the music and the laughter in the street outside got too loud to talk without hollering, and Harry cajoled Lilah into playing poker. As usual, he carried cards with him. They played a couple of rounds which he of course won. He *cheated,* but Harry would never cop to it. Tossing her cards onto the table, Lilah bellowed, "I quit!"

He only chortled in response.

Harry later dozed off on the faux-leather couch way too small for his frame, a dusty table fan blowing warm air onto him.

Sometime before daybreak, Lilah woke in her narrow bed. Almost immediately, there was a knock on her door. It was a wonder she even heard it what with the unrelenting noise from the streets. Harry was up—sweat plastering his dark hair to his scalp but the shadows in his face a great deal lighter. Standing under the dim yellow glow thrown by the single bulb, he muttered with his usual mischief that he wished he could hole up in the little house with her until the end of time, but it simply wasn't meant to be.

The moment the words were out, his gaze widened as though a wayward thought unexpectedly pushed its way into his conscious mind. His glance dropped to her lips before flicking quickly back to her eyes. Harry stared at her with a strange expression, a curious combination of riotous joy and aching passion and bleak futility.

Suddenly, Lilah was afraid of what he was going to say. *Don't,* she begged in silence.

An awkward hush descended. They hadn't done anything thus far which went against marriage vows. There was nothing—not even a handhold—she could point to as wrong, but none of it was right. Lilah couldn't let it go on. Harry wouldn't want to, either. Out of the corner of her eye, she watched him curl and uncurl his fingers a few times. It took him a couple of minutes to murmur, "Talk to you later," before striding out of the house into the slums of Bombay where the party was still on full blast.

Lilah spent the next few weeks telling herself the sooner the mission was over, the better for all concerned. When the call she was expecting came, it *would* be over. The last act of her time in India would begin, the confrontation with the criminal gang. Not long after, the network's charter would be signed. Then would come the final battle, the one with Temple and Godwin.

Chapter 34

Two months later, December 1987

Calcutta, India

The shrill double ring of the telephone jettisoned Alex from sleep. Switching on the bedside lamp in the hotel room, he mumbled into the handset, "Hello?"

"We have the merchandise," said Hoda. "Prince's people got it across the border at Ngur, and the minister has standing arrangements with check post officers along the way here. Until we move the stuff to China, it will be stored at a tea garden in Siliguri Netaji owns. The place has been closed a long time. Labor disputes."

"I'll be there."

Testily, Hoda said, "Not necessary. Sheila can inspect the merchandise since she was so picky about quality."

Alex was completely awake now. "She has already signed off on the quality. Tony and I can confirm the quantity. Fifteen million is a lot of money, Hoda. As our president is fond of saying, 'trust, but verify.' Plus, you'd better remind Netaji and the minister they also agreed to show up. If I'm risking my ass, *they're* damn well going to. No one's doing a double cross." Prince couldn't be around in person. He was someone on the Indian government's list of wanted criminals and couldn't be in the country for more than a few hours at a time without risking capture. His absence didn't really matter in terms of finding proof against him. Most of the world already knew he was a criminal, but he managed to evade the long arm of the law, anyway. The rest were going down. The U.S. would later attempt to get Prince extradited on the same charges.

Hoda snorted. "The minister and Netaji didn't survive this long in this trade by being stupid. Everyone involved needs to be on record on this. Like you said... less chance of double cross. Tony was at Pasighat. His little assistant has thus far kept her hands reasonably clean. But she needs to show up at least at the handover, or the whole deal's off."

Hell! Alex swore in his mind. *Now what, Harry?* He would be hearing the whole conversation over the phone line.

"We'll move the merchandise to China tomorrow night," said Hoda. "So Tony won't make it here in time, anyway."

#

Next morning

Siliguri, India

The signpost Alex spent an hour looking for lay corroding on the ground by the entrance to the tea garden. Liam got out of the Range Rover and gingerly put a hand on the rusting gates to push them open. The squeak was loud and harsh in the stillness of the empty street. There was a gatehouse inside, but it was empty.

They drove through and got to a cluster of buildings, one with a plaque proclaiming it as the office. As they parked, Liam asked, "What office?"

"When this place actually planted tea, I suppose," Alex muttered.

Breaths puffing white in the cold, they jogged to the building. A black Mercedes van with tinted windows sat next to the one-story structure.

Alex sneezed and brushed aside the cobwebs at the front door. A skinny spider scrambled to safety.

From one of the inner rooms, Hoda walked into the lobby. The union leader offered the other two men coffee spiked with rum. "We will stay here until evening, then drive to Nathu La. The observation post is not manned heavily after dark this time of the year. The minister is joining us there."

"What do you mean?" Alex asked, barely holding back curses. "I thought the minister was coming *here?* No funny business from your side, okay?" All the carefully made plans to whisk Sheila off as soon the minister and Netaji arrived at the gates... running a thumb lightly over his sweater, Alex made sure the wire was still there.

Hoda shook his head. "No, no. It's too risky *here*, but the minister will definitely be at the pass. We have friendly folks at the Indian post tonight. The Chinese don't have as good a view of our side from their side, so our mule packs should easily get through." He eyed Alex and Liam head to toe, all the way to the mountain boots and leather gloves. "You're dressed warm enough."

Before Alex could respond, a light-blue Ambassador car arrived. When Sheila walked in, clad in a voluminous red turtleneck and thick jeans and snow boots, Hoda said something in Hindi. Alex caught the word border post. Rekha stood at the door and frowned at the room in general.

Sheila barely glanced at Alex, but he spotted the suspicion of a trick by Hoda and gang. Casually, Alex brought his hand even with his head and waved a bit, hoping like hell she'd somehow figure out the military signal to advance. The CIA, Indian intelligence, Harry... they would all have heard the conversation. Either they'd call a halt to the operation and send officers to extract her, or they'd devise an alternative plan. Those in the building would wait and see what happened.

Turning to Hoda, Sheila instructed in English, "Here or at the border, make sure you deliver what you promised. Also, please get extra coats and earmuffs for the rest of us."

"Devil of a woman," Hoda said as she left the room in search of a latrine, Rekha in tow. "No expression at all. Like a ghost." He shuddered.

There were no surprise vehicles driving in, no soldiers thundering to Sheila's rescue. When it was time to leave, Alex inclined his head very slightly at her. Whatever the plan Harry and his associates had come up with, they would make sure she stayed safe.

"*She* can sit with the crates in the back of the van," Hoda said, nodding at Sheila. "There's space enough for her and the hijra. Since you trust Tony, you should have no problem trusting Sheila. And *I* need her as insurance."

Alex had no good response except to once again feel the wire through his sweater.

"Rekha and I will be fine," said Sheila.

Alex nodded. The ladies would be able to handle Hoda. Besides, both women were supposed to be packing heat.

The afternoon sun threw long, dark shadows across the entrance to the estate. Alex and Liam watched from the Range Rover as Hoda leaned out from his Mercedes and shouted in the direction of the gatehouse. A skinny young man with lanky hair and a pencil-thin mustache came running out and pushed the squeaky gates open. Hoda's black van drove out, followed by Alex's vehicle.

The sketch Harry later makes for the CIA of the drug route through India.

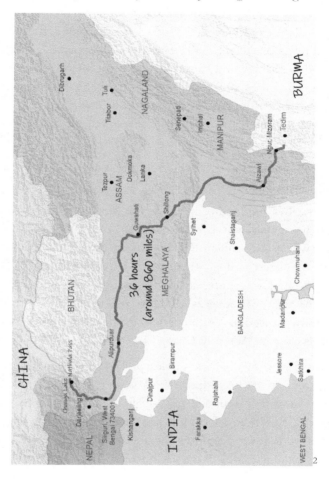

[2] *(DATASET CITATION: Tozer, B, Sandwell, D. T., Smith, W. H. F., Olson, C., Beale, J. R., & Wessel, P. (2019). Global bathymetry and topography at 15 arc sec: SRTM15+. Distributed by OpenTopography. https://doi.org/10.5069/G92R3PT9. Accessed: 2022-03-19*

NASA Shuttle Radar Topography Mission (SRTM)(2013). Shuttle Radar Topography Mission (SRTM) Global. Distributed by OpenTopography. https://doi.org/10.5069/G9445JDF. Accessed: 2022-03-19)

The road from Siliguri to Nathu La took them up the Himalaya Mountains, the trees packing the forest on either side getting shorter and shorter as they climbed. The sun soon disappeared. There was no moon in the sky and no streetlamps, but an almost unearthly glow drenched the night, the headlights from the two automobiles adding to it. Inside the Range Rover, it was pleasantly warm. Bollywood's version of disco music streamed out of the cassette player.

Liam hummed along, but Alex's heart was in his throat at the thought of the two women in the van.

About five hours into the drive, the Mercedes in front swung hard right, taking him by surprise. "What the—" Yanking the steering wheel, Alex took the Range Rover through the wide trail at the side of a large boulder where a wooden signpost read "Changu Lake." The path was short and ended next to a body of water frozen solid, the van's headlights glinting on the ice. Dark peaks surrounded the lagoon. "Another detour," he muttered into the wire under his clothes. "We're at Changu Lake."

Leaving his own lights on, Alex parked next to the Mercedes. Hoda stood at the back door of his vehicle, arguing with Sheila. Their quiet voices sounded ghostly in the utter silence of the mountains. Rekha stood behind her charge, not saying anything. Alex walked to them, Liam right behind. Both had their backpacks, weapons hidden inside. "What's happening?" Liam asked.

Nonchalantly, Hoda said, "The minister called me before we left. He's meeting us here, instead. Less risky."

Shit!

Another pair of headlights blinked farther into the detour, but no engines rumbled. The minister and his four guards walked from a shadowed vehicle, Netaji with them. "Tony's local contact?" the minister asked Hoda, nodding at Sheila and Rekha.

There was a rapid barrage of Hindi from Hoda before he went to the van. Dragging the crates out, he slit them open. Two of the bodyguards gestured at Alex and Liam, making them step back until they were almost at the edge of the lake. The remaining two muscle-bound thugs stuck close to the criminals. With the aid of a flashlight, the politician inspected the crates of individually wrapped cardboard boxes. Each held several one-kilogram packets of heroin powder for sale to subordinates. Sheila stood at the back door of the vehicle, watching the proceedings.

Alex's heart thumped slowly, painfully. *Where the... Harry, dammit! We need help here.* His submachine gun was in the backpack by his feet. He didn't dare reach for it, not with Sheila and Rekha around as potential hostages. No matter how many weapons the women carried, he didn't want to start an open gunfight and risk them.

"Rekha," Sheila called in a clipped voice, snapping out some order in Hindi. Tugging the lapels of her coat closer together, Rekha clambered into the cargo area of the van. Sheila closed the door and walked to the driver's side.

"Hey, what're you doing?" asked Hoda, irritated.

"We're cold," she told him, her voice no less freezing than the air. "I'm turning the heat on."

With an annoyed huff, Hoda said to Alex, "In that case, *you* count the packages and do the confirmation."

Within seconds after Sheila secured herself inside, a muffled report sounded. The guard in front of Alex collapsed to the ground. The military intelligence team! Finally!

Alex bent down and retrieved his weapon from his backpack the same moment the other bodyguard took a step rearward, shouting, "Hey."

The minister, Netaji, and Hoda looked up. So did the two thugs with them.

The van started. Liam had his gun out as well and aimed it at the fellow standing directly in front, shooting him point-blank.

Then, diving down, both Liam and Alex started shooting. Guns roared.

The politicians and the union leader had dropped to the ground as soon as they saw weapons in the hands of the Americans. Liam rolled to avoid the bullets coming his way, crowding Alex, who slipped onto the thick ice on the lake.

When the Mercedes moved away, Hoda crawled around and shot at the windows. "Go for the tires," screamed the minister. The loud bursts of the tires sounded like gunshots themselves.

The van swerved and went over the bank onto the frozen lake. It slid, unable to get traction. The headlights zigged and zagged. All the men watched, arrested by the same realization. If the vehicle hit a thin patch, if the ice cracked...

"The merchandise," howled Hoda.

The van didn't fall through. Instead, it continued sliding over the smooth surface straight at Alex. He rolled away as the wheels spun past barely an inch from his ear. Not even trying to stand, he continued firing. A third bodyguard crumpled.

Hitting the rocky bank, the out-of-control Mercedes came to a stop. Alex slid on his chest toward the enemy and got a few rounds off. There was a scream... sounded like Hoda, but the union leader was still crouching.

The remaining bodyguard was firing continuously as were the minister and Hoda. Netaji appeared unarmed. Alex tried to lift his head to check on Liam but dove back when a bullet scraped the sheet of ice next to him. The next one hit his shoulder. Blood stained the frozen surface of the lake.

"Don't let her take the merchandise," the minister shouted, scooting back toward the shadows. The spot was now lit by the van's lights, revealing what looked like an armored vehicle.

Oh, no, Alex thought, *you're not getting away.* Before he could fire, he heard Liam bellow he was hit.

The minister was screaming, too, scrambling into the back of the armored car. "Drive out!" he yelled. Netaji scrambled in after him.

The driver's side door opened, and Netaji's bespectacled assistant came out. In one fluid movement, he retrieved something from inside and bent toward the minister. Two shots. The minister slumped in his seat, a bullet hole in the middle of his forehead. Netaji gurgled once, twice, in surprise, before he, too, died.

The remaining bodyguard dropped his weapon and put his hands up. After a dazed look around him, so did Hoda. The assistant marched them at gunpoint to where Liam was. Behind him, Harry and his partner strode out from the cover of a large rock. Harry's gun was in his right hand, the left gripping the knife he used since his SEAL training days—a curvy beauty called Ari B'Lilah. He sprinted to the van, pulling open the driver's side door. "Are you all right?" he shouted.

There was an indecipherable mumble from inside.

Dragging himself to the bank, Alex clambered out and stumbled to Harry's side. His wounded shoulder was almost screaming in pain, but seeing "Sheila" more or less intact, Alex breathed, "Thank God."

"Rekha?" Harry called. The response in Hindi from the back of the Mercedes had him nodding, his relief apparent.

"Can I get some help here?" Sheila asked. "I don't want to risk stepping on thin ice."

In one quick move, Harry scooped her out and deposited her on safe ground. Rekha was assisted out by Liam.

Tapping Sheila's nose with his finger, Alex said, "At least you can get rid of the ridiculous prosthesis now. And *I* can go back to thinking of you as Lilah."

She laughed, the sound slightly jittery. As Netaji's apparent assistant—the one who saved the day by shooting his boss and the minister—strode toward her, she sketched a salute at the bespectacled fellow. "I'm fine, Shankar."

"You know him?" asked Alex. Turning to the chap, he redirected the question. "Who are you, man? I barely noticed you."

The assistant took off his spectacles. Somehow, he didn't look as humble and subservient as he did before. Crew-cut black hair, neat mustache under his nose, military stance. "Lieutenant General Shivshankar Mittal, Director of Military Intelligence. I'm the cousin of Lilah's who Harry talked to when you first contacted him about Hoda. We already had Hoda under surveillance as well as my 'boss,' Netaji, for suspected bribery of military personnel. We didn't know the minister was the kingpin until you set things into motion with your million-dollar donation."

Lilah and Rekha waited in the Range Rover while the rest cleaned up. The soldier with Harry handcuffed Hoda and the remaining bodyguard and tossed them in the armored car. The dead bodies were thrown into the back of the van. Mittal was wearing his own wire and talked to his team, updating them on the situation. The intelligence officers assigned to apprehend the criminals were still stuck at the crossing which was the previously intended handover location. Harry and his partner were supposed to come in only at the end to retrieve the Americans. Thankfully, his vehicle was not far behind Alex's and got to the lake in time to help.

"Here or at the border, the outcome would not have changed," said Mittal. "A trial would not have worked. They would've gone to any length to keep themselves out of jail... inciting riots, killing judges, whatever it took. Nor could we arrange straight-up assassinations without legal types getting their knickers in knots about civilian control. Now, the military has evidence of wrongdoing to show the authorities, and we can honestly claim the two crooks were killed in a shootout. The public... yeah, they wouldn't like it, but they're not going to know all the details. Tomorrow's newspapers will announce the deaths of the two esteemed leaders. They will be remembered as courageous civilians who sacrificed their lives, helping the army apprehend smugglers. Hell, they might even get posthumous recognition for bravery. Hoda is easier to take care of, especially since his bosses are no longer around."

Wrapping the handkerchief offered by Harry around his injured arm, Liam eyed Lilah. "So your 'boss'... Tony... is he CIA or Indian?"

"Tony's an agent with the Hong Kong police," Harry clarified. "The CIA contacted him. *I* called Shankar at his office and was told he'd be monitoring the situation from the Indian side. Couldn't tell you since he put both Lilah and me under a gag order."

"Thanks for all the help, Harry," said General Mittal, offering a handshake. "It was good working with you."

Turning the gesture into a one-armed hug, Harry said, "Same here, Shankar. I'll see you in Delhi before we wrap up and return home."

"I can't believe your own cousin let you get involved," muttered Alex, squinting blurrily at Lilah. Damn... his shoulder hurt. He flexed it a touch. *Oh,* yeah. It *hurt*. He needed to get it looked at as soon as they were done here.

"Why not?" General Mittal asked. "Harry insisted on someone he could completely trust, and so did I. And that someone needed to be able to blend in."

Alex only grunted in response, his annoyance making Rekha laugh.

Harry laughed as well, but the sound was shaky. He clapped Alex on the shoulder.

An electric bolt of pain shot through Alex's upper back and into his head. He blinked hard to clear his vision and saw his brother-in-law stare at the sticky blood coating his gloved hand. "Sonuvabitch," Alex mumbled. Then, for the first time in his life, Alex Kingsley fainted.

Chapter 35

A week later, December 31, 1987

Sikkim, India

Rumtek, the mountaintop monastery of Buddhist faith, was gorgeous. Alex walked with Lilah, their pace slow as she rotated the prayer wheels. Harry and Liam were strolling in front, talking in muted voices.

"What are you praying for?" Alex asked, flexing his shoulder and grimacing when sutures tightened across his wound. The bullet had been dug out, and the gash stitched by surgeons at the local army base. The Americans were asked to stay put in the region while the CIA and the Indian military collaborated, documenting the incident and deciding which details would be released to the public. Thankfully, there were guesthouses around the Buddhist shrine.

"I wasn't praying," she muttered, her thoughts seemingly far away. "Maybe I should. We could definitely use some divine intervention."

"With what?" Alex asked.

Lilah halted. "We need to be careful about security. Remember how many people wanted Sanders gone. We'll be bigger than he ever was... with more enemies... Hoda and Prince... God knows who else."

"True," Alex mused. "Prince is a friend of the Noriega regime. Everyone involved in the network will now need security... not only you and Brad... the rest of us, the board members..."

Eyes snapping wide open, Lilah stuttered, "The board? Yeah... and the chairman."

They weren't too far from the formation of a formal governing structure. The network's first meeting would happen soon, at which a board would be elected. "Whoever we pick as chairman will be in an extremely powerful position. The fellow will definitely need protection."

"Powerful," Lilah parroted. "Right." She glanced at Harry. He and Liam were now a few feet ahead but still within earshot. "We need to hire more guards," she repeated.

After a short time, the four of them sat on a cast-iron bench, the peak dropping off to a cliff mere inches beyond their feet. Tonsured monks in fluttering red robes walked about the large, open courtyard, uncaring of the freezing cold. Chants from inside the shrine-temple echoed through the pristine green forest behind. All around them, sun glinted off the snow-covered crests of the Himalayas.

"Peaceful," Harry murmured.

"Peace might be one of the things permanently lost to us," said Alex. At the inquiring looks on the other faces, he clarified, "Lilah thinks Prince might send Noriega after us."

Lilah glanced toward the buildings of the shrine. "Not just Noriega. There are other things to worry about. Power corrupts, and even the most well-meaning of us can make bad decisions. So we need to strengthen the checks and balances in our own charter. No matter who's at the top, the person should never be able to cross certain lines. Also, anyone who... umm... could be thinking of dethroning us might think again if leadership gets them nothing except responsibility."

"Make it so unpalatable so no one would want it?" Harry asked. "Might work to some extent. Ahem... talking about power corrupting... Alex, Rekha is terrorizing Dalal Street. The manager of the Bombay office made her security guard and gave her a pistol. She's very proud of it. Told some local thugs to go ahead and make her day."

Alex roared with laughter, the rest joining in. The sounds of their hilarity drew attention from a couple of passing monks, the dignified censure in their eyes causing the Americans to mumble apologies. Wiping her watery eyes, Lilah said, "I need to talk to the nuns. A girl I know in the local orphanage wants to study in America."

"Is this the same orphanage?" Alex asked Harry, remembering the story of the former SEAL's encounter with Sanders's misdeeds in India. One of the henchmen of the criminal oilman had a sideline in child sex trafficking, and fortunately for the girls involved, Harry happened on them. He took them to a children's home.

"The same," Harry said. "Gateway supports the home," he explained to Liam.

"Really?" asked Liam. "Verity never said anything."

"You work for Gateway, and you didn't know," Harry pointed out.

As Lilah went to the nuns' hostel, Harry said, "Rekha will be here any minute now. She's running some errands for me."

Laughing again, Liam said, "You'd better hope it doesn't get back to Verity. She's gonna think Rekha's the reason you've been flying to India almost every week. Aren't you supposed to be Rekha's... er... patron?"

"You should talk," retorted Harry. "Alex told me you introduced him to one of *your* friends."

A moment passed before Alex got it, then he groaned. "Lemme explain... he's talking about Lupe Valdez... Eden."

Liam stilled for a second at the mention of the strip club owner's name, his face turning slightly red. "Lupe's a good friend... nothing more and nothing less. The business she chose to run is simply that... a business."

"No insult intended," Harry said immediately. "The club of hers is precisely what I'm interested in."

Shaking his head, Alex elaborated, "He thinks Lupe would be a useful contact."

"Ahh," Liam murmured, understanding dawning in his eyes. "Her connections."

"I don't care," Alex said. "We're not going there, all right? I can just imagine trying to explain to my wife... we'll make do with a little less info."

"Lupe's not likely to agree, anyway," Liam said part-apologetically. "The club members wouldn't like it if she tattled."

"She must have picked up a lot of gossip about the people in DC," said Harry. "Politicians, lawyers, judges, diplomats... dirty deals, sexual games, family skeletons..."

"Good Lord," Liam muttered. "If Lupe ever talked about any of it, her life wouldn't be worth pennies. The people who go to her club are probably some of the most powerful men in the world."

Instant remorse clouded Harry's eyes. "You're right... my bad."

When Harry sauntered to the golden pillar in front of the monastery to examine the markings on it, Alex said to Liam, "Don't say anything to anyone about Lilah's presence here. Not even to Verity. Please?"

"Heh?" Liam frowned. "Was it supposed to be a secret she's in India? I thought her office staff knew."

Plus, Brad and the rest of the Kingsleys, Lilah's brother, and whoever else cared to check. Only, her real self and alter ego were kept disconnected, with the publicly visible Lilah Kingsley nowhere near where Alex or Harry happened to be at any given moment. "I mean, her part in this operation."

Liam snorted. "The CIA would throw my ass in jail if I blabbed. And you know Verity. When was my sister ever interested in anything to do with work?"

"Just making sure," Alex explained awkwardly. "There's been some gossip about Lilah and me. Those tabloids. You've seen the stories."

"Ahh."

"You'd expect family to understand, but they don't. Not always."

From ten feet away, Harry shouted, "Here she is." A sari-clad form hurried forward, the edge of the fabric draped over her head.

"Shh," said Rekha, handing Harry a large cloth bag.

"Come over here," Harry gestured to Alex and Liam. When they clustered around, Harry drew two bottles from the bag. A yellow-orange liquid. "It's New Year's Eve, and we're in this beautiful place. I thought we should celebrate. Rekha suggested the perfect way."

"What is it?" Alex asked.

Harry explained, "Bhang. It's buttermilk with mango and a touch of cinnamon."

"Milkshake?" Liam asked, tone dubious. "I don't—"

Harry grinned. "And a special ingredient: ground cannabis."

Liam gawked. "*Weed* milkshake?"

"Dude," Alex objected. "We just got done with..."

Rekha muttered something, translating it herself. "Silly... bhang not same as the other thing... other thing dangerous. Make young people sick. Prince bad man. You good men."

If Rekha first agreed to help the Americans only because of the request from Shawn Barrons, she now considered them her bosom pals. Not only did she have a steady job thanks to Alex and Harry, they defeated Prince! He was apparently a known figure in Goa, where Rekha hailed from. When Harry named the drug lord's Indian cousin, Rekha nodded vigorously. Said cousin owned a beach resort, and rumor had it Prince used the place to connect with other narco cartels. Rekha bemoaned what was becoming of her home state and insisted it was no coincidence Lilah ended up hiring a Goan as her guard. In His infinite wisdom, God surely directed the Americans to the right person.

"But bhang different!" Rekha concluded. "It's medicine! Holy medicine!"

"Huh?" said Liam.

With a laugh, Harry shook his head. "It's not illegal here." Apparently, the Indian government didn't include bhang in the definition of cannabis laid out in the Narcotic Drugs and Psychotropic Substances Act. Good thing, too. Folklore had it God himself brought it down to earth, and the population consumed it with great gusto to reach transcendental bliss or to cure ailments of all kinds. No politician would want to piss off deities... er... voters by banning bhang. "Rekha even got it from a government-approved store," finished Harry.

In silence, the four of them stared at the bottles. Finally, Alex said, "In some places, it is considered offensive if foreign guests refuse to partake in local customs. Rekha, please pour me a glass."

"True," agreed Liam. "We should be respectful of our hosts."

They settled on the ground in a quiet corner of the courtyard, the bottles and four steel tumblers in the center. It was far enough from the monks but close enough for Lilah to find them without much searching. A chilly breeze blew, making them all shiver.

Thick, creamy, and sweet, the liquid made its way down Alex's throat. The cold nearly froze his gullet. "Would have been perfect on a summer day," he said, wiping the traces off his lip with the back of his hand. He finished the drink and gestured at Rekha to pour him another. "So God brought it down?" Alex asked. "Why?"

"It was His favorite snack," Harry explained.

Topping up Alex's tumbler, Rekha asked something in Hindi.

Laughing, Harry interpreted, "She wants to know if you ever used *ghanja* before."

"Alex?" Liam chortled.

Affronted, Alex said, "I have, too. When I was twenty."

"Oh, yeah?" Harry asked.

"Brad caught us," confessed Alex. "Victor and me, I mean."

Harry poured more into his own tumbler, smacking the bottom of the first bottle with the heel of his hand to get every drop out. "We should keep some for Lilah." Gulping down more of the stuff, he asked, "So what happened when Brad found you and Victor?"

"Nothing," Alex said. "He looked so sad we swore never to do it again." Tears trickled down Alex's cheek, unnerving him. There was a heaviness in his chest, an incredible fear of getting caught. What the hell was he afraid of? He was a grown man now—free to do as he pleased.

"Sad!" shouted Liam.

"Phew," Harry said. "It's pretty hot for a winter in the Himalayas. I'm sweating." He stripped off his jacket and threw it to the side.

Chants rose from the shrine, ringing through the mountains. "Loud, aren't they?" someone complained from behind Alex. He twisted around, but no one was there. "Did you guys hear it?" he asked, turning back to his friends.

"Hear what?" Harry asked.

As Alex watched, Harry's body splintered into diamond-shaped shards, drifting apart.

"Hey," Alex screamed and leaped up. "Stop him."

"Stop who?" Liam looked up and down.

"He's..." Frantically, Alex grabbed at the shards, trying to put them back into the shape of Harry. "He's flying away."

Someone tugged at his arm, and he fell to the ground to see Harry in front. He appeared intact, with no missing pieces.

"You... you're still here." Alex giggled.

Rekha stood and belted out a song in Hindi, a wrist held dramatically to her forehead and her other hand on her hip.

Harry clapped, saying, *"Wah, wah."*

"Encore!" Liam exclaimed as though echoing Harry.

Holding onto Liam's shoulder for support, Harry heaved himself up and joined Rekha in singing and dancing.

"...*Hawa Hawaii,*" continued Rekha. "Song from movie," she explained. *"Mr. India."*

"*I* wanna dance," Alex whined, watching the leaps, the twirls, the heaving bosoms. *A kaleidoscope,* he thought a few minutes later. Or it could have been a few seconds. Or hours. He didn't know. As a child, he'd always wondered what it would be like to live inside a kaleidoscope. Now, he knew.

Visitors to the shrine, attracted by the noise, gathered around, pointing and laughing. Puzzled monks looked on. At the periphery of the crowd, Alex saw Lilah, her eyes first widening in shock, then shooting sparks.

When she pushed her way through the onlookers, Harry was in the middle of an energetic twirl. He spotted her and wobbled on his feet, grabbing her coat sleeve to keep himself upright. Grazing her chin with a knuckle, he switched to a soft croon. Unfortunately for him, Lilah did not appear impressed. Not even mildly amused.

Waggling his eyebrows, Harry asked, "Want some bhang? I saved some for you."

Okay, she was definitely unamused. Unless slitted eyes and flaring nostrils were barometers of mirth.

Rekha burped. "Uh oh."

Swaying on his feet, Liam tittered. "You wanna translate?"

Alex was aware of Lilah escorting them out with the help of the staff from the shrine. She and the monks dragged Rekha and the American men to the entrance of the guesthouse, Harry's weight hanging around Lilah's neck. Rekha planted a smooch on a young monk.

At the foot of the stairs, Alex looked up. The steps seemed to stretch into infinity.

Apparently, Harry agreed. "Too long," he complained.

There was a sudden yelp from him. Alex looked around to see Lilah's fingers twisting Harry's ear.

"Not nice," Alex chided.

"Get up there," she snapped.

One foot hovering over the bottom step, Liam whimpered, "She's scary."

Alex nodded in wholehearted agreement.

#

Sometime later

There was something heavy sitting on Alex's leg. *A dog?* He didn't have a dog. His lids seemed stuck to his eyeballs. With great difficulty, he raised his free foot and kicked out, hoping to dislodge the animal.

In less than a second, a heavy form landed on his chest, crushing the breath out of him. His eyes snapped open. Above the dark shadow hovering over him, lights floated around the ceiling, tilting one way, then the other. "Hey," he tried to shout, clawing at the grip around his throat.

Suddenly, the grip loosened. The shadow cursed in a familiar voice. When Alex blinked away the bleariness, the shadow morphed into Harry.

"What happened?" Alex croaked. "Why were you trying to kill me?"

Things came into sharper focus. They were in one of the spacious but modestly furnished rooms at the guesthouse. The sweet-and-sour smell of... something... clung to his clothes. He was in the same jeans and bulky jacket he wore for the walk around the monastery.

A groan rose from the floor. Harry slid off the bed the same moment Liam sat up on the carpet. "I'm hungry," he complained.

A few minutes later

Belly churning, Alex stared at the glasses of clear liquid aligned neatly on the table. Lilah was squeezing lemons into each, adding sugar and salt.

"Idiots," she exclaimed, irritation in the glance she swept over the three culprits sprawled in various positions. The fourth one cowered in a chair: Rekha with the kohl she habitually wore smudged, her skin sickly pale. Waving her arms about, Lilah berated the woman in rapid-fire Hindi, her pitch rising sky high at the end of each sentence. When Lilah paused to take a breath, Rekha attempted to respond, but she couldn't get a syllable out before Lilah resumed her tirade.

Spoon tinkled against glass as Lilah stirred the concoction violently enough to have a quarter of it spill to the floor. She strode to Alex's chair and thrust the drink under his nose.

Turning to the bed, she dragged the pillow off Harry's head and shouted, "You! You should've known better. Bhang! *Bhang!* One glass is supposed to be more potent than an entire bottle of ten-year-old single malt! What were you thinking?"

Harry hauled himself up, hair disheveled and face flushed. With both hands supporting his head, he begged, *"Chup kar, meri maa."*

There was sudden silence from Lilah. Then, she bent and screeched directly into Harry's ear. Alex jumped, his stomach threatening to upchuck the contents. Lilah stalked out, leaving Harry moaning in pain.

"Did you *have* to make her madder?" Liam grumbled. "What did you say?"

From the chair in the corner, Rekha muttered, "Harry saab call her *maa*. 'No talk, my mother.'"

Alex laughed but hurriedly stopped when an invisible mallet hammered his temples with each movement of his chest.

Tone doleful, Rekha murmured, *"Ghar jaana hai."*

The words made absolutely no sense to Alex, but Rekha's woebegone expression mirrored the sentiment in his heart. An intense yearning for home and hearth.

#

Hoda was set up for a quick trial and expected to be in prison for a long time. Thanks to the recordings made by the CIA, a New York court charged Prince with trying to import one thousand tons of heroin into the country, but Burma refused to extradite him.

On hearing the news, Harry, Alex, and Lilah glanced at each other, no one vocalizing the worry writ large on all their faces. Men like Prince didn't forget slights, let alone actual losses. The Kingsleys and Harry needed to keep their eyes open.

For now, they were busy with the final few details of their Asia campaign. The Peter Kingsley Network continued to hold forty percent ownership of the outfits they acquired quite legitimately. Alex's name was discussed a lot in capitals around the world. So was Harry's—the word "kingmaker" was tossed about with increasing frequency. Thus, when Alex brought the network's offer to other oil businesses, most were happy to accept.

"Phase three, complete," Alex said, tone jubilant.

"Mission accomplished," agreed Harry, a strange discomfort in his eyes instead of the triumph Alex expected. With a shake of his head, Harry grinned as though closing the door on some unwelcome thought. "The empire is complete... almost."

Only the charter remained to be signed. Once it was done...

Harry's markings on the world map at the end of the final phase.

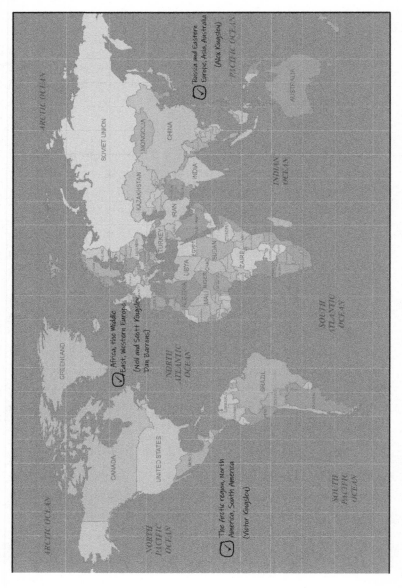

Part XI

Chapter 36

A month later, January 1988

Metropolitan Club, New York City

Every table at the dinner fundraiser was cluttered. Temple's held a tall glass vase wrapped in some sort of goldish material as centerpiece, creamy-white flowers and long green leaves stuck inside. A couple of leather-bound books were piled next to the vase, a small fishbowl on top. Temple imagined the trapped expression on the swimming critter was reflected in the faces of some of the writers gathered. There *were* some big names—the who's who of American literati—at the benefit. So was New York's *crème de la crème*, flashing wealth and glamor and glitter all around. Tuxedos, poufy hairdos, gowns in shiny fabric, sparkly jewelry... the clamor, the chatter, the laughter... damned hot, too, from all the folks crammed into the marble-walled hall at the club. The social events he hosted the last eight years at the White House seemed quite restful all of a sudden.

Godwin had rebuffed all efforts by the hostess to have his presence at the event. The expected attendance of the *nouveau riche* was enough to put him off. Andrew Barrons didn't have quite the same stick up his backside Godwin did about new money, but he also sent regrets.

Temple showed up because the presence of a former president lent prestige to such events, so the scholarship program for gifted young writers was likely to collect more money. Noah, as the author of a couple of well-regarded legal tomes, was also present.

But the main draw for both men was Brad's attendance, no Lilah, no brothers with him tonight. Temple wanted to talk to Brad without it looking like a planned encounter. Assured by the support of the former president in addition to the endorsement of his grandfather, Brad Kingsley would not dream Noah's words carried deceit.

Temple glanced across the hall where Brad was in conversation with the new chairman of the Federal Reserve. Lilah should've been at the event. If she deigned to attend a couple of such gatherings and show the public what she was... but no.

Lucky for their plans, Temple told himself. Both his instincts and the periodic updates he received indicated Lilah never shared her childhood trauma with her husband, but a last confirmation was needed before the next move could be played. Only then could the final battle over the network begin. If they didn't get the confirmation, plan B would involve direct attacks until one side or the other succeeded, the uncertainty of which Temple preferred to avoid.

An hour or so passed before Temple could excuse himself. Brad was already perusing the oak bookcases in the library on the second floor of the club when Temple and Noah walked in. They were the only people around thanks to Godwin's courtesy of reserving the use of it for Temple for the evening. Sounds receded as the security detail closed the door.

Temple, Noah, and Brad settled into the chairs set around the fireplace. The former president smiled at the Kingsley scion. "Sorry about calling you up here. It's been a while since we chatted is all."

A red flush worked its way up Brad's elegant face. "You can call me anytime, sir. My brothers and I owe you a great deal."

Temple could see why Godwin chose Brad as the clan's standard-bearer. The oldest of the Kingsley grandsons was also the one most open to listening to family elders. Lilah... she possessed every quality Temple looked for in the ruler of their alliance. If only she understood *realpolitik*. Once Harry was out of the picture, she *would* be forced to negotiate with the people who disagreed with her. She would start heeding the advice of those with more experience or risk losing control over the vast structure she built, something her conscience would balk at. With the lesson learned, Lilah would grow into the leader Temple knew she could be.

With a muted chuckle, Noah said, "Temple was considering visiting you in Panama. Unfortunately, even a former president has to follow security protocol. It would've messed with your schedule."

"I would've made time—" Brad started.

Waving a dismissive hand, Temple said, "You're a busy man."

"Especially since you're the only one at home," commented Noah. "All your brothers are out of the country currently if I'm not mistaken. There have been quite a few articles on how fast the network is growing, thanks to them."

"Managing home territory *is* hectic," said Brad. "And important."

"I agree," Noah said immediately. "Acquisitions get more attention, but protecting home ground is critical. I'm sure at least your CFO understands the fact... your wife. Godwin said something about her going to India. She has family there, right? I suppose she and Alex teamed up for the Asia part of the plan."

The color on Brad's face darkened. "Harry was with Alex. They're best friends, so they like to work together. Lilah was there only to sign off on the finances."

Noah threw a quick glance at Temple. Neither could figure out if Brad knew Lilah was in India on CIA business. He wasn't the sort to be calmly accepting of his wife's decision to go off on covert operations. Temple wasn't sure *he* was all right with it. Her safety...

especially with the Russians supposedly monitoring the situation... but the Indian government swore left and right she'd be protected.

Adjusting himself in the chair, Noah smiled at Brad. "Godwin said he talked to you about a drilling company located stateside."

"Yes," said Brad. "He's supposed to send the details."

Tone casual, Noah continued, "I'm going to Texas on other business, so Godwin asked me to broach the topic with the owner... if you're all right with it, of course."

"Thank you," Brad said, nodding.

"Pillar Oil," Noah said. "Owned by a retired colonel—Sheffield Parker. He's spent time in the Middle East according to your grandfather. Libya, I believe." One second passed. Two seconds. No hint of recognition of the rapist's name appeared on Brad's face. No shock, no anger.

Temple surreptitiously released his breath.

Chapter 37

A week later, February 1988

Cerro Azul, Panama

Smiling indulgently, Patrice accompanied Brad as he showed the former attorney general around the office complex. Brad had invited her to join him and his guest as she knew Noah from the time she lived with Peter. The lawyer once worked for Kingsley Corp, but as Temple's friend, Noah found himself treated more like family in the household. He'd even played a piece on his mandolin for Brad's christening. Patrice learned later that Noah dropped out of Juilliard and joined Yale to the tremendous displeasure of his parents, both musicians.

One thing everyone knew about Noah Andersen was he traveled every chance he got. When he returned home, it was always with fascinating stories and the hottest gossip from the hallways of power. The latest news was rather mundane, though. "I agree with Godwin," Noah said. "Pillar Oil would be a good acquisition for you."

Brad nodded. "Do you know how Grandfather got to hear of this company? It's funny how the name never popped up before. The number of documents my brothers and I reviewed... I could've sworn we went over each and every oil-related business in North America."

Clearing his throat, Noah said, "Pillar is a gem of a business, but it is small. Godwin came across it quite by accident, I believe. It happens."

"Yeah," said Brad. "Let me give Victor a call since he's in charge of the Americas. He was supposed to go to Texas, anyway, to talk to Major Armor." Pausing to frown mildly, Brad added, "Did I tell you Victor just got married?"

"Really?" Noah came to a halt in the middle of the anteroom in Brad's office suite. "Godwin didn't mention anything."

"It was very recent," Brad explained. "Vegas wedding. Come to think of it, Victor might not appreciate being given more work now. I should wait until Alex returns."

Noah held up a hand. "Actually, I was going to suggest you negotiate with Parker yourself. Alex and Victor did the heavy lifting thus far, and it will be good for your wife to know *you're* also willing to get your hands dirty. Keep it a pleasant surprise for her and your brothers."

Patrice frowned. The way the former attorney general was phrasing it—

Brad's secretary came out of her room to tell him Lilah was on the phone.

"Finally!" Brad said, brows drawn once again. Excusing himself, he went inside his private office.

"Brad's wife is still in India, I take it?" Noah asked, settling into the large, comfortable leather couch in the anteroom. There was a *faux* fireplace next to the couch. All the executive suites got one, thanks to the architect's fancy.

Patrice took the chair at one end of the couch. "Lilah is done with her work there, but she has relatives in a small town called Kampil. It's somewhere in the north, close to the capital. Family visits... she'll be back home in a couple of days."

Brad came out, face flushed under the stubble beard he'd recently taken to sporting. His mouth was set in a thin line.

Not again, Patrice despaired. Lilah had gratefully accepted her mother-in-law's offer to help run the household, but it meant Patrice was privy to every piece of gossip among the staff. The separate sleeping arrangements and the daily arguments between the couple were fodder for entertainment for the household. Most of the quarrels centered around Alex. Patrice found the idea laughable... anyone who knew the supposed star-crossed lovers should've laughed, too. Clearly, both moved on from their initial attraction. But Lilah wasn't helping matters with her prolonged absence. Apparently, Brad had pleaded with her to return, reasoned, even ordered... all to no avail. The two of them needed to get their act together. Their marriage didn't involve merely a husband and a wife, for God's sake! A global empire depended on them.

"Short conversation," Noah commented.

Brad adjusted his glasses. "Yes... she was busy."

Gently, Noah smiled. "To be expected since she's combining work and fun. Was Alex with her when you talked?"

Noah's face... he was almost... Patrice couldn't put her finger on it, but she didn't like the sneer.

"Yes," Brad said, voice curt.

"Hopefully, they'll both decide they enjoyed enough vacation and return home soon."

No, Patrice wasn't mistaken... that was definitely a dirty insinuation. "Excuse me, but what do you mean—"

The older man shifted to face her when she started speaking, and at her frown, his eyes turned to hard green emeralds. "Which is fine, since it gave me time to reacquaint myself with you, Patrice. I meant to tell you how well your eldest son is thought of even in a relatively small place like Corpus Christi."

Corpus Christi? Blood drained from her face, leaving her cold. Her mouth dried. *Corpus Christi? He couldn't know... he simply couldn't!*

"All children are dear to a mother, of course, but the firstborn is always special," Noah said, a warning in his gaze. "You must be proud of him."

Through stiff lips, she tried to form words, her mouth twisting in a feeble imitation of a smile. *How can he know? Did Mr. Temple tell him? Oh, God, what's going on?*

"Mother?" Brad touched a gentle hand to her shoulder. "Are you all right?"

Patrice stared at Noah, unable to blink, unable to breathe. *Lilah... he doesn't want me to defend Lilah.* As though in a fog, Patrice turned to face Brad. *God... oh, God, what will I do? I can't let them find out.*

"Perhaps she needs some rest," Noah suggested. "After all, she's been handling everything since Lilah's been gone to help Sabrina through Alex's absence."

Patrice's head jerked around. The lawyer's only response was a soft smile. Shaking with fear, Patrice stayed mute.

"Lemme contact your doctor," Brad said to her. "In the meantime, I want you to lie down." Calling his secretary, he asked her to accompany Patrice to her wing.

At the door, Patrice turned to look at Noah. His bright eyes dared her to reveal all, to put an end to whatever harm he was attempting to inflict on Lilah. *Corpus Christi... how did he find... why...* thoughts whirled in Patrice's mind, none of it adding up. Her gaze shifted to her son. Noah wanted Brad to go to Texas. Patrice couldn't let it happen. As long as Brad stayed away from Corpus Christi, everything would be fine.

Patrice nodded to both men and left them alone. Much later, she would wonder if that was the moment she could've changed destiny.

Chapter 38

A week later, mid February 1988

Corpus Christi, Texas

The plane was ready to land. Through her window, Lilah eyed the puffy white clouds and smiled wistfully at the memory of the months in India. But it was over. The network's charter would soon be signed. The final confrontation loomed, and she needed to make her moves.

She'd already gritted her teeth and called Brad to discuss an important change to the network's corporate charter. The chief executive's office would carry painful responsibility with very little privilege. Temple and Godwin would realize control of the network carried only the burden of accountability.

Also, there was the position of the chairman of the board. Voice clipped, Lilah brought up the reluctance shown by Gateway affiliates. The CEO of the Peter Kingsley Company would remain the CEO of the network up to such a day in the future when they made changes to the leadership structure to allow for some kind of rotation. Until then, any anxieties among other member companies about the Kingsleys turning into autocrats needed to be soothed. The alliance would add a clause to the charter which would force the CEO to follow the elected chairman's instructions or obtain two-thirds majority from the entire board to supersede.

Brad didn't seem resistant to the idea, but of the three people he was most likely to nominate as chairman, Lilah would have to veto all three. Temple or Godwin... no way. There was the man who extolled Brad Kingsley's virtues at every media event. Brad wouldn't imagine a scenario where Harry opposed him. Unfortunately, pushing it through right at the moment meant practically inviting Temple and Godwin to attack Harry. And of course, Harry's was the first name Brad came up with.

Lilah simply stated they could thrash out the particulars at the next meeting of senior executives, but no matter who graced the position, some modifications to the hierarchy were needed. In the back of her mind was another thought she didn't want to acknowledge. There was a chance Harry would end up dead in his attempt to take down her enemies. She didn't know if she would have the strength to carry on after. Even if she did, Brad was not likely to follow her directions, but the changes she proposed would limit the CEO's actions to a great extent.

An hour later, Lilah was in the presidential suite of a magnificent hotel in downtown Corpus Christi. She smiled warmly at the girl Victor introduced as his wife. Lilah didn't know why she was under the impression Victor was still mourning his former girlfriend and mother of his son, Gabe, but it was clearly not the case. Victor, who was generally drawn to the wounded bird type, wouldn't have known what hit him when Luisa Valencia exploded into his life. She almost vibrated with passion. Fashionable, too... her steel gray power suit with shoulder pads was most certainly *haute couture*.

Lilah glanced down at her flight-crumpled shirt and pants with a rueful smile. Luisa laughed and offered use of her wardrobe if Lilah so wanted. They seemed to be more or less the same size.

"I love her already," Lilah said to Victor and Shawn, setting them all laughing.

As the four of them gathered in the living area of the suite, Victor said, "Thanks for agreeing to help with Major Armor. I don't trust him and Steven not to pull a fast one. You can give me expert opinion on the wells *and* the books."

"I was waiting to board when you called."

Lilah was at Bombay's international airport, strategizing tactics in her mind, when the overhead system announced there was a phone call for her. Victor Kingsley was on the line. The conversation was short—Lilah was needed in Texas. She canceled the flight to New York to visit her old schoolmates.

The trip to Corpus Christi would serve one other purpose. The ongoing investigation on Amber Barrons and Godwin and Temple's half-brother... there was one person Lilah needed to talk to about it, one person with a slim possibility of having answers. Shawn Barrons, Andrew's biological son. He was in Texas with Victor and his bride. Apparently, Shawn served as Victor's best man and heard Lilah would be in Corpus Christi. Wanting to meet her, Shawn accompanied the newlyweds to the city.

"Sorry, Lilah," said Victor, tone regretful. "I'm sure you were hoping to take a break. Brad said he'd handle Armor, but Mother fainted when he was about to leave."

"What?" Lilah exclaimed. "Oh, my God! Is Patrice okay?"

"The doctor said he can't find anything wrong. Brad thinks it may only be stress, but she's insisting he stay with her while she recuperates."

Lilah frowned. Patrice, the tough-minded woman she knew, fainted from stress? Just when Brad had been about to meet the major. The same man who'd—as Alex recounted to Sabrina—played such an important role in the Kingsley brothers' childhood. With an inward grimace, Lilah tried to dismiss the suspicion she'd shared with Sabrina, the wild conclusions reached by their collective imagination. Why would Patrice stop Brad when she knew either Victor or Alex would step in? It didn't make any sense.

Waving a hand, Shawn said, "Rich really ain't a bad sort. He was with me at West Point. We did our time under General Potts together." Which would put Shawn and the major at almost thirty-nine to Victor's thirty-five and Lilah's thirty-one.

"Old man made it tough for you, huh?" Victor's tone was mock-sympathetic. "What did he do? Ask you to take your beads off?"

Fingering the amber beads he habitually wore around his neck, Shawn admitted, "As a matter of fact, yes, and I refused. They kicked me out for insubordination."

Victor howled. "Seriously? What reason did you give the general?"

"Told them it was my mother's."

Lilah huffed. "Right... as though you couldn't have told me all those times I asked about the beads. Fine, you keep your secrets." Glaring at Victor, she added, "I can't believe you talked me into this silly idea... investing with Major Armor with all the bad blood between him and you!" The younger four Kingsley brothers were completely tickled by the scheme. When even Brad didn't object, Lilah couldn't find a reason to vote against it. Armor's company *was* a profitable enterprise, and he *was* involved in the murder attempt on the brothers. Having to answer to the same men was small potatoes in terms of punishment.

Victor opened a folder and tossed some papers across the small table. Turning to Shawn, Victor explained, "This particular outfit was part of Sanders's holdings, but by the time we heard of it, Armor got first refusal. Fortunately for us, the bank didn't consider him qualified enough for a loan, and he didn't ask Steven for help. So we got together a venture capital firm instead, which offered funds to him."

"The major had no idea who the people behind it were," said Lilah.

The surprise on Shawn's face turned to mirth.

Guffawing, Victor said, "We told Armor after the fact. He ain't happy about it, but there's nothing he can do now. Watch what happens at the meeting tomorrow."

A couple of hours later

Neither Shawn nor Lilah wanted to intrude on the newlyweds' privacy, so excusing themselves, they opted for a steakhouse. The décor was rustic with a low, wood-beamed ceiling and rough-hewn tables arranged around a central bar. Fishing and hunting knick-knacks were scattered everywhere, including a buck head staring at customers with a baleful eye. Lilah shuddered, wondering how anyone could eat with the thing glaring down.

Shawn followed her gaze to the wall and laughed. "Ignore him. The food is good."

"What's this business you were talking about?" she asked, popping a fry into her mouth. The salt and the grease were exactly right.

"The internet," Shawn said from across the restaurant table. "Imagine... every household in the world linked to millions of others, instantaneously sharing information. Each one of us will be connected to more than five billion others."

"Scary thought."

"There are a few companies looking at opening up the internet to commercial use. I have some money invested in one of them. You want in?"

Lilah waggled her fingers. "Information, Shawn. Financials, business plan, and all those boring details."

Shawn sighed. "You have no romance in your soul. Look at it as a quest. Venturing into the great unknown. You could end up on top of the world."

"Or I could lose my shirt," Lilah said hardheartedly.

With a grin, he dug out a folder from his backpack and handed it over. "Do I know you or what?" Tone deliberate, he added, "And Lilah? Let Sabrina take a look."

Lilah was perusing the documents and jerked up at his words.

"I figured it out," he said. "The hacker community is not very big."

Fear. Pure and simple.

Shawn saw it. "Nope, the feds don't know," he clarified. "They have to work within the law, but I don't. When you refused to tell me who digitized your records, I took a look at the résumés of your IT team. None of them is capable of that level of complexity. The only other person I found in your entire setup was Sabrina. I did a little digging around at her alma mater. She hung out with a group of hackers at Hunter College."

Lilah was outraged. "You *snooped?*"

"Chill," said Shawn, waving his fork around. "Sabrina has been sticking her nose into other people's business—*government* business. She should expect similar treatment. Tell her to be careful, though."

Her inner self shaking from the shock of discovery, Lilah took a gulp of the cold soda. "You said the feds don't know."

"Only because they haven't seen the fingerprints." At Lilah's look of incomprehension, he explained, "Every hacker has his—or her—favored technique. I saw Sabrina's work during my 'snooping,' and when Harry asked me to check into those drug dealers in India, I needed help from a buddy who works for the FBI. I recognized Knight-errant's handiwork. I was sure she couldn't have done what she did without someone letting her access a sophisticated system. So..."

"It could have been Alex who helped," Lilah pointed out.

Shawn grinned. "Alex Kingsley would have a stroke if he knew. You, on the other hand... you might ignore a little bending of a rule or two."

"Alex does know Sabrina likes to work with computers, but I doubt he realizes the extent of her activities. Still, thank you. Not many people say that about me." Lilah smiled in guilty delight, making Shawn laugh. "Sabrina says it's only public service to let the FBI know their systems are weak. Plus, she's made sure not to wander into any of the critical sections. Also, she hasn't done any hacking after the law was passed."

"Good," said Shawn, look of relief plain on his face. "With her kind of talent, she could do her own *legitimate* thing. Her professors said she was versatile—programming and networking."

"She has her own absurd justifications, but I think she actually prefers it that way. Look at her, Shawn. She never got a chance to finish college and went from being Harry's sister to Alex's wife.

Even the gossip magazines don't see her. They link her husband to *me!* I think this is her way of maintaining an identity."

Shawn wiped his mouth with a pristine white napkin and twisted off the cap on the Bud Light. "Some of us cope with our secrets; some use secrets to cope?"

"Precisely." Lilah bit her lip. "Shawn, talking about secrets... I meant to ask you. Do you know anything about Ambrosia Barrons?"

Shawn was taking a swig and coughed when beer went down the wrong way. Lilah stood to slap him between shoulder blades.

He waved away her concern, smiling apologetically at the waiter who materialized next to the table. "I'm fine."

Lilah settled back into her chair, asking, "So... about Amber?"

He wiped the moisture from his shirt, seemingly hesitant to answer. Eyes on the faint stain on the lapel, he muttered, "I thought you said 'Ambrosia.'"

"A nickname—Ambrosia 'Amber' Barrons," Lilah said. "You *have* heard of her?"

"Very little," said Shawn. "She died right around the time I was born. The staff at home were instructed not to say anything in my presence. They didn't want me scared, I guess. I didn't know anything about her until I was almost out of high school. Why are you asking?"

Lilah and Harry had ruled out involving Andrew Barrons—Shawn's father—in their plans against Temple and Godwin. There really was no way to tell if Andrew were also part of the president's scheme to control the world. Shawn... Lilah learned enough about him to know there was next to nil communication between him and his father. Still, to suggest to him Andrew might be part of a murder plot was risky, but she was at a point where there was no choice except at least to subtly probe Shawn for info.

"We found her picture with some of the Kingsley stuff." Lilah eyed the beads around Shawn's neck. "She was wearing a necklace very like yours."

"Not 'like' mine... the same one," Shawn admitted. "When I heard about her, I went hunting for more details and found the thing. Amber beads for Amber Barrons. She left this and the suicide note on her bed before hanging herself."

"You put the beads around your neck?" Lilah asked, shuddering.

"Why not?"

"Don't you find it... I don't know... *morbid?*"

"No, I'm keeping her memory alive," Shawn said, his eyes solemn. "She was still in her teens when she died. Who knows what might have happened if she lived? She was a feisty girl by all accounts. Championship swimmer, planning to go to Columbia, never backed away from a fight. Popular, too. She might have married, had more children..."

Food forgotten, Lilah stared at him, saddened by the picture he was painting. The loss of potential.

"I didn't mean to make you cry," he said, flicking his fingers at her cheek.

Wiping off the wetness, Lilah said, "Brothers are allowed."

"It's strange," Shawn said, slicing himself a piece of medium-rare T-bone steak. "I'm pretty sure you don't think of Andrew and Caroline as your parents, but you call me 'brother.'"

Shawn was more of a sibling to the adopted twins than Caroline who actually was their half-sister. Lilah smiled wistfully, then used her fingers to hide the yawn that took her by surprise.

"Jetlag," said Shawn. "You need to get some rest. Victor needs you to rescue him from big, bad Major Armor tomorrow."

"I have more questions," she complained, stifling a second yawn. "Why did you tell General Potts the beads were your mother's?"

For a few seconds, Shawn chewed on the meat, his face thoughtful as he seemed to wonder how to answer. "I lied," he finally admitted. "I didn't want to take them off. I didn't want to get kicked out, either, and it was the first excuse which came to mind."

"Why *didn't* you want to take them off?"

"I just didn't. The army allows religious symbols under the uniform, so why not my beads?"

"Because your beads have nothing to do with religion?"

"Why are *we* arguing about this?"

Laughing, Lilah threw her hands in the air. "I have no idea... I only meant to ask you if you knew why Amber killed herself. Just because her boyfriend refused to marry her? The man was already married, for God's sake. With a mistress on the side and a child with her. And he was a drunk. What *did* she see in him?"

It was Shawn's turn to laugh. "Are you planning to write a novel about it or something?"

Hurriedly, Lilah grabbed the napkin, dabbing her lips with it. "Amber's story resonated with me," she said, keeping her voice light. Another yawn burst forth. Her eyes watered.

Face crinkling in sympathy, Shawn said, "I understand. I've told you all I know. And you really need to get to bed."

Chapter 39

Next morning

Corpus Christi, Texas

Hostility churned the air around the conference table as Lilah went through the last of the accounts of Armor Drilling Company. "Thank you. Everything seems to be in order. Good to know our investments are going well." With a smile, she returned the folder to the young clerk. Shawn was also present, brought along as someone who could meet Armor on friendlier footing than the Kingsleys.

Richard Armor glowered. The door hadn't yet shut behind the clerk, a young woman, when he said in a tight voice, "I take care of my property, Mrs. Kingsley."

Deciding not to engage the irate man, Lilah was collecting her papers in silence when Victor responded, "Bearing in mind forty percent of it is owned by our venture capital firm, I would say it's *our* property, as well."

Ignoring Victor, Armor asked Lilah, and not for the first time, "Will you consider selling it back to me? You'll make damn good money off it."

Victor capped his pen and slid it into the pocket of his blazer. "No. We already make decent return on investment from this firm, and oil prices are going up. Returns are going to be even higher. Why would we give it up for short-term benefit?"

"Kingsley!" The metal table shook as Armor slammed a fist on it. "I went looking for outside investors because you and your brothers pressured the banks into refusing to loan me money. If I knew you were behind the venture capital firm—"

"Banks are in the business of making profit, Armor." Victor was pitiless. "If they thought you were creditworthy, they would've given you the loan no matter what anyone else said. Also, you didn't have to use venture capitalists. You could've asked your friend Steven. Why didn't you?"

Lilah intervened, "Let's leave, Victor. Mr. Armor is obviously upset."

"*Major* Armor if you please," the man snapped, teeth clenched.

Lilah narrowed her eyes, remembering the first time she ran into him... the Barrons party where she was officially introduced to the Kingsleys. He'd said the same thing that day. Richard Armor clearly had a problem being considered a regular old civilian.

Armor continued his tirade. "I was a military officer with a record even your brother would envy before I worked as judge advocate in the JAG Corps. Then, I successfully ran Steven's Texas division. Which of these rendered me a high credit risk in your opinion? None of you three brothers—"

"Five," Victor interrupted. "There are five of us."

"Whatever," the major said bitterly. "None of you had the kind of résumé I did, but no one hesitated to give you what you needed. Your friend Harry was still in his teens when his family managed to start Gateway. *Of course* the banks took your word I'm not creditworthy. The good ol' boys' network strikes again."

Victor spat, "Oh, yeah? You have nerve! My brothers and I were dirt poor when we returned to the family home, Armor. You damn well knew it and decided to help your rich buddy, Steven, get back at us for the crime of merely existing. So don't give me your sob stories about the evil rich guy versus the poor man. Besides, there's no one who's more 'good ol' boy' than Steven. Why didn't you ask him for help?"

"Steven already gave me something more valuable than money," Armor said. "When you and your brothers called me 'the chauffeur's son,' he called me 'friend.'"

"'The chauffeur's son,'" Victor mimicked. "You know what your problem is, Armor? It ain't about us insulting you. It's that you consider it an insult to be a chauffeur's son. You think you're better than your father, than us, than *everyone* else. When others don't bow and scrape before the heroic Major Armor, you get angry. You hated it when Alex turned out to be a better officer. You hate the fact we outsmarted you with the venture capital firm."

"On any day, I *am* better than you," Armor snarled. "Unlike you and your brothers and Mrs. Kingsley, I have ethics."

"What the hell do you mean?" asked Victor.

Armor laughed. "I was there at the beginning, remember? Mrs. Kingsley—your sister-in-law here—was slobbering all over the golden boy, but she chose to marry the CEO." He turned to Lilah, face twisted into a mocking smile. "The *Journal* called it a 'political alliance,' but the rest of the world knew it for what it was—legalized prostitution."

Leaping to his feet, Victor roared. "*Armor...* I'll slice off your damn tongue!"

Shawn stood, face flaming in anger.

"Enough," snapped Lilah. Her body threatened to explode from inside out. Her eyes burned with rage. "Sit," she said, gesturing at Victor and Shawn. With venom she didn't know she carried, Lilah smiled at their adversary. "I'm told you're a lawyer by training, *Mister* Armor. All I can think is you're a very bad one, or you were desperate for money. Because no lawyer worth the ink on his diploma would have signed the contract with the venture capital firm." She paused, smoothening her voice. "I'm going to walk out of here with my team. Once we're gone, I suggest you take another look at the terms. We have only forty percent, but every last cent of it is ours to keep or sell as we wish. One word from me is all it will take for those shares to be sold to the most unpleasant customer on the planet. Someone who—unlike the Kingsley brothers—will bleed you dry. Remember it well the next time you're tempted to call me names."

In under a minute, Armor got a minion to escort the visitors out the door.

"That was terrible," Lilah muttered as she strode down the hallway, a baleful eye on Victor's guffawing form.

"Are you kidding me?" Victor gasped, coming to a halt by the elevator door. "The only way it could've gone better is if you ended your little speech with 'you bastard son of a chauffeur.'"

"Victor," she snapped.

"Don't beat yourself up," Shawn said. "Rich deserved it... richly."

Holding on to the wall, Victor howled.

Lilah threw her hands in the air. "Gimme a break."

"Give yourself a break," Shawn said, grinning. "You did nothing wrong."

"Don't you think the major has reason to be upset with us?" Lilah asked, frowning. "We did trick our way into the company. Plus, he's a small business owner, and we're currently the biggest fish in the ocean. Not an even match. What we did is not right, Victor. We should sell our shares back."

"Hell, no," Victor said, wiping tears of mirth from his eyes as the elevator doors swished open. "Let Armor stew about it. It's time he ate some crow."

Lilah said, "I know there was childhood rivalry between you and him, but—"

Victor waved her into the elevator. "Childhood rivalry? Guess it's one way of describing events. Personally, I would call it attempted murder. Forgive me if I don't find his relative lack of money a redeeming factor."

"*Steven* tried to kill you and your brothers," Lilah corrected.

Victor snorted. "Rich has done the thinking for Steven ever since they met. The murder attempt was also a collaboration."

Jabbing the button to the lobby, she asked. "You have proof?"

"Now, you sound like Mother," Victor said. "She never lets us say a word against the poor orphan."

Lilah sighed, feeling even worse. Her mind kept returning to the same ridiculous thought, but the idea was not worth entertaining. Patrice felt sorry for Richard Armor and was making up for her sons' bad behavior. That was it. Patrice Kingsley was not the sort to deceive her sons—*all* her sons—for decades on end.

Shawn held the elevator door open for Lilah, his warm brown eyes strangely sad. *But then,* she thought, *everyone lies.* Some—like Sabrina—lied with their silence. Some—like Shawn—lied with words as he did with the military.

Stepping out of the elevator and into the crowded lobby, Victor handed Lilah a dossier. "One last man to see before we head to Panama. Lilah, you must be tired... return if you want, please. I can handle this one on my own."

Lilah frowned. "I'd thought Major Armor was the last on our list."

"So did I," said Victor. "Brad called this morning. Seems Grandfather told him about this drilling company with great potential, and he was waiting until Mother got better to do the negotiations himself. Brad says Mother's still feeling jittery about being left alone in the mansion. Since I was coming to Corpus Christi for Armor anyway, he thought I could check out Pillar Oil, as well."

Luisa was waiting in the lobby and joined them. They headed to the Mexican restaurant across the street. The WALK sign lit up. Victor pulled Luisa along, the girl almost skipping. Shawn followed, laughing at their antics. The blinking yellow man announced there were only a few seconds before lights changed again. Musing about lies, Lilah hurried behind, opening the folder as she walked.

A name leaped out of the document. Every thought of Patrice and her potential for deception flew out of Lilah's mind.

Horns blew loudly as she came to a halt in the middle of the pedestrian crossing. A cabbie cursed fluently, shaking a fist at her through the driver's side window. "Lilah!" shouted Victor. Running, he swung her out of the way of an approaching bike.

Almost as though disembodied, Lilah watched the scene. She understood little of the commotion. The name on the paper had whisked her back to the darkest moment in her life: Colonel Sheffield Parker, the criminal who assaulted her in Libya.

Part XII

Chapter 40

Three weeks later, March 1988

Cerro Azul, Panama

The monster was back. Lilah was once again tossed into a never-ending nightmare. Fear for her best friend's life was the only thing keeping her grip on sanity.

The afternoon in Texas, she grabbed the excuse of being jet-lagged to avoid accompanying Victor to Pillar Oil's offices and immediately flew to Panama. She spent days trying to think things through. Temple and Godwin clearly expected Harry to go after Parker and be killed in the process. Lilah could move heaven and earth to protect Harry from the enemy, but how could she keep him safe from himself?

A face-off between Harry and Parker could not be allowed to happen. She tossed out every objection to Pillar Oil she could imagine at the executive meeting of the Peter Kingsley Company—insinuations of financial irregularities in Parker's business, mockery of the quantity and quality of the oil produced. Nothing worked. The Kingsley patriarch had proclaimed it a gem of a company, and neither Brad nor his brothers needed to hear anything more. She raised the fact that the business was small enough not to make a difference to the network, only to be shot down with the retort they were also small once. As CFO, if she refused to sign off on the deal, the brothers would involve Harry.

She was only vaguely aware of the discussions about the chairman of the board. None of the brothers objected to the clause which gave the elected chairman some authority over the CEO. They all knew it would provide further reassurance to the member companies that they wouldn't be reduced to vassals. Voting for the chairman's position would happen at the first ever meeting of the member companies to be held in a few months' time, in the same gathering that the charter formalizing the network would be signed. When Alex brought up Harry's name, Lilah stiffened.

"Not him," she objected. Until Temple and Godwin were forced to stand down, Harry couldn't be nominated as chairman without making him a bigger target. Not at this time.

"I like Harry," said Scott, the youngest of the Kingsley brothers.

Despite her worries, Lilah smiled a little. She contended Harry's name was too closely aligned with the Kingsleys and would fail to project the image of a democratic process. Nor could the senior executives propose anyone else connected to themselves to serve in the capacity... including Temple and Godwin. Member companies needed to be allowed to bring up names before voting. She threw in her idea of nominating the energy secretary.

The American government would welcome the move since it would give the authorities a say in such a powerful structure. The political nature of appointments to secretary positions meant the person would usually serve a maximum of eight years, the same duration as the president. It also meant Temple and Godwin couldn't be sure of playing puppet masters without risking public exposure. Once both enemies were finished, and after the first chairman left his political office, she could bring up Harry's name. The day he was appointed, she'd leave whether he liked it or not.

"Harry is well known," Scott spoke again, his tone stubborn. "I'm sure the members will agree."

"They might even bring up his name on their own," contributed Victor.

"Perhaps," Lilah said, inclining her head. "But we as chief executives probably shouldn't do the nominating."

They left it there, no consensus reached.

Weeks went by. Lilah managed to hide the criminal's name from documents sent to Harry, but there would come a point when he found out. A phone conversation with Alex... with Brad... any of the Kingsleys could bring up the company's name. If Harry heard, his next call would be to Lilah. Her heart thudded in panic each time her private line rang. Her terrified mind kept going in circles without zooming in on solutions. The deal with the monster's business was signed only days before for the party thrown by Brad to celebrate their accomplishments.

#

A month later, April 1988

Cerro Azul, Panama

The girl in Lilah's office smiled happily at Harry before turning to Brad. "I'm sorry, Mr. Kingsley. Mrs. Kingsley has told me no one is allowed in her safe." The intern's eyes were wide at the sight of the CEO, but her tone was quite firm.

"I'm certain she did not mean the order to include me, young lady," Brad said, sounding partly amused, partly irritated. He said to Harry, "Hema is from India."

Harry bowed gravely to the oldest of the sixteen girls he once rescued. "Why don't you ask Mrs. Kingsley for permission to let us take a look at the final list of investors? We can wait a few minutes."

As Hema left, Brad grunted and took out his own keys to open the strongbox. "Finally! Don't know why Lilah tucked it in here. And I have no idea why she sent last year's copies to all the departments. Someone should've noticed the error!"

"The admin staff likely assumed the info was accurate and up to date," Harry soothed. "It did come straight from the CFO." Allowing none of the strange jitteriness in his chest to seep into the words, Harry asked, "Where *is* Lilah?"

"Talking to some of the other American expats," explained Brad. "We're all concerned about the situation with Noriega. I don't think she knows you're here. Here it is." Brad handed over the folder.

Harry sank into one of the chairs and mentally shook himself. The time in India really did a number on his brain, but there would be no more of the stupidity. Lilah's love and loyalties were Brad's to claim, and Harry... he had his own commitments.

Verity seemed to have backed off on her demands to start a family. Dante's doing, of course. He'd called her the night Harry walked out in the middle of a snowstorm and showed up at his boss's doorstep. Whatever Dante said to Verity, Harry was grateful. Traveling to India as frequently as he did this last year would've been painful with Verity complaining nonstop. Nor did he want to explain to her planning a child was a bad idea when he didn't know if he'd live to see the infant born.

It was even beginning to look like he wouldn't be able to fulfill the vow he made to bring the rapist to justice. After all these years of searching fruitlessly, the only conclusion Harry could come to was the criminal died somewhere in a sewer. Confirmation was what Harry needed. If the monster had indeed been punished by the universe, Harry wanted Lilah to at least have proof.

Closure on the most horrific chapter of her life was the minimum she deserved for shouldering the responsibilities of the network. Lilah would govern the global empire with the few people she dared trust separated from her by death and destiny. Harry would be gone, and she refused to risk Dan's life by involving him in the dirty power games. There would be many more such games... many would-be Sanderses with their eyes on her throne.

Harry muttered a curse under his breath. The Kingsleys already designed the network's power structure to bring little privilege to its leaders even in the presence of enormous responsibility. The move would discourage external attacks to some extent. Temple and Godwin wouldn't be deterred, but Harry would make damned sure the network stayed safe from the most devious of its enemies. Afterward, it wouldn't matter if he wasn't around. The Kingsley clan was quite capable of defending one of their own *and* the network, and with Lilah in charge, there was no reason to fear the structure would morph into a tyranny. She would never let the empire be used as a weapon against humanity. There was nothing for Harry to worry about.

Opening the folder, he looked through the names of the investors. There was a commotion at the door, and he turned to see Lilah standing there, her face flushed and breathing faintly audible.

"There you are!" she exclaimed. "Patrice wants to talk to both of you. Right away."

Brad stood, and so did Harry. Gaze skittering, Lilah smiled vaguely at them.

You're lying to me? Harry asked silently. *What about?*

#

The same night

At the evening's event, Lilah was standing near a potted plant talking to Victor and Luisa when she heard her name called. Brad sauntered up with the former attorney general, both men holding glasses of wine.

"My wife," Brad said and threw his arm around her shoulders. Lilah stretched her lips into a smile, her muscles clenched in the effort not to shove him away.

Noah raised his glass. "Mrs. Kingsley, I admire the way you've handled things. You have all the Kingsley men working hard to get the network to this point. You must be proud of them. Particularly of Alex. I hear he did some good things in Asia."

Inclining her head, Lilah said, "He contributed quite a lot to the effort."

"Alex is just as ardent about you... about what you do on the home front. Both you and Brad, of course." Noah's tone indicated amusement.

"I'm afraid I don't underst—" Brad's fingers bit painfully into the soft flesh of her upper arm, unseen by anyone else. The pressure released so abruptly she was left wondering if she imagined it. Before she could say anything, they were joined by Alex and Harry.

"I saw you at the graduation ceremony at West Point a couple of years back, but we were never introduced," Harry told Noah as they shook hands.

Smiling at the group, Harry's gaze collided with Lilah's, and his brows drew together at whatever he saw in her eyes.

No other way... she needed to tell Harry, prepare him for the confrontation.

A few minutes later

Lilah stood facing the mountains, elbows resting on the railing of the balcony. There was a muffled snap behind, and the sounds of the party receded as though someone just shut the glass doors to the great hall. A shift in the air, a warm presence at her side... Harry, but she didn't acknowledge him.

Hummingbirds hovered at the feeders, their buzzing mingling with the muted music and chatter from the hall. The fragrance of jasmine clung to the air. From where they stood, they could see the rolling hills below, blanketed by dense rainforest. The sun was on its way down, casting large shadows across the landscape. Lilah shivered. April evenings in the Central American mountains could be cool.

Finally, when the fiery reds and oranges of twilight gave way to the glittery blackness of the night sky, she asked, "Harry, do you trust me?"

"With my life."

"If I ask you to do something you find hateful, will you do it because I asked you to?"

He was quiet for a few seconds, then said, "The list."

Silently, she took the folded piece of paper from her pocket and handed it to him. He scanned it quickly under the yellow bulb illuminating the balcony. A third of the way down, his eyes halted. She knew what name he'd seen—Pillar Oil Explorers, owned and operated by Colonel Sheffield Parker.

Harry pushed off from the railing, stance coiled. Lilah clapped a hand over his mouth, muffling the roar of rage threatening to erupt. She dragged him into the shadows of the back corner and out of sight of the other guests.

Obediently, he breathed in and out as she told him. He listened to what she had to say about the acquisition, about Temple's plans.

When the violent haze in his eyes lifted, Harry said, "I'm going to kill the bastard."

"No," Lilah snapped, shoving him by his shoulders. "You are not."

"Damn it, Lilah. I thought you wanted justice."

"I do. But not at the expense of your *life!*" She stepped away quickly and back into the light, clumsy in her movements. Facing the garden, she said, "Godwin and Temple are watching you, waiting for you to make a move. If you physically attack Parker, you'll play right into their hands. If you go after Parker like we did with Sanders, the other members of the network will mobilize against you, perhaps kick you out of the organization."

With a muted groan, Harry slammed his fist into one of the concrete columns. "If I do neither, what then? Do you imagine Godwin and Temple don't have a plan B?"

"Who's Parker?" Alex asked from the door. "What do you mean about Grandfather and Mr. Temple?"

Chapter 41

Later the same night

Lilah continued to play the part of the perfect hostess by Brad's side. Out of the corner of her eye, she watched the balcony where Alex and Harry were still talking. Harry faced the shadowy mountains, hands resting on the railing. Alex was pacing. He already knew about the attack she survived, but neither Lilah nor Harry ever mentioned the name of the rapist to the Kingsley grandson. The omission was not deliberate. Harry already had access to all the resources Alex could offer to track the monster.

In a few minutes, Alex stalked back into the crowd, ignoring the polite greetings coming his way as he left the hall. Puzzled eyes of the guests followed him, switching to Harry returning from the balcony.

Still later, Lilah snapped on safety goggles and earmuffs before going through the airlock doors in one corner of Alex's wing. He stood in the indoor booths of the shooting range immediately outside the mansion, Galatz pointed at the target a hundred yards away. He fired at a sustained rate, eyes locked on the silhouette. A storm of bullets sped downrange. The figure fell. Switching positions, he kept shooting. After systematically destroying every one of the targets, he stopped to reload.

"Alex," she called softly.

Twisting around abruptly, he cursed at her. Then, he threw his rifle to the side and ripped off the safety equipment. Voice guttural, he insisted, "Grandfather is not the enemy."

"Alex," she tried again.

"No." He held his hand up. "You've got it all wrong about Grandfather. He's been a father to us all these years. You're simply wrong."

"What if you're the one who's wrong? Are you willing to risk Harry's life?"

Gripping her shoulders, Alex said, "I won't let anything happen to Harry, but Grandfather is not our enemy."

Not looking away from Alex's gaze, she inclined her head. "Believe what you will but understand *this* as well: family ties matter, but you, Brad, the rest of your brothers... you owe it to the people who trust you with power to put everything aside and focus on what is right. You owe it to Harry, you owe it to me, and you owe it to every man, woman, and child who's part of your business empire."

Alex ptchaaed. "Lilah—"

"All right," Harry said from the open doorway. "Let's say you're right about Godwin, but will you promise me something? If I'm not around for whatever reason, can I trust you to protect the people who're important to me? In case you turn out to be wrong, will you put aside everything and defend Lilah?"

"I'm *not* wrong," Alex said, letting go of his grip on Lilah's arms.

"Your word, Alex," demanded Harry. "There can be no difference between us in this. You must do what *I* would for Lilah. Hell, you *have* to be me."

"Fine," said Alex. "You need a pledge? I swear I will do whatever it takes to defend her."

When Harry threw a quick sideways glance at her, Lilah nodded. There wouldn't be any more concessions from Alex until they shoved concrete evidence under his nose.

Alex continued, "I shouldn't have to remind you, Harry. You went with me a couple of times when I visited Grandfather. You remember how he talked to you every damn time? He made it clear the kind of esteem he holds you in."

Harry shook his head. "Godwin's a smart man. Shrewd. He's not going to—"

Tone emphatic, Alex said, "My grandfather meant every word of what he said. Believe me... he doesn't easily hand out compliments. Actually, you don't need to take my word for it. We now know where Parker's been hiding all these years. So let's do our own investigation into how he managed to stay under the radar for so long, who he's pally with, etcetera."

"I'm planning on it," agreed Harry. "We'll thrash out details in the morning."

As they walked back from the indoor-outdoor range, Lilah said to the men, "I should talk to Brad... about Godwin and Parker, I mean."

Alex halted, forcing the other two to stop as well. "Are you kidding me?"

Biting her bottom lip, Lilah said, "Parker's outfit is small. From a financial or strategic point of view, it doesn't make a difference whether he's part of the network or not. The main reason you and your brothers insisted on including the company is that Godwin suggested the purchase. Once Brad understands exactly what's going on... if he agrees, we could simply kick Parker out... by selling back the percentage we bought, I mean. Even at a loss, the business is small enough that the trade will be painless. It has to be done before the network is finalized, or we'll need permission from the board. I... umm... didn't think Brad would take my word against Godwin's, so I was waiting to talk to Harry first." It was unlikely Brad would take even Harry's word about it, but she couldn't see any other way of stopping the looming catastrophe.

Alex sighed. "Let me ask you something. Have you told Brad about what happened in Libya? Does he know you were there?"

"He knows about the... umm... assault, not the specifics of where, when, and who." Lilah swallowed hard, not wanting to divulge what had happened after the conversation. "It's been hard for me to talk about, that's all."

Raking his fingers through his hair, Alex said, "I didn't think you could've said anything to Brad about Libya, or he'd have been the first one you went to after Parker popped back up. You'd have said something without bringing up Grandfather. As things stand, you'll have to start your discussion with a secret you kept for years. Even if you talk about Parker without mentioning your ridiculous theories about my family, the first thing Brad will do is run to Grandfather for advice. Let's say we kick Parker out. We still will need to figure out if there is someone behind him. If I were in Brad's place, I'd want to be part of the investigation. Your concerns about our grandfather... at some point, Brad will figure out what you're thinking, who you're looking at. Relationships will be irrevocably ruined. Don't do it, please."

"Let's worry about ruined relationships later," said Lilah. "Parker—and whoever is behind him—is relying on me not saying anything to Brad. Just like you, they think if I say anything about Godwin, the alliance will fall apart."

"I bet they believe I won't risk it," mused Harry.

Lilah nodded. "Yeah... nor will *they* want to risk the network before the charter is signed. There won't be any attacks until then. Once it's done, Parker and his pals are not going to wait until we come up with some new trick, some way of ripping him apart without making it obvious to the other members. They're going to force a confrontation at the meeting. Brad can kick Parker out before it happens."

"To begin with," Harry said. "Afterward—"

"I am not letting you go after him personally no matter when," snapped Lilah.

Alex held up a hand. "Okay, so this Parker character is going to pop up at the conference and confront Harry. *I'm* betting Parker came out of hiding because he's counting on the network itself to protect him. Mutual protection *is* part of our charter. Whatever he tries, the three of us can make sure he fails. And you'll see for yourself Grandfather has no part in any of it. Afterward, we'll talk to Brad. Once Grandfather's in the clear, Brad will willingly help us figure out what to do about the criminal. Whatever you want will be fine, Lilah... quietly bankrupt him, go public... whatever. But we need to wait until after the conference, or you'll forever suspect my family of plotting against you."

"Listen to me, Alex," said Lilah. "The chairmanship of the board... we talked about nominating the energy secretary. I've been wondering if Temple plans to nominate Godwin."

"And if he does?" asked Alex. "Grandfather is eminently qualified." When Lilah started to speak, he held up both hands. "I know... you'll immediately see it as a part of this grand conspiracy to take over the network... even if it happens to be a good-faith proposal. Well... you can object to it, can't you? You can announce at the meeting exactly what you said to my brothers and me. The chairman needs to be someone not closely associated with the Kingsleys so the member companies feel comfortable."

"Which is when Parker will speak up," Harry said, realization dawning in his eyes. "It's highly likely Parker will have friends who will help him start a ruckus at the meeting in support of Godwin. Temple and Godwin believe if Parker's past crimes alone don't make me go after him, I'll do it to stop them from taking over. It's their plan B. Parker as close associate of the people running the network... perhaps Lilah forced into working with him... they know I won't be able to stand the idea. Alex, I can't let it happen."

"I can't, either," said Alex. "Not because I don't want my grandfather in charge. You two will then never accept he didn't have anything to do with Parker showing up. Lilah, if Mr. Temple or anyone else thinks to nominate Grandfather as chairman, *I* will join you in objecting. Good enough?"

Lilah studied the Kingsley grandson for a moment or two. With a huff, she glanced at Harry.

"Trust me," pleaded Alex. "Both Grandfather and Mr. Temple will withdraw when they hear our reasons, Parker or no Parker. Only then you'll realize you were wrong about them. There's no need to involve Brad until it's all done. Talking to him right now will be counterproductive."

"So we speak to him after the meeting?" she asked.

Hesitation obvious, Harry nodded.

When the three of them were at the side door she usually used to get into her wing, Alex started walking toward his own home. "Let's go, dude," he called to Harry. As always, Harry was staying with his sister and brother-in-law.

"I'll catch up." Harry turned back to Lilah and took her hand in his. Standing in the glow of the yellow lightbulb, he peered into her face. "I should've asked before... are you all right?"

She inclined her head. "I'm fine."

"Really fine?" probed Harry. "You know you don't have to pretend with me."

Sudden tears welled. Blinking them back, she smiled. "I've been too worried about you, dumbass."

"You don't need to be," Harry said. "I swear I'll do things exactly as you want. At the meeting, we'll finally get proof of Godwin's involvement." Squinting in the direction of his brother-in-law's home, Harry added, "Once Alex sees his grandfather for what he is, we'll have a decent chance of winning this battle. Let's use the time until then to gather information."

Chapter 42

A few weeks later, July 1988

Panama

Lilah and Harry continued their years-long probe into Godwin Kingsley, hunting for something—*any*thing—they could use against him. Their search for evidence of foul play in Amber Barrons's death yielded zilch. The inquiry into Colonel Sheffield Parker took off on a new trajectory. Harry was certain someone deliberately blocked his investigation all these years. There was no way the criminal could've hid for so long without help. Harry asked Grayson Sheppard, the Peter Kingsley Company's legal officer, to look into the matter, impressing upon him this was a private concern for Harry and therefore to be kept quiet from the Kingsleys. Neither he nor Lilah wanted to involve an outside detective in the problem, and personally investigating the colonel at this point would put Harry in danger. Of all the people he and Lilah knew, Grayson was the only man with reason to ask for info on a member of the network and also less likely to be under watch by Temple and gang.

Brad increased security in and around their residences and offices, citing the need to avoid any untoward incident which might upset their plans. None of it made a difference to Lilah's psyche. Her nightmares about the assault returned, except the monster now stalked *Harry* while she watched helplessly from behind a glass window. The images of the tribespeople in Argentina haunted her every waking moment. Lilah became so jittery that every sudden noise, every shadow in the corner, made her jump. Tense weeks passed.

One night, the phone rang in Lilah's home office. She spoke in short, terse sentences to Harry, jotting the address of a motel on a notepad. Drawing on a light jacket, she stepped out the side door into the garden, thus avoiding her guards. Alex was waiting for her in the garage, unseen by anyone else. She could trust him to keep her safe.

She didn't know there was a man watching through the window in her office. She didn't see her husband pick up the notepad by the phone and read the address.

#

An hour later

Panama City, Panama

Harry stood next to the window, listening to Grayson's words. Alex and Lilah sat on the plastic chairs in the cheap motel room Grayson rented to ensure privacy. At the small table, the old lawyer opened folders one by one and read from the documents. "Once Sanders figured out where you were headed, he stationed people in every town on every possible route from Libya to Egypt. It was your bad luck Parker was the man you asked for help in Qasr Libya. I don't understand why he didn't get you arrested right away, though."

I know why, Harry thought in cold rage.

Parker took one look at Lilah and decided the arrest would wait until he... Harry stupidly left her alone to go look for a vehicle they could use, believing her to be safe at the American Club. Parker got his chance to brutally assault Lilah, but Harry returned while the rapist was out contacting Sanders's thugs to take the teens prisoners. All these years... Harry and Lilah had been imagining Sanders carried only peripheral responsibility for the rape... all these *damned* years.

Out loud, Harry repeated the lie he put in the official report. "Parker may not have had time to get things in place when I made my appearance, so he assaulted me to keep me from going too far. But I escaped." Harry's eyes burned with fury as he remembered the anguish of the weeks he spent in the back room of the church, praying desperately for Lilah to heal. "How is it possible he escaped our notice this far? I went through every record the army kept on him. No one in the military had a clue he was back in the States? No one knew he was affiliated with Sanders?"

"Sanders kept Parker hidden," Grayson said. "If you accused him of attacking you, the U.S. Army might have intervened. A former officer assaulting a teenager wouldn't have looked good, especially with all the protests against the military back then."

"Why would Sanders care?" Alex asked. "Parker was simply another minion."

"Sanders did protect his own whatever his other faults," Grayson said. "Plus, what if Parker turned? Sanders wouldn't have wanted to take the chance, and he wouldn't have killed Parker himself to cover up because it could cause trouble among the rest of his flunkies. Loyalty in the ranks is important."

"It explains why Sanders decided to help," Harry said, tone hard. "But what about after he went to prison? Parker worked in the oil sector—"

"Under his own name," interjected Alex. "But I suppose he didn't change it because no one expected Sanders to lose. Then, it was too late."

Harry nodded. "Also, Parker's drilling outfit is small but not insignificant enough to be invisible. How did he continue hiding from me when I was actively looking for him all this time? Unless someone was working to block me from our side, as well. But for what purpose?"

"Part of what kept him hidden was you, Harry," Grayson said. When Harry stared, Grayson explained, "You never said much about him. If anyone in Gateway heard about Parker, they probably didn't make the connection. Another thing I don't understand is why he came out of hiding *now.*"

Alex answered, "Parker probably decided to brazen it out. He doesn't have Jared Sanders backing him any longer, but as a member of the network, we're obligated to protect him."

Harry said, "There is another possibility. The people who blocked me from finding him likely figured out the details of our encounter. They could've encouraged him to come out of hiding, expecting to provoke me into an attack. Parker probably knows I've been looking for him and figures this is going to be his best chance to finish me before I attack him."

Alex shook his head but did not say anything to counter the opinion.

Grayson continued, "A large part of Parker's military record was sealed until a few weeks back. So I agree, Harry... it does look as though someone was concerned you might find him; but now, not so much. Or perhaps they *want* you to know. Also, Parker was a big part of those attacks on the old Sheppard business, Genesis Oil."

"The accidents?" Harry asked.

"Yes." Grayson shook his head in disgust. "The rest of the folder will tell you why Sanders employed him. He was a criminal and a pervert of the first order. Did you know when he was a recruit, he was accused by his commanding officer's wife of rape?"

"How did he escape charges?" Harry asked.

"The usual tactic," Grayson said. "He told the army brass she invited him into the house. She protested it was because he came to the door feeling sick. It became a 'he said, she said' story. There were more accusations."

It took another hour to go through all the available paperwork on the colonel. Crickets set up a cacophony as Harry walked out of the motel with Lilah and Alex. The night air was hot and muggy in Panama City unlike the cool and comfortable temperatures in Cerro Azul. Harry called, "Wait."

Alex stopped with his hand on the car door. Lilah was already in the passenger seat and turned to eye the men.

Harry rested his elbow on top of the vehicle. "I envy your faith in your family, Alex. I'm not sure I can trust mine." Lilah drew the lapels of her coat together but didn't say anything in response. Harry explained, "You know what happened to Dan and Neil in Morocco. I need to tell you both something else about it." He went over what he discovered after his investigation into Gateway's accounting. "Hector says he had nothing to do with McCoy's thievery, but he admitted to contacting almost every single business which popped up on the list. Those events and now this mess with Parker. Are they connected? My immediate family is aware Lilah was in Libya with me. If one of them got access to Parker's military records, it wouldn't have been difficult to figure out what happened. I still think Temple and Godwin are the most likely culprits, but what if the Sheppards are also involved? Did Hector do what he did out of some sort of spite toward Lilah?"

Alex laughed incredulously. "C'mon, dude. You believe your brother is plotting against you and Lilah? For what? Also, what would he get from killing Dan and Neil?"

Harry pinched the bridge of his nose. "Perhaps you're right, and Hector had nothing to do with the murder attempt or the embezzlement, but he did collude with Gateway's partners behind my back to slow down the network."

Huffing, Alex said, "Maybe Hector didn't want Gateway too closely associated with our side because of Steven. They're friends.

Hell... didn't Hector host a fundraiser for Helen's husband's reelection? You know... Steven's sister, Helen."

"I don't think it was because of Steven," muttered Harry. "My father said *he* asked Hector to talk to those people. Then, the embezzlement... I'm not sure the Sheppards would have qualms about sacrificing Lilah to protect the family business."

Getting out, Lilah slammed the car door. "I lost my faith in the Sheppards the day they handed me over to Andrew Barrons." Harry flinched. "I was seventeen," she reminded him. "Barely more than a child, and they were the only family I had left. Uncle Ryan used to call my papa his best friend. None of it mattered. So forgive my lack of surprise at how things are turning out with them. Maybe they didn't have any part in attacking my brother and Neil... they wouldn't want to push Andrew that far. But the embezzlement... yeah, not surprised."

Drowning in misery, Harry said, "Lilah—"

She held up a hand, voice shaking in fury. "Don't you dare apologize for the adoption. It was my pride or your life. I understand that part. I gladly made the choice. The *right* choice. Afterward, it was as though I didn't exist for the Sheppards. I was just... invisible. Except to you and Sabrina."

What defense did Harry have against truth?

Lilah continued, "I don't trust any of them, but we're not without resources of our own. Security has already been reinforced. As for Parker..." Her voice hardened. "He might have bought himself some time. Doesn't mean he's going to escape justice. I won't let him."

#

An hour later

The sky was turning the pink of dawn when Lilah returned to her room, covering a yawn with her hand.

"Where were you?" came a voice from the corner.

Startled, Lilah jerked around, her shirt half unbuttoned. "Brad," she said, "I didn't expect..."

"It's obvious. Where were you?"

"I had to go out urgently to deal with a problem. A company matter."

"This time of the night?" he asked and crossed the room to face her. "Without your security? Not even one of your six guards?"

"Brad..." Gesturing helplessly with her hands, she shook her head.

"What *was* the business issue? Since I'm the CEO, I ought to know."

Mutely, she stared at him and massaged her brow with her fingers. Alex claimed Brad would never believe... what could she say to...

"I only suspected until now..." Brad said, his tone bitter. Under the stubble beard, his face was pale. "You... with my own *brother.*"

"I swear I haven't cheated." The defensiveness of the words... Lilah cringed inwardly.

Brad's lips twisted in an ugly sneer. "I think you actually expect me to believe it. Or maybe you don't care what I believe. I can't do a single thing to you because of the pre-nup, and Alex... if I confront him this close to finalization of the network... we can't afford a split in the family. No matter. My brother will come to his senses soon. He's going to see you for what you are." Eyes glittering, Brad reached out to cup her cheek. "Do you think your beauty is enough to blind everyone around to how ugly—how *evil*—you are beneath your skin?"

Lilah bit the inside of her cheek, fighting nausea as he ran a thumb across her lip. Brad's fingers traced their way down her throat and to her chest. Hands on her hips, he jerked her hard against him.

"Let go," she hissed. "Or swear to God I'll kill you." Pushing hard against him, Lilah freed herself. "Get out of my room."

"Why? You're still my wife. You know what they call me? The luckiest man in the world... married to the perfect woman. Perfect hair, perfect lips, perfect body. Didn't one article claim you have almost no hair on your perfect body? I wonder how the author knew."

Her full weight was behind her slap, and Brad stumbled to the carpet. Pivoting on her heel, Lilah strode out. She spent what remained of the night huddled on a bench overlooking a patch of ginger lilies, the palatial home with its expensive furniture and soft beds looming behind.

Part XIII

Chapter 43

Two months later, September 1988

Cerro Azul, Panama

Security was tight when investors in the Peter Kingsley Network gathered to elect a board of directors. Governments around the world insisted on it. Any problem with one or more of the assembled VIPs could send shock waves through the global economy. Southcom was placed on high alert. Local law enforcement officials made frequent rounds, and an army of private guards patrolled the Kingsley compound.

Elaborate provisions were made to deal with crises that might arise—any trauma, unexpected health problems, even terrorist attacks. Evacuation plans were in place, including the fleet of MedEvac choppers kept ready on premises. The local clinic was retained to treat minor ailments, but a temporary hospital with full emergency care facilities was erected on Southcom grounds. Transport aircraft with in-flight ICU capabilities stood ready to move a patient or more back to the United States.

Technically, Victor, Alex, and Harry were members of the security team and were permitted to carry their weapons at all times. Lilah prayed they wouldn't need to use any of it.

The entire Kingsley clan would attend the event, including the hated cousins. The Sheppards were there along with the Barronses, all enjoying Brad Kingsley's hospitality in the massive guesthouse on the family property. Former President Temple and his security detail were staying with Brad and Lilah. Temple didn't talk much at dinner the night before the meeting. He never even glanced in Lilah's direction. She wasn't sure what she'd have done if he dared address her.

On the morning of the conference, Lilah stood at the back entrance to the hall, watching as the movers and shakers of the energy sector gathered in one room. Temple was seated with Godwin and the other Kingsleys. Accompanying Steven were his brother Charles and his friend Richard Armor. The Kingsley coloring ran strong in the men of the family—brown hair and either gray or blue eyes. Good-looking lot... except Charles gave off vulgar vibes without saying even a word. Something about his posture, the near-constant leer on his face...

At the same table was General Potts, the former dean from West Point, and his son, Phillip. David and Grace Kingsley—Steven's parents—were there as well, along with Grace's brother who worked for Kingsley Corp as an accountant.

Gateway brought a sizable representation to the conference, and they were seated right next to the Kingsley family. The Barrons men—including Shawn who was there on Lilah's invitation—sat with Brad and his brothers. Patrice declined to attend the event and was babysitting Michael.

Lilah felt rather than saw Harry walk to her. "This is it," she said.

"This is it," he agreed, eyes scanning the room. In a second, he snarled. "Colonel Parker." The two of them watched the man take a seat at the opposite end of the hall, chatting casually with the others at the table.

Lilah stiffened. The monster's face... from this distance, she couldn't see the demonic glee in the stony eyes, but she'd never been able to forget. In her nightmares, she still heard the threats. The memory of the smell still made her gag.

"Are you all right?" Harry asked, the thread of tension in his voice evident to her ears.

She waited for rage... panic... *some* violent emotion to crash into her. To Lilah's relief, there was no out-of-control agitation. That came when she first saw the criminal's name. "I believe I *am* fine," she murmured. Her priority now was to get the criminal out of her home with no harm done to Harry. "Neither Parker nor Godwin is taking any notice of each other," she observed.

"Maybe Alex is right," Harry said. "Godwin's not looking for chairmanship."

"Do you actually believe it?"

"No, but the only way to keep Alex's support is to let this play out. Once the conference is done, he will update Brad and the rest." Taking a deep breath, Harry said, "Afterward—"

"No," Lilah said instantly. "You're *not* going after Godwin and Temple."

"I'm not going anywhere until you get—"

Luisa, Victor's wife, joined them. "Showtime."

#

Half hour later

Harry huffed in relief and settled deeper into his seat. So far, so good. The charter was signed, and the board of directors was chosen without significant conflict. Now, it was time to elect the chairman.

Alex had kept his word all these months. While the Kingsley brothers were all okay with the idea of nominating the energy secretary of the United States as chairman, Alex was the one who took concrete steps to contact the American government about it. The feds informed Brad the decision would be quite all right, but the choice needed to be democratically made by the member companies.

Leaning to the side, Brad asked his grandfather if he wanted to be the first to make a recommendation since he was the senior-most of the oil sector officials in the room.

Lilah sat up. So did Alex.

Before anyone could state exactly who was supposed to be nominated, Godwin Kingsley picked up the microphone at his table. "I nominate Harry Sheppard from Gateway, Incorporated."

Harry jerked in shock.

Polite murmurs of agreement rose from the group in the room. Alex scooted his chair back to nod jubilantly at Lilah. She was staring at Godwin, her eyes wide in disbelief.

"We'd thought..." started Brad, blinking.

Lilah opened her mouth as though to—

Scott stood, nearly knocking over the glass of water in front of him. "I... ahh... second the nomination. Harry is the best man for it."

Turning slightly in her chair, Lilah threw a glance at Harry. Writ clear on her face was the frantic question: *what now?*

Thoughts whirled in his mind, but he shook his head very slightly. They could do nothing at all. If he asked the Kingsleys to withdraw the nomination and eventually died at the enemy's hands, Godwin would remain blameless in his grandsons' eyes. To leave Lilah even the smallest hope of convincing the Kingsley brothers, the best option was for Harry to let the game play out and see where Godwin was going with this proposal.

"My brothers and I did come up with a few possibilities," said Brad, nodding at his grandfather and Scott as they returned to their seats. "But I agree with Scott. Harry would be a great choice for the position of chairman. He *is* the most qualified. We'll have a vote once we put up all the suggestions—"

"Wait a minute," came a voice from the side. "I object to this. On what basis are you calling Sheppard the most qualified to chair a network this size?" Colonel Sheffield Parker had finally spoken.

Gritting his teeth, Harry counted his heartbeats until they slowed and steadied. The mind was a Navy SEAL's most powerful weapon, and he needed to keep it clear. The enemy was about to launch his attack.

Parker marched to the front of the conference room and addressed the assembled executives. "Hello. Only some of you know me. I'm Colonel Parker from Pillar Oil Explorers. It's a small company. When Brad Kingsley sent his brother to talk to me about the proposed network, I agreed. We all know about the volatility of the sector and the ability of rogue nations and stray events to impact our livelihood. I thought we would finally be able to take some collective action about it."

The man turned a one-eighty.

"What kind of a network are we building if we put someone like Harry Sheppard in charge?" Parker asked. "Do any of us know this man? Who is he?"

The rapist paused, his arm sweeping dramatically in Harry's direction.

"What are his credentials?" Parker demanded. "He has no technical training. He has no formal business education. He doesn't even have a college degree! Yet the Kingsleys chose him from among a room full of Ivy League-educated businessmen and women."

The colonel turned to the Sheppards.

Pointing at Harry's family, Parker asked, "Is he the CEO of Gateway, Incorporated? The Kingsleys could have nominated Ryan Sheppard if it were the case. Petty Officer Sheppard certainly isn't the most experienced here; the honor would go to Godwin

Kingsley. If the Kingsleys were merely looking for a well-wisher, why not Barrons or his sons? Barrons O & G is one of the largest drillers in the world, and Andrew Barrons is Brad Kingsley's father-in-law."

Parker walked to where Temple was seated.

"For God's sake, we have a former president of the United States right here. Why didn't they nominate him? Can you imagine the clout this network would have with Mr. Temple as the chairman? How about General Potts or his son? The Kingsleys are certainly familiar with both. The general was the dean of West Point."

Parker circled the presidential table and got to Brad and entourage. Face stiff, Lilah stared straight ahead.

"I thought Brad Kingsley was a leader worth following," the criminal said, one finger jabbing at the air. "What I see *now* are immaturity and poor judgment, and I'm being charitable. I feel he lacks business ethics if his first act as CEO of the Peter Kingsley Network is to appoint someone like Harry Sheppard as chairman."

The audience listened, stunned into silence by this unexpected turn of events.

Parker turned back to the rest of the oil executives. "Either we vote down the nomination, or I'm out of this network. I strongly suggest the rest of you consider doing the same."

Brad stood and opened his mouth to speak. Before he could utter a word, a rumble started in the hall, gathering within seconds into a roar so loud not a syllable could be heard. Parker was striding to his own table. Pushing his chair back, Brad chased after the colonel.

Holding up a hand to request silence, Godwin stood. "Hold on, Brad. Please return to your seat. I have something to say. Ladies and gentlemen, I acknowledge the concerns raised by Colonel Parker, but let me remind you most here have had dealings with Harry

Sheppard at some point. Some of you have come worse off for it, but have any of you failed to be impressed by him? He could teach *me* a thing or two... as old as I am." Smiling in condescension, Godwin continued, "I admit he doesn't fit the usual profile of a well-qualified business executive. Unlike most of us, he was educated at the school of hard knocks. Now, if this audience feels his lack of credentials makes him ineligible to be the chairman, of course you must do what you feel is right."

Harry glanced at the Kingsley table where Lilah was watching the proceedings, dismay on her face. As though aware of his scrutiny, she turned in his direction. Harry nodded. This was Godwin's strategy. A show-crowning of Harry followed by a bloodless coup. In the same speech praising Harry, Godwin declared the nominee possessed none of the usual qualifications and urged people to vote their consciences if they felt he was unfit. Godwin and Parker would force Harry out of chairmanship, then possibly from the network itself. Harry would be killed at a more convenient time. The Kingsley patriarch's reputation would still remain unblemished. The brilliance with which Godwin played his part in the drama would allow no one, not even Alex, to suspect skullduggery.

"Excuse me," Scott called, grabbing the microphone from the center of his table. "I... I seconded his nomination. Harry is a... ahh... a good person. Smart."

The din resumed.

Scott tried again to speak. Finally, he shouted, "Silence!"

The audience fell quiet.

"Stop arguing... please..." Scott begged. "Let us take a vote."

Without any others on the ballot, Scott called out names and the percentage of voting shares. Each investor answered aye or nay for Harry's nomination. As the representative of Kingsley Corp,

Godwin was expected to vote aye. This, he did. In the end, Harry was elected chairman of the board by a narrow margin. It was closer than he would've imagined. The comments accompanying the votes made it quite clear there were lingering resentments from the fall of Sanders. There was also the knee-jerk antipathy toward a stronger entity. With Parker now giving voice to the simmering anger, more were willing to speak publicly against Harry and the Kingsley brothers. He threw a glance at the villain, waiting for the next move.

Parker stood again. "This vote shows us close to half the investors here do not want Sheppard as the chairman. What does it say about the trust we have in Kingsley's decisions? I want a vote of no-confidence in Brad Kingsley's leadership, or I want the contract between the network and my company voided. I'm not going to be held in this system at gunpoint. I urge you good folks who are not happy about the outcome to do the same."

Every eye in the hall swung to Brad Kingsley.

"All the years of effort." Brad was mumbling, but his words were clear to the audience thanks to the microphone. He turned to Godwin. "What do we do, Grandfather?"

Leaning casually back in the chair, Harry flipped his pen around with his fingers. If Parker could not defeat Harry by election, he would threaten the network itself. Either Harry would abdicate to keep the network safe, or he'd be asked to leave by Brad. Eventually, the same reasons would be used to nullify Harry in the power structure.

His voice clear, Godwin stated, "Harry will take care of this. As chairman, he must deal with such disagreements. Harry can finish this fool off."

Ahh. Harry smiled grimly to himself. Once he was driven out, his enemies did expect him to go on the attack. Parker trusted his new benefactors to protect him. Every man and woman present at this meeting would testify to the events which led to the attempted killing of Parker. No one would believe it was in retaliation for a crime perpetrated many years ago. Lilah's claims about all of it being a conspiracy would fall on deaf ears. This game was not meant merely to send Harry to prison or the electric chair; it would quash any arguments Lilah might make.

Once again, Parker strode to the front. "This old man says Sheppard was educated at the school of hard knocks. What's he talking about? Those stories about the escape from Libya? Do any of you know what Sheppard did there? How many he killed—yes, *killed*—in his attempt to save his own skin? There are multiple warrants out for him in the country for the murders of many, including a woman. Buhthah... her name was Buhthah."

Hers was the first of many faces to haunt Harry's nightmares— the assassin who tried to kill him with poison and ended up dying at his hands. Now, there was a name to call her by.

"There was wanton destruction of property," continued Parker. "Thievery of government vehicles. The bombing near the Halfaya Pass was a last-ditch attempt by Libyan forces to get this criminal. How many Bedouins died for him to escape?"

Parker paused for a second to let the information sink in. The audience murmured.

Flinging a hand up, the rapist continued, "Petty Officer Sheppard blamed Sanders for what happened to his family's old business, Genesis Oil... as though Sanders needed the two-bit company when he owned the largest private oil network in the world. I worked for Jared Sanders. He was—is—a great man. Unlike what this criminal made the world believe, Sanders was fair in his treatment of partners. If Sheppard wanted to beat Sanders, why didn't he go about it the honest way?"

There was no mention of Argentina. Parker either believed the stories about Sanders being responsible for the slaughter, or the colonel's current bosses told him to keep his mouth shut about it. After all, it would implicate them, as well.

Parker swung to face Godwin.

"This old fool who supports the criminal," the colonel said, pointing at the Kingsley patriarch. "What does *he* know about ethical behavior? Oh, the stories I've heard about Godwin Kingsley would shock most decent people. Has anyone here asked him why he never got married? Why there have been no whispers about him with women? Couldn't he rise to the occasion?" Parker laughed crudely. "Or is he hiding some perversion? What *does* the Kingsley family know about ethics? I heard his alcoholic half-brother got yet another girl pregnant before he died. Mr. Brad Kingsley, your grandfather is the master of misdirection. All his lofty talk about ethics is only a distraction while he feeds on your hard work."

Through Parker's long tirade about Godwin, Harry didn't move from his position, but his eyes narrowed. Parker was attacking the former justice? For what? They were supposed to be in cahoots.

Victor stood, face red and angry. "I'm going to beat the shit out of you."

"Sit down, son," Godwin barked. "This is a corporate meeting, not a barroom brawl. As chairman of the board, Harry will take care of things. I'm quite surprised he's been silent so far."

Harry flicked another glance at Lilah at Godwin's continued baiting. Her eyelids lowered in a silent request for calm. Harry acknowledged it with a slight nod.

Parker continued to ridicule Godwin. "You're nothing in Kingsley Corp. No shares... you exist in the business at the will and pleasure of others."

Godwin was unperturbed. "True enough. It's also true none of these CEOs can match me in experience or skill."

A few of the irritated businessmen called for Godwin to shut up.

So this is how Godwin gets to stop arguing for me. The surprising nomination of Harry as chairman coming from the very people who wanted him dead, this last attack on Godwin by his own weapon... all of it was designed to make sure no blame fell on the main conspirators.

Harry stood.

"Enough," he said, voice ringing across the hall. The decibel level in the room went instantly down. "For now, I'm the duly elected chairman of this board. Like any other board, we have protocol we will follow. Colonel Parker has elaborated on why he believes I'm not the right person for this position, so let's hold another vote. According to our charter, more than fifty percent support is enough to win the chairmanship, but two-thirds majority is needed for the person in question to defeat a no-confidence motion. If I don't get to sixty-seven percent, I will be out. Let me make it very clear this vote will only be on *my* leadership, not Kingsley's. Brad Kingsley was educated at West Point. Godwin is his grandfather, and Mr. Temple is more or less an uncle. Brad's wife is Andrew Barrons's daughter. Brad grew his company from a small setup to the powerhouse it is today. He and his brothers organized this network. Brad has the education, the connections, and the skill to run this organization. There's no reason for any of you to have doubts about his leadership. Vote *me* out and pick another chairman if you so wish."

Murmurs of agreement rose from the listeners. In a matter of seconds, the mood shifted from incensed to rational.

Harry continued, "Before the vote, there are a few facts you need to hear. The things the colonel mentioned about Libya... the female *assassin* he accused me of killing, the thievery... the U.S. government has been aware of all of it for a long time. The authorities understand I was trying to escape death at the hands of a power-hungry madman and his pet dictator. *Sanders* bombed the border crossing between Egypt and Libya in his attempt to kill me. The deaths of the Bedouins were from the same attack, and Jared Sanders alone bears responsibility for the lives lost. There is evidence for everything I mentioned... you don't have to take my word for any of it. Furthermore, the very fact I'm fortunate enough to call one of the Bedouins—Saeed al-Obeidi—my friend should tell you something. Several Gaddafi officials were in Sanders's pocket, so of course, the Libyan government has arrest warrants out on me. The concerned authorities in the U.S. have thus far protected me precisely because they do not feel I did anything unjustified. Also, please be aware Colonel Parker has a history with Genesis Oil and the Sheppard family."

Parker's head snapped back, a small smirk appearing on his face. Godwin sat up as did the president.

Harry nodded. "Recently, I got the opportunity to go back and study the events leading to our abandonment of the business in Sirtica... the various accidents and calamities befalling our old company, Genesis Oil. Funnily enough, the name of a Colonel Parker popped up in nearly all those incidents. Oh, there's no proof he caused any of it, but when you see a common thread running through what appear to be completely unrelated events, logical people wonder."

Tone cautious, Alex called, "Harry." He shoved his chair back as though to approach Harry and stop him from responding to Parker's provocations. Sabrina's hand shot out, grabbing Alex by the wrist.

Ignoring the byplay, Harry said, "There's also the matter of your personal history, Colonel. Why did you leave the army? Would you care to tell these folks? Was it an honorable discharge? Why not? Would the fiancé of an influential sheik in Libya have a tale to tell, Colonel? Or the wife of your CO when you were a recruit?"

Parker swept his arm in a wide arc. "People, I give you the hero of the oil sector and the pride of the U.S. Navy SEALs, Harry Sheppard. He brings up the names of women to discredit me. Neither an officer nor a gentleman! Go on, Sheppard. Let's put all the information in front of those gathered here and have another vote. I'll fight you. Not even for myself. I'll fight you only for the opportunity to see someone capable and deserving in the spot you now occupy."

"As you wish," said Brad. "We'll vote tomorrow. The delay will give us sufficient opportunity to consider both sides of the argument."

There were shouted yeses from the oil executives. Chatter rose.

Parker started striding back to his seat and paused by Harry so they were standing shoulder to shoulder, facing away from each other. In a whispered taunt only Harry could hear, Parker mumbled, "You called her 'Harry,' I remember. After yourself? How sweet! So she was, by the way. Very sweet. A tender fifteen or sixteen at the time, am I right?"

Harry clenched his fists. *One... two... three...* he focused on his heartbeats until the criminal walked away.

#

Five minutes later

Steven scooted his chair back. "Come," he said to his friend, Richard Armor. "We need to have a chat with the colonel."

Accompanied by Charles, Steven and Richard strode to Parker's table. The rest of the audience was now milling around, chattering in excitement. There were many glancing toward Parker, but no one seemed to want to talk to him and associate themselves with a potential problem. Steven could talk to the man without being overheard.

"What's the game?" Steven asked, eyeing the colonel up and down. Parker had obviously maintained himself even after retirement from the military. Still, the profusion of gray in his hair and the crow's feet surrounding the stony eyes suggested age at least in the fifties.

"The game is to get Sheppard out of his position," Parker said, gathering his papers. "He's a troublemaker. What if he decides one day one of us isn't ethical enough to suit him? Are we going to kowtow to him and his ideas for utopia? As though he follows any rules or ethics himself! We all saw what he did to Sanders."

"It will still leave Brad in charge," Steven said.

"Once Sheppard's out of the picture, we can put in someone as chair who's more... understanding," Parker said. "We'll deal with Brad later. Work with me here. Talk to people. We don't have much time. The vote is tomorrow."

As the gathering dispersed, Steven invited Parker to join them for dinner before the entertainment organized for the evening.

"I have plans," he said, flicking a glance in the direction of the Kingsley table and smiling to himself.

Chapter 44

Same evening

Arrangements were made for a light-and-sound show dramatizing the history of the castle housing the Kingsley family. It was to be a tale of love, betrayal, and revenge. The young wife of the Spanish general in charge of the fortress made the mistake of starting an affair with a captain under her husband's command. The pair of lovers vanished one day. Stories abounded about their disappearance, but no one openly challenged the general's claim his wife returned to Spain. The captain was supposedly transferred to

Cuba. Many years after the general died, a curious American soldier found two skeletons walled in the dungeons. Both bore bullet holes in their skulls. Locals whispered how on foggy nights, you could see the shadows of a man in a soldier's uniform and a woman in flowing, gauzy robes running across the roof, between the turrets. Sometimes, they were laughing in love play. Sometimes, they were fighting a third person, a man.

Inside Brad Kingsley's wing, footsteps sounded on the stairway used by the serving staff. The man wearing the uniform of the catering company waited nervously with a deep tray holding wine bottles. Money exchanged hands. "In her room at this time," said the waiter. "The guards are around, but my contact in the regular staff says her husband asks everyone else to get out when they start fighting. It happens almost daily, so watch for your chance."

#

An hour later

Why *did I return here?* Lilah asked the image in the dressing-table mirror. The woman clad in the cowl-neck gown in shimmery vermillion appeared composed, not a hair out of place, none of her turbulent thoughts showing on her face.

Behind her was Brad, fixing his bowtie while griping about her failure to speak up in support of him at the meeting. "...not a single word!" He paused for a breath and adjusted the glasses on his nose.

"I have a few papers to look over," Lilah said abruptly. The low stool clattered to the floor when she stood and grabbed the colorful scarf from the table.

Without waiting for a response, she practically sprinted out of the suite. All six of her guards were waiting on the other side of the door and fell in behind as she strode to the office, stiletto heels clickety-clacking on the floor. Something—perhaps the unnatural stiffness of the security officers—told her Brad was following. At the door to the office suite, he dismissed the men, and Lilah resigned herself to a prolonged fight.

Fortunately, Hema—Lilah's intern—was at her desk, still in her preferred work clothes of pants and shirt. The Nepali girl usually stayed in Patrice's wing, but she was very diligent about her job. She'd waited in Lilah's office until after the meeting without bothering to get ready for the night's entertainment. Brad glanced at Hema and apparently decided not to continue the quarrel. Thankful he left, Lilah did take a couple of minutes to peruse a document or two. But the reports on Amber Barrons were already reviewed a million times.

Tossing the folder back onto her desk, Lilah said, "Hema, we don't have much time before the show starts. You need to get changed."

"I have my dress right here," said Hema, smiling widely in excitement. It would be her first time attending an event this large.

"Lilah," someone called from behind.

Turning around, Lilah murmured in surprise, "Patrice."

"I heard what happened at the meeting," said Patrice. "Bits and pieces of it... what's going to happen now?"

"Gimme a moment," Lilah said. "Hema, please put the papers away and get ready while Patrice and I chat. We can go to the show together."

Leaving Hema to don the modest frock she picked for the evening, the other two women used the private corridor which led to the garden. They stood right next to the French doors, talking. Lilah braided the colorful scarf into her hair, her only accessory for the event.

"I'm sure Harry can reason with the investors," she soothed.

"All this time and effort, and some crazy fellow..." Patrice fretted.

The melancholic tune from a Native American flute echoed across castle grounds. "Are you sure you won't go with me and Hema?" Lilah asked, a new thought occurring. Patrice popped up in the office *sans* the two men supposed to be keeping her safe. Thanks to Brad's little snit, Lilah's guards weren't present, either. Since the Kingsleys were expected to move around with their own protection, the rest of the security officials would turn their attention to wherever the guests happened to be at the moment—currently in the amphitheater or resting in the guesthouse. It meant Lilah needed to call the security chief to provide escort for herself and Hema. For Patrice, too. "Go with us," Lilah suggested. "The troupe we hired has promised it'll be spectacular."

"I would stick out like a sore thumb." The dress code was black tie—tuxedos and evening gowns and enough glitter to rival the night sky. Patrice waved a dismissive hand. "Besides, most of these acts simply give rich people what they expect. No authenticity."

"In that case," Lilah started, "will you stay in the office until—"

A loud scream echoed out from the building. Startled, Lilah stilled, as did Patrice. At the same instant, both pivoted and ran inside. Lilah grabbed the iron poker from the *faux* fireplace in the anteroom of her suite. Shoving open the door to the inner office, Lilah exploded in.

Hema was cowering in the farthest corner, papers and shattered pieces of glass scattered all around. A man stood not three feet from her. Parker.

The room blurred. Lilah was suddenly in the American Club in Libya. *"Please!"* She held out a hand to the maid at the doorway, begging for rescue. *"Help!"*

The man astride her turned his head and yelled at the woman to get the hell out and shut up if she knew what was good for her.

"Help!" Hema screamed, jolting Lilah back.

"Get away from her," Patrice yelled.

Parker whirled. "There you are," he said to Lilah. "I was actually looking for you when I ran across this tidbit. Who knew she'd screech so loud?"

"What?" Patrice spat. "Do you know this man, Lilah?"

"Oh, she knows me very well." Parker smirked. "I wanted to make sure there are no hard feelings. After all, we're going to be working closely together."

Hema was still huddled in the corner. From beneath the protective shield of the girl's crossed arms, Lilah could see bare skin where the shirt was torn. She looked at the sniggering man standing directly in front. Rage set fire to her blood, sending it boiling through her veins. "Not one more woman," Lilah said in a hard voice. Raising the poker, she swung it with all her might at his neck.

Chapter 45

The slow, steady beat of the powwow drum pulsed through the air. Singers chanted their respects to the Great Spirit who gave the first drum to the women of the native nations. Drummers beat the stretched skin with their sticks while women in tribal clothing swayed around the flame pit. The heartbeat of the Indian nation came together with the heartbeat of Mother Earth.

Lilah's heart skipped a time or two, then beat in rhythm with the music. Righteous wrath churned within. The monster had turned at the last moment and escaped the blow to his neck. Lifting her weapon again, she brought it down on him. He fell, howling in pain, blood trickling from his scalp.

Outside the office window, the last rays of the sun vanished. A full moon lit the night sky. Billions of stars burned all across the heavens. Far away on the stage, the choir called to the ancient spirits, their voices echoing across the velvet blackness.

An ancient fury filled Lilah, turning her body into a crucible. Her arms hardened to steel, lending her strength to destroy evil. The metal rod came down again and again as the demon twisted and turned on the carpet. Roaring in thwarted lust and rage, he grabbed the weapon. Lilah slashed out with her foot, her pointed heel gashing his hand. Blood spurted. He screamed once more in pain and ire.

The castle glowed golden. The first strains of "Bolero" sounded. Clarinet music accompanied by military snare drums played in the background while the shadow army marched across the fortress. The captain arrived, ready to report for duty.

In the outdoor audience, Harry looked for Lilah, but the seat next to Brad's was empty. Briefly, Harry wondered if she would skip the event. She wouldn't want to encounter the—where was Parker? Dread exploded... sudden, acute terror. Harry stood. When Verity caught his arm with a questioning look, he shook himself loose, saying, "I have to go."

He broke into a run, toppling chairs and pushing aside those standing in the aisles. When he got to the last row of seats, he saw Hema running to him, hands clutching the edges of her shirt together. Catching her by the elbows, he asked, "Lilah?"

She gasped, "Help," and pointed back at the house.

The music changed to a loud and lively fandango. Clapping and Spanish guitars accompanied the singers. The performers danced across the roof, ingenious lighting showing them only as mysterious silhouettes, twirling, bending, and dipping. On the turret, a shadowed woman fell to her knees in despair. She looked back at her departing husband, defiantly tossing her head before joining the crowd of dancers.

Back in the castle, the monster rose from the carpet, wounded and enraged. He grabbed Lilah by the forearm, wrenching it as hard as he could. "Oh, no, you don't," the beast said, using his other hand to grip her windpipe.

Patrice rained futile blows on him, screaming loudly for help, but there was no one in the building to hear. As he started to squeeze precious air out of Lilah, she gasped to Patrice, "Run."

Trumpets blared. The young *señora* was ordered away from the dance by her lord and master. She turned to look at the audience as she was dragged away, her arm stretched out in entreaty.

Lilah was heaved out of the house, over the graveled garden path and into the shadows, her arm still clutching the poker. She clawed at the monster with her other hand. Then, he made a mistake. He dragged her upright. Raising her knee, she slammed it hard into his groin. She bent her elbow and rammed it into his solar plexus while bringing the sharp point of her heel down on his foot. As he shouted in pain and let go, she wheezed in huge gulps of air. While he was bent over, she shifted her grip on the pointed rod and gouged his face.

Thundering ovation filled the air as the first dance of the show came to an end. Shadows ran in synchronized fashion across the roof and back into the dressing areas.

Lilah ran toward the distant sounds of applause, toward the light, wanting the world to put this madman away for all eternity. A flight of stairs loomed before her, stones loose. The old fortress. She ran up, her panic not letting her recognize where it led. She could hear loud grunting close behind. Bursting into a brightly lit open space, she looked around in confusion. Below her was the rooftop where the troupe gathered for the next part of the performance.

The curious audience glanced from one scene to the other. Background dancers swayed gently on the lower roof. On the upper roof, the shadows showed two figures meeting in battle. Barely audible screams of rage added to the drama.

Patrice ran blindly into the gathering. Panting, she looked around for someone, *any*one, who could help. "Alex," she sobbed, spotting her son. She brushed past a man and apologized out of habit, not pausing to check who it was.

Richard Armor straightened from his stumble as the middle-aged woman rushed past. He glanced back in irritation and narrowed his eyes when Alex Kingsley leaped from his chair to sprint out. Richard marched to his friends and placed a hand on Steven's shoulder. "Something's going down."

Tango music played. The clarinet sounded. The couple on the lower roof danced passionately, forgetting vows, pledges, and honor. They twisted and whirled between turrets, faces unseen.

Above them, a macabre dance of life and death ensued. The woman spun across the crenelated terrace, holding her weapon in front. She edged back as the monster stalked her, hands held menacingly out.

No one? Lilah thought in anger. Was there no one in the audience to come to her aid? She straightened. The fire which birthed her at the Egypt-Libya border rendered her strong enough. "*I* will stop you," Lilah said, pivoting. "I am *meant* to stop you." She swung her weapon hard. Blood sprayed from the monster's neck. As he screamed and clutched at his wound, she swung again. "Justice," she sentenced with the collective voices of ages past pouring through her. "For everyone before me and everyone who came after— justice."

Through the stairway door burst another shadow. Holding the weapon trained on the demon, Harry stepped around him and jogged to Lilah's side.

Music rose to a crescendo. Cymbals crashed. The captain held his inamorata close, fingers splayed at her waist. She wrapped her leg high around his thigh, and they swayed back and forth to the primal rhythm of Argentine slum-dwellers, the world forgotten.

Above them, the hunter was now the hunted. Harry held his gun on Parker while Lilah closed in on him, poker raised.

Alex ran up the stairs and onto the roof. Taking in the scene with a single glance, he waited for Lilah to finish off the monster.

Just behind him, three men erupted into the light. "Parker," Charles yelled as his companions turned to him to say no. A shiny black object flew across the roof. Parker caught it.

As he raised his arms to point the pistol at Lilah, Alex roared and bounded forward. Fury in her eyes and weapon in her hands, she faced down death.

Harry sprinted with almost superhuman speed, his gun still locked on his target. Time slowed. His lungs burned in excruciating agony. Heart thumped painfully against the rib cage. Everything blurred as he leaped. Then, he was in front of Lilah, shielding her with his own body. His weapon discharged.

Red balls of fire spun across the roof, each projectile striking the threatening shadow in the head. At the same instant, a blue light erupted from the monster's hand and pierced the other man.

Harry's body jerked as the bullet tore into his torso. He continued to shoot while somehow managing to draw his knife from the ankle sheath. Barely aware of the pain in his chest, Harry threw the Ari B'Lilah. The blade whirled through the air, spinning faster and faster until it resembled a lethal wheel to his fuzzy eyes. Parker was already falling, but the weapon landed squarely in his neck, splattering blood and gore.

Many in the audience were standing now, shouting in alarm. Brad asked Victor, "What's happening?" They looked around and at each other. Verity searched frantically for Harry. Patrice continued to peer up at the roof, praying incoherently.

Harry wheezed. He couldn't get any air. Screams surrounded him. The gun fell from his fingers, and the world tilted. He saw Alex running toward him, taking his hand in a tight grip. Slender arms enveloped Harry from behind as his head lay on Lilah's lap. She pressed her scarf against his chest in a futile attempt to stem the bleeding. Harry kept his eyes pinned on her dearly familiar features. Both Alex and Lilah were begging Harry to stay awake, to please stay with them. Their words echoed. Faces blurred. He tried to speak, to tell her... the voices faded.

The stage lights dimmed, shrouding the world in darkness. A woman's agonized scream rent the night. *"Harry!"*

Part XIV

Chapter 46

Don't you dare die, Harry! Quaking in wild fear, Lilah pressed her scarf against the ugly wound on his chest. Warm blood soaked the thin silk as desperate sobs echoed in her mind.

Over the terrace, a giant bolt of lightning tore the black sky, followed by a deafening crash. Hidden by dark clouds, the moon was no longer visible. Power blinked out without warning. Footsteps thundered up the stairs, and with flashlights piercing the darkness, Kingsley security officers burst through the door, followed by the emergency personnel hired for the board meeting. The beeps of the portable medical equipment sounded ghostly in the moonless night. There was more lightning, and for a few seconds, the roof was lit, revealing more figures running to the scene.

The heavens opened, rain sweeping across the fortress and its grounds. Water slammed Lilah's head, pouring down her face and nearly blinding her. A tarp was erected quickly on the roof, but the people beneath it were already soaked to the skin.

Blood, so much blood. Technicians shouted out orders, but Lilah hardly heard any of it. Under the scrap of fabric she held against Harry's chest, Lilah felt his heart continue to thump, her existence narrowing to its rhythm. Counting each precious beat, she pleaded with God to give him another.

Lilah was vaguely aware of the doctor from the presidential entourage saying something to her, then to Alex. She barely felt Alex wrap his arms around her shoulders. Sitting on the gray stone floor under the same tarp shielding Harry from the deluge, Alex pulled Lilah to his chest.

The doctor inserted a narrow tube through the patient's mouth, squeezing air into his lungs. A familiar face was with the doctor... Neil Kingsley. The two surgeons from the emergency medical team were also around. The techs were unmindful of the pelting rain while they waited for instructions from the medics kneeling over the wounded hero.

Wet evening gown clinging to her form, Lilah shook violently from the icy downpour. Sharp needles pierced her lungs with each wheezing breath she took. At her side, Alex was in no better condition.

Sabrina appeared at the top of the stairs. Dan and Shawn were right behind, both men shouting Lilah's name. With an anguished gasp, Sabrina ran to her brother's body. Dan bounded toward his twin, but he was stopped by one of the security officers. Shawn joined him, the storm drenching all of them. They kept calling Lilah, demanding to know if she were all right and what was happening with Harry, but she couldn't answer. Sabrina dropped to her knees next to Lilah and asked her husband wild, hysterical questions, but her words were drowned out by the squall. Alex's responses were equally incoherent.

Alex shifted Lilah from his embrace to Sabrina's and scrambled to the medics. "Did the bleeding stop?" he asked frantically.

"I need space," snapped the surgeon examining the patient. Harry's body jerked in a soundless cough. Red, frothy fluid trickled out of the corner of his mouth. The surgeon growled. Not sparing the others a glance, he turned to his colleagues. "If we wait for MedEvac, he won't make it."

"Punctured lung?" asked Neil.

"Tension pneumothorax," one of the other doctors responded, nodding.

Rapidly cutting away Harry's wet tuxedo and dress shirt, the medical team inserted a needle between his ribs.

"He'll be okay," Alex said as though trying to convince himself as well as the women huddled next to him. "He's tough. He *will* get through this."

In the middle of the uproar, a small whimper penetrated the fog clouding Lilah's mind. Harry's wife, Verity, stood at the entrance to the terrace, her shell-shocked eyes on the prostrate form. His parents and brother were also there. At the sight of the Sheppards, the jumbled thoughts ricocheting around Lilah's mind came into sharp focus.

Rain continued to come down in sheets. Through the translucent curtain of water sluicing down the awning at the entrance, Lilah stared at the people clustered under the shelter of the canopy. What Harry said about his brother's role in the trouble at Gateway... did Hector Sheppard have a part in what happened? Hot rage churned in her chest.

"Lilah," Dan shouted again. She turned her head toward him and nodded, letting him know she was okay.

A little away from the group, Kingsley security guards helped cops in waterproof gear zip Parker's remains into a body bag.

When the sounds of the MedEvac chopper got louder, Lilah peered at the night sky. The red cross on white background was lit up. The aircraft settled onto the terrace, and uniformed men ran out, bending almost double. Medics strapped Harry to the stretcher, and Verity touched his fingers briefly before he was lifted into the helicopter.

Lilah's teeth chattered from the cold wind generated by the chopper blades. Icy water sprayed in her face, and she blinked rapidly to clear her vision. Lights came on as the backup generator finally powered up.

Gusts of wind blew leaves and twigs across the landscape. Umbrellas protected the crowd in the garden as they watched the rooftop drama. Brad and Victor were trying to herd the curious guests toward the glass-walled lobby of the corporate building. Muttering something about helping, Shawn hustled Dan from the scene.

Holding on to each other, Lilah and Sabrina watched the helicopter lift off, carrying Harry to the hospital on Southcom's grounds.

Chapter 47

A few minutes later

A second chopper waited on the rooftop for Harry's family, blades rotating slowly. The rain ebbed to a drizzle, but water had already washed the red stains from the rough stones where Harry's body lay only a few minutes ago. The tarp that protected him from the storm was kicked to the side. The remains of the dead rapist were already on the way to the morgue.

Blinking away the drops clinging to her lashes, Lilah called, voice steely, "Hector..." Alex and Sabrina followed closely as Lilah strode toward Hector Sheppard. Harsh lights threw Hector's face into threatening shadows. Facing down the former pugilist, she said with a blatant note of command in her tone, "In the hospital, Harry's security will be arranged by the Peter Kingsley Network. No one will have access without guards present."

"Excuse me?" Hector said incredulously, his eyes going to Alex's supportive hand on her shoulder.

"Not for a minute," Lilah insisted.

"He's my brother," growled Hector. "We can take care of him."

"Harry is the chairman of this network," she reminded the elder son of the Sheppard family. "He was injured in an attack by a madman who was *also* a member of the network. I have a responsibility to ensure his safety, and I can't simply take people at their word. Round-the-clock security will be arranged with limited access to visitors."

Sabrina made a muffled sound of confusion but didn't object. The senior Sheppards were next to the chopper and turned at the antagonistic conversation. Voice soothing, Ryan said, "It's a family matter now, Lilah. Let *us* handle it."

"Since when were family and friendship enough to secure the loyalties of the Sheppards, Uncle Ryan? If you decide to make things difficult, no one—and that includes you—will get anywhere near Harry until he recovers."

"Just how are you planning to carry out this threat? I'm his father."

Smiling coldly, she said, "*I* won't; Alex will. By the authority of having Harry's power of attorney."

Alex's hand tightened on her shoulder.

The local clinic called to say they were ready for Lilah's X-rays. "Dante and Hema," she insisted, shivering violently in the waterlogged gown. Someone wrapped a large, dry towel around her shoulders. "They need to go with me." A dozen guards accompanied them.

In one corner of the private waiting room, Lilah held a whispered conference with Dante, rattling off instructions. "We cannot afford delays on this," she said. "The Kingsley jet should be ready for you by now. Go, please."

Shock clear on his face, Dante nodded and marched off.

Hema was huddled in a chair toward the far end, an oversized shirt covering her from chin to knees. Smiling tremulously at her intern, Lilah was about to call her when there was a thundering of fists on the door.

The doctor entered, followed by Panamanian cops. The officers did a quick interview of Lilah while she was getting treated. Hema was also examined by the medics and declared shaken but uninjured.

It was almost dawn when they returned to Lilah's office suite. The guards stationed themselves outside. Wet gown slapping against her calves, she walked in. Muddy footprints marked the beige carpet. Next to the window, the wide-mouthed glass bowl lay broken on the carpet, blue lotuses strewn around. Papers were scattered all over.

Left arm in a sling, Lilah made a call on the internal line. Dan informed her all his appointments for the next week were canceled. Until he saw for himself her security arrangements were satisfactory—better than what they currently were—he wasn't leaving. No, not even for the China trip the next month which was particularly important to Barrons O & G. Lilah finally lied, claiming she was going to rest.

Quickly, she dialed a second number. "Alex," she said in lowered tones, darting a quick glance at the library in the suite where Hema was napping. "We need to take care of it now... before anyone finds out."

Half an hour later, she ripped the sheet off the typewriter and handed it to Alex. "Here... sign it."

Like Lilah, Alex was still a soggy mess from the evening, his tux wet and dark-brown hair plastered to his head. Bloodstains showed on his shirt as they did on her dress. "This is illegal," he argued, eyes wild.

"We can't let anyone get to Harry while he's unable to defend himself. I'm a lawyer licensed to practice in the state of New York. Didn't he ask you to do what he would when we first discussed Parker's reappearance? 'You *have* to be me' were his exact words. This is my legal opinion. Harry gave you power of attorney. When he wakes up, if he decides to sue me for malpractice, he can. Sign it."

Alex groaned but signed the document and watched Lilah endorse it as the grantor, Harry Sheppard. "Watch... we'll both be in prison for fraud. Hector is Sabrina's *brother*, for God's sake! You seriously expect me to tell him to stay away from Harry?"

"If you want Harry to survive, you'd better do exactly that. I'll explain to Sabrina."

"This is crazy," Alex said, shoving both hands into his hair. "You're wrong. I can't believe Hector would—"

"Hector, Temple, Godwin—we cannot afford to trust any of them."

Alex glared. "How can you possibly blame Grandfather for what Parker tried to do?" At her mutinous silence, he huffed in disbelief. "*You're* crazy." Shaking his head, he said, "Never mind. I'll indulge you for now... until Harry wakes up. Not a second after. And I don't want to hear any more of your ridiculous theories about my grandfather." He strode out, muttering through clenched teeth.

Before the door shut behind him, Sabrina called with information from the hospital. The trauma surgeons successfully stopped the hemorrhaging. Harry was on a ventilator, more tubes inserted into his chest to keep the lung expanded, but he was deemed stable enough to be moved to Miami. Full recovery was the prognosis given by the medical team. No, there wouldn't be time for Lilah to visit before the transport aircraft took off.

He would live, and that was enough for her. Whispering a prayer of gratitude to the Almighty, Lilah hung up. She continued to stay in the office, watching the first rays of the sun come up. Her poor guards remained outside the door. She tried to analyze what happened, but images of Harry's bloodied body crowded her mind.

When Hema brought her a cup of coffee, Lilah took it with gratitude. "You know what we are going to do?" When Hema's brows drew together in a silent question, Lilah elaborated, "Set you up with some self-defense lessons."

For a few moments, Hema simply stared. "I'd like that," she said. Tears suddenly sparkled on her lashes. "You killed him... the horrible man."

Lilah stood with alacrity and went around the desk to wrap the girl in a hug. "I'm so very sorry about what happened," she whispered. "I wish... God, I wish... you haven't seen much justice in your life, have you? You believed you'd be safe here. We need to make sure you *are* safe. As soon as the whole mess settles down, we're going to see about getting you martial arts lessons. Plus, Alex can teach you how to shoot." Letting Hema go, Lilah mustered a playful smile. "Who knows? Maybe you'll go into that line of work. A police officer or some such."

The remark got an answering smile from Hema. "Thank you," she said.

When Lilah returned to her chair, the girl went to the carpet and collected the papers scattered on the rug, carefully avoiding the sharp pieces of glass from the broken bowl. Wet patches had made the ink spread on some of the sheets.

Lilah's eyes followed Hema as she slid the documents back into the slim plastic folder.

"Are those the papers I left with you before..." Lilah asked. When the intern nodded, Lilah held out a hand. "Leave them on the desk to dry out... I'll put them away later. *You* need to go to bed."

The cops might ask to inspect the office. Lilah didn't want anyone else seeing the info on Amber and unnecessarily starting fresh gossip about a dead woman. The story didn't turn out to be the weapon Lilah hoped for, and there was no longer any point in disturbing Amber's ghost.

Temple and Godwin had succeeded in bringing another ghost into the open, one from Lilah's past. Parker did his best to squeeze Harry out, but whether the rapist won or failed, it wouldn't have mattered. Temple could have waited until Harry went after Parker in some way. So why did Parker try to kill her? Well... he attacked Hema first, but he wouldn't have done so and left Lilah alive as witness. The intern simply happened to be in the wrong place at the wrong time. Lilah was Parker's target. Was it how the enemy planned to provoke Harry? *But the death beneficiary clause in the pre-nup... did they decide it doesn't matter since there won't be any children?*

Closing her eyes, Lilah tried to study the enemy's strategy. The pieces on the chessboard, every move perfectly timed... her death, followed immediately by Harry's... the prenup, her old will, inheritance laws... Harry would have his own will.

Lilah rubbed her brow with a finger. Temple and Godwin were surely behind it all. Still, her thoughts kept circling back to Harry's family, back to Hector Sheppard and the embezzlement.

Part XV

Chapter 48

The next morning

Cerro Azul, Panama

At the breakfast table in the guest suite, the former president kept his eyes on the television as Brad's secretary reported Godwin's departure the night before. Barely checking his rage, Temple thanked the woman. She wished them a pleasant day and left the well-lit room.

"Son of a..." Temple ground out. Legal experts on CNN continued weighing in on the incident involving the titans of the oil and gas industry. Next to Temple, Noah buttered a croissant and stayed silent. "Noah, tell me you didn't have a hand in it."

The table knife made no sound as Noah placed it carefully on his plate. Dangerous anger glittered in his eyes when he met his friend's glare. "No. If I chose to go after Lilah, it would've been a clean kill. I would *not* have contracted a suspected rapist like Parker to attack her."

Thumping the table with a fist, Temple said, "So it's Godwin."

"Let's think this through, logically."

Filling his mug with coffee, Temple's mind replayed the events of the night before. The chief of police had already reported there were no guns on Parker except the one registered to Charles Kingsley. Only security personnel were supposed to carry weapons to the event, but the idiot of the Kingsley clan hid one in his blind father's luggage, and the disabled man was waved in without much scrutiny.

Perhaps Parker didn't attempt something similar because he never imagined Lilah would be able to fight back. Perhaps the absence of firearms was meant to bolster any claims of innocence he might later make in the matter of her death. The police might have bought the story, but Harry wouldn't have. He'd have completely lost it.

Temple's hand shook, and hot liquid splashed onto the cream lace tablecloth. "Has to be Godwin's doing. Who else?" Perhaps when Lilah did fight back, Parker's criminal insanity made him chase her into a public arena.

Noah blotted the coffee stain with a tissue. "The police have no idea Parker was not acting on his own, but if they did, the first person they looked at would be her husband."

"Brad?" Temple exclaimed. "He's not a violent fellow."

Noah sighed. "Haven't we both seen enough of the world to know better? Any man pushed hard enough can be vicious. Brad thinks his wife's having an affair with his own brother. Why would you rule him out?"

Temple slashed the air with his hand. "The pre-nup... Brad would not have risked it. He's a rational man. Also, Brad had no clue of Parker's connection to Lilah."

"Could he have figured it some other way? Someone else told him, perhaps? Jared Sanders, for one. Or Parker himself."

"If Parker or Sanders appealed to Brad, Godwin would've heard about it. Brad would not blindly believe either of the scoundrels. He would've asked his grandfather for advice which leads us to the same conclusion. Godwin had a hand in this. Plus, what could Parker or Sanders have said to Brad about Lilah to prompt such a brutal response toward *her*? If anything, he should've beaten Parker black and blue."

"True." Noah scrunched up the tissue and threw it neatly into the trash can. "What about the troubles in Gateway? Parker might have been double-dipping."

Temple huffed. "If Parker was paid by one of the thieves who embezzled from Gateway, it means that person was aware of Harry's history with Parker. I won't rule out Ryan Sheppard as the embezzler, but I highly doubt he contracted someone to kill his own son. Before you ask, Hector has no idea about Parker and no reason to kill Lilah or Harry."

"You can't be sure Hector was unaware of Parker's existence," Noah argued. "If Hector *was* the embezzler, he did have reason to kill. Lilah might have been bait to draw out Harry. In fact, any one of Harry's enemies could have done the same."

Temple thought about the probabilities for a few seconds. "Parker wanted protection from Harry. Apart from us, the only people who could promise it were—Hector as Harry's brother, their father, Godwin, and Brad. There's little to no possibility of Harry's father or Brad being involved. I'm flying to New York tonight. Before I talk to Hector, I'm going to meet Godwin... but why... we could've easily controlled her after Harry..."

Noah frowned. "You know, I bought into your assumption Lilah could be sidelined once Harry was gone. Godwin never did. Temple, step back for a moment and think. What do you think Lilah will do if Harry dies? Godwin's surely on top of *her* list of suspects, and so are you. She might or might not know about my involvement. She could claim to the cops we orchestrated the whole thing."

"She can claim, but it's not going to be easy to prove. Not with Parker out of the picture and unable to give evidence."

"Are you sure she's as powerless as you insist?" Noah asked. "Or are you saying it because in your mind, she's your daughter? You don't want to admit she could and would make trouble for all of us, including Godwin. If the police don't take her seriously, she could launch a counterattack on her own. She still has enough votes in the company and the network to make life difficult for the rest of the leadership. You don't want to admit *she* might need to go, not just Harry. Godwin never had any such blind spots."

Temple froze. "But the pre-nup?"

"We know Harry is her beneficiary. Imagine if the deaths were specifically timed for Lilah to go first, then Harry."

"His property would pass to his missus," Temple said, connecting the dots. "And Hector Sheppard would willingly help Godwin direct the young lady's actions."

"Godwin might even have planned to have one of his other grandsons—Steven, perhaps—marry Harry's widow." Thus cementing Kingsley control of the entire sector. "All conjecture, of course," Noah added.

Snarling, Temple said, "If last night's attack was Godwin's idea, I'm responsible for it. It was my support that made him think... he believed I wouldn't dare a say word after. I *will* talk to him. No more attacks on Lilah *or* Harry. They might not be looking for advice from us, but both have proven themselves quite competent. If they stumble, they'll recalibrate."

Noah whistled softly. "You old hypocrite. All your talk about attachment being illusion... it was fine when Harry was the planned sacrifice, but because *your* child got hurt, you want to stop the game."

Nostrils flaring, Temple drew a deep breath. "Perhaps I *am* one... but it's not just about Lilah. Noah, the idea behind the network was to create stability. If Godwin set up what happened yesterday, it was purely out of ambition... greed to the point of cold-blooded murder. I need to make it clear last night's incident cannot ever be repeated. Where are *you* on it?"

Noah set his cup down. "I've had my doubts for some time. After last night... no, we need to end this here."

"All right, I'll speak with Lilah and let her know she has our support."

"Temple..."

"What?"

"She has no reason to believe you. Wait until Harry recovers completely and talk to both."

Temple rubbed his jaw. "What if the person behind Parker attempts another attack?"

"Have a chat with Brad," suggested Noah. "Let him know to watch out for tricks from the Kingsleys, but I don't know if he'll believe anything bad about Godwin even coming from you."

"He won't," said Temple. "But I *can* ask him not to indulge in any hostilities with Kingsley Corp. Plus, beef up Lilah's protection. I hope he does. Thanks to us, things are not pretty in their marriage."

"His wife was just attacked. He can surely put aside his insecurities for a few weeks to make sure she's safe. After all, as you said, Brad Kingsley is a rational man."

Chapter 49

A week later, September 1988

Cerro Azul, Panama

During the next few days, most of the guests left, including the Barrons men. The police asked Charles and Steven Kingsley as well as Richard Armor to remain available for further questioning. Stanley, Steven's uncle, stayed back with them. Their suite of rooms in the guesthouse was luxurious but still a prison with guards at every exit.

Steven and his entourage gathered in the living room to discuss options, but Charles had started drinking early in the day and was in no shape to carry on a conversation. Looming over the couch, Steven waved away the fumes of alcohol wafting from his brother. "Because of *you,* we're stuck here, watching Cousin Brad rule the oil sector."

Charles grunted. On the second couch across the coffee table, Uncle Stanley stayed silent, content to be a supportive presence.

Not bothering to hide his bitterness, Steven said, "That whiny, sanctimonious idiot is now the most powerful man in the world. What do people see in him? President Temple, a military hero like Harry Sheppard... all of them support Brad. What has he done to deserve any of it? Even his wife was handed to him on a platter!"

From the chair to the side, Richard laughed, his eyes closed. "Envy your cousin however much you want, Steven... but not for his wife."

Steven loved Richard like a brother, but understanding the workings of his mind was another matter. "What do you mean?"

"We both know she married him because he was going to be CEO."

"So?" Steven asked. "Have you *seen* the woman?"

Richard sat up. "I have. According to the tabloids, Brad's brothers have seen *all* of her."

Steven snorted. "The *paparazzi* will say almost anything to sell copies."

"Maybe," Richard acknowledged. "But she was with Victor in Texas. The way she ordered him around... I haven't seen Victor jump the way he did for any other woman. Also, I heard rumors she was in India with Alex. She's not merely a sister-in-law."

Flinging a hand up, Steven said, "She is *not* merely their sister-in-law. She's the CFO of the company and the whole damn network."

"Don't be naïve, my friend," Richard said. "I've worked with women. They don't behave the way Mrs. Kingsley does except with husbands and boyfriends. Some of the papers say she's married to all five brothers."

"Oh, for—" Steven huffed. "Tell me you're not stupid enough to buy it."

"No, but there's *something* going on," Richard insisted.

"Whatever, man. Hell, I wish I could get her to stop the 'something' and switch sides. The Barronses and the Sheppards are with Brad only because of her. Imagine where Kingsley Corp would've been if she'd been with *us*." Steven liked ladies who were easy on the eye just as much as the average male, but he made it a point to avoid the kind more interested in his last name. Still, to be where Brad currently was... oh, yeah... a little less affection was small price to pay.

Richard retorted, "Imagine living like your cousin, knowing the rest of the world believes your wife's sleeping with your brothers. Would you feel like a man?"

"Feel like a—you know what, I don't give a flying—" Steven said. "I want to get out of this place. Unfortunately, we can't go anywhere because of Charlie." Turning to his brother, Steven asked, "Whatever made you throw the gun to the idiot? In full view of everyone!"

Morosely, Charles said, "Leave me alone."

"What if Parker killed Lilah?" Steven continued to berate his brother. "Do you realize we would've been accessories to her murder?"

"She's not dead, is she?" Charles asked, tugging at his collar with a finger.

"No thanks to you," Steven shouted. "Be grateful Sheppard decided to jump in."

"He took a bullet for her," said Richard. "Wonder what your cousin thinks of the whole thing."

"Huh?" Steven glanced at the chair where his friend was sitting.

Charles giggled.

Irritated, Steven said, "I doubt Brad would've been happier to have his wife die. And Sheppard is friends with the woman. *We're* friends, and I'd take a bullet for you."

Richard's face softened into a genuine smile. "I'm aware of it. And grateful. Somehow, I have a hard time seeing Mrs. Kingsley and Harry Sheppard as another version of you and me."

Steven slashed the air with his hand. "I couldn't care less if the two of them were making out on Brad's desk. Right now, what we need to do is figure a way out of here."

"There's nothing to figure," Uncle Stanley contributed. "The police already know Charlie was drunk when it happened. Leave it as is, and you three should be okay."

"God, I hope so," Steven said.

"It's not like people don't know about our Charlie's drinking problem," continued Uncle Stanley. His eyes were on the empty beer bottles spilling out of the trash can.

Charles ignored his relative. Holding a bottle by the neck, he stood and swayed. "Where'sh the bastard, Brad? *I'll* tell him... we dem... dem... I wanna go home!" Lurching every which way leaving the suite, he screamed, "Braaaad!"

"I'm going with him," Steven said to the other two. "Who knows what else he's going to start?"

Outside, Charles held on to the doorjamb and sneered at the guard. "I'm going for a walk," he announced and took another swig from his bottle. Losing his footing, he fell against the glass wall on the right, beyond which was the conservatory. The guard bit back a smile and offered a hand up. "Pah," said Charles, heaving himself erect. He staggered about and finally found the exit to the garden. There would be more guards there.

Steven followed his brother. It was a glorious fall morning in the mountains. The blue waters of the pool sparkled under the sun. Birds flitted about, chirping incessantly. A few feet away, Steven spotted Lilah walking in their direction, her arm in a sling. She was surrounded by her security detail. Charles hadn't seen her yet, his bloodshot eyes squinting at a grove in the distance.

Steven grimaced. While he loathed his cousins, he really had nothing against Lilah. An apology, perhaps? What the hell did he say? *I'm sorry my brother tried to get you murdered? It wasn't personal... Charlie's just a simple drunk who gets his kicks from hurting women?* When Lilah got close enough to his location by the pool, Steven called out, "How's your arm?"

She slowed enough to incline her head but didn't speak.

"And Sheppard?" he inquired. "Harry, I mean." Steven had nothing against Harry Sheppard, either, except for annoyance over his support for Cousin Brad. Plus, Harry was Hector's brother. Some concern was owed.

"Stable," Lilah said, voice clipped.

Steven tried again, "Heard they moved him to New York."

"It was more convenient for the Sheppards than Miami."

Charles stumbled around, noticing Lilah's presence for the first time. "Looky hoos here," he said, leering at Lilah with a drunken giggle and weaving about.

She wrinkled her nose at the strong fruity odor emanating from him. It seemed he was going to fall on her neck. Lilah stepped quickly to the side, but Charles's momentum kept him going.

Steven muttered under his breath and moved forward to catch Charles before Lilah's guards slammed him to the floor. Unfortunately for Steven, Charles wasn't in the mood to be helped and pushed his brother to the side.

Steven's foot slipped out from under him. The sky tilted. He waved his arms about, trying to hold on to something, but his fingers grasped only air. With a splash, he fell into the pool. Chlorinated water rushed over his face, stinging his eyes, choking him. Frantically, he splashed about and tried to swim to the side, but there seemed to be a weight on his shoulders, pulling him down. His clothes. He tried to scream for help, but only gurgles came out. His stomach churned.

A hand grasped Steven's arm, halting his descent. As the guards fished him out, someone snapped, "Calm down."

There was loud laughter, masculine in timbre.

"Blind idiot," another male voice muttered.

"Escort him back to the guesthouse, please," Lilah said to her security detail, the impatience in her tone clearly directed at the clumsy guest, not her guards.

Staring straight ahead, Steven marched his sodden self back to his room. Charles followed, slapping his thigh and howling like a hyena.

"Steven!" exclaimed Richard, leaping from his chair. "What happened?"

"Fell into the pool." The admission set Charles off again. Ignoring him, Steven said, "I want to get back to my own place where I don't have to put up with the likes of Delilah Kingsley." He peeled off his wet shirt and threw it to the carpet, explaining quickly how he was rescued from his unintended swim. "What does she think of herself? Laughing at me!"

"She laughed at you for falling into the pool?" Richard asked, eyebrows drawn in puzzlement.

"And called me blind." Steven suppressed the memory it was a *man* laughing, likely Charlie or one of the guards. The remark about Steven being blind was definitely made by a masculine voice. "Can you believe it? What kind of a woman insults... both my parents *are* nearly blind." His father lost most of his vision from childhood measles, and his mother's bad migraine made it necessary for her to wear glasses so thick they blocked almost all light.

"Steven," called Stanley. "Calm down, son. She probably blurted it without thinking. It's a common enough thing to say."

"I don't care," Steven raged. "She crossed a line."

"The woman doesn't know her place," Richard agreed. "She thinks she can get away with anything. Your idiot cousin *lets* her."

Steven said, stalking to the bedroom. "Maybe she *is* sleeping with all five brothers. And Sheppard. And does anyone here care she was ready to kill Colonel Parker? Not a single mention of the fact."

Stanley called out, "Well, it was quite obvious he was about to attack her."

A towel wrapped around his hips, Steven returned to the living room. Richard and Uncle Stanley were back in their respective seats. Charles was collapsed on the couch and snoring. "I was there, wasn't I?" asked Steven. "What was going on was beyond self-defense. I wouldn't have cared, but when I... all I wanted was to keep my position in the company. If that makes me a criminal, why is it different for whatshername? Everything these people do is somehow divinely ordained!"

"Why are you so frustrated?" Stanley asked. "We'll be out of here in a couple of days, and Kingsley Corp is doing well by any measure."

"Because this network should have been mine, dammit! Grandfather and Mr. Temple helped them build it."

"Godwin *is* heavily involved in the network." Stanley wiggled himself deeper into the chair. "You know he faxed over some numbers for me to review."

"Uncle Stanley," his nephew said, thoroughly annoyed by now. "You're an accountant in the company. It's your *job*."

"No, these weren't Kingsley Corp books. Computer printouts from the Peter Kingsley Company."

Steven drew up the chair next to Richard's, and both leaned forward. "Why would Grandfather have the information?" asked Steven.

"I'm not certain," Stanley admitted. "Godwin Kingsley is a smart man. Be careful he doesn't sell out Kingsley Corp and join Brad."

"Doesn't make sense," Richard said. "Why would the justice hand the papers to a Kingsley Corp accountant if he's planning to defect? Ask him, Steven."

Steven said, "Grandfather is not going to tell me a thing. I'm going to talk to Father. Maybe *he* knows something."

Stretching out in his chair, Richard closed his eyes. "Perhaps there *is* a way to get back at Mrs. Kingsley."

"For what?" Steven asked.

Richard chuckled. "For laughing at you. What else?"

Chapter 50

Two weeks later, September 1988

New York, New York

As expected, the Panamanian police decided Charles was an idiot drunk and his cohorts guilty only of being in the wrong place at the wrong time. When Steven returned to New York and the Kingsley mansion, he found his father in complete ignorance of the workings of the Peter Kingsley Company and the network. "I'll ask Aaron," David finally said. Aaron Kingsley, illegitimate son of the Kingsley clan and half-brother to both David and Peter, was one of the senior executives in the family business. Steven's father was supposedly the CEO, but the patriarch ran everything with Aaron's help.

"What's the point of going to Uncle Aaron?" Steven asked bitterly. "He always takes Brad's side." Aaron's heart melted at the thought of the fatherless boys... probably because he, too, grew up without a father.

Come to think of it, Charles took after the biological grandfather he never met. Like the old fellow, Charles went around drunk to the gills most of the time and let his plumbing make the decisions. But the dead alcoholic was never accused of violence or force. Charles... there were a couple of incidents with the maids... then, a cruise ship employee... thank God for the Kingsley cash, or Charles would've been dead or in jail. Why he felt the need to go after domestic help was something Steven would never understand. The weaker the woman's status, the more excited Charles got.

The company he kept wasn't helping. Their sister's husband, for one. Steven wished he paid more attention when Helen got engaged to the perv, but he'd only been a teenager at the time. Richard said something, warning Steven to keep an eye on things. Apparently, Richard's father, the family chauffeur, went to the Kingsley elders with the information before the wedding, but no one gave a damn. The man was rich and connected and was considered a White House prospect. Steven always made sure to check on Helen, and she seemed to be doing all right. Charles, on the other hand, latched on to the perv, going on exotic trips with him every few months. These days, Hector Sheppard went along when he could with Helen's husband and Charles. Hector used such occasions to indulge his fondness for fine drinks, but he also managed to keep Charles out of trouble. No one dared go against the orders of the boxer... not Charles, not the politician who was the Kingsley son-in-law.

Steven wished like hell he'd stowed Charles with Hector before running to check what was going on with Parker. It *was* simply a matter of wrong place, wrong time.

The explanation wouldn't hold water with Godwin or Aaron. Neither man was happy with Steven and Charles at the moment. Aaron Kingsley wasn't about to answer Steven's questions.

"Asking Aaron is our only option," David said.

Aaron was as surprised as they were by the news and equally determined to investigate the patriarch's involvement in Brad's company. Steven accompanied Aaron when he went in search of Godwin. The Kingsley scion watched as his aged grandfather ordered workmen about from the top of the steps, shivering slightly in the chilly morning. "Over there," the old man yelled. He was proud of his family home and kept tight control over how it was maintained.

Aaron laughed and affectionately grabbed Godwin by the shoulders. "Father, they've been doing this every year at least since I was born. I believe they know to the last inch what they need to do."

Godwin grumpily consented to leave the staff alone and walked with his adopted son and grandson to the home office. The aroma of fresh-roasted Arabica wafted to the door where Steven waited in silence while Godwin poured himself coffee. It was only recently and after much cajoling that the retired justice agreed to use an automated coffee maker instead of ringing the kitchen every time he wanted a cup.

The rest of the office remained furnished as it was since the home was originally built in the eighteen-hundreds. Damask covered the walls, and an antique globe with its brass meridian and mahogany base stood in one corner of the room. The large carved desk always seemed to have a chessboard on top, handmade pieces in genuine ivory and ebony ready for a brand-new game.

"Father," Aaron started, his tone careful, "David was asking me if we're somehow involved in the network. Steven... ahh... found some papers from Brad's company."

Godwin set the carafe back, taking care not to spill even a drop on the counter. "Brad is my grandson, too, just like Steven and the rest. When he has questions, I try my best to help him is all."

"You help them," Steven exclaimed. "The Barronses help them. Harry Sheppard helps them. Even the former president went to pay respects to the emperor of the oil sector. The woman... Lilah... she had the audacity to laugh at me for falling into the pool! Colonel Parker was killed in front of dozens of witnesses. Nothing... *nothing's* going to happen to Harry Sheppard. You know why?"

"Son," called Aaron, placing a soothing hand on his nephew's shoulder.

Steven swatted it away. "If Sheppard didn't have support from Brad and his brothers... Brad! *Brad!* He's now big enough to rescue Harry Sheppard from the government."

"I don't believe Harry needs rescuing in this instance," Aaron said mildly. "Everyone who was there saw what happened."

"It's not the damn point," ground out Steven. "One word from Brad, and both governments simply accepted Parker was a bad man who needed to die. You think the cops would've bothered to check further if Richard or I said something to the contrary? Brad is now in a position where he... you helped put him there, Grandfather. And you're *still* helping him."

Saying nothing, Godwin took a seat in the leather chair behind the desk, his eyes on the chessboard.

Steven stalked forward and rested his palms on the edge of the table. "I learned from you how to run this company. You always claim a sense of rivalry is crucial in growing a business. If you're going to work with our competitors, how can I or anyone else expect Kingsley Corp to grow?"

Godwin nodded at Aaron. "I'll handle this." Tilting his head slightly in acknowledgment, Aaron left. As he disappeared around the corner, Godwin said to his grandson, "Close the door, Steven. I have something to discuss with you."

Steven huffed in irritation. Another lecture on why Cousin Brad was the chosen one, of course! Shutting the door with exaggerated care, Steven returned.

"Coffee?" asked Godwin.

"Let's get it over with." Steven collapsed into the second chair, brooding. "List all the ways Brad is a worthy heir to the Kingsley empire, and I'm not."

"Kingsley Corp is hardly an empire, Steven. It is only one company under the umbrella of the Peter Kingsley Network."

Steven laughed bitterly. "If you'd put in half the effort for Kingsley Corp you did for Brad, we *would* be ruling the empire."

"True," mused Godwin. "Peter Kingsley Company and the network should belong to the Kingsleys. Not to upstarts like Lilah and Harry."

"Lilah and Har—what?"

"Harry Sheppard is the chairman of the board, son. Can you imagine your cousin showing enough spine to stand up to him even if Kingsley interests were at stake?"

Steven heard the words, but they didn't make any sense. "What?" he repeated.

The patriarch took a leisurely sip of the beverage and recited the Kingsley genealogy, starting with the ancestor who braved the North Atlantic gales to seek out opportunities in the new world.

Surreal! What did a pilgrim on the *Mayflower* have to do with the network?

"The blood of monarchs flows through our veins," continued Godwin. "They came from different continents, from different cultures, but all had one thing in common. They were royal. My mother came from the higher ranks of Austrian aristocracy. The Kingsleys are royal."

"Not me," said Steven. "My great-grandmother was a lobsterman's daughter from Maine. Remember her? President Temple's mother? Your stepmother?"

Godwin's gaze skittered. "Yes, well. My father lost his head... can't blame him; she was a beautiful woman." The swivel chair squeaked. Godwin left the coffee mug on the table and got up to retrieve a framed photograph from the wall. "Cunning, too. She made sure *her* son got all of Kingsley Corp. Thank God, I was kept on as president, or my dear half-brother would've sold the business for the price of another drink."

"You're talking about my real grandfather," Steven said, eyes narrowing at the trace of malice in Godwin's voice.

The former justice laughed. "Consider yourself lucky your *real* grandfather didn't live long enough to see you born. Another year under his tender mercies, even *I* wouldn't have been able to rescue the company. But no matter... what's important is we survived. Unfortunately, Sanders was ruling the sector by then. It took a lot of planning for us to return to where we were."

Steven cursed under his breath. "You just agreed... Grandfather, *we're* not where we were. Kingsley Corp is only one company. The *network* is ruled by Brad and his brothers."

Godwin's glittering gaze was fixed on the picture of his father and stepmother on their wedding day. "Sadly, even that's not true. Understand statecraft, Steven. Real power is something exercised behind the scenes and beyond scrutiny. Brad doesn't run their empire; Lilah does, with Harry's support."

Bursting into laughter, Steven said, "I'll bite. Tell me more. How are they doing it? Mind control?"

Godwin's nostrils flared. "Do you believe I find disrespect amusing?" He tossed the photograph to the carpet. "Steven, your cousin might be an idiot, but he's at least willing to take guidance. You're stupid *and* arrogant. Understand this. Lilah has the last say on every penny moving in and out of the business. Her office acts as liaison for anyone who calls with a complaint. There's very little Brad can do without her signing off on it."

Steven sat up. "Why? He's the CEO."

Ignoring the picture he'd left on the floor, Godwin walked to the table and stared at the chessboard. He spat out complaints about Brad and Lilah's pre-nup and Harry's influence and something about years of planning going down the drain.

Once as a young child of five, Steven wandered into the hedge maze in the Kingsley gardens. Lost in the labyrinth, he screamed in terror until the chauffeur's nine-year-old son came to his rescue, igniting a friendship between the boys. Listening to Godwin Kingsley go on about the network made Steven as disoriented as he felt at the time. How could Godwin have planned the network for years when it started with the alliance between the Peter Kingsley Company and Lilah's family?

When Brad was working for Kingsley Corp, he'd only been one among the many heirs, and the Barronses would never have agreed to the scheme without making certain Lilah got to be the queen. The chances of it happening would have been at best fifty-fifty. Even if Godwin anointed Brad as CEO, Steven would have retained enough clout to create problems—if the company had not split. Kingsley Corp would not have split if the animosity between cousins did not get to the point of attempted murder. The alliance couldn't have been planned prior to the murder attempt... could it?

The patriarch continued to explain the terms of the pre-nup, his fingers on the white queen's pawn.

Images from his childhood flitted through Steven's mind, the return of the barely remembered relatives. Brad's overall suck-uppery annoyed the hell out of Steven. Victor and Alex would've been all right, but thanks to Charles, neither wanted anything to do with Steven. He remembered the quarrels—petty in hindsight—blown out of proportion by the adults in their lives, the rage when he was the only one punished.

"I was hoping your idiot cousin would learn how to control his wife and property." Godwin brooded. "What a waste of time."

Idiot cousin? Steven tried to focus, but memories bombarded him.

Moving the pieces from both sides on the board, Godwin droned on about Lilah's intransigence. The white queen's pawn opened, and black responded with the Dutch defense. The game continued with both black and white adding to a stonewall. *"Real power is something exercised behind the scenes,"* Godwin had said.

Abruptly, Steven asked, "Did you do it on purpose?"

"Do what?" Godwin moved the white knight kingside.

"Were you manipulating us, Grandfather? All those fights while we were growing up, I mean. Was it your way of controlling us? Or did you seriously not realize ridicule of one party was not the way to peaceful coexistence?"

"Does it matter? You weren't too fond of them to begin with."

Shock. Steven was glad he was sitting down. Even as he asked the question, he didn't really believe it, but the chilling lack of concern on the patriarch's face sent Steven reeling. He watched his grandfather's fingers hovering over the chessboard, studying the pawns. Boys, once mercilessly maneuvered, were now aligned against each other as men. Blood against blood. Brother against brother. "Psychopath," Steven whispered.

Godwin's head jerked up. His unblinking stare bored holes into Steven. "Careful, son," he murmured. "You should be grateful. Do you think you would have gotten to this position if Brad still worked with us?"

Foggy mind trying to untangle the decades-long deceit, Steven asked, "Are you claiming you did it for me? I'm not Cousin Brad to blindly believe you."

The cold anger in Godwin's eyes caused the hair on Steven's forearms to rise. For the first time in his life, he felt real fear. Heart-stopping fear. A minute passed with Godwin saying nothing.

Steven's eyes dropped, drifting to the chessboard. "You moved the white knight too far down," he blurted.

When there was only silence in response, Steven was afraid he'd again said the wrong thing. Then, Godwin spoke, "I didn't know you kept up with chess."

"I happen to remember a few moves is all," Steven said. "The black bishop can attack the pawn on h2 and checkmate the white king."

"The bishop? Oh, you mean the priest."

"Huh?"

"For the king to have power, the priest needs to bless him. Kings without the backing of the church are easily dethroned. Fortunately for us, the priest hasn't realized the game is not over. It won't be until the grandmaster says so."

Bizarre.

Abandoning the board, Godwin picked up the ancient photograph from the floor and spent a few moments hanging it on the wall and aligning it perfectly into its previous position. "Nor does anyone know which side the grandmaster is on. Steven, a true grandmaster will play both white and black. Whichever side loses, he will win."

Steven wondered if the old man were going senile, but the former justice's eyes carried the same sharpness as always. His words flowed easily even when they seemed to be shifting between the world of humans and the squares on the chessboard. "Why?" Steven asked finally.

"Why what?"

"Why all these games? And why are you telling me about it?"

"My motive has always been plain. To get power back into the hands of the rightful heirs."

The rightful heirs... the Kingsleys... Godwin would've been the first in the line to the throne if it weren't for his stepmother. In any case, he had only a few years left to rule, and Steven was the sole half-way decent successor remaining within the family fold. Picking up the pencil cup, he raised it. "To the Kingsleys, in whom the blood flows imperial blue. What's your next move?"

Godwin outlined his strategy.

Like tongues of fire, excitement licked its way through Steven's veins. "A multi-pronged attack," he whispered.

"Yes, and before Harry recovers. After the heroism he showed at the meeting, a no-confidence motion will not win. If he's allowed to get back, he'll have veto power over your cousins' decisions. Harry will make sure *we* get nowhere near the network. Also, Temple has been calling me... I can hold him off for a while, but we need to move quickly."

"What about Brad?" Steven asked. "And his brothers?"

His grandfather said in an irritated tone, "Didn't you hear me? The fact Brad bears the title of CEO is immaterial. The family is what matters."

With the back of his hand, Steven wiped the sweat from his upper lip. "Grandfather, I'm not a fool like Brad. You're telling me this because you need me as cover. I'm your fall guy if the plan fails. You want my cooperation? Pay my price. I want to be president and CEO of the network. Brad and his brothers have to go, not just Harry and Lilah."

Godwin eyed his grandson for long moments, unblinking, unspeaking. Then, he swept the pieces from the chessboard onto the table. As Steven stared in confusion, Godwin muttered, "I've been playing the wrong game all along. I should've seen it. What we need is a better gambit... the sacrifice of the piece who thought himself king." He strode to the antique globe at the back of the room and spun it, jabbing at a speck in the Atlantic. "The Cuban Gambit."

Part XVI

Chapter 51

A week later, October 1988

Upper East Side, New York City

In a private room at New York Hospital, the monitor beeped, showing strong, healthy heartbeats. The tubes had been removed a couple of days ago, and the ventilator turned off, but the patient continued to toss restlessly in drug-induced slumber, sweat-drenched dark hair stark against white pillows.

Watching Harry from the door, Dante said a prayer for the irreverent teenager he met so long ago. As a young man from Harlem, Dante knew nothing about the oil business, but when the opportunity came up, he grabbed it with both hands. Ryan Sheppard was clear—the pay wasn't much, the hours were long, and the only assistance Dante got would be from his gofer, a fourteen-year-old boy called Harry. Oh, and the secretary was expected to live with the family. Dante didn't care. With a wife and a toddler son, he needed the job. Plus, he was ambitious, and this job assisting a small oilman would be the first rung up the corporate ladder. He gave himself two to three years tops before moving on to bigger and better things. He never imagined he'd still be working for the Sheppards nearly twenty years later, albeit as the COO. He never imagined he would get this attached to the smartass who nicknamed him "old man" the day they were introduced.

Dante nodded to the armed guard sitting on alert in one corner. There were a couple of security officers outside the door, too. Harry's wife was curled in a chair, sleeping. Sympathy welled as it did each time Dante encountered Verity. Also, a strong urge to plant his boot on Harry's backside for the way he was treating the poor girl. Marriage vows meant something, dammit.

After Harry showed up at Dante's apartment in the middle of a blizzard, Dante was the one who let Verity know where her husband was. The young lady sobbed out something about Lilah, enough to tell Dante there were insecurities lurking in Verity's mind. He assured her how Lilah was merely Harry's childhood friend and asked why they wouldn't have simply married each other if there were anything more. Verity seemed soothed by the thought... which of course made it clear Harry never told her anything about the political pact leading to the alliance. Now, Verity was going to have questions Dante wasn't sure he could answer.

He patted the young woman on the shoulder, and she woke with a start, gray-blue eyes crinkling in a smile as she saw him.

Leaving the guards with Harry, they went to the deli on York Avenue. The fall morning was damp and gloomy. Birds fluttered about the open space outside the shop, pecking at the crumbs on the ground. They sat at one of the high-top tables in the deli. "Harry was thrashing about so much the nurses gave him sedation," Verity said, using a scrunchie to pull her white-blonde hair into a short ponytail. "But the surgeon said the fever's going down." She took a sip of her tea. "Dante, can I ask you something?"

He had an inkling of what was coming but still said, "Go ahead."

Verity looked sideways. Fat pigeons crooned outside the glass wall, setting up a gentle cacophony. Men and women in business suits hurried to get to work. Some of the hospital staff were also on the streets, stealing a smoke or getting breakfast. "He took a bullet for her," Verity whispered. "Literally."

Taking her cold fingers in his hand, Dante said, "Once a SEAL, always a sailor who runs into harm's way. Verity, it's in Harry's blood to defend. Also, Lilah was not some random stranger in trouble. *Of course* he jumped in front. He'll tell you the same when he wakes."

Verity withdrew her hand. "Is that why he keeps calling for her whenever the sedation wears off?" The lilting voice was now tinged with bitterness and mockery. Wiping away tears, Harry's wife said, "He asks for Alex, too. Why aren't those two here? They're supposed to be Harry's friends."

Dante remembered his long conversation with Lilah the night Harry was shot. Shivering in the damp clothes and long, dark hair plastered messily to her scalp, she'd weaved a fantastic tale for him. *"I have no option, Dante. The network is already formed, and I* can't *let Godwin and Temple take over. I have to be here to protect it."*

Dazed by the twists and turns her story took, he did the only thing he could: be at Harry's side as she asked, guarding the former SEAL against harm. In the two weeks since the fateful night, Dante thought long and hard about what Lilah said. He was sure she was wrong—at least about the Sheppards. Yeah, sure... they were a mercenary lot and prone to infighting, but to plot against *Harry*, one of their own... no way. Once Harry recovered enough, he needed to clarify the situation.

Aloud, Dante said, "Both Alex and Lilah are helping Brad hold the fort. They're relying on you to take care of Harry. Verity, please talk to him when he's not drugged out of his mind."

"I will, but I'm not letting anyone fool me," she said, her tone hard.

Chapter 52

Later in the morning

Cerro Azul, Panama

The daily report sent to Alex by the chief of the security company was on Lilah's desk. She hadn't gone through it yet, but the caller on the phone enlightened her as to its contents. No one, not even Harry's wife, could be in his room without armed guards present. "Try to imagine how she feels." Dante's irate voice came through loud and clear.

In the chair across the desk, Sabrina stayed silent, but Lilah knew she could hear every word. "We can't tell Verity anything," Lilah said, feeling bone-weary.

"She's not part of any plot, dammit!" Dante snapped.

"I agree, but she has no reason to believe what Alex and I have to tell her. Will she keep other people away from Harry?"

"Listen to yourself! You really believe Hector and the rest of the Sheppards are out to get Harry. You're *paranoid*."

"I will not risk Harry's life. Until *he* explains to Verity exactly what's going on, we can't involve her."

"*We*? Or do you mean *you* don't want her involved?"

Flinching, Lilah said, "I cannot afford to care what people think, you included. Please... when Harry is awake, I need to talk to him. We must figure this out."

"Ask your *husband* to figure it out. Let Harry worry about his wife, instead." The loud click told her Dante hung up.

Lilah placed the phone back on the cradle. Too tired even to bother defending herself, she said to Sabrina, "Go on."

"Go on with what?"

Sabrina had witnessed Lilah ordering Hector to keep away from Harry. It could only have been the shock of Harry's injury which kept his sister silent about what Lilah did. "You heard what Dante said," Lilah mumbled. "Don't you also want to tell me I'm paranoid?"

"You mean the part about Hector and the rest of my family plotting against Harry? You *are*, kind of."

It hurt. Gritting her teeth, Lilah said, "Sabrina—"

"Before you say, *'Et tu, Brute?'* let me list what I know." Sabrina held up a finger. "Fact number one: Parker tried to have Harry ousted from his position. Fact number two: after the criminal failed, he attacked *you*. Fact three: we don't know what he hoped to gain from it. Fact four: without knowing the motive, it's impossible to conclude there will be no other attacks. Fact five: Temple and Godwin have been plotting against Harry. Finally, fact six: Harry is unable to defend himself at this time." She sat forward, elbows on the desk. "So while I agree with Dante you're wrong about the Sheppards, I'd rather you go overboard with security. I want both my brother and you safe. When Harry wakes up, he can sort it out." Sabrina smiled. "I will expect a big apology once you see how wrong you were."

Lilah's eyes filled. With a half-laugh, she promised, "I'll take an ad out in *The New York Times*."

"It has to say, 'Sabrina Kingsley is always right.'" Smile fading, she asked, "What if there's another attack before Harry gets better? On *you*, I mean. And the network."

Lilah looked at the door to the office beyond which a dozen former soldiers stood guard. After what transpired, Brad wouldn't dare order them away even for a minute. "I'm safe... I think." She *did* make some changes to her will... just in case.

She didn't share Dante's faith in the familial loyalties of the Sheppards, but he was on the mark about one thing. Lilah needed to talk to the one person who could end the tussle over the empire once and for all... *if* he chose to believe her.

#

In the afternoon, she was in her office, trying to devise a way to enlist Brad's help. Absent eyes on the shallow pond overflowing with blue lotuses right outside the window, Lilah rubbed small circles over her eyebrow. If what she had to say planted at least a kernel of doubt in Brad's mind, he might think twice before accepting Godwin's advice. And once Harry was back on his feet, he could exercise his chairman powers—no, it wasn't enough.

Greed loomed whichever way Lilah whirled, turning blood against blood. Godwin's manipulations, his callous disregard for his grandsons' lives... Steven's crimes... Hector Sheppard's plans to marry off his sister to a wannabe murderer... the embezzlement in Gateway... there was also Temple. Corrupted by the prospect of absolute power, the former president plotted to kill a sailor under his command. The empire they built brought out the worst instincts in the people involved.

In us, too, Lilah thought grimly. Harry had his own sins to repent, and she... her hands were as bloody as everyone else's.

The network needed to be destroyed. It was the only solution. But Harry... somehow, she needed to convince him it was the only way to stop the never-ending struggle over power, the wanton spilling of blood.

Harry's life, gushing out into her hands... at the memory, Lilah closed her eyes. His face, ashen and cold. Lilah shuddered. She tried to reassure herself Harry was under round-the-clock guard. Without turning, she called, "Hema."

"Ma'am?" came Hema's subdued voice.

"When you've finished filing those reports, please go to Alex's office. Let him know I'd like to meet him here when he has time." He could take a trip to New York and personally check on the security arrangements for Harry. As Hema murmured acknowledgment, Lilah added, "Make certain you deliver the message in person and confidentially. I don't want his secretary to overhear."

The intern left. "Excuse me, sir," Lilah heard her say politely to someone at the door.

Lilah turned. "Brad," she said, somewhat surprised by the visit.

He held a hand up and walked to her desk. Blue eyes hard, he said, "Sit down, Lilah. I need to talk to you." Her husband's face was pale under the facial hair.

Lilah sighed mentally and did as commanded. This was already not looking good.

Brad continued, "I came here to ask you about the power of attorney Harry signed in favor of Alex. They're best friends, so I get why Harry did it. What I want to hear is how *you* got to know of it and what you plan to do. What happens if Harry dies?"

Lilah flinched.

"Cut the bull crap, Brad," Alex warned from the doorway. "I don't like the insinuation." Red-faced in anger, he strode in.

"And if I don't follow orders?" Brad asked as though goaded beyond control. "You're *de facto* chairman; are you and my loyal wife planning to oust me?"

The other brothers were crowded around the door. Wondering why they were in her office, Lilah again massaged her eyebrow. "Brad, just let me talk to you," she whispered.

"The time to talk was before the two of you pulled this trick," Brad said.

"Enough!" said Victor. "Brad, Alex, in my office. *Pronto.* We need to thrash some things out."

Chapter 53

Five minutes later

Alex didn't know where to begin. Not one of his brothers would believe Lilah's nonsense about their grandfather plotting against them, and he didn't want to cause their current hostility toward her to go through the roof.

"Bro, you must admit it doesn't look good," Victor said somberly. "I was the one telling Brad to cut her some slack on all the rumors, but now, I don't know what to believe."

"You have no clue..." Alex huffed. "The power of attorney was only to keep Harry safe. She's worried about the Sheppards and... some other people. She's wrong, of course, but she really is afraid."

"You don't seem to understand," Victor said, voice rising. "If Lilah approached you with a problem, you should've told her to go to Brad. She's his wife, not some... *thing* he'll hand over just because you decide you want it."

"God, Victor," Alex exclaimed, shoving both hands into his hair. "What a load of... Brad has no reason to doubt either Lilah or me." He looked around at the faces of his brothers and laughed in frustration at the obvious disbelief. "How could you possibly think... Brad, you have to trust Lilah. She's the kind who'll keep her vows whether you're worth it or not."

Brad snarled.

Victor stepped between them. "Alex, we're your flesh and blood. We've gone through a lot together. Lilah is a wonderful woman, but Brad still must be your priority. Family first, remember?"

Alex slashed at the air and groaned. Finally, he went to Brad and held him by the shoulders for a moment or two. "Dude, family has always been number one for me, and it will continue to be so."

"Is it why you went with her to a motel?" Brad asked, voice trembling. "Don't lie to me, Alex. I saw her go to the garage... then, your car came out."

"*What?*" Alex needed to think a moment before he understood. "Oh, for—what have you been imagining this whole—yes, I did go with her but to meet Grayson and Harry. Check with Grayson if you want." The whole story about Parker would come out. Maybe it was time. Maybe hearing the tale would shock Brad into thinking straight.

Brad stared unblinkingly for a few seconds before nodding. "You wouldn't lie to me... I'd know if you did. We don't need to involve Grayson. I'll take your word for it."

"*My* word?" Alex puffed out an exasperated breath. "Did you bother asking Lilah?" When Brad looked away, Alex said, "Let me get her. I want everything out in the open."

Brad said, "No. I can deal with my own wife."

Alex hesitated for a second. No, it wasn't his place to divulge Lilah's secrets. He never mentioned any of it even to Sabrina. "As you wish."

"I need you to do something for me," Brad said. "It's time Lilah learned who's in charge."

"'*In charge*'?" Alex ground out.

"Let me," said Victor, holding up a hand. Pulling Alex to the far corner of the room, Victor said, "We need to let Brad do this." At Alex's glare, Victor added, "I know what he said sounds bad, but he loves her. Haven't you ever looked at his face when they're together? He used to gape at Father the same way... you know... kinda hopelessly."

Alex did see the look Victor described, but he always took it for straightforward affection.

Victor continued, "I mean... she agreed to marry Brad for the business. It must sting. Then, there's all the gossip about her and you. Talk in the papers is you and I did the heavy lifting in the network. Plus, this power of attorney business between Harry and you. Brad probably feels he has something to prove. Give him room for now. I know Lilah's worried about the stuff which happened, but he's not in any shape to help. He won't be until he knows his position is safe—both as CEO and as husband. *He* needs to be our priority right now. Nothing will happen to Lilah in the meantime... she's got at least a dozen guards around her at any given point."

Hesitantly, Alex nodded.

Victor turned to their other brothers and announced, "Family first. Alex knows it as well as the rest of us. What do you want us to do, Brad?"

Part XVII

Chapter 54

Later in the afternoon

Lilah sat in her office the rest of the day, unable to focus on work. Outside the window, the sky was darkening to the lovely pink of twilight when a knock sounded on the door. "Lilah?" Sabrina called softly. "I went to your wing. Brad said you were still here."

Shaking her head, Lilah was about to let Sabrina know Brad hadn't even been willing to let her speak when the anxiety on Sabrina's face registered.

"Dante called," Sabrina said. "Harry is back on the ventilator. A blood clot or something."

Lilah stood, the swivel chair rolling back and hitting the cabinets with a thump. Sabrina was still talking, but her voice echoed strangely around the room. Lilah was vaguely aware of the younger woman urging her to sit but could see nothing except the darkness she'd been plunged into. A vise gripped her chest, crushing the life out of her. From a distance, she heard Sabrina repeatedly call her name.

Lilah wasn't aware of being moved across the room until Sabrina firmly pushed her onto the couch. "He's okay," Sabrina was saying. Warm hands cupped Lilah's cheeks. "Shh. He's fine... Lilah, can you hear me? Look at me. Listen to what I'm saying. Harry's okay."

After long moments, Lilah nodded, unable to say a word.

"The clot is small. They didn't want to take any chances." A moment later, Sabrina added, green eyes incredibly sympathetic, "Oh, Lilah."

Lilah tried to speak, to explain away her reaction. Her throat clogged. "I..." She gestured weakly. "It's good... Harry..." Voice catching, Lilah stopped and looked at Sabrina. "Harry..." Lilah tried again and bit her lip when a tear ran down her cheek. "Harry..." she said a third time and cried helplessly, chanting his name over and over like a prayer. Gulping sobs racked her body. Covering her face, she attempted to hide her anguish, but the fear and pain she'd managed to hold at bay came gushing out. Sabrina's arms encircled Lilah as she wept. Between tears, Lilah babbled, "I could handle it all... as long as I knew he... how could he? He should have..."

Sabrina didn't respond except to croon softly as a mother would to a distraught child.

Lilah eventually ran out of words and sat there in silence, head on Sabrina's shoulder, muted whimpers escaping now and then. When the sounds of the cleaning crew making rounds in the garden filtered in, Lilah shifted and called hesitantly, "Sabrina."

"You don't need to explain. I've known for a long time."

Chapter 55

A few days later, 2nd week of October 1988

Cerro Azul, Panama

Lilah couldn't fly to New York to hear for herself from Harry's doctors that the blood clot was, indeed, "not a big deal." Something was up, something the Kingsleys brothers were keeping from her.

Ever since the scene in her office, Alex avoided her. So did Brad, having moved into Victor's wing. She attempted calling on the phone, but with an uncomfortable sigh, Victor asked her to try later.

The only place she could catch Brad was at work, but even here, he put up roadblocks.

"Who's he with?" Lilah asked Brad's secretary.

"I'm not at liberty to disclose," said the secretary, her stony face daring Lilah to object.

"All right, Barbara," Lilah said, pasting on a pleasant smile. "I will make myself at home right here." She plunked herself down on the fabric settee in the reception area and picked up the morning's edition of *Wall Street Journal* from the coffee table. There would be more gossip after this stunt. From the amount of snickering Lilah encountered, the employees were already talking at home and in the office, but she was beyond being embarrassed.

Glancing between the CEO's door and Lilah, the secretary ground her teeth. "Mr. Kingsley will not like this," she warned.

"We'll see," Lilah muttered. She drummed her fingers on the arm of the couch. "Is it Gander, again?"

Stanley Gander, uncle to Steven Kingsley, already visited once before. "*Godwin wants me to run some ideas by you, Brad,*" he'd said, taking a seat across from the CEO. When Brad dismissed her with a nod, Lilah had no choice but to leave with a polite smile or risk looking completely unhinged. The two men flew stateside the same evening, Brad returning in a day with suppressed excitement on his face.

This would be Gander's second visit in one week. "*Is* it Gander?" Lilah repeated her question to Brad's secretary.

The secretary's eyes flickered. Shifting in annoyance, she said, "Ma'am—"

Lilah got her answer.

The door swung open, and Brad gestured Gander—a slight man with features to match—out. Seeing his wife waiting in the foyer, Brad's steps faltered.

Lilah stood, throwing the newspaper aside. "We need to talk," she said to her husband, not bothering to greet Gander.

Brad smiled apologetically at his companion and turned to Lilah. "It will have to wait. Mr. Gander and I are flying to New York in half hour."

"Again?" she exclaimed. "Brad, this is important."

Brad's face darkened. "Give me a minute," he said to his guest. He marched her by the elbow to his office, shutting the door behind. "Are you intent on humiliating me?" he asked through clenched teeth. "Haven't you already done enough?"

"Brad, please," she begged, ready at the moment to put every negative emotion she carried about this man behind her if only he would listen. "You cannot trust Gander. He's up to something."

Brad laughed, incredulity in every note. "What the hell do you know about the man to make such ridiculous claims? *Grandfather* sent him here. Mr. Temple advised me not to respond in case of any provocation from Kingsley Corp... even he couldn't have imagined how well things were going to turn out."

"Your grandfather," Lilah exclaimed, throwing her hands in the air. "Temple... Brad, they're not... don't do anything until you talk to Harry."

"What is the matter with you?" Brad shouted. Shaking his finger, he said, "Mr. Gander's here with an opportunity for me to almost double our profits. I'm not about to wait for Harry to return."

"D-double?" she asked, voice shaking. "Why would you believe such wild promises? That also from Steven's uncle? Don't trust them, Brad."

"My *grandfather* is involved in it," Brad snapped.

Lilah nodded frantically. "Him, Gander. Something's going on."

"Something *is* going on," Brad agreed. "I finally have an opportunity to prove myself, and you don't want to let it happen. It would take away every excuse you ever used to justify your preference for my brother."

"Stop, Brad," she beseeched, eyes tearing in frustration. "This has nothing to do with Alex. Please... just listen!"

Stabbing at her chest with a finger, Brad snarled, "Enough, *darling.* You've taken away my manhood. I'm the laughingstock of every tabloid in the country. I won't let you take away my business, too. If the deal they offer me is good, the papers will be signed before I return home."

"How can you sign anything this big without me?" she shouted. "I'm a major shareholder of this company. *And* the CFO."

"I call the shots in this outfit. Not Victor, not Alex, and certainly not you. Let me see if I can run this place without your expertise."

"All right," she said desperately. "Don't believe me. Ask someone else." Frantically, she racked her brains for someone whose word Brad would trust. "Your mother!"

"My mother?" asked Brad, tone furious. "I don't need a babysitter. If the deal turns sour, it's on me. I'll consider it my fate."

He stalked out. As the door swung open, she saw Alex and Victor in the outer room of the office suite, talking to Brad's secretary. As soon as Alex caught her eye, he turned away.

When the door shut, Lilah ran to Brad's desk and tugged at the drawers. Locked. She emptied the trash can, searching frantically through the papers for some clue as to what was being planned. Except for the annual report from a small company in Venezuela she'd already seen, there was nothing. Exhaling in desperation, Lilah knelt on the carpet, fingertips to her forehead.

"You need help," Alex said from the door. Behind him was Victor, concerned eyes scanning her.

Lilah scrambled up. "Alex, I'm so glad you're finally... Victor, you, too." She dragged them in and closed the door. "I don't know what's going on with Brad and Stanley Gander, but it doesn't sound good. Stop your brother before something happens."

Huffing, Victor said, "Listen to what you're saying, Lilah. Brad's not just our brother... he's our *boss.*"

Lilah bit her lip hard, trying to stop herself from screaming in exasperation. "Brad is working with Steven's uncle! Whatever Steven promised you... kicking me out, kicking Harry out... you think it's going to end there?"

"My God," said Alex. "It's come to the point you imagine even Victor and I are plotting against you?"

"No, but you both know this thing with Gander is a trap... no way you don't. But you're following along, no questions asked... because Brad said so. You should *not* put up with it, brother or boss." Taking a deep breath, Lilah turned to Alex. "You promised Harry you wouldn't let family ties get in the way of doing what's right. You *swore* you'd defend me."

"And?" Alex asked. "Parker was an outsider who attacked one of us. Nothing happened *within* the family which could harm you except you have slightly less power in the network than you're used to. All your conspiracy theories... you've been under a lot of stress, Lilah. The answer is to get professional help, not attack Brad for having his own problems. As far as he's concerned... give him time and space to recognize no one's trying to steal his wife or his business from him, and things will return to normal."

Heaving in an angry breath, Lilah said, "I didn't want to do this because Verity... the Sheppards don't want me in New York. Unfortunately, I don't have another option. I'm going there. As soon as Harry is off the ventilator, I'll have him call. Someone needs to talk sense into all of you."

Striding out, she found herself jerked back by her elbow. Lilah gasped, teetering on her heels, and glared into the furious face of Alex Kingsley. "No," he said.

Lilah swung, forearm raised, striking his throat with her entire body weight. Surprised by the counterattack, he let go and stumbled back. "Don't you dare," she warned, shaking in fury.

Alex coughed hard, trying to recover his breath.

"Get out of my way, Victor," Lilah ordered.

"I didn't mean to hurt you," Alex apologized, wheezing between the words.

Without a response, she tried to squeeze her way past Victor, but he wouldn't budge.

Alex staggered over. "I'm sorry, Lilah. You can leave the office, you can even fly to New York, but you won't be able to talk to Harry. I won't let you—or anyone you enlist—embarrass Brad."

"You cannot stop me from meeting Harry," she said.

"Yes, I can," Alex retorted. "I have his power of attorney."

Chapter 56

Mid October 1988

"No, Dan hasn't called back," Lilah said to Sabrina.

He was in China with the U.S. delegation. The enhanced security measures around her had convinced Dan she would be safe while he helped the American government negotiate with Beijing on stopping weapons sales to Iran. One way to get attention from the Chinese was by threatening to interfere with international trade as corporate titans such as the Barronses could do. Shawn went along, hoping to pick up some business. Not wanting either of her brothers drawn into the tussle over the network, Lilah had encouraged them to leave.

Call, call, call, Lilah now sent thoughts to her twin. *Right away.* He could perhaps use Barrons O & G to stall Brad's insane scheme until Harry recovered. Threats to create trouble for the Kingsleys in critical regions of the world, a lawsuit, something... Dan could at least force a delay. There was a time Barrons O & G could've compelled Brad Kingsley to stop altogether, but as CEO of the network, he'd gone beyond the control of the original partners. Only the chairman possessed such power now.

"Alex won't even let *me* bring up the topic," Sabrina said, a frown on her face. With an absent hand, she patted Michael's sleeping form on the couch in Lilah's office. "Or visit Harry. That power of attorney..."

The cordless phone glued to her ear, Lilah paced the room, waiting for Dante to pick up.

"I know you don't trust my family, but I tried calling my father," Sabrina said. "He absolutely refuses to believe anything you say. I talked to Patrice, too. Apparently, her pet project, Richard Armor, made a personal call to convince her. He told her it would be the best chance they got to bury the hatchet."

"Godwin and Temple are closing every escape route," Lilah fretted. She'd even considered going public, but when she couldn't give details of this deal of Gander's, the rest of the world would also dismiss her worries as the babbling of a woman cracking under pressure. End result would be her ouster on psychological grounds, leaving the field clear for the enemy in case something happened to

Harry. "Why can't anyone—Dante, thank God." Moments later, Lilah begged, a hand to her forehead, "Please... listen!"

"No," said Dante. "If there is a problem in your business, talk to your husband. He's the CEO."

"Brad won't believe me," she admitted.

"Can you blame him? What you're saying is unbelievable."

"Not just about this. We... we've been having some personal problems."

"Work things out with him. When did your marital troubles become Harry's concern?"

"Dante!" Lilah tried a deep breath. "I'm not talking about my marriage. If Godwin and Steven are plotting, trust me, they're going to account for Harry. Remember what happened at the conference."

Dante was adamant. "There's nothing here for you to worry about. I'm pretty sure you got the reports from this morning. Harry is still on pain meds, but they took him off the ventilator. The security team does not leave him unguarded for a second. Precisely because of what happened last month, he needs time alone with his wife. Stay away for a while, Lilah."

"If you don't want me talking to him, let Sabrina. Or *you* tell him."

Dante explained patiently, "No. The minute Harry hears of the possibility of danger, he'll charge to your rescue. He feels some responsibility toward you and the Kingsleys, but his primary obligation must be to his wife. As for the situation with you, I know the place is well-guarded. Whatever the problems between you and your husband, I'm sure he's not stupid enough to risk your personal safety."

"This network was Harry's dream."

"Maybe, but Brad is the CEO; it's his problem, not Harry's." Voice firm, Dante added, "Lilah, I've always wanted the best for Harry *and* you. What both of you need at this time is some tough love. You made your choices a long time ago. Now, *move on.* Your partners deserve better than this."

"Dante, please—"

Ignoring her interruption, Dante continued, "Alex called me. He specifically asked me not to let anyone into the hospital room without his permission. He said that includes you and whoever comes here on your behalf. I was surprised at the time but not now. You know what I think? That you're messing up your marriage the same way Harry's messing up his. Fix things at home, Lilah. Let Harry worry about his own life."

Huffing in desperation, Lilah tried one last time, "What if one of the Sheppards..." She paused, glancing at Sabrina.

Sabrina's eyes were dull from lack of sleep, dark circles surrounding them. She didn't say anything.

"Stop," snapped Dante. "Hector's not trying to kill Harry. Even Alex agrees with me. He gave consent to let Harry's family have limited access."

"What?" Lilah shrieked.

Dante hung up.

Lilah gritted her teeth and turned to her sister-in-law. "Help me," she pleaded.

Chapter 57

3rd week of October 1988

In Alex Kingsley's wing at the family mansion, the door to the air-conditioned utility room shut. Inside, a panel opened, and

Sabrina took out what looked like an off-white suitcase. Quickly and efficiently, wires were connected, and power was turned on. Interrupting the electronic darkness, the portable computer introduced itself: Compaq SLT/286.

"Do *you* think I'm losing it?" Lilah asked, dragging a chair next to Sabrina's.

"My family has nothing to do with any of it," Sabrina insisted, fingers flying over the keyboard. "But as I said before... better be overcautious about safety until we know what's going on."

Lilah sighed. "You're the only one who even halfway believes me. Alex has already told me I need to see a shrink; so has Dante. I've wondered myself..."

Sabrina threw her a sharp look. "What?"

"I used to have nightmares, you know," Lilah said.

Sabrina paused, then proceeded with her work.

The rhythm of the keystrokes soothed Lilah. "It took me a long time to get over it."

"Were you attacked?" asked Sabrina, voice gentle. Lilah had left out one crucial part from the story she told Harry's sister. Still, Sabrina had to have guessed. There were enough clues in Lilah's behavior.

"Let me call it what it was," Lilah said. "Rape. I was sixteen." She took a deep breath. "Parker."

There was a smothered gasp from Sabrina, but she continued to punch in code, eyes on the equipment.

Almost to herself, Lilah whispered, "I hated the idea that I was so... helpless. A victim. So I pretended it never happened. There were days when I thought I was over it. Within seconds, something would trigger my fear, and I would be back where I began. Finally, I tried going to a psychiatrist, even took pills for anxiety for a while.

I told myself I accepted it, promised myself I would move on. You know what finally made me do it?"

Sabrina asked, voice gruff, "What?"

"The discovery I couldn't have children. It left me with no choice but to face reality."

"Mmm," Sabrina mumbled as though unable to speak.

"In a way, it gave me the strength to deal with Parker. Who knows? I might have gone to pieces, otherwise. When I first heard about him being part of the network, all I wanted to do was make sure Harry stayed safe. Then, I saw Parker attack Hema, and I wanted to make sure he never got a chance to do it to someone else." Lilah continued, voice hard, "I'm *not* insane."

Sabrina hmphed. "Told you so already."

"I did wonder for a while," Lilah admitted, "if this were some sort of a waking nightmare. That maybe seeing Parker again made me snap. That all the voices in my head screaming warnings were imaginary."

"What Parker did here was not a figment of your imagination."

"No," said Lilah. "Neither is the fact Stanley Gander was sent by Godwin to start mischief. Too bad none of the Kingsleys can see it. They prefer believing I'm crazy. Except for my husband; he thinks I'm merely immoral, unethical, and out to get him."

Sabrina muttered something under her breath, the tone enough to convey her contempt for the five brothers. Then, she swiveled around in the chair, mouth pursed and eyes narrowed. "Hold on a minute. Did you say you hear voices?"

Lilah glared. "Figure of speech, you... you..." Both laughed until tears sprouted. "Thank you," Lilah said. Two minutes with a friend did more for her than all the years of telling herself she was in control.

Sabrina returned her attention to the portable computer. "Thank me for this." She sneered in the general direction of the office complex. "Your purchasing people bought technology for show instead of functionality. But no matter... *I* did my job." The machine hummed. Over the next hour, Sabrina showed her sister-in-law everything she accomplished in the last seven days. Handing over a folded sheet of paper, she said, "I've set a few obvious passwords—any one of them will trigger the program. It's relatively straightforward but impossible to eradicate without the right key."

Lilah had no idea what the numbers scrolling across the screen meant. "Are you sure it will work?" she asked, brows furrowed.

"Trust me... no one will be able to access your systems without your permission." Sabrina asked, "Lilah, I'm worried... we secured the digital data, but what if Temple and Godwin fake a couple of papers? I mean, you sign hundreds of documents as CFO."

"I can claim fraud and hold up proceedings for a long time." Lilah nodded at the computer. "This is where I'm most vulnerable. Are you sure you can get to the other machines in the office?"

"I'm Knight-errant," Sabrina bragged. "Of course I can. And I already did. The system is clean for now. I'll disconnect your devices from the grid in a minute." She groaned. "What do you think is going to happen?"

"I doubt anyone will try another direct assault this soon after the Parker debacle... not without some criminal like him to take the fall. My best guess would be Godwin and Temple sent Gander with a lure for Brad. All of them want me out of leadership. The one way I can see is if they could prove financial malpractice on my part."

"Brad would do that to you?" Sabrina asked. "Alex wouldn't go along. Victor wouldn't, either."

"Not on purpose, but they're letting themselves be duped."

Tone broody, Sabrina said, "Without their cooperation, it's going to be almost impossible for us to account for... there are so many variables here. So many things could go wrong. Both you and Harry will remain in danger until Brad decides to listen to you or Harry gets the five idiots to do what they're told."

"The moment he's taken off pain meds, he'll demand to know what's going on here," Lilah assured Sabrina. "He *will* call. Dante won't be able to stop him. Nor will Alex."

Chapter 58

Last week of October 1988

New York, New York

"Will you just bring me a phone, old man?" Harry slammed the plastic breathing device provided by the hospital on the side table. A piece broke off and bounced on the linoleum floor. "I'm not calling to chat! This is important."

The nurse walked in, the air around her vibrating in disapproval. The men waited until she completed her lecture and brought in new lung therapy equipment. "Don't upset my patient," she snapped at Dante. Even after he stopped needing machines to keep him breathing, Harry spent days in the private room, rehab specialists helping him regain his strength.

As soon as the nurse left, Dante exclaimed, "Both of you need to stop, Harry. You and Lilah feed each other's obsession." Voice gentling, Dante added, "Lilah told me about Parker and what happened in Libya. Don't you think meeting the rapist again might have provoked something in her? Some sort of paranoia?"

Harry growled. "Lilah didn't hire the guards only because of the bastard. She doesn't know who to trust, and neither do I. Dammit, old man, we're wasting time. There are things I need to... enough is enough. I'm signing myself out. Don't you realize Lilah may still be in danger?"

"Yeah? Why would Temple and Godwin attempt another attack now? Parker's gone, and they have no one else to take the blame. Also, why would they risk retaliation by killing her and leaving you alive? As long as you're safe, so is she. Plus, Lilah has her *husband* at her side."

"Brad?"

Dante threw his hands in the air. "Of course Brad. How many other husbands does she have?"

"How did *he* figure out they were trying to kill her? Did Alex say something?"

Irate, Dante said, "I don't know; he probably did."

If Alex apprised Brad of what their grandfather and the former president did, the enemy could no longer harm the network. With it, the threat to Lilah's and Harry's personal safety also vanished.

Dante pleaded, "Harry, try to understand how Verity must feel. After everything, she needs reassurance about your marriage."

Guilt settled on Harry's shoulders like heavy bricks. He did owe Verity an explanation.

"Focus on her for a change," Dante said firmly. "You married her, Harry. 'For better, for worse,' remember? She has a right to your loyalty. Fix your marriage."

Verity did deserve better from her husband.

Watching him waver, Dante's eyes softened. "I know you care for Lilah, but it's time to let go. Brad Kingsley is a powerful man. He has four brothers just as capable of protecting their own family."

Lilah didn't really need Harry. Not with Alex at her side. Brad, too.

Part XVIII

Chapter 59

October 31, 1988

Cerro Azul, Panama

Tapping the tip of her pen on the folder, Lilah reviewed the sparse notes. Brad's staff and the Kingsley brothers remained tight-lipped about the plans with Gander. Without more info, the only defense she could mount was Sabrina's digital magic.

"No answer from China yet, Hema?" Lilah asked. Her brothers were still in Beijing with the U.S. delegation.

"No, ma'am," said the intern.

"Anything from the hospital?"

"Nothing this morning," Hema said. "The fax machines are not working."

Not that the reports from the doctors treating Harry were very informative these days. The patient was stable... Mr. Alex Kingsley gave specific instructions on who could get details... and sorry, Lilah was not on the approved list. The Sheppards were equally reticent with Sabrina. It didn't matter. If Harry were not drugged to keep the pain at bay, he'd have called.

"What about the lawyer?" asked Hema.

"Huh?" Frowning, Lilah asked, "What lawyer?"

"You know, your uncle—Grayson Sheppard. I heard he used to be a big person in New York. Also, he's old. Mister Alex can't tell *him* to get out, can he? Mister Grayson could talk to Mister Harry when he wakes."

#

The way the office complex was structured, the front entrance led to a huge lobby with glass walls on three sides. All senior executives occupied suites on the lower floor with their own private exits to the garden. Besides them, security offices were located on the lower floor as were a couple of large conference rooms. The staff worked mostly on the upper floors.

Grayson Sheppard had opted for a small suite toward the back of the main floor, the one with the best view of the mountains bordering the compound. Because of its location, it was also the best place for a private conversation.

In ten minutes, Lilah was contemplating the elderly gentleman across the desk, wondering how much she could divulge. Uncle Gray—Grayson Sheppard—was a former chairman of the New York Stock Exchange and on Harry's request, came out of retirement to join the Peter Kingsley Company as its legal officer. Grayson was powerful, to be sure, but Temple and Godwin were much more so.

"Spit it out," Uncle Gray said, eyes twinkling. "Problems with the husband?" Of course he'd heard. The entire office now knew about her marital problems.

She smiled awkwardly. "Brad is not the reason for my visit, Uncle Gray."

Grayson examined his nails. "You sure you don't want any advice? I know I'm a bachelor, but back in college, I used to write a relationship column."

"Really?" asked Lilah, diverted for a second. She shook her head. "Never mind my marriage for now. There's something else. Uncle Gray, what do you know about Stanley Gander?"

"The chap who's been hanging around Brad? Isn't he one of Godwin's accountants? Brad was saying Godwin sent him to discuss a deal."

"What deal? Why are they so intent on keeping me out?"

"Keep you out?" exclaimed Grayson. "They can't. You're not only a major shareholder... you're the CFO. You *have* to sign off on money transfers."

Lilah massaged her brow with a finger. "I said so to Brad, but..."

"He won't listen to you because the two of you had a fight," finished Grayson.

If only it were as simple. Steepling her fingers, she said, "Brad is claiming he can almost double our profits with this deal."

"What?" Grayson laughed. "Tell him not to be an idiot."

"I did," Lilah said. "No one wants to hear it. Not Brad, not his brothers."

"*I'll* talk to them." Grayson stood, shoving his chair back.

"Uncle Gray, they're beyond listening to reason. We need Harry. Can you go to New York?" She explained the situation without going into personal details. They needed the chairman's veto power. Even if the deal involved only the company and not the network, Harry's objections would force the Kingsley brothers to think twice.

There was a commotion outside the door. With a surprised exclamation, Grayson shuffled to check. In the anteroom, his equally elderly secretary was struggling to keep Lilah's intern from barging in. In calmer moments, Hema could make herself understood, but right now, she was babbling in a peculiar mix of Hindi and thickly accented English. Lilah's guards stood where she left them, puzzled looks on their faces.

"What's going on here?" asked Grayson, voice stern.

Spotting Lilah behind the old lawyer, Hema took deep breaths. "Oh, thank God... come quickly."

"Hold on, Hema," Lilah said. Grayson moved aside to let her through. "Did something happen?"

"No, no," Hema panted. "Your brother, Mister Dan, is calling."

"Transfer it here," said Lilah.

"Something wrong with the phone, ma'am. You have to go to the telecommunications office. Hurry up."

#

Ten minutes later

"Dan," Lilah shouted into the phone but to no avail. The connection was lost.

"We've been having trouble all morning even with local calls," the operator offered, voice apologetic as she fiddled with the switchboard. "This was from *Beijing*."

"Let's call him back at the same number," Lilah directed.

"Sorry, Mrs. Kingsley, we haven't been able to dial out from the compound since noon." Around them, the company's communications technicians were tinkering with the equipment, attempting to plug lines together.

"I don't understand what happened," the manager said, wringing his hands. "Everything was fine when I left last night. Now, the entire system seems to be down."

"What about cell phones, car phones... anything at all?" Lilah asked. Their senior executives used the large and clunky mobile devices mainly while traveling. Sabrina had been talking about some machine small enough to be carried in purses. It wasn't out in the market yet, but surely, one or two of the staff owned something that could be used to—

"Nothing is working within the walls of the compound," fretted the manager. "Even the two-way radios the guards use. I don't see how it can be a problem with the internal systems. Got to be something at the telephone company."

"Have you contacted them?" Lilah asked.

"Of course," said the manager. "They already sent someone to check *our* lines first."

"Keep me posted, please," Lilah said. "If Dan calls again, have someone get me from my office."

"It seems to be getting worse," the manager said. "His was the only incoming call in the last thirty minutes." Impossible for a busy enterprise like theirs.

"Dan is still in China?" Grayson asked. He had finally caught up with her. Around them, Lilah's guards simply waited in silence.

"Yes, with Shawn."

"Too bad," mused Grayson. "What about Andrew Barrons? He could talk to Brad."

"Andrew and Caroline are on a cruise," Lilah lied. She had no idea if her brother-in-law was also involved in Temple's plans.

A piece of paper fluttered on the carpet. Tools hanging from his work belt, a young man grabbed it. He wore a dark-blue uniform shirt and khaki pants.

"Sorry," he said, chewing gum. "I'm from the telephone company. The receipt is for the manager."

"Can you fix it today?" Lilah asked.

He frowned. "Can't figure out what's wrong. I'm gonna have to bring my engineer."

"Please make it quick," she instructed, dismissing him. "Uncle Gray, I'd better return to my office."

"We'll sort it out, Lilah," Grayson said. "As soon as we hear Harry is awake, I'll have my secretary put me on a flight to New York. He'll take care of it."

"Actually," she said, "will you consider leaving tonight? You could talk to Dante... he might listen to you."

Grayson shook his head in confusion. "Okay, what do I tell Dante? The same thing about this deal of Brad's?"

"Yes. Maybe Dante can get the doctors to take Harry off meds for a while... until he manages to register an official veto of whatever Brad is planning."

"You're really worried," observed Grayson.

"Yes... enough to ask you to leave the building right now and keep driving until you get to a telephone booth."

After a contemplative moment, Grayson nodded and shuffled off.

The security detail marched alongside Lilah as she made her way back to her suite. Twelve men, but if Brad chose to order them away, she would have no guards. *I have no husband now, no children,* she thought in slight bitterness. *No brothers or parents, either. I don't even have Harry.*

Lilah stopped dead in her tracks in the middle of the glass-walled lobby. She looked around herself, heart pounding. She was isolated, truly isolated.

Chapter 60

Same day

New York, New York

"Finally," Harry muttered as the surgeons at New York Hospital told him he was ready for discharge. They'd been dangling the particular carrot in front of him for the last couple of days. The lead physician now talked to Verity, giving her instructions on how to care for the wound which was not completely healed.

Apart from that, Harry was home free. In more ways than one. He'd been working on a plan to get Parker as well as Godwin and Temple when fortune made it happen without the need for a suicide attack. Lilah finally got the justice she deserved, and the network was safe. Harry no longer needed to watch for hidden assassins. He glanced toward the chairs where the two guards waited. There would be two more outside. He didn't really need them now. *Tomorrow,* he promised himself. He'd call the security company and terminate the coverage.

The nurse bustled in. Extracting the intravenous catheter from Harry's forearm, she chattered about how excited Harry must be to finally go home. He should've been. Instead, there was an emptiness within his chest, a restlessness in his limbs.

The network... the reach of it... not as though he didn't already recognize how big the empire was. Perhaps the reality of it finally sank into his chest along with the bullet from Parker's gun. Temple and Godwin might have been disarmed, but power spawned countless such enemies. The many tyrants around the world were surely waiting for a chance to dethrone Lilah. She would need to be constantly on her guard. The immense authority of the network in the wrong hands... the risk to Lilah's life... Harry reminded himself the situation wasn't as bad as he expected only a few months ago. He was still above ground and able to help Lilah with anything she might need. The Kingsley brothers, too. They could even start grooming future leaders of the network to be public servants first and foremost.

The nurse applied a bandage to the IV site. "Do you need help getting dressed, Mr. Sheppard?"

Clutching the edges of the hospital gown together at the top of his butt, Harry heaved off the bed and headed to the latrine. "I believe I can manage."

The plastic bag holding the belongings he arrived with was almost empty, the clothes he wore having been taken as evidence. The SIG and the Ari B'Lilah were also with the cops. He'd requested Dante to get a replacement gun, but no way in hell would Harry let the police toss the knife in some bin to be forgotten until the end of the world. The blade had saved his life far too many times. His wallet was in the bag, along with some loose change. There was also a piece of fabric, stiff with dried blood. A scarf? Harry stared at it for a few moments.

"You all right in there?" the nurse's voice came from outside.

"Yeah." Harry set the bag aside and shoved his arms into a Polo tee, grimacing when sore muscles stretched under the thick bandage. "Mind over body," he muttered to himself. Every Navy SEAL knew it.

According to the surgeon, the scar was unlikely to completely fade away. One more souvenir of... funny how most of Harry's scars had something to do with Lilah. He wondered how she was doing. Dante claimed she was fine except for a sprain. Emotionally... *did* she find closure? She should've.

Harry pulled on the sweatpants and returned to the hospital room, somehow feeling even more on edge.

What he needed was company. Where the hell was Alex? Watching Verity sign the forms releasing him, Harry was racked by fresh guilt. She did love him in her own way. Dante was right; he needed to make an effort.

Within an hour, Harry was back in his apartment and sitting in his own bed, propped up by plump pillows. As Verity smiled her thanks at the ambulance men who helped settle him in bed, he closed his eyes and leaned back. He wasn't cleared to drive yet, and it hurt like hell to move his arm, but his two good legs could've carried him into and out of Verity's car. Dante was the one who insisted on getting the paramedics.

Harry heard the ambulance men moving out of the room, and then, the front door closed. Two guards would be in the living room, and two right outside the apartment.

Blessed calm descended. Soft footfalls told him his wife was back in the bedroom.

"I know I'm injured, but you can go ahead and give me a hug," he teased, eyes still closed. At the complete silence greeting this remark, Harry turned his head to look at her. She was at the window, the sun behind her throwing her into silhouette. "Verity?" he called, holding out his hand.

She walked closer and sat at the edge of the mattress, ignoring his outstretched arm. "I promised someone I'd wait until you feel better, but I can't. I need to know... or I can't sleep." She looked him in the eye. "Do you love her?"

His heart stopped for a second. The question, the response to which he'd buried under layers of duty and responsibility. He didn't want to answer, but nor could he leave it unanswered. He couldn't even pretend not to know who they were talking about.

Dropping his arm to the bed, Harry started to say something, but Verity held up a hand. "I want to know how you feel about her, Harry. Don't give me stories about your childhood friendship or the stupid network."

He tried again to speak, his voice still hoarse from the tube inserted to help him breathe. Try as he might, he could not force the denial through his teeth. As he continued to stare helplessly, Verity bit her lower lip, uttering an angry half-laugh, half-sob.

She stood, her eyes going to the framed pictures on the side table. She picked up the one with them feeding wedding cake to each other and stared at it for long moments, a tear finally dropping on the metal frame. With an angry snarl, she flung it against the wall.

The glass shattered. Harry flinched as the photograph fluttered to the floor.

"Why did you marry me?" she demanded, her voice throbbing and chest heaving with contained emotion.

He looked at her in silence, uncertain of what he could say to soothe the hurt.

"Answer me," she raged at him. "You owe me that."

"When we met again at my parents' home, I thought you were beautiful," he said. "Sweet." He swung his legs out and sat up on the mattress.

"And stupid. God, how stupid! I *threw* myself at you. At a man who never loved me."

"I did... I do... you're my wife," he said urgently.

"Don't tell me that," she shouted, angry tears streaming down her cheeks. "I want to hear that you don't love... that woman. Can you say that to me?" Verity collapsed onto her knees in front of him. Clutching at his shirt with both of her hands, she shook him. "Tell me," she demanded. "Tell me you don't."

Bowing his head, Harry closed his eyes, unable to answer. She buried her face in the crook of her elbow, her hands still fisted in his shirt. Loud sobs racked her frame.

After long minutes, Verity asked, "Why didn't you marry her? She's beautiful."

"Is she?" he murmured. "I don't know."

Verity raised disbelieving eyes up to him.

Almost to himself, he whispered, "When she was a girl, people told me she's beautiful. I couldn't see it. I've never been able to see it. She was just Lilah. Perhaps fifty years from now, people will say she's old. I'm probably not going to see any wrinkles, either. She'll always be just Lilah to me."

Later, when Dante came to the apartment to stay with Harry, Verity returned to the bedroom.

Once again, Harry started to speak, and again, she stopped him. "There's nothing left to say." She swiped at her cheeks with the heel of her hand. "You could've lied to make me feel better, but you couldn't bring yourself to do even that. I deserve better than you. Someday, I hope to find someone who'll talk about me the way you talk about Lilah. Someone who'll look at me and only see the woman he loves."

#

An hour later

"Nothing to say, old man?" Harry asked as he settled on the couch next to Dante. They were alone. All four guards had stepped out as requested. They were told Harry would terminate the contract in the morning but still insisted on keeping at least two outside the front door until they were officially off the case.

Dante sighed in resignation, running fingers through his thinning mop. "I would've said plenty if I thought it would do any good. Or if I knew some way to change things."

On Dante's insistence, Harry called his family. The frigidity in his father's tone didn't improve when he received the news of Verity's departure. Sophia Sheppard was no more empathetic than her husband. "I think you should take this time to re-evaluate priorities," his mother said before hanging up.

"Go back home, Dante," Harry said. "You don't need to babysit me while I feel sorry for myself."

"Your wound," Dante demurred.

"The finest doctors in the world claim I'll be fine."

Shrugging on his jacket, Dante said, "Don't burden Lilah with it. This is not her doing."

Harry inclined his head and stayed put on the couch as Dante exited. Forget bothering Lilah, Harry needed to figure out some way of making sure the reason behind his wife's departure never reached Brad or his family. If it did, Alex would vouch for the fact there was never anything inappropriate in Harry's behavior. Still, some unpleasantness was bound to—

Dante poked his head back in. "Harry, did Alex call you?"

"No. Why?"

"The guards are saying he asked them to leave tonight. Apparently, Hector didn't like being told he couldn't visit his own brother." Irony in his tone, Dante added, "Just imagine!"

Harry smiled. "Alex probably decided I could take care of myself since all the bad guys have been defanged. Go home, old man. I'll be fine."

When the door closed, Harry went to the window. Costumed crowds were already gathering for the Halloween parade. Shouts, laughter, honks. Party time for the city.

He growled. Maybe it was a mistake to ask Dante to go home. Harry desperately needed friendly conversation to fill the emptiness. Snatching the cordless phone from the countertop, Harry dialed Alex's number.

"Todos los circuitos están ocupados. Por favor, inténtelo de nuevo más tarde," the phone intoned, asking the caller to try again later as all circuits were busy. Alex's mobile gave the same message.

Frowning, Harry tried to make the call from his own mobile. At the low-pitched, rapid tone, he hung up, swearing mildly about unreliable telephone services.

Collapsing onto the couch, he groaned and buried his face in his hands. It occurred to him how very alone he was at the moment. *No family, no wife, no friends.*

He sat up on a sudden realization. He was isolated. Completely isolated.

Part XIX

Chapter 61

October 31, 1988

5:45 PM, Eastern Standard Time

New York, New York

A metallic slam. The sound of the steel door to the stairwell echoed into the apartment. Harry stood, pulse pounding. Dialing 9-1-1, he listened to the thundering footsteps getting closer. At the busy signal, he cursed. *Impossible.*

The loud thud of a heavy weight landed on the front door. Wood panels trembled as the intruder tried to force his way in.

Harry sprinted to the bedroom and grabbed his gun and keys from the side table drawer. Thank God Dante got the replacement SIG as requested. Tucking the weapon into his belt, Harry ran back and opened the sash window. Cold wind rushed in, slapping at his face. His jacket hung on the coat hook by the window. Harry tugged it out and stepped onto the fire escape before slamming the frame.

The phone rang. He hesitated for a second, eyeing the blinking light. From his perch on the emergency stairs, he saw the deadbolt on the door jiggle.

Metal clanging loudly, Harry ran down the steel steps and dropped to the ground. The parade crowd wasn't in the least interested in what he was doing. Young girls dressed in sexy devil costumes laughed drunkenly from the doorway of the CBGB. Street musicians continued to play on drums, beating fast and furious rhythms.

A shout from the fifth-floor window told Harry his escape had been discovered. An assassin—dressed in a business suit of all things—was climbing out.

Harry's hand went to the gun. No, he couldn't use it in the crowd and risk hitting civilians. On the plus side, nor could any assassin fire weapons at this range without drawing attention. Harry turned a quick three-sixty, looking for his car. *Damn...* the streets were cordoned off. There were cops around, but if Harry went to them or shouted into the crowd for help, he'd first be hauled to the precinct before being allowed to make phone calls. And the enemy had surely accounted for the possibility of police intervention. God only knew what arrangements were made to counter such a move. Harry didn't have the time to deal with all of it. He needed to call Lilah... warn her to hide.

He ran along the sidewalk, pushing through the pedestrians, causing annoyed shouts. Colors blurred, and voices blended. His own harsh, raspy breathing echoed in his ears.

A vending cart selling shish kebobs and roasted peanuts stood at the end of the street, blocking his way. Harry pushed the vendor aside and shoved the cart back the way he came. It rolled down the street. People jumped to get out of the way. The crowd screamed and flung obscenities.

Harry continued running hard. An elbow collided with the left side of his chest, right where the still-healing wound was. Flaming hot pain arced across his ribs, but he couldn't stop.

"Watch it, you..." A Harlequin cussed colorfully as Harry bumped into it.

A group of bulldogs barked loudly at him, all dressed in Superman capes. Strangely, their minder was decked out as Cruella de Vil. Stopping short, Harry pivoted and dug into the pocket of his jacket. "Here's a twenty," Harry said to Cruella, nodding in the direction of the assassin who was giving chase. "Block his... *their* way." The thug who'd climbed out of Harry's window seemed to have two friends with him, all dressed similarly in dark suits.

"Whatever." Cruella shrugged and snatched the bill out of Harry's hands.

While the three attackers were kept busy by the barking pooches, Harry grabbed the curious Harlequin by the arm and dragged him into an alley, their location at least temporarily concealed by the crowd. Leaving the man counting twenties, Harry continued walking briskly up Spring Street, hoping to go undetected in the jester's costume. There was a sharp twinge in his left chest. He put a light hand on his rib cage. The open nerve endings screamed. His vision grayed.

Harry jogged along as fast as he could. Another sharp bolt of pain shot across his chest, making him wheeze. He stumbled to his knees, and people laughed at the sight of the tall man in the black-and-white Harlequin costume drunkenly wobbling about the street.

"I see him," came an angry shout from behind.

#

11:45 PM, local time

Brussels-National Airport

Travelers hurrying through Pier B were shoved aside by cops in bulletproof gear galloping down the hallway.

"Step aside," shouted the team leader, pushing his way through a group of backpackers. An elderly woman screamed when he reached toward her. Moving past the old lady, his gloved hand landed on the shoulder of a passenger in a dark suit jiggling the buttons on a payphone.

"What the hell," the passenger exclaimed, turning.

"Daniel Barrons?" queried the cop. "Brussels police."

"Wha... what's going on?" asked Dan, eyeing the men surrounding him.

"Dan," someone shouted from the gate. A sandy-haired man sprinted toward the group.

"Stay where you are," the cop bellowed. "Police business."

"Shawn Barrons, his brother," one of the policemen said to the leader. "His name was not on the message."

"What message?" Shawn asked.

"It doesn't matter," said the leader. "You're with him; we have to detain you as well until we sort it out."

A young officer gestured at Shawn with his rifle, shoving him toward Dan when compliance was not fast enough.

"Step back," the leader hollered at a group of gawking tourists.

Airport security appeared on scene with a bullhorn. "The area is being cordoned off. You will be able to catch your flights at different gates. The numbers will be announced soon. Follow the instructions of the security team."

Dan and Shawn looked around in shock as the security men herded waiting passengers, shouting orders at them to avoid hindering the apprehension of two suspected terrorists. "Terrorists?" Dan echoed.

The brothers were thrown into the interrogation room. "It's those phone calls you were trying to make to Lilah," Shawn said. "Got to be. Something bad is going on."

"Of course something bad is going on," Dan said wildly. "My God, Lilah was leaving messages at the embassy every day. How could they not let me know?" The only reason Dan found out was he went there to meet his contact, an old friend from West Point. The contact also tipped Dan off on something else, something incredible.

Shawn nodded. "The Iran thing... I thought it was some stupid bureaucratic error, but if we've been arrested over it..."

"Yeah." Dan massaged the back of his neck with a hand. "Brad *is* involved with the Iranians."

#

5:45 PM, local time

Cerro Azul, Panama

In the library attached to Lilah's office, Michael Kingsley scribbled on a coloring sheet. He could see his mama through the door, typing on the portable computer. Of all the rooms in the corp... corp... work building, this was the one Michael liked best. Lilah's big books were here, but she also kept lots of stuff for Michael, like all kinds of toys and art supplies. There was even a small television for his cartoons—*Garfield* was Michael's favorite. He was usually brought straight here after a busy day in kindergarten so his mama could keep an eye on him while she did her work in Lilah's office.

They called the large hall outside the office the ant-y room, though Michael never saw any ants there. One of the mysteries of the grown-up world, he decided, just like deadbeat dads who were alive.

Turning back to his artwork, Michael ran a critical eye over it. The kitten's teeth were too long. And crooked. Did cats go to dentists? Smoothing the paper, he padded out, ready to gift Mama the masterpiece. He frowned when she ruffled his hair and thanked him without taking the time to admire his efforts. She wasn't payin' ttenshun.

She called Hema in from the ant-y room before crouching next to him. "Mikey, stay with Hema, okay? We'll go out for dinner after I put my computer back."

Once more in the library, he sat at the table, Hema drawing a picture for him with crayons, but Michael was bored with art. He wanted to find his daddy. They were supposed to play with Michael's toy bow and arrows. Daddy ackshually wanted to teach Michael to shoot a gun, but Mama wouldn't hear of it.

Mama thought he was still a baby. Swallowing a manly chuckle, Michael looked longingly at the blue skies beyond the window. There would be bunnies hopping about the garden, but he'd promised not to wander off by himself. Grunting, he pulled a heavy chair to the window. He climbed on it and plastered his nose and hands to the glass to watch people walk around the compound.

Big black vans came roaring in, startling Michael. Black-clad men rushed from them and thundered toward the front entrance. One of them held large, fierce-looking dogs on leashes, all the animals barking like crazy. Michael liked dogs, but these were frightening beasts with mean looks in their eyes, spit spraying from their jaws. And big, sharp, scary teeth. Did dogs go to dentists?

Michael's eyes rounded. The men had masks on and carried big rifles. "S, W, A, T," he read the large yellow letters on the backs of their jackets.

Hema stopped coloring when the commotion started outside. Hearing him spell, she said, "Mikey, you know your letters. Big boy!" She joined him at the window and frowned in confusion as she saw the policemen.

"Hema," Michael asked, voice quavering. "What's going on?" Something was beating very fast in his chest, like the drum set Uncle Victor got for him. Mama hadn't liked the gift at all.

"I don't know, Mikey," Hema whispered. "Let's go find Lilah." But all three rooms were empty except for them.

From the main door to the office suite, they watched the scene in increasing panic. The girls at the reception desk screamed continually as men held them at gunpoint.

"Stand down," the cops hollered at the security guards running forward to block the intruders. "This is the police. Put down your weapons." The SWAT team shoved the workers into one corner of the lobby, shouting, "Hands behind your heads."

Muddy shoe prints dirtied the carpet. Furniture was flung aside, the visitors' register confiscated. The policemen spread out, going into every room in the office complex and hauling the evening staff to the hall. Angry shouts and frightened screams filled the building. Squawks from police radios added to the confusion while the officers walked from room to room.

"Get out there," one of the cops bellowed at Hema as she pushed Michael behind her.

She stood unmoving until the policeman tugged her by the arm into the reception area. She looked over her shoulder and mouthed at the child to hide, but no one noticed the terrified little boy standing by the door, anyway.

The potted plant right outside the ant-y room was large enough to conceal him. From his hiding place, Michael could see both the office suite and the lobby with its glass walls on three sides. He watched as large shadows marched up and down, their heavy boots echoing frighteningly. Some of them went inside Lilah's suite, ripping open desk drawers. Someone was coiling the wires to the computers. "You're not supposed to touch them," Michael offered timidly. No one heard.

There was noise, so much noise. Michael liked making noises, but these were the kind that made him scared. His tummy hurt. It always hurt when he was scared. He whimpered. He wanted Mummy, but she was on her way home to leave her computer there.

Lilah was supposed to be in the office, wasn't she? But she was also not around.

#

6:15 PM

New York, New York

Something's going down... Lilah... Harry needed to call her... warn her. Weaving his way in and out of the crowd, he chanced a glance behind. The three suit-clad attackers were in pursuit, thirty, maybe thirty-five feet away.

The parade was at least ten feet deep at the entrance to Sixth Avenue. Harry elbowed his way through, prompting more curses and yells. When he got to the giant skeleton puppets mounted on poles, he knocked over a walking condom which called him a name more appropriate for itself.

The telephone booths along the way were packed with people watching the spectacle. They hung over balconies, climbed trees, and sat on fences. Every now and then, cops came and moved them out, but the spots would quickly fill up.

A hard thud landed on Harry's thigh. His feet slipped out from under him. The tarred road rushed up to meet his face as a metallic clang zinged across his skull. The trash can he'd collided with rolled down the street, spilling garbage. Harry's palms burned, scraped raw on the asphalt. The shouts of the pursuers got closer. Fear balling into a tight knot in his abdomen, he clambered up and continued to run.

As Gregorian chants echoed from the church on the left, Harry's mind raced. He needed to get to a phone without being spotted. Nausea churned at the thought of what might already be going on in Panama. Cold sweat beading from pain and panic, Harry shivered violently as he ran.

The Halloween parade in Manhattan stopped at Sixteenth Street, but the party spilled onto the streets nearby. Harry was slowing now, the repeated jolts of pain arcing across his left chest leaving him trembling. He stumbled another time before gritting his teeth and thundering forward. *Mind over body,* he told himself. A Navy SEAL would not surrender... not to the enemy, not to his own weaknesses.

"Keep going," someone said from Harry's right. "They're still behind us." Virgil, Dante's son.

"How?" Harry asked, continuing to run.

"Dad sent me to make sure you're all right. I was just outside your building when you started the circus act on the fire escape. I've been behind you ever since. Thought it might be better if your friends back there didn't know you have help."

"We need a vehicle," Harry said. "The only way we're going to shake them."

"In *this* traffic?"

"My bike... the Harley... it can get us through the crowds. I have the keys, but it's in a garage near work."

Virgil spat out a curse. "Not happening, bud. We'll have to take the subway even to get to the bike."

As Harry and Virgil got to the subway station and pushed through the shoulder-to-shoulder crowds, the N train rolled in with a loud blast. Ignoring the curses and shouts of the other passengers, the duo elbowed their way in. Harry counted every one of the thirty seconds it took for the train doors to swish shut. Through the glass windows, he kept an eye on the stairs outside, but with hundreds moving up and down, it was impossible to say with certainty the killers hadn't yet made it there.

The train jolted into movement.

Hanging on to one of the steel poles, Virgil said, "Dad got worried about the guards being dismissed and tried to get Alex on the phone, but the lines were busy. I offered to check on you. Good thing I did."

Harry continued to scan the crowd, checking the car behind through the glass panels on the connecting double doors. Three suit-clad figures were pushing their way forward. "*Shit...* they're on the train."

#

6:15 PM

Cerro Azul, Panama

"Alex Kingsley," one of the policemen shouted as his friend checked off something on a list. The former sniper was dragged from his office.

Confused why his daddy did not beat up the bad men, Michael watched them thrust him against the wall. Wrenching his arms behind, the SWAT team restrained Alex. Two of the cops patted him down and confiscated the gun they found. When he objected, they jerked his head back by the hair. Alex grunted.

At a roar from Victor, Michael started. "Stop," Victor shouted. "You have no reason to manhandle him." An evil-looking rifle was pointed at his neck. He was shoved back.

Breath hitched in Michael's throat. *Don't kill Uncle Victor,* he wanted to shout. His other uncles were thrust against the wall, too, pinned there by weapons pointed at them.

"Lilah Kingsley... where is she?" asked one of the men.

Lilah came striding from Uncle Brad's office suite, her face hard and flushed. Michael wanted to scream at her to hide, but the sound wouldn't come out. His throat felt like there were needles poked in.

All the employees—including Lilah's security officers—were herded into the conference rooms. Armed policemen stood outside. The five Kingsley brothers and Lilah were kept in the glass-walled lobby under gunpoint. Luisa, Victor's wife, was also there. Until now, the child standing next to the potted plant went unnoticed.

"This is a mistake," Brad said.

"We have our warrant," the captain told him. "Keep your hands where we can see them. We're searching the premises."

"You!" a cop yelled at Luisa. "Inside... with the employees."

She opened her mouth, eyes spitting fire, but at a nod from Victor, went to the closest conference room.

"Officer, this is an illegal search," Lilah said. "We have a right to see the warrant."

"Oh, do you now?" called a voice from the main entrance, the tone a mixture of resentment and glee he made no attempt to hide.

Moving aside a leaf, Michael peeked at the new arrival. The man had funny hair. Grandma Patrice called it the color of the sun when she pointed him out to Michael the day of the big conf... conf... big party with all the people. If Grandma Patrice liked him, he was surely a nice man. Did he arrive to save them? He was close to where Michael was now, enough to show the mean smile. His glance swept across the lobby, arresting for a second near the potted plant. Michael held his breath until the man moved on. Air whooshed out of Michael's lungs, strangely followed by a churning in his belly. Was he going to puke? He *couldn't* puke. The bad men would surely notice.

"Officers, we've come to join the party," said the man. "I'm Major Richard Armor of the U.S. Army JAG Corps, currently working with the counterintelligence division."

#

6:45 PM

New York, New York

Frankenstein monsters and clowns and witches swarmed the train, providing Harry and Virgil with cover as they shouldered through the throng, away from the assassins in pursuit. Virgil tugged open the door at the end of the car. Pungent smells from the tracks assaulted their noses as they walked across the shaky connection between cars, the train lurching and shuddering. Virgil opened the second door, and they squeezed in. When the train stopped at a station, they sprinted out and doubled back to one of the carriages behind.

Twice more, they needed to play the game before exiting at Whitehall.

The garage was a few blocks away. Vehicles weren't allowed this evening on this street, but costumed partiers thronged the block. Two bulky men patrolled the entrance to the garage, different ones than the three who chased Harry through the parade.

Harry pulled Virgil back by the elbow, hiding amid the mass of humanity. "They were expecting you to go for the bike," mumbled Virgil.

"Yeah," said Harry.

The mastermind of the plan obviously studied his target very well. He knew about the bike's location and knew the assassins wouldn't be able to get to it without the key to the locked section of the garage. The mastermind knew the only two keys would be with the latest owner of the garage—Harry. Which was why the criminals were patrolling the entrance. There were likely to be more of them inside. Thanks to the jester costume, Harry went unrecognized by the new set of thugs, but if he tried to walk in—

"In there," Harry said, and he and Virgil went into the pub across the crowded street. Passing a twenty to the bartender, a college student with a big red clown nose and red-and-white-striped hat, Harry asked for use of the phone.

"Todos los circuitos están ocupados. Por favor, inténtelo de nuevo más tarde."

Busy? *Still?* How was it possible? Cursing, Harry tried another number. "Dante," he said when the call was answered. Quickly, Harry explained his predicament and asked for help.

By the time he hung up, Virgil heeded the bartender's meaningful coughs and ordered brews.

"God knows how long it will take Dante to find backup," Harry muttered. If escape were all he wanted, he could simply hide. But the enemy was savvy enough to know Harry would be desperate to contact the Kingsleys. Those who wanted him dead would have accounted for every step he could possibly take. Without someone trusted at his back—and a decent getaway ride—there was little Harry could do.

"Harry, what if the first set of thugs let these guys know you escaped?" asked Virgil. "Won't they check the bars around here to see if you're waiting for a chance to get into the garage? We should wait someplace else."

"You're right." Harry gestured the bartender close. "Buddy, I need to get out the kitchen door. Ex-girlfriend outside."

"Ahh." The young fellow nodded in perfect understanding.

More partiers were in the street behind. Harry and Virgil skirted the tables and the costumed diners to go to the alley between two buildings which connected the two streets. Under the cover of shadows, Harry watched the garage.

Half an hour passed. The two killers did go into the bars, but one was always guarding the garage, and there was surely at least one more inside, next to where the bike was.

"Great," Harry muttered, seeing Dante walk to the bar Harry called from. There was another man with him, the hood of his sweatshirt drawn over his blond head. "Exactly who I need right this minute. Verity's brother."

Concealing himself amid the crowd, Harry jogged to intercept Dante and saw one of the goons throwing something. Metal glinted as the knife cut through evening air. Liam staggered forward with a shout, collapsing to his knees at the door.

#

7:45 PM

Cerro Azul, Panama

In the glass-walled lobby, men in military uniforms dumped documents—thick folders, loose papers, receipts, brochures—into waiting carts. Those in lab coats handled the computers.

Lilah and the five Kingsley brothers watched in shock as their office was stripped nearly bare. Face red with anger, she turned to the enemy. "By what authority are you doing this, Major? We're entitled to know. All of us are United States citizens, protected by the law of the land."

An open palm struck the side of Lilah's face. She stumbled and fell to her knees.

"Son of a bitch," Alex roared and lunged, his hands still in cuffs. A menacing-looking rifle stopped him, and a couple of cops pinned him to the wall.

Lilah scrambled to get up. Thick red blood trickled from her nose. She touched her fingers to it.

Charles Kingsley stood above her, smiling in anticipation.

Michael wanted to run to her, to punch Charles. He tried to make himself move, but his body wouldn't listen. His legs felt like Jell-O. Silent sobs wracked his chest as he watched Lilah bleed.

"Don't touch her, you goddamned bastard," bellowed Alex, struggling against the men restraining him.

"We're not in the United States, Captain Kingsley." Major Armor growled in malevolent satisfaction. "This *son of a chauffeur* is the one giving orders here."

At a snap of the major's fingers, Alex was slammed face first into the wall. Plaster crumbled, and he slid to the floor. The cops dragged him upright.

Fat tears rolled down Michael's cheeks as he watched the bad men. What were they going to do with his daddy? Were they going to kill him?

In the cavernous lobby of the Kingsley offices, the stillness was absolute. No one moved a muscle as they stared in horror at Lilah's battered face and Alex Kingsley's limp body held up by two cops.

#

7:45 PM

New York, New York

A thin blade stuck out from Liam's shoulder, causing a dark stain to spread across the back of his jacket. Virgil hissed and sprinted toward the injured man. People spilled out from the bar to help Liam.

Hiding in the crowd, Harry strode to catch up. With screams and yells, some of the patrons looked around for the culprits. The street was so packed this evening it was impossible to tell who threw the weapon. Harry and Virgil joined the group surrounding the knifing victim.

Liam was conscious. Kneeling next to him, Harry leaned close. "We'll get you to a hospital."

Liam turned his head, eyes bright with acute pain. "It's above the shoulder blade... I can feel it."

So the major internal organs were likely safe. Thank God. "Still can't pull it out," Harry said.

"I get it." Liam groaned. "Dante said someone's after you. Did they do this... the knife?"

"Yeah," said Harry. The assassins probably recognized Dante. Liam's hoodie... they couldn't see his hair and assumed it was Harry.

Dante was on Liam's other side. "They're now in the middle of the street, looking this way. Trying to see what's happening with Liam, I bet. They're not quite sure who they got."

Harry nodded acknowledgment. Sirens blared not too far in the distance. Red light whirling, the ambulance rolled to a stop outside the bar. Lucky for Liam, New York's emergency personnel stayed vigilant and ready to respond at a moment's notice on days such as this. "Virgil will go with you to the E.R.," said Harry.

"What about you?" Liam asked. "Don't you need help?"

"I have an idea." Not explaining further, Harry stood and signaled Virgil and Dante to follow. The three of them slipped behind a pillar. "Virgil, you go with Liam and make sure nothing else happens, okay? I'm going to need your father's help... his boat is the one place I could hide in." It was a recent purchase not many knew about, Dante's idea of getting away from it all. Plus, his phone line worked, unlike Harry's.

"Can't we just talk to the cops?" Virgil asked. "Someone's bound to have called them by now."

"No," Harry said. "Whoever arranged the hit would have plans for the possibility... not testing it." Chances were Harry would somehow end up dead in police custody, and Lilah... "I need to get to the Kingsleys."

Nodding in the direction of the ambulance, Dante ordered, "Go, Virgil. I'll be all right."

The killers were now at the edge of the crowd—*three* of them, not two. Which meant they were pretty sure they got Harry, and the one inside joined his mates.

Jogging around the crowd and behind the wannabe killers, Harry and Dante slipped into the garage. In complete silence, they concealed themselves behind other parked cars and made their way to the locked section. The noise from the streets echoed in, but without the sweating hordes, temperature dropped.

Harry cursed under his breath and put his arm out, bringing Dante's stealthy creep to a halt. One man in a business suit stood next to a parked vehicle not far from where the bike was. Innocent bystander or yet another assassin?

Eyeing the layout of the place, Harry calculated. "I need a distraction," he said to Dante, voice as low as he could possibly make.

"Heh—me?"

"Unless *you* want to try and knock out the fellow."

In under three minutes, Dante was casually strolling to the waiting businessman. "Excuse me," he said.

The man turned.

The split-second recognition in his demeanor was all the confirmation Harry waited for. Sprinting from behind a nearby car, he delivered one-two knockout chops to the sides of the man's neck. He collapsed soundlessly to the ground.

With a yelp, Dante leaped back. "Is he?"

"No," said Harry. The pain on his left pectoral was a constant now, intensifying with every movement of his arm.

Tossing the unconscious thug into the locked area, Harry and Dante wheeled the bike to the exit.

"We need to wait," Harry said. Only when white police cars swung into the street, lights flashing, did the bike roar out of the garage. The remaining killers were still at the periphery of the crowd around Liam, but they wouldn't dare start shooting right in front of the NYPD. By the time the assassins got to their vehicle to give chase, the Harley would be far, far away.

Flying along the streets of Manhattan, Harry said, "Damned wound... it's hurting like hell." Another wave of pain screamed across his nerve endings.

Even over the whistling wind, Dante heard. "Let's go to City Island first," he said urgently. "Your parents."

"Can't risk it," said Harry. "They may have people watching." Nor could he be sure one of the Sheppards didn't arrange the hit.

#

3 AM

Brussels-National Airport

In one of the many buildings of the airport in Belgium, Daniel shook the bars of the cell in frustration. "I keep telling you we're Americans, working for Barrons Oil & Gas. My brother-in-law is the CEO of the company. All you need to do is call him."

The chief of police was unmoved. "My department does not particularly care even if your brother-in-law is the pope, sir. A terrorist is a terrorist. We have been given information indicating you were planning a bomb explosion on the flight. You will have to wait until the investigation is complete."

"You'll hear from the American government," threatened Shawn. "Your superiors will not be happy."

Unfazed, the chief repeated, "You will have to wait." He nodded at the guard and pivoted to leave.

Dan demanded, "We want a lawyer." He punched the wall in frustration when the chief exited without deigning to respond. Discarding his blazer, he joined Shawn on the narrow bench.

"They can't hold us forever," Shawn said. "Heads will roll when Andrew finds out you've been arrested."

"C'mon, man," Dan said as he'd done many times before. "You're his son."

As usual, Shawn laughed in mild mockery, but his laughter stopped abruptly. He whispered, "Dan."

"What?"

"Look." Shawn nodded at the main door of the holding area. The security chief had left it slightly ajar.

Through the narrow slit, the two of them watched as the former dean of West Point shook hands with the chief. "Brigadier General Potts." Daniel snarled in disbelief. "He's the one behind this?"

"I don't understand," Shawn said. "Is it because... the general doesn't like Andrew. You've heard the story."

"Yeah." Years ago, Andrew had ignored the general—an old college friend—when he needed financial assistance. Then, there was the skirmish over a Venezuelan oil company which Andrew lost. "General Potts is not stupid," Dan muttered. "He wouldn't get you and me arrested simply for an old slight. It's the mess with Brad and the Iranians. Got to be."

"Doesn't make sense. Potts wouldn't have anything to do with the Iran problem. He's only a retired dean."

"Not anymore," Dan said. "He's the head of army intelligence."

Shawn loosened his tie, his hand shaking. "Army intelligence? My God, what did Brad do?"

#

9 PM

Upper West Side, New York City

Harry parked the bike in a lot near Boat Basin. Stripping off his costume, he threw it in the trash.

Dante's eyes went to the small red stain on Harry's tee. "Here," he said, shrugging off his jacket. "You don't want people seeing."

Quietly, they moved through the rotunda and the café. Late diners were enjoying the crisp fall evening on the Hudson River. Music boomed and laughter pealed from the anchored crafts, but none of the occupants were outside to see Harry almost tumbling down the polished wood steps of Dante's brand-new forty-seven-foot Vagabond ketch, *Triumphant*. "Let's hope the thugs don't know about your boat," Harry said. "Where's the phone? If I can't reach the Kingsleys, my asset in Panama can take a trip to their place."

"Sit," ordered Dante. "You can make calls while I check the wound."

Harry stripped off his shirt and grimaced when he saw blood seeping through the gauze bandages. Letting his boss apply fresh dressing to the injury, Harry made his calls. "Dammit. How can they block Southcom's lines?" The United States Southern Command functioned under the Department of Defense. No way would an enemy—even if he were a former American president—be able to disrupt military communications without backing from a whole lotta people along the chain of command. Temple wouldn't dare go as far. He'd be worried about leaks. "More likely they're doing this from our end."

"Who's 'they'?" Dante sat back on his haunches after he put the last tape on Harry's chest. "Temple and Godwin? Why are they blocking *my* phone line?"

"Shit... they *do* know—" started Harry. The boat shuddered and rolled. Footsteps thundered above, drowning out sounds from the revelers in other crafts. Harry shot Dante a warning look. Grabbing their jackets and weapons, they ran aft to the narrow hatch. When they heard the rattling of the fore hatch, Harry opened the one on their side and hauled himself out.

Wound screaming in agony, he lay flat under the cover of the dark night. *Mind over body,* he told himself. Turning his head, he watched the killers disappear down the brightly lit stairs to the cabins.

With a grunt, Dante followed Harry to the deck.

"Six men inside," Harry said. "How many hatches?"

"Four," said Dante.

Shouts from the cabins echoed up. "Secure the rest," Harry muttered.

Leaving Dante to this job, Harry waited at the hatch, his weapon ready in his hand.

"They left this way," came a voice from below.

A face looked up the hatch and appeared shocked to find Harry still there. Before he could shout a warning, Harry fired. The pursuer crumpled to the floor, a hole in the center of his forehead. Another man appeared and peered up. In an instant, he, too, fell dead.

"Four left," Harry told Dante who was back after securing all other exits. He had his own gun drawn and ready.

The four inside were trapped, with all exits now blocked, but—

"We need to leave," Harry said. "I need to get in touch with the Kingsleys, somehow."

"Down," Dante shouted, and he dived for cover.

A bullet pinged the mast next to Harry's ear.

Harry dropped to his hands and knees and slammed the remaining hatch.

"More killers?" bellowed Dante.

"To the wheel," Harry roared. "Turn on the engine."

Scrambling on all fours to the dock lines, he ducked every few seconds to avoid getting shot and released all but the spring and stern lines. There were hardly any sounds from the gunfire. The thugs clearly came prepared with suppressors, but the din from the Halloween parties was anyway loud enough to drown out the sounds of weapons.

The engine rumbled on.

Releasing the tether, Harry hollered, "Hard to port."

Dante rotated the wheel counterclockwise. The stern kicked out.

"Reverse," Harry shouted, bringing the spring line on board. Bullets continued to ping around them, causing them to duck every few seconds. Taking cover, they fired back at the motorboat from which the new group of killers appeared to be shooting. "We won't get out alive like this," Harry said. "At some point, we're going to run out of ammo. Dante, get me closer."

"What?"

"Just do it." Dante revved up the engine. "Can't this go any faster?" Harry asked. "We're barely at seven knots."

"My ketch is not a navy patrol boat. This is as fast as she gets."

Harry looked around. "Reverse engine."

"It will stop us dead!"

"Do it."

As lights turned off, and the big vessel plunged into darkness, an angry voice from the motorboat carried over the water. "What the hell?"

Within minutes, Harry and Dante had lowered the dinghy at the back into the water and climbed in. They came roaring out from behind the ketch, spray drenching the two of them. Dante steered the dinghy straight at the other watercraft. "Keep your head down," Harry shouted and lay flat on his abdomen, shooting at the attackers.

With yells and shouts, the gunmen redirected their fire at the smaller boat.

Dante groaned.

"What's wrong?" Harry asked.

"I'm hit," Dante said, tone pained. "My hand."

Harry twisted around. "Those sons of a—"

"Aaahhh," Dante cried, clutching his arm.

"Dammit, they're gunning specifically at you. Dante, if you can still steer, keep your head down and set course straight for them."

The dinghy sped toward the criminals. "They're going to collide with us," yelled the same angry voice from before.

"He's insane," screamed someone else.

Above the roar of engines and the spray, Harry tried to listen, to place the vaguely familiar male sound.

"Sheppard," shouted the first voice. "We have your father."

Harry jerked up.

"Stop your boat, or he dies," the enemy threatened. A flashlight went on in the other boat. Harry could make out the shadowy forms of four men, one of them staggering as another yanked him up. Harry cursed. Ryan Sheppard was screwing his eyes against the bright light directed on to his face. "We want only you," continued the enemy. "Surrender, and we'll let your father go."

Slowing the boat, Dante asked, "What now?"

"Full speed ahead," said Harry. "Get them as hard as you can."

Ducking to avoid gunfire, Dante revved up. Harry tucked his gun back into his belt and made himself flat on the deck, gripping tightly onto the edge. Dante hung on to the wheel and rammed into the side of the other boat. Both vessels rolled from side to side, water sloshing inside. The men in the enemy boat staggered and stumbled.

"Jump, Father," Harry roared.

Ryan Sheppard leaped into the icy waters of the Hudson River.

Fingers locking on to the edge of the hull, Harry dragged himself into the enemy craft. The men were still trying to regain their balance. Wresting the rifle from one of them, he kicked hard at the chest of another. With a loud shout, the second man fell into the water. Harry hit the first one in the head with the butt of the weapon. As the hostage-taker was trying to get up, Harry shot him in the head, then shot the one in the water.

The last man on the boat—the one at the wheel—was scrambling to get his rifle. Harry kicked out and snarled in satisfaction as the weapon disappeared into the inky darkness of the river. Before he could get the rifle in his hands trained on the enemy, the other man rose in rage and punched him across the jaw. The weapon in Harry's hands fired. An enraged roar came from the attacker. He came at Harry again, driving a fist into the chest.

A wet warmth spurted under the bandages Dante applied. Pain, immeasurable pain. Darkness encroached on Harry's field of vision. He let his body go lax and fell off the side into the river. The freezing water shocked him back into consciousness. He swam a little and wiped the wetness off his face.

Ryan Sheppard was in Harry's dinghy, holding the last remaining killer at bay with the aid of Dante's gun while Dante steered toward Harry. Hefting himself in, Harry sat on the plastic seat. He leaned forward, breathing heavy, icy water sluicing down his body.

The enemy boat turned and disappeared into the darkness. Harry knew the escaping thug. Grimly, he stared after Phillip Potts, the son of the former dean of West Point. Hector, the Pottses... how many people were involved in Temple and Godwin's scheme?

"Where are we?" Ryan asked, interrupting Harry's thoughts.

"Somewhere around Inwood, I think," Dante said. "Let's get back to the ketch."

"No," Harry said. "Too dangerous. If they know about your boat, they don't plan for anyone to be left alive to be identified."

"What do you mean?" Dante asked.

A loud blast rocked the waters as they spoke. A red-orange ball of fire shot into the sky. The *Triumphant* burned, destroying all evidence of the attack on Harry.

#

10:15 PM

Cerro Azul, Panama

"My grandson is in the office building," Patrice pleaded for the thousandth time, voice hoarse. The entire household staff had been detained in Alex's wing for hours, Patrice and Sabrina with them. The cops declined to answer their questions but did confirm the child was still in the lobby.

"I should have brought him back with me," Sabrina agonized. "I should have... my God, what's happening there?" She shook the shoulder of an armed guard twice her size, uncaring of any danger. "Let me get my baby... he's only five." She was thrust back into the room. Hand to her forehead, she resumed pacing. "Oh, God, Mikey... my baby."

The radio crackled. "We have what we need, Officer," said a voice. "You can let her come and get the kid, but no one is allowed to leave the compound yet."

Patrice followed Sabrina into the night, sprinting as fast as she could behind the young woman. She managed to catch up as Sabrina was reversing the car out of the garage. It took only two minutes to reach the office complex. Black-clad men guarded the entrance, letting them through with some impatience. Patrice staggered to a halt at the scene in front.

Policemen in SWAT gear swarmed the brightly lit glass-walled lobby. Haggard, tired employees were shoved into conference rooms, cops preventing escape. Her sons were lined up against the wall, all in handcuffs. There was a bruise on Alex's forehead. Lilah, dried blood on her face, defiantly confronted a man with close-cropped blond hair and icy-blue eyes—Major Richard Armor.

"No," whimpered Patrice.

"Mikey," screamed Sabrina, whirling around in search of her son. She ran in the direction of Lilah's office suite and came to an abrupt stop by the potted plant next to the door. "Mikey," she screamed again, grabbing the small form hidden by the leaves. Sinking to her knees, she ran her hands over the mute little boy before hugging him to her bosom.

Eyes groggy, Alex took a stumbling step toward his wife and child before being stopped by the cops.

Patrice marched to the major, her vision blurry with tears. "What is going on here?" she demanded. "Why are you arresting my sons?"

Major Armor hesitated, then snapped, "This is a government matter, ma'am. Please step aside." Turning to his subordinates, he growled, "I said you could let the kid's mother in, no one else. Why is *she* here?"

A hard vise compressed Patrice's throat. Words struggled to escape.

"Sorry, Major," said a SWAT cop. "Should we send her back? The chopper's almost here."

"Makes no difference at this point," the major said.

In painful silence, Patrice watched Richard Armor order his men to take the prisoners outside. One by one, all the Kingsley brothers were hauled into the dark night. Steel handcuffs were placed around Lilah's slender wrists. She wobbled a bit as she was dragged by her elbow. Men in military uniforms carted out documents. Gloved technicians loaded computers and discs into the police vehicle. The major and his team followed them.

Patrice ran to the glass panels and saw the lights of the SWAT helicopter descend, the whirling blades slowing to a stop. She could barely make out her sons and Lilah in the middle of the crowd stomping across the dark garden.

"Down," someone barked over a bullhorn.

The six prisoners—Lilah and the Kingsley brothers—were pushed to their knees in the pool of light thrown by the chopper. Hoods were placed on their heads. Bound and blindfolded, they were dragged up the steps to the helicopter and shoved inside.

Chapter 62

11 PM

New York, New York

Dante piloted the motorized dinghy across the Bronx Kill and through the East River. He was moaning on about the loss of his boat, completely ignoring the gunshot wounds on his left hand and arm. Harry's own injury was throbbing continuously now.

"The assassins would've preferred for me to die from a bullet," said Harry, scanning the waters. "Maybe an accident. Something not very difficult to explain, but since I'm alive, they didn't have a choice. The thugs we trapped in the ketch could've led us and the authorities back to those who ordered the killing. Phillip Potts most likely set off the explosive with a remote."

"What?" exclaimed Dante. "They rigged my ketch before we even got there?"

Harry nodded. "They guessed I might ask you for help. Look at it this way... it was either us or the ketch. If they'd managed to kill us, they wouldn't have had to destroy it."

Ryan Sheppard swore succinctly.

The dinghy cut through the water, passing the penitentiary on Rikers Island. Harry asked his father, "How did they get you when Hector lives right next door?"

"I was sent a message to meet you at your apartment."

Harry looked back at the heavily guarded buildings of the prison complex. "Hector knew *nothing?*"

With an angry huff, Ryan said, "You can't stop blaming him, can you? What's he going to get out of this?"

"I have no idea, Father," Harry snapped back. "Why was he trying to marry Sabrina to Steven?"

"Cut it out, you two," said Dante. "Save it for when we're safe."

"Right," conceded Harry. "First things first. I have to call Panama. Land us a little away, Dante. Before we go in, I want to make certain the house isn't being watched."

They docked at the tip of City Island with minimum noise. The streets were quiet, trick-or-treaters having long gone to bed. There were no strange faces around the Sheppard home. Perhaps the mastermind imagined Harry was already done for. Perhaps Phillip Potts hadn't yet gotten the opportunity to inform his bosses the intended victim was still alive.

Well, Harry planned to remain in the land of the living. He inclined his head at the other two men. Shivering violently, they dragged themselves up the short flight of steps to the house. Harry kept his weapon drawn, and so did Dante.

The front door opened to a light touch from Dante's fingers. The door to the kitchen was only half closed, both Sophia Sheppard and Hector visible through the crack. They were sitting at the table and jerked up at the sounds.

"Harry," his mother yelped, standing in a hurry. She ran to him and placed her hands on his chest. "Grayson has been calling. Something's going on in Panama. He said he'll call back."

Half an hour later

The call to the media informing them the explosion on the river involved Dante's boat was done. With the press sniffing around, the mastermind would think twice before launching another attack on Harry. But Lilah... the Kingsleys... after what Grayson said to Sophia Sheppard about a military raid, Harry didn't dare make anything else public without knowing details.

He leaned forward, supporting himself with his hands on the edge of the kitchen table, the phone cradled on his shoulder. His mother reapplied dressing to his chest, working around him while he talked to airport officials.

"I'm sorry, sir," came the unapologetic voice of the airport clerk. "You've been placed on a temporary no-fly-list. The aircraft owned by your company have been secured. You cannot fly, domestically or internationally."

Hanging up, Harry beat a rapid tattoo on the tabletop with his fingers.

Dante winced while Hector cleaned his wounds. "I don't see any bullet fragments," Hector said. "You're lucky."

"Harry, I'm worried about Sabrina and Michael," said Sophia. "Can't you call Southcom to get help?"

Bleakness attacking, her son turned to her. "They have me essentially jailed, Mother." Catching Dante's eye, Harry remembered a similar night so long ago. When Ryan and Sophia Sheppard were arrested, Lilah offered to help. Only *this* time, it was Lilah who needed them. "We can't give up. I'm going to drive down."

"I'll go with you." Eyes miserable, Dante cursed. "Should've believed her."

It was near dawn when Grayson called again. "I'm sorry, Harry. I was outside the compound, trying to reach Dante, when the raid happened. No one from the mansion has been allowed to communicate with anyone else. None of the workers have been permitted to go home. I haven't been allowed in. I don't have any more information."

Terror quaking his insides, Harry asked, "Anything from the Panamanian government?"

"They're refusing to talk." Grayson added, "I'm worried. Neighbors tell me they saw a chopper lift off."

Dante and Harry stayed in the home office making arrangements for their travel while the rest of the family went to bed. The phone rang shrilly, making them both jump. Harry grabbed it. "Sheppard residence."

"Harry?" came Daniel's voice. "Oh, thank God."

Chapter 63

Two days later

California

It took Harry and Dante forty hours on the road to reach Los Angeles airport, where Dan and Shawn waited. During the time, Grayson obtained for them the barebones details of what happened in Panama—American military police raided the Kingsley office and home for reasons unknown. The entire leadership of the Peter Kingsley Company had been arrested and taken to an undisclosed destination for interrogation. Southcom confirmed the happenings but warned of national security implications if the info was leaked to the press. Unless Harry wanted to waste a few years in jail while Lilah dealt with the enemy on her own, he'd have to keep his mouth shut.

Much like Harry and Dante, Dan and Shawn looked haggard with shadows around their eyes and stubble on their cheeks. "How did you get the Brussels police to let you go?" Harry asked. When Dan called the Sheppard home, Harry didn't have much time to interrogate. "Andrew?"

"Uncle Gray," Dan explained from the back seat of the rented Ford Bronco. "When he couldn't get hold of any of us, he called Mr. Temple."

Harry was climbing back into the driver's seat and stilled.

"Mr. Temple tracked us down at the Brussels airport and got us out," Dan said. "He was able to get permission for us to fly back home, but nothing more. We're also supposed to be on a no-fly list until the investigation is done."

It didn't make sense Temple would help—actually, it did. With the Barrons heir, the former president would want to continue the pretense of being a benevolent statesman.

The SUV sped along the coastal route. The Pacific Ocean was moody and gray, reflecting the autumn sky. Terrifying surf crashed onto rocky shores. "Hope they don't detain us at the border," Dante muttered.

"We're going from San Diego to Tijuana," Shawn said. "No one checks IDs."

From Mexico, they flew to Panama City. There was no talk of no-fly lists in either country. The car they rented at the Panama airport easily took the mountain route to Cerro Azul. The vehicle jolted as Dante sent the rear wheel into a pothole.

"What did Southcom claim was the reason for the arrest?" Dan eventually asked.

"They're not talking," Harry said, knuckles drumming the glass window on the passenger side. "My man at the Panama base was reported missing two days ago. I'm waiting to hear back from someone at the CIA."

Shawn hissed. "Do you think your contact at the base is...?"

"Don't know," Harry said. He hoped like hell the fellow was simply detained on some pretext or the other.

Tires squealing, Dante drove through the gates of the Kingsley family compound. Not a single soul was to be found. No family members, no employees, and no policemen. "A ghost town," Dante whispered.

Harry and Daniel ran into the office. It was deserted. "Alex's," Harry said. They drove across the grounds.

Grayson was waiting outside with a tearful Patrice by his side. Harry placed a hand on his aunt's shoulder and brushed past her. The other men jogged in after.

Sabrina was in the living room, Michael next to her. Victor's wife, Luisa, was also on the couch. The only employee present was Hema, Lilah's intern. All looked like they never slept in the last two days.

"Where are they?" Sabrina asked, voice breaking.

Harry could offer no answer. No one knew where the Kingsley brothers had been taken. No one knew where Lilah was.

Chapter 64

Same time

Somewhere over the North Atlantic

Darkness. Not a sliver of light could be seen from under the hood. Lilah tugged hard against the cuffs. Locked as her arms were to the bar above the seat, her muscles stretched unbearably. The angry wheezes spewing from her lips were drowned out by the loud, steady drone of the helicopter. Finally, she stopped, her struggles ending in a sob of exhaustion.

Without warning, the cramping struck again. She whimpered out loud as the hard, tight spasms of her womb doubled her over. Behind the hood, hot tears ran down her jaw. When sour fluid coated her mouth, she prayed wildly not to throw up again. The last time she did, their jailors never noticed until the next meal break. The acidic smell still lingered on her face and hair.

"I need..." she tried to scream, but the words sucked the cotton covering her head through her lips, choking her. Black fabric clung to her nose with every breath she took. Lilah once imagined she knew what terror was, but nothing—*nothing*—compared to this shroud she was forced to wear.

Carefully spitting out the cloth, she tried to take short spurts of air to calm herself. Someone grunted next to her. Sounded like Victor.

Their captors placed the former boxer next to her when they were first shoved in. Since then, the six prisoners were moved around from place to place. Sometimes, they would land and be left alone and handcuffed for long periods while the guards simply disappeared. At other times, the chopper would take off again within minutes. Except for when they were allowed to eat, the hoods stayed on. *"Disorientation tactics,"* Alex murmured at one point when Neil asked why they were touching down again and again, seemingly without reason. It was working. Lilah couldn't tell how many days passed. Just one or a whole week? Menstrual pain had yet to end its assault on her, so it couldn't have been more.

The chopper shuddered as it settled. The handcuffs were taken off, and she was dragged upright. There was a pressure on the small of her back, pushing her forward. The high heels... Lilah lost balance and tumbled down what felt like a short flight of steps. Somehow, she managed to stretch out her arms and fall on her all fours. Rough hands hauled her up and finally pulled the cloth off her head.

The light was bright... too bright. Her eyes hurt. Squinting, Lilah looked around. On the horizon, the sun beat mercilessly down on low hills dotted with sparse vegetation. In front of them loomed tall chain-link fencing topped by razor wire, beyond which was a guard tower. Other than the guards and her fellow prisoners, the tarred road was deserted. Somewhere far away, the ocean roared. Or was it her imagination? Lilah took a deep breath and coughed when dust irritated her already raw throat.

Glasses dangling from one ear, Brad was next to her. So were the other four brothers. The bruise on Alex's forehead was now green. All of them looked as dazed as she felt... as scared.

Lilah took a wobbly step forward and nearly stumbled again. Victor caught her elbow, steadying her.

Security personnel verified the identification of their captors and examined the papers they were given. *"Ustedes pueden entrar. Las instalaciones requeridas están listas. El personal de investigación ya está ahí."* Lilah knew enough Spanish to get the gist of what the man said— you can go in. The facilities you requested are ready. The investigation team is already there.

The gate swung open. She glanced at the board above.

United States Naval Base

Guantanamo Bay, Republic of Cuba

Part XX

Chapter 65

A few minutes later

Naval Station Guantanamo Bay

The wall calendar in the office told Lilah it was the third day of their arrest. "Let's go," said a baby-faced fellow in fatigues, the patch on top of his pocket flap announcing him as a marine.

Armed guards escorted the prisoners into a passageway with Lilah behind the men. The blood-red silk blouse from Monday smelled rank and clung to her sweaty skin. The black color of her knee-length skirt could guard her privacy only so far, but she still tried to pretend no one could see her predicament, that no one could see the congealed blood on her legs.

"Señora," called a gruff voice.

Lilah wobbled to a stop and turned toward the sound. The young marine waited with her as his comrades ordered the Kingsley brothers to keep moving. A plump woman approached the waiting duo, her dark skin glowing with perspiration. A civilian... perhaps a local who worked at the base.

"This way," said the Cuban woman, handing something to Lilah.

Cheeks heating in embarrassment, Lilah took the proffered sanitary pad and change of clothes, including the pair of slip-ons. "Thank you," she said in a whispered croak, profound gratitude welling.

"What's going on over there?" shouted a now-familiar voice from the far end of the passageway. Major Richard Armor, in crisp uniform, was accompanied by his cohorts, Steven and Charles Kingsley. Passing Brad and his brothers on their way down, Charles sneered. Armor was the first to reach Lilah.

The Cuban employee stammered, "Sir, she is... they tell me... *oh, Dios mío*, I only do what they tell me."

"Stop blabbering, woman," ordered Charles.

The baby-faced marine leaned close to the major and mumbled something. Armor's sharp eyes scanned Lilah, not bothering to hide his amusement when he noticed the red splotches on her stockings. "Mrs. Kingsley needs to change her clothes, Charlie," he said, chuckling.

"*Sí, señor*," said the Cuban woman, nodding eagerly. "The officer from the helicopter also say she ask for something *para el dolor*—the pain."

"Heh?" Charles frowned. "*Oh.*" Chortling, he inquired, "Did she say please? Pretty please?"

There was a small sound of distress from the young marine who updated Armor, but the rest of the group made no noise. There was no objection, no reprimand.

"Don't waste time," Armor warned Lilah. "Changed or not, you'll appear in court."

Court? What kind of military arrest took prisoners straight to court?

Charles guffawed, slapping his thigh. "I'll make sure she shows up... even if she's *naked.*"

"Shut up, Charlie," growled Steven, not meeting Lilah's eyes.

Ignoring the overdue admonition, Charles shot out his hand. Before Lilah even realized what was happening, rough knuckles grazed the sweaty skin on her neck. One hard tug on her lapel... shirt buttons popped. Fabric ripped. With a startled gasp, Lilah stumbled back. Her arms came up to shield her bra-covered breasts. Fear... panic... her mind tumbled momentarily into the horrors of the past before she yanked it back to the here and now.

Steven gulped, and the Cuban woman clapped a hand to her mouth, her eyes wide in shock.

"Sir," shouted the young marine. Any further objections from him were stopped cold by a stern stare from Armor.

Lilah's vision took on a reddish hue. Muscles coiled, urging her to rip the Kingsley criminal limb from limb. "You'll pay for this," she spat at Charles, heart thundering painfully against her ribs.

The demonic mirth on his face morphed into open disappointment. Turning to his comrades, he complained, "She ain't crying. Stupid woman. She should be begging us for help."

Lilah struggled to bring her thoughts to order, to focus, to understand that the moment she attacked, she'd be asking for a bullet to her brain. She couldn't fight back. Not physically. Raising her chin, she looked through the men in front. The enemy might seize the company, the network, everything she and the Kingsley brothers spent sweat and blood building. Temple and Godwin might even succeed in executing her. The one thing they wouldn't have was her self-respect. They would never see her cower in fear. They would never hear her plead for mercy.

"I believe our prisoner already got the point," said Major Armor, tone relaxed. "She is not the queen any longer. This place is not part of her empire. *We* make the rules here. If she doesn't follow orders, she will face consequences." He nodded at the young guard and snapped out a command to check on the status of a colleague in Quantico. When the fellow was out of earshot, Armor laughed jubilantly, clearly not giving a damn what the Cuban employee heard. "Steven, we both know the truth about Mrs. Kingsley. Five brothers! C'mon... she's no better than the whores in Times Square. Let Charlie strip her naked and drag her to court. What difference would it make to someone like her?"

In the next few moments of thick silence, Lilah took the measure of the man Richard Armor was—petty in attitude, criminal in action. "I want to talk to the people in charge," she stated. It couldn't be the major. He was a lawyer and mentioned showing up in court, but surely, Armor wasn't high enough in the hierarchy to be the commander of the setup. "This naval base might not be part of my 'empire,' but it *is* United States territory. I have rights here as an American citizen, Mr. Armor. Your superiors will hear what you said."

Armor's face darkened in annoyance. "*Major* Armor," he corrected. "You'll get to meet the officers in charge. I'll make sure of it. Today will be the day all the stories about you—the *myths*—come crashing down. The world will see your true colors. You're nothing without your money and the men who prop you up."

The sound of boots alerted them the marine was back. Coming to stiff attention, he reported in a voice as deep as the youth could muster, "No updates from Quantico, sir."

"Thank you, Private," Armor said. Turning to the Cuban employee, he barked, "Get her cleaned."

When the major and his cronies marched away, Lilah stared after them. The enemy didn't seem bothered in the least by the prospect of their misdeeds being brought to light. Whatever it was they had on her, it was big enough to eclipse any complaint she raised about assault under custody.

The Cuban woman tugged at Lilah's arm. The tiny restroom she was shown to didn't have a lock on its door, but the space was spotless. Leaning against the wall, Lilah peeled off her blood-stained skirt and hose and tossed them into the empty trash can. The torn blouse was next, followed by undergarments. Water trickled from the tap in the stainless-steel sink. She wiped herself with damp paper towels and pulled on what was clearly prison clothing. The olive-green pants and shirt were drab, but they felt clean against her skin... comfortable. With trembling fingers, she braided her unkempt hair and splashed water on her face, whimpering when it stung. There was no mirror to examine the injury left on her cheek by Charles Kingsley's vicious blow at the time of the arrest.

The same young private and the Cuban woman led Lilah to the room where the five Kingsley brothers were being held. She collapsed onto the bench. All she wanted was to take one sweet breath after the other without inhaling the vomit-encrusted cotton of the black hood. And sleep. She wanted to sleep. She was so tired. When the Cuban woman's footsteps faded away, Lilah scanned the room with bleary eyes.

Gray concrete walls surrounded the holding cell on three sides. Sunlight filtered in through a small window set high. Beyond the chain-link door barricading the prisoners was a long, narrow passageway with only a wall clock to relieve the unrelenting bleakness. Lilah took note of the time... early afternoon. The brothers sprawled in various positions on metal benches nailed to the ground, unshaven and still clad in the same crumpled business suits from the day of the arrest. Brad was cleaning his glasses with the hem of his shirt.

Forcing herself to speak, Lilah asked Brad, "What did you do?"

Anger warred with bafflement on his face. "You're blaming me?"

The same bewildered expression was on the other men. They didn't know? How could they not?

Sudden adrenaline surge making her fingers quiver, Lilah rubbed the inner corners of her eyes. Were all the brothers targets, or were they brought to Cuba only to testify against her? No, Steven would want all five out. The plan was surely to get everyone at the same time. But how?

At the back of the cell, there was a small table with a pitcher and Styrofoam cups. Limping to it, Lilah poured herself some water.

Harry... oh, God, did they get him as well? Back on the metal bench, she took a sip of water, trying to calm herself. "We need to get out of here," she said, enunciating each word, "so you're going to have to come clean. Brad, I need to know what kind of scam you walked into."

Anger flared again in his blue irises. "This is not about the deal. Steven and Armor are pulling some kind of trick. Instead of understanding the real problem, you prefer to attack me."

Alex murmured indistinctly. The other brothers stayed mute, watching the argument.

"Steven and Armor?" Lilah snarled at Brad. "Where was this insight when *Steven's uncle* sweet-talked you into stupidity?"

"This has nothing to do with the deal," Brad insisted, his face set. "Grandfather okayed it. *This* is about Steven and Armor and their trickery."

With a desperate huff, Lilah glanced heavenward for a moment. "How could you possibly imagine the two things are unrelated— okay, fine. Let's say you're right, and I'm wrong. On the one in a million chance *I* have it right, just tell me *what the deal was about.*" She knew she was shouting, but she couldn't help herself.

His mouth twisting in mockery, Brad said, "I told you before. I don't want you anywhere near it. If anything goes wrong, it's on me."

"But—"

"Not one of you will tell her anything," Brad said, shaking a finger at his brothers.

"Alex?" Lilah called. "Victor? Are you really going to let him do this? You're not stupid enough to think this arrest is coincidental. Neil? Scott?"

"*Grandfather* sent Stanley Gander," Brad reminded his brothers.

With a small sound of discomfort, Victor sat forward. "Lilah, it *must* be coincidence. Grandfather would never knowingly let us get arrested."

"Oh, my God," she said, rubbing her temple with a finger. "Even if Godwin held a gun to your heads, you'd find an excuse for him." She glanced at Alex. "You won't talk to me, either?"

Misery on his face, Alex said, "Someone's going to have to tell us what the charges are. Let's wait until then before deciding who's at fault."

Flopping her head back, Lilah groaned. Still, Alex was right about one thing. Sooner or later, they'd know what the charges were.

Unfortunately, no one came by to speak to them. Every now and then, military personnel marched up and down, but no one glanced in their direction. The clock on the wall ticked away. Ten minutes... thirty... an hour... the air grew thicker with every passing moment.

Two guards in fatigues appeared at the door. "You!" one of them shouted. "You're wanted for questioning." He came in and dragged Scott up by the collar. "The judge is waiting."

It was the same baby-faced marine who witnessed Lilah's encounter with Armor and his two Kingsley sidekicks. In fact... Lilah squinted, recalling the raid at the corporate office in Panama. The members of the SWAT team had worn uniforms somewhat similar to those of American cops, but they communicated in the slightly accented English of the local police. Besides Major Armor and Charles Kingsley, the only one whose attire clearly proclaimed him a part of the U.S. military was a young man standing behind the two officers. His expression had held shock when Charles slapped Lilah.

Yeah... she was sure it was the same fellow who functioned as guard while she changed into clean clothes. Major Armor had addressed the marine by his rank of private. Someone this junior was allowed to be part of such high-profile arrests? Someone this green was appointed as court escort in a place like Guantanamo Bay? The boy shoving Scott Kingsley toward the door barely seemed old enough to drive.

Scott waved down his brothers. "I'll be okay," he murmured and ambled off. Victor stood and walked to the door, watching until the youngest of the family disappeared around the corner.

Almost a half hour passed before guards returned to get Neil. With an impatient sound, he shrugged off the guard's hold on his elbow. *Thwack.* The marine's hand landed hard on Neil's nape. He fell to his knees.

Victor and Alex leaped from their seats. "What are you doing?" Brad snarled, hard gaze on his brothers. Slowly, Alex and Victor sank back to their seats.

When Neil heaved himself up, hand on the wall next to him, metal cuffs were snapped around his wrists. His brothers watched in anger as the guard poked at his back with the butt of a rifle to push him along. Victor strode to the door and raised his hands as if to tear down the metal barrier. "Stop," said Alex. "We can't afford for you to get into trouble, too."

Over the course of two hours, the four younger Kingsley brothers were taken. Complete silence reigned for some time before Brad jeered at Lilah. "Since you're worried, maybe you should use those skills everyone talks about... leave a button or two open... show some skin. You could even cry a little in front of whoever's doing the questioning."

Shock... maybe she shouldn't have been shocked after living with the man for the last six years, but she somehow was. Lilah battled the desire to chop him into little pieces. She couldn't afford to get distracted.

Before Brad could come up with more taunts, the guards returned. As the door shut for the fifth time, Lilah closed her eyes and pictured herself at the edge of a cliff... a steep, dangerous precipice, with sharp rocks which could impale a climber. She *would* get to the ground in one piece. If she failed, she'd fight all the way down to her last breath. *Harry,* she whispered in her mind. *Stay safe wherever you are.*

When boots sounded along the corridor, Lilah was mentally prepared. Looking up, her eyes narrowed.

Accompanying the baby-faced fellow was Charles Kingsley. "Come along, your highness," Charles mocked, openly ogling her chest. "Your turn now."

Nostrils flaring, she asked the marine, "Aren't you supposed to provide female guards? I'm not going anywhere with *him.*"

Charles guffawed. "You're a prisoner here, your majesty. You do what I tell you."

Throwing an uneasy glance at Charles, the young marine said, "*I'm* escorting you, Mrs. Kingsley, not the captain." When Lilah continued to hesitate, he added, "It's only a short walk, and I'll be with you until we're in front of the judge."

What option did she have except to comply? Lilah staggered to the door on unsteady legs. Charles grabbed her elbow, jerking her out through the narrow opening. She stumbled against him. A hand landed on her breast, squeezing hard. Lilah gasped in pain. Shoving him away, she ground out, "Touch me again, and I'll kill you!"

The marine was saying something, but Lilah could barely hear over the drumming within her skull. She took a step backward. Her knees buckled. Before she crumpled to the floor, Charles's boots appeared next to her. His hand landed on her nape, hauling her up by her hair.

"Aaahhh," she screamed, pain and rage pulsing through her veins.

The guard shouted, "Captain Kingsley, no!"

Lilah twisted to face Charles, her braided hair still wound in his grip. Every inch of her scalp burned. A kaleidoscope of colors danced in front of her eyes. Charles's sneer blurred, then the image sharpened. "Wretch," she snarled, raising her arm. Her entire weight in the blow, she slammed the heel of her hand up under his nose.

Bones crunched. Blood spurted. With a high-pitched shriek that echoed down the hallway, Charles let go.

Breath coming in angry wheezes, Lilah bolted, only to stagger to a halt when faced with an ugly gun.

"Stop, or I'll shoot," the guard warned, his young voice quavering. He was sweating profusely.

She spun in a semicircle, head jerking wildly between the two men. There was a door to her right a few feet away. "Help!" she screamed, her skin hot and tight. Blood seeping between the fingers he held to his nose, Charles lunged. Lilah darted just outside his reach.

To her surprise, the guard didn't swivel to keep his weapon pointed at her. The gun was aimed at his actual target—Charles Kingsley. "Captain," called the young man. "I'm responsible for the safety of prisoners. Please don't make me shoot you."

"Son of a bitch," Charles spat. "Get out of my way."

The guard didn't lower the muzzle. "Remember, the court is going to see what shape Mrs. Kingsley is in. She looks bad enough already."

"Prater," bellowed a voice behind them. "What the hell is going on?"

The men spun, straightening automatically. Gulping air, Lilah swatted the hair hanging in front of her eyes. Yet another fellow in uniform stood at the door... a superior officer from the way Charles and the guard stiffened.

"She fell," Charles blurted.

"Bring her in," the officer at the door said, frowning at the blood on Charles's face but not commenting on it. "The colonel is waiting."

Chapter 66

"Thank you, Private Prater," the judge at the bench said to the guard.

Clothes stained with Charles's blood, Lilah strode to the middle of the room. Her legs trembled halfway there. Halting, she placed a hand on a table behind and let it take some of her weight. Her braid had come undone, so Lilah needed to tuck strands behind her ear before glancing around what appeared to be a makeshift courtroom.

The chamber was painted a dull off-white, and cheap wood furniture formed a hollow square. A single ceiling fan twirled lazily, circulating warm air. A picture of President Reagan hung on the wall across from her. In front of the photograph was a yellow-fringed stars-and-stripes banner mounted on a short staff. To the right of the flag was a judge's bench with two men, the silver eagles on their shoulders identifying both as lieutenant colonels. There were also a few others in military uniform, one of them sitting behind a typewriter—clerks, perhaps, and a court reporter who would transcribe the proceedings. Armed guards stood at strategic points.

Lilah looked to her right. Steven Kingsley was at that table, glowering. She noted his uncle, Stanley, perusing some papers next to Steven and Richard Armor. Charles was marching toward his comrades, blood soaking the tissue held to his nose. *Someday,* Lilah swore, staring hard. *You will pay for what you did.* Charles took his seat by Armor... *Major* Armor, who was eyeing her up and down with a cynical expression. There was a portable projector screen next to the men.

As she looked around, she saw Godwin and David Kingsley at a table to the left along with Grace Kingsley, David's wife. The woman wore the same dark glasses she always did... something to do with migraine attacks. David was already nearly blind from some childhood illness. Next to the couple was Brigadier General Potts. Godwin glanced from Lilah to Charles, the flash of annoyance on his face replaced within seconds by impassivity. Aaron was at his father's side, looking confused and panicked. He was talking in hushed tones to a young man Lilah didn't recognize, both of them regarding her with patent unease. The presence of nearly the entire Kingsley family in the courtroom cemented Lilah's suspicions into certainty. Godwin and Temple arranged this, using Steven as weapon. Where was Temple, though? Why wasn't he here to make sure his plan worked?

Finally, Lilah looked behind her at the table she was holding on to. There were five men, all now clad in prison uniforms of the same olive-green color as Lilah's clothes. Clearly, none of them were given the chance to shave. And none of them would meet her eyes—not Brad, not Victor, Alex, Neil, nor Scott.

"What happened out there?" asked one of the colonels at the bench, squinting at Charles's bleeding snout, then at the red stains on Lilah's shirt.

"My... er... my..." Charles sputtered, tone indistinct. "... nose... accident... it got on her."

"Mrs. Kingsley?" called the colonel, clearly unconvinced by Charles's explanation. "Are you all right?"

The two senior officers in charge... were they on the take? The one speaking seemed genuinely concerned for her. Also, when everyone else around was a Kingsley or a family crony, Godwin and Temple would want a couple of outsiders to lend legitimacy. The colonels were the only ones with even a remote chance of being impartial.

"How could anyone be all right under the circumstances, sir?" Lilah asked. She *could* report Charles now... or wait for the right moment to present itself. "But I'm well enough to hear what exactly brought us here. To *Cuba* of all places."

"If you're sure you're able to continue..." The colonel inclined his head. "The interrogation will now commence."

Interrogation?

Before Lilah could ask for clarification, Godwin spoke, leaning back against his chair and steepling his fingers. "Lilah, do you understand the charges being considered against you?"

"What charges?" she responded. "No one has said anything to me."

Tone somber, Godwin said, "It seems Russian intelligence was keeping an eye on Alex since he went to Siberia, and they reported certain... suspicious activities to the justice department. Lilah, you and the company got a mafia leader off the hook in India."

"That was part of an undercover sting. And since when do we take the KGB at its word?"

"Are you claiming the Russians lied about you giving a million dollars to a known criminal with ties to the Noriega government's drug syndicate?"

Mystified by the line of attack, Lilah responded, "No, but both the CIA and military intelligence in India were notified of what we were doing, and they signed off on it. The money came from the CIA."

"Hmm." Godwin picked up a pen from the table and uncapped it. "Are you then claiming the CIA continued to bless the antics of the senior staff from the Peter Kingsley Company when they partook of some... how shall I put it... hallucinogenic material afterward? When a known transgender prostitute was entertaining all of you? When the singing and dancing got so loud and out of control the monks at the monastery were forced to get the entire party to a safe place?"

Godwin was making it sound as though they'd had an orgy, complete with sex, drugs, and rock 'n' roll. "The CIA had nothing to do with the 'party' as you called it." Lilah arched an eyebrow. "I find it hard to believe the *Russians* found this noteworthy. A couple of men in their thirties celebrating New Year's Eve by indulging in some foolishness?"

Godwin smiled, his eyes bright with malice. "It was not only the one time, was it?"

"What do you mean?" she asked.

"Scott?" called Godwin. "Do you want to tell us again what you were doing in Amsterdam?"

Startled, Lilah pivoted toward Scott. Glasses askew on the bridge of his nose, Scott kept his eyes fixed on his feet. He didn't utter a word. With a sigh, Godwin signaled a clerk. The legs of the chair scratched the floor as the clerk stood and brought Lilah a folder.

She scanned it, irritation mounting at the information. Marijuana was found in Scott's hotel room, along with evidence of his having visited the red-light district. The tabloids would have a field day if any of it leaked. Handing the folder back to the clerk, Lilah stated, "Hardly something for the military to worry itself about."

"You're not denying any of it?" Godwin asked.

"Why would I? The report clearly states Dutch cops found marijuana in Scott's room, but it's legal there. The stuff in India was bhang, which is also a cannabis concoction. It's a part of the local culture. As far as I know, a local woman—the same one you just labeled a prostitute—got it from a *government-approved* store. Besides, I don't believe the use of cannabis is enough justification for the American government to assert jurisdiction over the conduct of private American citizens in foreign countries." Any agency which tried to would likely be laughed out of court.

Scribbling on a notepad, Godwin said, "Nevertheless, it was enough to trigger some alarms with the FBI. What does a woman like Delilah Kingsley know about opium trade? Why were you posing as a chemist with expertise in heroin smuggling? What were you doing at a drug binge?"

"Is the FBI accusing me of running drugs?" Lilah queried. "Using my chemical engineering degree to drown the world in hemp-induced bliss?"

"Lilah." Godwin sighed. "I'm trying to help you." He extended a hand toward her, palm up.

Inclining her head, she said, "Thank you, sir. But I'm sure we can find someone in the CIA to vouch for me." It was hard to believe Godwin would've opted to attack her on something so easily disproved.

Godwin's eyelids flickered. "It won't be necessary. This interrogation is not about the mischief created by you and your friends. In the course of the inquiry, the FBI ran into other things and contacted military intelligence."

Ahh. So the purpose of the narration had been to destroy her credibility in preparation for greater accusations to come. "Oh, but I insist," she said smoothly. "Since the idea that I might be a drug smuggler has been introduced by no less a personage than a former supreme court justice, I feel this intense need to disprove it. Color me crazy, but I resent the insinuation."

"Mrs. Kingsley," called one of the colonels at the judicial bench. "This court understands you're offended, but there's no need to be impertinent to someone of Justice Kingsley's stature. We will check with the CIA. For now, let's move on with the matter at hand. I'll be presiding over this interrogation, and my colleague is here in advisory capacity."

"If this is an interrogation, why is Justice Kingsley here?" she asked.

The colonel said, "In case this court sees the need to take action against you or the Peter Kingsley Company, we need to make certain the network and the oil sector do not become destabilized. Justice Kingsley can take over if necessary. He has extensive experience in the industry."

There it was. Godwin's endgame, openly stated.

With a regal tilt of his head, Godwin said, "As I said to the colonel, I'm also going to do my best to help you. Within the law of course."

She arched a mocking eyebrow. "So as a senior member of the family, you'll be advocating for us? I should thank you... and the court for allowing such bias in favor of us."

With a smile, the colonel said, "The court has full faith in the justice's knowledge of law and respect for the constitution."

"I hadn't expected to be in this position at my age." Godwin rocked back in his chair, disappointed eyes on Brad and his brothers.

Her belly cramped hard once, then settled. Lips curling in feral imitation of a smile, Lilah hobbled forward to face the colonel. "What about the presence of Steven Kingsley? And the rest of the family?"

Godwin answered, "Steven is here as witness for the prosecution. The FBI contacted General Potts with their findings since he's the current head of Army Intelligence and Security Command. The military asked Steven and Mr. Gander to assist them with a sting. The family needed to be involved for believability. Your detention comes as a result of the investigation in which our entire clan helped. The Kingsleys have always stood with the truth even when some of our own were on the other side."

Lilah asked, "Steven and his uncle helped the army investigate my husband and family? Is the court aware Steven once tried to kill them? He's a criminal... a wannabe murderer." Ignoring the tiny mewl of distress from Grace Kingsley—Steven's mother—Lilah continued, "The former justice certainly knows the details of that little example of Kingsley truth."

"I understand your concern, my dear," Godwin said, eyes sympathetic. "But allegations of past crimes against Steven are unproven and will not change anything about the matter currently under investigation."

A muscle twitched under her eyelid. "Once again, why are we in *Cuba*? Whatever the planned charges, why is this interrogation being done in a military court? May I respectfully remind the esteemed people in this room we are citizens of the United States and entitled to a *civilian* trial in open court?"

Major Armor sat forward. With his tone scrubbed clean of the glee he exhibited when encouraging Charles to strip her naked, Armor said, "Not when the charges include treason."

Chapter 67

The words echoed around the stone walls. Shock surged. "What?" Lilah asked numbly.

Armor smiled, unable to completely conceal his malevolent satisfaction. "Mrs. Kingsley, you and your family were detained because of the grave concerns the army had about your activities. I'm the trial counsel—the prosecutor—and will be conducting the interrogation. Captain Charles Kingsley is acting as my paralegal will read out the offense under investigation."

Charles stood. "Delilah Kingsley and the Kingsley brothers were detained on suspicion of treason against the United States, which aided and abetted the enemy state of Iran. If we find sufficient evidence to charge them with this crime, there will be an Article 32 hearing, following which the charges will be referred to a general court-martial."

Shaking with disbelief, Lilah spun to face her husband. Brad stayed silent. None of his brothers said a word.

"Mrs. Kingsley, you can be considered an unlawful combatant," said Armor. "Especially so since the Peter Kingsley Company is a defense contractor. The 1942 supreme court ruling, *Ex parte* Quirin, did say unlawful combatants can be subjected to trial and punishment by military tribunals."

In roiling anger, she watched her husband stay mute, not contesting the allegation. "Were you drunk?" she snarled, blurting the first question which came to mind.

Titters rose. Brad's lips thinned, but he didn't speak.

She pivoted back to the court. Wild with dismay, she pointed behind and demanded, "Ask this gambler who else was involved in his stupidity... I certainly wasn't."

The snickering from Charles Kingsley turned into gleeful guffaws, subdued only by admonishing glances from the colonels. Triumph was writ large on the faces of Steven and Armor... their certainty that along with the rest of their enemies, Lilah would be crushed.

Struggling to hold on to her reasoning capacity, Lilah said, "*I*, sir, am not a traitor to my country. If you must accuse me of treason, the ruling cited by the prosecutor concerns a *declared* war, and military tribunals are tools which can be applied against unlawful combatants only under such specific circumstances. May I ask the court if the United States Congress has declared war on Iran? In the absence of such a declaration, the constitution we all swear allegiance to demands a public, *civilian* process. Moreover, Article 32 hearing is also usually a public undertaking. Why are we being subjected to this clandestine proceeding in Cuba?"

Armor cleared his throat. "Are you claiming to be an expert on military law, madam?"

"I wouldn't dare," she said. "Not in such exalted company. Still, as you said, the Peter Kingsley Company is a defense contractor. I've tried to stay updated on the Uniform Code of Military Justice to avoid any accidental missteps."

Inclining his head, Armor said, "So you should realize treason is considered an egregious enough crime to warrant a military trial whether or not there is an ongoing war. And there are national security reasons to close this to the public. Justice Kingsley is convinced of the constitutionality of this interrogation."

"Constitutional?" Lilah asked, glancing between Godwin and the colonels on the bench. "Do the senior officers of this court honestly believe this is constitutional? This *farce* with someone who once tried to kill my husband and his brothers as one of the witnesses?"

"Mrs. Kingsley," the colonel snapped, making no effort to hide his displeasure. "You have already been informed why the Kingsley family is here."

As though there had been no interruption, Armor continued, "I've been entrusted with this proceeding, Mrs. Kingsley. You will be provided with court-appointed defense counsel. First Lieutenant Vincenzo has been assigned to represent you." He gestured at the young man she'd noticed standing next to Aaron Kingsley. "You seem to be defending yourself. Are you the attorney for the Kingsley brothers, as well?"

The court-appointed lawyer looked ready to bolt. He was blinking rapidly and staring through tortoise-shell glasses. A greenhorn as guard/escort and a rookie as legal representative... the enemy side planned their attack well. Lilah needed to think clearly to mount an adequate defense. She smiled reassuringly at the defense counsel. "The lieutenant must know what he's doing, or the military wouldn't have appointed him to the job. Still, he hasn't been given an opportunity to confer with his clients. I hope he won't mind if I speak up."

There was only the barest hint of an eye roll from Armor. "*I* hope you're aware of what they call lawyers who defend themselves." More snickers went around the room. Other than Brad and his brothers, only Grace Kingsley was silent, but there was no gesture of support from her, nothing to indicate she sympathized with Lilah. Armor continued, "Our CID contact, Major Potts, was expected to be present at this interrogation. We don't know what's keeping him, but I have the evidence he's collected thus far and will be presenting it to this court."

On the screen behind the prosecuting team, a picture snapped on which showed Brad shaking hands with a turbaned man. "Do you recognize the individual your husband is talking to, Mrs. Kingsley?" Armor asked, using the tips of his fingers to slide the glass of water in front a little to the side.

Keeping her eyes on the bench, she answered, "No, I do not."

Next to the major, Stanley Gander coughed. "Forgive me, Mrs. Kingsley," said the slender man, his voice hesitant but cultured at the same time. "It's hard to believe you do not recognize the CEO of one of the biggest Iranian oil companies, especially when the Peter Kingsley Company signed a check for over one billion U.S. dollars to him only last week."

A bil... billion *dollars?* Lilah's head swam. Lips stiff with the effort to hide her desperation, she said, "Mr. Gander, I'm not sure where you're getting your information, but you are wrong. The Peter Kingsley Company has not given any money to him, certainly not on that scale."

"Mrs. Kingsley, we have evidence you did sign a billion-dollar contract with the Iranians to develop the offshore fields near Sirri Island," Stanley said, bringing out some papers from a satchel. "As an accountant in the oil sector, I was asked to look at some of the numbers. You're welcome to examine them yourself."

Lilah took the pages the clerk brought and glanced at them. She laughed, forcing derision into every note. "First of all, *my* signature is not on it. Only those of Brad and his brothers. Secondly, how do I know this is not forged?" She tossed the material back at the clerk.

Steven spoke up, "Lilah, Brad has already admitted to dealing with the Iranians." He drummed his fingers on the table. "As far as I understand, the way your company is organized, all the major shareholders—which means the five brothers and you—have to certify deals once the dollar value crosses a certain limit. Brad and the rest signed off on this particular contract. All the brothers have acknowledged you control the movement of funds in and out of your company."

Lilah turned to Brad. He kept his eyes down. One by one, she glared at each of the Kingsley brothers. No one looked up.

Steven continued, "The cash movement did happen, so one might assume the CFO—you—gave consent. One might also argue how the same consent can be taken as your approval of the deal as a shareholder. You're claiming you did not even know about it. If Brad faked the consent of a major shareholder and CFO, then he committed fraud as well as treason. He and his brothers are lying to the court. Is it what you're suggesting?"

The colonel interjected, "Mr. Steven Kingsley, you're here as a witness. Let the counsel do the talking."

Keeping her tone steady, Lilah said, "I will answer Steven's question, sir. I have not authorized any such money transfer, and Brad knows it. So do his brothers. If they somehow implied my consent and signed the contract without me, they did commit fraud—*internal* fraud—and *I'll* sue them in *civilian* court. So will the other stakeholders in our business... they will rightly see it as breach of ethics, if not corporate regulations. The chief executive's job is to safeguard the interests of the company—shareholders, partners, employees, and customers included—not act as though he's divinely ordained to do what he pleases."

"Senior executives have the power to make decisions for the business," said Godwin. "Except the American government has objections to what Brad and the rest of you did."

"Power..." Lilah nodded, gripping the edge of the table where the Kingsley brothers sat. "It's always been a misunderstood, misused concept. With authority—be it political, legal, corporate, or anything else—comes the *responsibility* to act as good custodians of the security and well-being of every man and woman who's a part of the community served. Power *is* responsibility... duty... the privileges which come with the job should be just rewards for work well done, perks to make burdens easier to bear. Power should not mean a blanket license to act as an authoritarian. Once the executive loses sight of this truth, he has lost himself. He should no longer have such power and should not be allowed to make decisions for those reliant on him."

The colonel presiding over the proceedings leaned forward, a look of interest on his face.

"Yet it's not how the system works, is it?" asked Armor. "Brad did retain his powers, and he misused them. His brothers went along. What remains to be clarified for this court is your part in the illegal deal."

"If there is such a contract with my name on it, it *is* fraud," said Lilah. "Even then, dealing with Iran is not a matter for the military. I mean... the oil embargo on them was lifted years ago. So why are we here?"

Armor spoke again, "Dealing with Iran is quite legal, but being involved in nuclear arms technology sales to an enemy state is definitely illegal."

Lilah was thankful her hand was on the table. Her sweat-slicked fingers convulsed once. Behind her, Brad gulped audibly. Ignoring him and the prosecutor, she addressed the court, "The Peter Kingsley Company deals in oil and gas. We have nothing to do with nuclear energy or arms technology."

"We have proof," Armor said. Another picture snapped on which showed Brad in conversation with a man of South Asian descent dressed in a gray suit.

Lilah swallowed hard. She didn't dare look toward her husband, but her hands itched to grab him by the lapels and shake him until her arms refused to stay up.

"Mrs. Kingsley, I see from your expression the Sri Lankan fellow in the picture is someone you do recognize," the prosecutor said. "Because of his known connections to nuclear traffickers, he's been under surveillance by British intelligence. When Brad Kingsley met with him and the CEO of the petroleum company in Iran, what exactly were they discussing if not a very beneficial three-way swap? The Peter Kingsley Company buys the oil field from the bankrupt Iranians for a billion dollars. The Sri Lankan who brokered the deal for Kingsley gets the use of the merchant ships owned by the oil field to transport uranium enrichment equipment from Pakistan to Iran. Part of the money paid by Brad Kingsley was meant to compensate the suppliers."

She walked in front of the colonel in charge, wiping her sweaty palms on her olive-green pants. "They could've been discussing world cup soccer for all *Mister* Armor knows. I don't believe for a moment Brad was involved in any nuclear deals. Let the prosecution produce something other than innuendo."

Armor chuckled. "Does Mrs. Kingsley expect us to believe her husband's meeting with an internationally known criminal happened purely by chance? I submit to the court that the CEO of the Peter Kingsley Company pimped out the business for a chance at developing the Persian oil fields. Metaphorically speaking, but it was an immoral act all the same... against the organization, against the network, against the United States of America."

"*Pimped* out?" Lilah's lips curled unpleasantly. "The prosecutor too knows many unsavory characters. Some are right in this courtroom—his friends, Steven and Charles. Yet *Mister* Armor chose to throw his support behind them. If anyone has been bought and paid for, it is *Mister* Armor."

With a frown, the colonel presiding over the interrogation opened his mouth to speak. Before he could say anything, Armor snapped, "*Major* Armor, if you please. And I'm my own man. Also, unlike your husband, I have never sold out my country and its people."

"Major," called the presiding officer. "Be careful with your choice of words. The same goes for you, Mrs. Kingsley. Decorum must be maintained in the courtroom."

The major immediately expressed regret.

"I apologize—" Lilah started.

"The word Rich—Richard—used is now the problem?" Steven asked incredulously. "Why don't you ask your husband to deny dealing with that criminal? You must have noticed he hasn't said a single thing in his own defense."

"Mr. Steven Kingsley!" the colonel exclaimed. "I have already asked you to stay silent."

Lilah asked, "Why should Brad say anything? The onus to furnish proof is on the prosecution. The defendants do not have to oblige the trial counsel."

"No," agreed the major. "The constitution allows you to refuse to answer on the grounds that doing so may incriminate you. Are you admitting to criminal behavior, Mrs. Kingsley?"

Lilah laughed, injecting scorn into the sound. "The prosecutor—I'm sorry, *the trial counsel*—has suddenly discovered the existence of a document called the American constitution." Somehow... she needed to find some way... Lilah turned to Godwin. "With the permission of the court, may I address Justice Kingsley?" Voice loud and clear, she asked the family patriarch, "Sir, the prosecutor alleges unethicality and illegality on the part of Brad Kingsley—"

Gravely inclining his head, Godwin interjected, "If found true, Brad's actions would indeed be against the law."

"And a betrayal of the trust vested in him by everyone who in some fashion worked with the company," agreed Lilah. "The privilege enjoyed by elites like us is real. On a societal level, privilege will never go away, and in many cases, it shouldn't. Because hard work and ingenuity need to be rewarded, or humanity itself will not prosper. Regardless, there used to be an idea taught to the upper crust... *noblesse oblige*. It has come to mean generosity toward those less fortunate. Generosity! No, it's about the responsibility which comes with power... the obligation to act ethically, regardless of self-centered desires. Once we forget this responsibility, we lose ourselves. We should then lose the privilege of command. Such a chief executive should not retain the right to act for the business and its employees, nor such officials for the nation."

The second colonel—the one who was present in advisory capacity—leaned close to his colleague and muttered something inaudible. The presiding officer nodded his agreement with whatever was said.

"Is there a point to this lecture, Mrs. Kingsley?" asked Armor.

Ignoring him, Lilah continued, "But the prosecutor and his team are doing precisely what they *allege* Brad Kingsley to have done. I accept what the court said about the presence of the Kingsleys in this interrogation, but has the prosecutor disclosed his close relationship with the family to the judges? Has he been upfront about his long-standing personal involvement with the same people who tried to kill my husband and his brothers, the same group of wealthy men who're witnesses in this case? His investigation team is misusing a ruling meant to be applied in times of war to try us in a secret military court, all under the pretext of national security. There is also the open abuse of governmental authority to deny us the presumption of innocence guaranteed by the U.S. constitution. The six of us are American citizens, and we're being stripped of our rights on U.S. territory."

"What is she trying to—" started Steven.

"Doesn't it mean the investigators have lost sight of their responsibility to be scrupulous in their dealings?" asked Lilah. "Doesn't all this add up to intentional misconduct on the part of the prosecutor to deliver to his rich friends what they want? Shouldn't the prosecutor's authority in this case end right this minute?

Someone else should be looking into the accusations, someone ethical and impartial."

"You would like for all of us to go away, wouldn't you?" exclaimed Steven.

Lilah kept her eyes on Godwin Kingsley, but she could see the colonels in the periphery of her visual field. Both officers were listening intently. "Instead, the prosecutor insults the dignity of this court by claiming what he's doing is moral. Is morality now about abuse of power, or is it something precious and subtle, rooted in universal and self-evident truths?"

Godwin inclined his head. "Morality, constitutionality... these things are indeed subtle and best left to interpretation by experts in the judicial system. But any judge can tell you in a court of law, morality goes hand in hand with the power of evidence, which in this case, supports the prosecution. Sorry, Lilah. I submit to this court I don't see any grounds for the removal of Major Armor from the case. But you will get due process."

"How can you say we're getting due process?" Lilah asked. "Article III Section 3 of the constitution says, and I quote, 'no person shall be convicted of treason unless on the testimony of two witnesses to the same overt act or on confession in open court.' *I* haven't confessed to anything, and there are no witnesses against me. The prosecutor has *no* proof against me and is merely indulging in a fishing expedition to please his friends. The only power I see him having is what was conferred by money and connections, and morality cannot be whatever the mighty decree it to be."

Armor hissed through clenched teeth. "Once again... the Peter Kingsley Company's regulations say your signature is needed on all invoices over a certain amount. Also, you've been screaming you're not involved, but your husband has stayed silent. What does it tell you?"

"*Argumentum ex silentio, argumentum ad ignorantiam...* you're committing multiple logical fallacies," said Lilah. "Brad's silence is not evidence of my guilt. No such evidence exists, but I'm being presumed guilty because there is no evidence to prove I am *not* guilty. Well, the law of the land demands the exact opposite... the law you're obligated to uphold... innocent until proven otherwise. The burden of proof is on you as the prosecutor, not me. Being Brad's wife and the CFO of the company is not adequate evidence against me. Even Brad only admitted to the oil deal, and it's not illegal. Has he confessed to the *nuclear* deal? Yet another logical fallacy... a *non sequitur*... one deal cannot automatically be assumed to follow the other. Where is your evidence against my husband? Why is he being presumed guilty? I submit to this court the prosecution has no proof against any of us. I submit to this court the presence of the Kingsley family with whose members the trial counsel is closely affiliated screams conflict of interest. I further respectfully submit to this court the whole setup reeks of misconduct. Finally, I submit to this court the entire proceeding is unconstitutional."

"This is not the Harvard debate society, madam," said Armor. "The real world works differently. Some amount of extrapolation is allowed in judicial matters."

Diffidently, the court-appointed attorney asked, "If I may? The trial counsel has not presented anything which even hints at Mrs. Kingsley's participation in the Iran deal to extrapolate from. Major Armor asked if she needed to be party to such contracts in the normal course of events, and Mr. Brad Kingsley and his brothers answered in the affirmative. It's her job description, not suggestion of wrongdoing."

The major jeered, "You've found your tongue finally, young man. Congratulations! But perhaps you're not aware of the Marital Privilege Law? No one can testify against a spouse. Brad Kingsley cannot say anything of his wife's involvement in the matter."

The young lawyer gulped.

Tone mocking, Steven interrupted, "Let's ask Brad directly, Major. Was she involved or not? If he admits he faked her consent, she can walk out of here, can't she?"

"Brad can't testify to her involvement, but he's quite free to deny it," answered the major.

"Right." The patriarch glanced at his eldest grandson who was sitting rigidly in his spot, staring down at nothing in particular. "Brad can acknowledge the woman who's his wife and subordinate in the company operates beyond his authority."

"If not him, one of his brothers can attest she was not involved," said Armor.

"C'mon, Alex, Victor," Steven taunted. "Speak up. Brad will face charges of fraud as well as treason, but it would be a fair outcome."

Lilah glanced at the five men.

Turning to Brad, Victor said, "Maybe we should—" Alex's hand landed on Victor's shoulder, stopping any declaration he might've made.

"The bastards are waiting for us to break," Alex muttered. He kept his eyes averted from Lilah.

She looked away, not letting the hurt show.

"Furthermore," the major continued, "we all saw Mrs. Kingsley's reaction to the nuclear trafficker's picture. No way she didn't realize what was going on. Even if Victor and Alex didn't know who the man was—which I highly doubt given what they used to do in the army—she certainly did. She would've told the rest. They all knew and are guilty. Once I present hard evidence of her participation, conviction of all six accused will happen soon enough."

Of course Victor and Alex never knew Brad met the trafficker. Or they *would* have recognized him and called a halt to the deal. But they didn't demand any details from their brother out of some warped idea of family unity.

"Major," called the colonel, shuffling the papers in front of him. "I allowed this unusual interrogation only because I was told there would be proof of imminent danger to the nation from the chief executives of the Peter Kingsley Company. This court sat through your examination of all five brothers and..." He shook his head. "I shouldn't have to remind you... innocent until proven guilty *beyond reasonable doubt* is a bedrock principle of our criminal justice system. I'm not opposed to extrapolations, but they need to be fair. Thus far, I haven't heard any argument from you about Mrs. Kingsley's involvement which meets our high legal standards of beyond reasonable doubt. Without such evidence, this proceeding risks devolving into exactly what Mrs. Kingsley labels it... abuse of power."

Standing, Armor assured the court. "The prosecution *does* have other evidence against the Kingsley brothers and their CFO. Mrs. Kingsley managed to sidetrack us for a while with her sermonizing, but it's time to hear some facts." The major pivoted to his team. "Captain Kingsley, is the technical crew ready with Mrs. Kingsley's computer?"

Chapter 68

The technician came in carrying the device and set it on one of the desks. "We haven't been able to get into the system, sir. It's encrypted."

A shudder went through Lilah before she caught herself. Her speculation that this would be where the enemy targeted her turned out to be accurate. There was something in the computer, something planted to implicate her in the crime.

"Our investigators previously accessed it," the major stated, clearly irritated.

His subordinate said, "Yes, Major. We verified access on site before moving the machine here, but it was running at the time. The devices were unplugged for transport, and the shutdown seems to have triggered an encryption change in this particular one. Now when we attempt to log back in, we're having trouble. Each time we enter the wrong password more than twice, it turns off for fifteen minutes. We *could* hire an outside expert, but it will take time."

"Mrs. Kingsley, this is your chance to prove us wrong," Armor said. "The court could compel you to disclose your password, or you could do so of your own volition. Demonstrate for us there's nothing in your computer to show you committed a crime."

"Your Honor," called Lilah. "The major is once again trying to circumvent the law... and right in front of the court! I'm sure by now his team has been through every bit of paper and electronic data in my office. With paper, I can easily disprove any claims a signature is mine. With computers, it's not as easy. I suspect evidence has been planted against me. Under the scenario, I'm invoking the Fifth Amendment... I cannot be compelled to disclose anything that might incriminate me."

"The Fifth Amendment doesn't apply in this case," ground out Armor. "If you decide not to cooperate, you will be held in contempt. Prison time, Mrs. Kingsley."

"Go ahead," retorted Lilah. "I'll take it all the way to the Supreme Court. If you insist on cheating your way to a trial, I'll make sure the American public knows about it." Every darned tabloid would be salivating over seeing her in shackles. Their breathless reporting would carry the tale to the common man. The enemy wouldn't like it one bit because the chatter could put pressure on the political class to respond.

The prosecutor pivoted to the bench. "Your Honor?"

The presiding officer and his associate conferred for a few moments. Then, the colonel in charge spoke, "Major, you're surely aware President Ronald Reagan signed The Civil Liberties Act a few weeks ago. The nation issued a public apology to Japanese-Americans who lost their property and liberty due to the actions of the United States government around the World War II period. Oh, there were plenty of rationalizations at the time, all short-sighted. Whatever the proof you expect to find, this court has a..." He stopped for a moment and inclined his head toward Lilah. "...larger responsibility, the obligation to exercise its power ethically. Or we risk betraying the founding principles of the union. We risk losing that which makes us who we are. My colleague and I agree we cannot allow Mrs. Kingsley's civil liberties to be violated because the prosecution finds it convenient to do so. Her right to remain silent includes her password."

Armor gritted his teeth for a second or two before asking the technicians, "What passwords have you tried so far?"

They read out from a sheet. Names, birthdays, and last names in various combinations were listed. Names of schools, places, the year she got married—they had all been tried. Her husband's name, Alex Kingsley's name, even Michael's. Harry—his name, as well.

Pursing his lips, the prosecutor considered the defiant woman and the family sitting behind in complete silence. "You think very highly of yourself, don't you, Mrs. Kingsley? But people are quite predictable, you included." Pulling his chair back with more force than warranted, Armor seated himself. "All those names and numbers my team tried... no, it wouldn't be as easy. Also, not so difficult... others would need access to your computer in case of emergencies." Armor scribbled on a piece of paper and said to Charles, "Captain Kingsley, try this."

"What is this?" Charles asked.

"An educated guess," the prosecutor said.

In her memory, Lilah saw blurred images of letters and numbers. That day in Cerro Azul, Sabrina had handed over a folded sheet of paper. *'I've set a few obvious passwords—any one of them will trigger the program.'*

Watching Charles enter the numbers, Lilah wiped the sweat from her cheek with the back of her hand. Her fingers trembled.

Eight, one, eighteen, eighteen, twenty-five. With each stroke of the keyboard, she whispered in her mind, *H-A-R-R-Y.* Unheard by anyone, her lips formed his name. The key to her secrets. Her last defense.

Excited mutters and muted cheers went up as the operating system hummed. The colonels and the senior Kingsleys sat forward. Aaron and Vincenzo looked worried. The Kingsley brothers watched with dulled eyes.

Lilah tried not to imagine what would happen if Sabrina's trick didn't work. If Armor retrieved the planted evidence, the six prisoners would be shut away for life. Not to see the world ever again, not to watch Michael grow up... not to visit her brothers or chat with Sabrina or meet old friends. Not to ever argue with Harry...

"It's working," Charles Kingsley said.

The glee in his voice jerked Lilah back to the interrogation room.

White letters flashed on blue screen. Microsoft Windows Version 2.1. "WELCOME BACK, DELILAH KINGSLEY," the computer intoned.

Lilah forced herself to stay perfectly still, but her heart continued hammering against her rib cage.

"Get to it, Charles," Armor said, speech cracking in triumphant spite. "I've been preached at enough about my immorality in daring to go after Lilah Kingsley, fearless protector of the powerless! All lies... this pretend virtue is merely her cover for the greed which led to the Iran deal. Let's strip it all bare right now."

Shooting a displeased half-glance at the prosecutor, the colonel in charge leaned forward to stare at the computer. Everyone else around was doing the same, even Grace Kingsley, the silent witness to this crime being perpetrated by her sons on another woman. The thick glasses remained on her face, hiding her expression from the world.

Charles clicked on one of the folders.

Sabrina's magic triggered the logic bomb.

Violent color exploded onto the screen, from glittering garnet to the crimson of blood. Chants started, sonorous and mystical.

"What the hell is this?" said the prosecutor. "Where are the documents?"

1s and 0s sped across magnetic material, imprinting new information. For every layer that was uncovered, new data was laid in, protecting Lilah's secrets.

The chaos on screen organized itself into flames, swirling in mind-bending shapes.

Mutters of surprise and annoyance went around the room. The colonel asked, "What is this, Major Armor? Some kind of video game?"

"Not sure," said Armor. "Charles, try again, please."

"Stupid computer," said Charles Kingsley. He clicked repeatedly all over the screen.

The program started replicating at a faster rate. Sheets of numbers fell across the coating on the hard disk, masking the ugly treachery of the Kingsley clan from the world.

The chants got deeper in tone, faster, more threatening.

"Do a reboot," Armor ordered.

"What's going on?" asked David Kingsley, speaking for the first time since Lilah walked in. He peered in the direction of the computer and blinked rapidly. "Why isn't it opening?" His wife stayed silent. Her dark glasses remained on her nose, but she didn't turn away from the monitor, not even for a moment.

"I don't know," Aaron answered. "Something seems to be wrong with the computer."

"I can't shut it down," Charles said, jiggling a foot. "It's stuck." He pivoted in his chair and reached for the power cord. "Lemme try it this way." Before anyone could protest, he pulled the cord out and plugged it back into the outlet.

Steven Kingsley was glaring at his younger brother as he entered the password a second time. Glancing toward the middle of the room where Lilah stood, Steven stilled. Her stiffness must have given her away. Tone uneasy, he murmured, "Rich."

The machine whirred again. Reams of random data were written rapidly.

The flames reappeared with greater ferocity. When the chanting resumed, Steven swung back to the computer.

On the monitor, the ribbons of heat and light twisted themselves into a vortex. The more Charles clicked, the faster they churned. The cadence of the song changed, morphing into battle music... Sabrina's sense of drama. The gazes in the courtroom swung between Lilah and the blaze torching the computer screen.

"I don't know what's happening," Charles growled. "I can't stop it."

Armor cursed. "There's some sort of virus overwriting the files. Stop it right now, Charles. Shut it down."

"I can't," Charles said helplessly. "It won't let me."

The room erupted into noisy disarray. "What's going on?" asked the colonel. "I thought you said you had evidence."

"Seems to be slowing," Charles said. "Stupid song sounds like it's almost done."

The technician who'd brought in the device offered his opinion. "The data has most likely been overwritten, sir. My team can take another look, but I doubt we'll recover anything useful."

"What about the other devices?" Armor asked. "There must be something we can use. Shared files or some such."

"They've already been checked, Major. This was a standalone."

"What do you mean?" the prosecutor demanded, teeth clenched.

The technician explained, "There was some networking of the company's computers, but the digital setup in Mrs. Kingsley's office suite seems to have been completely separate from the rest of the enterprise. Given what happened just now, I assume the same self-destruct feature has been programmed into every device belonging to her and her staff. Even if there's something on the other computers in the building, you'd need to prove she had physical access... as in she or someone she appointed walked to the devices, put in passwords to access them, and for some reason, stored potential evidence against herself in places she couldn't directly protect. Information entered under someone else's profile will be even weaker evidence. I'm no lawyer, but I'd think such info would be inadmissible."

Lilah couldn't help heaving her chest in a full breath. David and Grace Kingsley slumped back into their chairs while Godwin's stare threatened to drill holes into the computer tech.

Pounding the table, Armor asked, "Why the hell wasn't I informed of this?"

"I didn't realize..." The technician shook his head in obvious confusion. "My team did exactly what you asked, sir."

Armor ground out to Charles, "Take her back to the cell. We'll have to question her later."

"Take me—wait a minute." Lilah pivoted to the court. "How can they continue to hold me here without charges, without even evidence?"

Armor growled. "She deliberately infected the system. This is obstruction of justice. Mrs. Kingsley is an attorney; she knows this. The court cannot let her go!"

"Obstruction of justice?" Lilah asked. "The system was the private property of the Peter Kingsley Company until the investigation team confiscated it. While it was in my custody, it was perfectly legal for me to protect my data against malicious intrusions, which is what I did. I didn't ask anyone to use that particular password. I'm not responsible for the trial counsel's lack of judgment."

Godwin's voice held an edge when he said, "Your knowledge of the law is exemplary, Lilah, but you very cleverly erased all the computer data right under the court's nose. How can we believe you're innocent after what just happened?"

There was a suppressed squawk from Alex, ignored by his grandfather. The former sniper stared at the Kingsley patriarch, hurt and shock in his eyes. After everything was said, after the lack of evidence against Lilah was blatantly clear, Alex perhaps imagined Godwin would let her go. But all her arguments and all the things she did to protect herself from attacks... none of it seemed to be enough.

"Besides, *you* quoted Article III Section 3 of the constitution earlier," Godwin said to Lilah. "No person shall be convicted of treason unless on the testimony of two witnesses to the same overt act or on confession in open court. The refusal of Brad and his brothers to speak up in support of your innocence indicates they're witnesses against you... not two as the constitution demands... *four* of them. Brad cannot testify against you, but his brothers can."

"Really?" Lilah mocked, no longer bothering to conceal her contempt. "Their silence is now evidence?" At the very least, she would expose Justice Godwin Kingsley's true nature to the world. Her testimony would let the public know what happened in this kangaroo court. His responses would also be on record. Surely, the news media would be interested in the transcripts. Surely, a journalist or two would have the courage to point out Godwin misused the rules meant to be the foundation of the American justice system.

The colonel seemed about to say something, but Godwin interjected. "Legally speaking, their refusal to speak cannot be used against you. But certain leeway is allowed in case of emergencies to hold accused individuals without charges, and threats to national security would indeed qualify. Engineers from technology firms need to be hired. There must be someone who can salvage the lost data. Time will take care of it, and during the time, you—*all* of you— need to be in a secure facility. I'm sorry, Lilah. I cannot put family relationships ahead of the nation. Peter's sons are *my* grandsons— the grandsons of a former supreme court justice—but traitors, however well connected, deserve the highest punishment the nation can mete out."

"The highest punishment?" Lilah asked. "Death penalty? I'm to be condemned to die simply because my husband refuses to admit he committed fraud? Because his brothers refuse to testify against him?"

"Say something, Brad," Victor begged tearfully. "Tell them she had nothing to do with the deal, CFO or not. They won't be able to do one goddamn thing to her if you just tell the court what happened."

Continued silence was Brad's only response. Alex finally looked away from Godwin, gaze colliding with Lilah's.

Coward, she taunted silently.

A mocking smile played on the prosecutor's face. "Seems none of the Kingsleys care to speak up for you, ma'am. Perhaps *you* should have exercised better judgment in your choice of spouses. You would not have been standing here as a criminal accused of treason."

"Major," the colonel warned. "Avoid personal attacks. I will not ask you a third time to watch your words."

"Brad, say something," Victor pleaded again. "They'll at least let *her* go."

The other sons of Peter Kingsley remained silent, eyes directed downward.

"Not one of them," derided Armor.

"How can Brad and the rest possibly say anything?" Lilah asked. "The Kingsley brothers are worried about repercussions. Even their confessions were obtained under duress. All of it should be considered inadmissible."

"What duress?" asked the major. "I mean... look around. They're in a military court, but Brad Kingsley's grandfather, the former justice, is present. Brigadier General Potts is right here. Anyone from West Point will tell you the general has always been a well-wisher to Alex and his brothers. I'm curious... has there been an interrogation like this in the entire history of the United States where the accused have this much support among the same people in charge of the investigation? If they still refuse to speak up—"

Lilah addressed the presiding colonel. "Sir, I understand this is only an interrogation, not a hearing, but with the court's permission, may I ask Private Prater a few questions?"

Chapter 69

After the marine assigned as guard took a seat, Lilah asked, "Private, where did you first see me?"

"At your company's office in Panama, ma'am."

"You were with the prosecutor when he met up with the SWAT cops, were you not?" Lilah asked.

"Yes, ma'am."

"SWAT cops who are part of the Panamanian police force?"

"Er, yes, ma'am."

Lilah gestured with her hands. "I'm only a civilian lawyer. So tell me, is it usual for the U.S. Army to use foreign police to detain Americans?"

"It depends. In your case, we could have asked for the Delta force, but the SWAT team was easier to arrange."

Lilah arched a disbelieving eyebrow. "*Who* thought it would be easier to use Noriega's police force? Was the person aware President Reagan has been trying to get Noriega on drug charges?"

The private's eyes darted between her and the prosecutor. "I... er... I'm not sure."

The colonel's reprimand was swift. "Mrs. Kingsley, you can't expect him to read minds."

With a gracious nod, she retreated and realigned. "Private, can you describe for this court my interaction with the prosecutor at the Kingsley office and how it ended?"

The young marine swallowed. "I... I..."

Gently, Lilah said, "May I remind you, Private, that you serve the United States and its people, not the prosecutor?"

Prater testified. The speed with which events unfolded and the tension enveloping the Kingsley corporate office that day were clear from his words. He took the court through Lilah's conversation with Armor. "Then..." the young man stopped, grimacing nervously.

"Then what, Private Prater?" demanded the colonel.

"Then, Captain Kingsley slapped her," Prater finished, tone barely audible.

Charles Kingsley stood, his knee bumping the table. Papers scattered on the floor. "She was resisting," he erupted.

"Sit down, Captain Kingsley," ordered the colonel.

"Was I resisting?" Lilah asked, lips curling in mockery. "How? By questioning your authority in arresting us?" She turned to the private and instructed, "Mr. Prater, please detail for the court your observations on the assault."

His eyes fixed on the floor, he said, "Mrs. Kingsley fell. She was bleeding."

"What was the prosecutor's response to this?" Lilah asked. "Did he reprimand his subordinate for use of excessive force?"

"No," the young man whispered. "The major reminded Mrs. Kingsley he was in charge."

The colonel muttered something under his breath. Armor gritted his teeth and stared straight ahead.

"What happened afterward?" Lilah pressed.

"Mr. Kingsley—Mr. Alex Kingsley—protested," said Prater. "He, er, needed to be restrained."

Lilah stretched her lips into a grim smile. "By slamming his face into the wall?"

"He was rightly considered a threat, ma'am," the private insisted.

"Major Armor, we'll have to talk about this," the colonel said. "Private Prater, you will step down."

"Your Honor, I'm not done with him," Lilah said. "May I continue?"

A barely perceptible nod granted permission, and a glare from the colonel nailed the witness to his chair.

"Private," called Lilah. "You were present when I first arrived at the naval base, and you accompanied me to this hall along with Captain Kingsley, did you not?"

"Yes, ma'am." The guard clearly knew what was coming and took a sip of water.

Charles growled.

Tone steady, Lilah said, "Please describe for this court what Captain Kingsley did both times."

The guard recounted the first encounter, the torn shirt. He described the short walk from the cell to the courtroom, Charles's attempt to grope Lilah, her fall, and his fist in her hair, trying to pull her up.

Through her lashes, Lilah took a quick glance around. Shock was evident on the faces of the officers presiding, misery on Aaron Kingsley's. The court-appointed lawyer was gawking at the witness in near horror. Sounds of distress came from behind Lilah—from Alex and his brothers. Everyone else... with varying degrees of anger and frustration, the Kingsleys and their sidekicks glared at Charles. Except Grace Kingsley. Her face swiveled between her criminal child and the family patriarch. She was almost out of her chair, ready to defend her worthless offspring from Godwin's wrath. Let alone offer the assaulted woman a glance of sympathy, Grace didn't as much as exclaim in disbelief Charles could've done this.

Wondering why on earth she ever imagined Grace would feel empathy, Lilah returned her attention to the witness. "What made Captain Kingsley stop his assault?"

The private's cheek twitched in an obvious effort to suppress a grin. "You hit him. I think you broke his nose."

"No, she didn't," Charles yowled in humiliation and fury. "I let her go because we were at the door."

The colonel leaned forward. "Do you mean to say you dragged her by her hair all the way here, Captain Kingsley?" Silence filled the courtroom as Charles looked from the colonel to Lilah and back. Sweating, he turned to his brother and Armor. The prosecutor's hand covered his mouth, and his eyes were closed.

Lilah addressed the colonel again. "Brad Kingsley, my husband, took his cousins and their uncle—Mr. Stanley Gander—at their word. Brad wouldn't have expected Mr. Gander to send cops to our home in Panama. We were all confused and terrified that day. We all saw how the prosecutor and his team demonstrated complete disregard for the laws of the United States. When I dared ask about a warrant, I was subjected to brutal violence. The prosecutor's aide manhandled me in front of my family and employees for the crime of questioning his authority. Finally, when we were brought here, all my family was taken away, and I was alone in the holding cell. When they left, I was tired and somewhat unkempt, but I certainly wasn't splattered with blood. Brad would know something happened in the short time I was alone. How can the prosecuting attorney claim Brad Kingsley is not under duress? As far as Brad knows, if we object, if we resist, we can come to harm. As far as he knows, anything less than complete compliance can mean a death sentence. How is this not duress?"

No response. Just... silence. Lilah looked around. The colonel leaned forward with his elbows on the table. Godwin Kingsley stared unblinkingly at her. Richard Armor, the court-appointed defense lawyer, the assorted Kingsleys... none of them said a word. Seconds ticked by, but a hush continued in the chamber.

Then, there was a muffled sound from behind. Her name was uttered in tones of profound regret—Alex. "With your permission, Colonel?" he asked in a louder voice.

Every eye in the room swung to him. Except for Lilah's. She refused to glance at him, refused to have an iota of faith.

There was the sound of a chair scratching the floor, of a throat being cleared. "She was not involved in the original oil deal," Alex stated.

Once again, there was silence... complete silence except for the whirring of the ceiling fan's blades and a gulp from Victor.

Alex addressed the court, voice growing stronger with conviction, "Brad Kingsley, our CEO, thought he had all the right in the world to treat the business as his personal property. Four of the principal stockholders, the brothers you see here, were informed of the deal, but we did not challenge him. Unfortunately, Brad had no way of spotting the nuclear trafficker. His work in the company always involved the home front where he didn't meet the criminal sort. Out of the six major shareholders in our business, only Lilah, Victor, and I would have been able to identify the nuclear trafficker as such. The three of us made it a point to study the miscreants we might encounter while in the course of our work. Brad never had a need to do the same. He might have asked me or Victor for counsel, but he didn't. We didn't participate in the negotiations or meet any of the people involved. All we were told to do was not say anything to Lilah and sign on the dotted line as though we did discuss it. Brad made it clear to us he *would not* seek consent from the CFO. We were stupid enough to agree. Travel logs and company records of meetings will corroborate what I said. I contest any evidence presented by Major Armor which says otherwise. For our mute compliance with fraud, Lilah Kingsley should take us to court. For our blind obedience to Brad's orders, we—his brothers alone and not Lilah—deserve to be condemned by the nation."

Chapter 70

Victor's sobs stopped Alex's speech. Something flickered to life in Lilah's mind. *Please,* she implored, not knowing exactly who she was addressing.

"Thank God," Aaron Kingsley muttered. The court-appointed lawyer took off his glasses, blinking rapidly as though he couldn't believe his luck. Pushing his chair back, Godwin Kingsley half rose.

Please, Lilah begged again. She didn't have any more tricks up her sleeve. If the court refused to accept Alex's word, the only thing left for her to do would be to somehow survive whatever Godwin's minions had in mind and pray Harry was still alive to do something from the outside. Dan... he'd try. She hoped he wouldn't. Her brother didn't have any part in the mess to deserve the painful death the Kingsleys would surely mete out.

The lead colonel said, "Mrs. Kingsley, it seems your claim to innocence has support."

"Alex," Godwin walked around the table to face his grandson. "You know... remember, your brother..." Misery and guilt writ large on his face, Alex looked toward the colonel, refusing to meet his grandfather's eyes. Smiling gently through fury, the former supreme court justice said, "As I was about to say, Brad's pic—"

Outside, a dog howled, followed immediately by two or three more. "K9 unit," someone said. The animals set up a cacophony of barking.

"Someone shut those creatures up," the colonel said irritably.

Another fatigue-clad fellow marched into the courtroom and whispered in the colonel's ear. At a nod from the officer, the man went to the former justice with a note. The Kingsley patriarch pivoted from Alex in obvious annoyance, snatching the piece of paper.

As Godwin Kingsley scanned the message, blood drained from his face, then rushed back. His eyes swung to Lilah. The panic in his gaze... Godwin's rapid breathing...

Harry? Is it about Harry? There was a roar within Lilah's skull.

In the courtyard, dogs started howling even more loudly... perhaps the time for their meal grew near. The colonel snapped at his clerk, "What *is* with all the noise? This is supposed to be an interrogation."

Godwin said curtly, "If Alex also supports Lilah's claim, we should consider putting a stop to this investigation."

After a moment's confusion, Lilah gaped at Godwin. The rest of the courtroom was also staring wide-eyed at him.

"What?" Steven asked on a yelp.

Brows drawn together, the prosecutor asked the former justice, "I'm sure you don't mean to set her free, sir. They're suspected traitors." Voice tinged with annoyance, the major called the guard. "With the court's permission, I want them back in the cell."

Lilah gathered her thoughts together and pivoted to the prosecutor. "*Mister* Armor, you asked for one witness to confirm I wasn't involved. So he has. Now, let me go. In fact, you need to let all the Kingsley brothers go. Beyond the original oil deal, there is no proof anything illegal has occurred over which the nation needs to intervene. The fraud committed by Brad is the company's internal problem. None of your business."

Armor turned to Godwin. "Sir—"

"No, Major," Godwin said. "My recommendation to the court would be to let them go. Time for this to end."

"Grandfather!" snapped Steven Kingsley.

David walked around the table to stand next to the patriarch. He squinted at the note before turning to his wife. She glanced at the message before whispering something in his ear. There was a moment's stillness from David. Then, blinking rapidly, he spoke to the court, "I... ahh... agree with my father." Without a trace of embarrassment, he added, "It's because I really think my nephews are innocent. Poor boys."

There was a buzz in Lilah's brain. The enemy's acquiescence had been so swift as to be almost comical. Who sent the note? Was it Harry? What was in the message?

The colonel nodded. "I agree, Justice Kingsley. The evidence presented has been weak at best, and I feel the military wasted more than enough money and resources over this farce."

Mutters and exclamations rose. The prosecutor and his team conferred among themselves. Aaron Kingsley's sigh of relief was loud. The court-appointed lawyer strode to Brad and his brothers.

Amid the clamor, Lilah contemplated Godwin. His son David took the note from his father's unresisting fingers and scrunched it up. Lilah's eyes followed David to the garbage can. The wad never went in. She watched him tuck it surreptitiously into his pocket. As Grace and David Kingsley walked out of the room without even a word of regret for the crimes of their sons, Lilah swore, *Someday.* The couple had been in on the plan, cooperated eagerly with Steven's schemes. Until the security of her world was somehow threatened by the note, Grace remained mute.

Lilah shook her head, unable to fathom why Grace's cold selfishness was bothering her so much when they hardly knew each other. Plus, the Kingsley men were the main culprits, not Grace. Her sons, her husband... all would pay dearly for what they tried to do. Grace would also weep, remembering her own complicity was one of the reasons behind her family's downfall.

"Mrs. Kingsley," the colonel called. When Lilah turned, he inclined his head. "I'm sorry. It seems you have suffered unnecessarily." He nodded in Brad's direction. "You, too, Mr. Kingsley." The colonel said to the room, "I do not find any probable cause. Mrs. Kingsley and the Kingsley brothers are free to leave."

Chapter 71

Brad stood. For the first time since Lilah walked into the courtroom, he spoke. "What do we need to do now?"

"Nothing much," the colonel said, gesturing toward one of the clerks on his right. "My staff will get the paperwork ready, and afterward, you'll be free to return home." He warned, "I'm sure you're aware the authorities will be keeping an eye on things. They might buy the excuse of ignorance once, but not another time."

"I understand, sir," said Brad. "It won't happen again. And thank you." Without as much as a word of gratitude to Lilah, without a single glance of contrition, he approached the clerk. Throwing furtive looks toward her, his brothers followed.

"Colonel," she called. "I have a request."

"You've had a rough experience," the colonel said. "Whatever I can do to make it up to you, I will."

"I'd like to wipe the legal slate clean so to speak," she said. "You can absolve us of this crime we were alleged to have committed."

"There were no official charges, so acquittal is not necessary," said the colonel. "I hope you can look beyond the events of today.

The United States military had the defense of our people in mind. Nothing else."

Lilah closed her eyes in desperate disappointment. She already knew there was no chance of an acquittal. After all, they were never tried. But she'd hoped... oh, God, how she'd hoped the brutality of the interrogation would prompt the colonel to close the doors on further investigation. Perhaps some kind of immunity.

She was no longer worried about herself. The prosecution possessed no evidence against her, and while Brad's brothers broke company regulations, their stupidity was not an offense to be prosecuted by the military. But there was one card she hadn't been able to shred: Brad's picture with the nuclear trafficker, from which she managed to sidetrack the courtroom.

Godwin had started to say something about it before the note forced him to back down. Perhaps the failure with the planted evidence and the trouble Armor got into because of Charles caused the prosecutor to forget the photograph for the moment. But it wouldn't be long before he remembered. Could the same note sent to the former justice fend off Armor? If he got Brad arrested a second time... Lilah couldn't take the chance.

Brad was critical to her plans. He was still the CEO of the network she helped create. If not the former president and his stepbrother, there would always be some criminal lured by the promise of almost unlimited power. It was no longer enough to leave Harry as chairman who could exercise control over Brad. The network needed to be destroyed, and she could see no way of making it happen without Brad's presence. If he got arrested, Lilah would've won the battle and lost the war.

Chapter 72

Hurry! Lilah willed the uniformed clerk helping Brad with the paperwork. Every scrape of the chair's legs grated on her nerves when the colonel got to his feet.

If she could spirit Brad away before an arrest happened, they could get temporary legal protections in place. Dan would be back from China, and Harry... she prayed he was alive. Between Gateway and Barrons O & G, she could convince Brad the best way to ward off an arrest would be to start the process of dismantling the network. Once it was gone, there would be no more reason for anyone to attack. They could even try to keep things under the radar... as much as possible, that is.

But once the arrest happened, political support for Brad would drop to zero. With him in military prison... the leadership of the network... there was no way to be certain what the courts would decide.

The colonel and his entourage were on their way out, including Charles and the military clerk who was taking care of the paperwork. With a sigh of relief, Lilah took one step toward the brothers, ready to hustle them out.

Another man approached the brothers—Aaron, their uncle. More delay. Lilah's heart sank.

"Brad," called Godwin. He and General Potts joined the group around Brad.

Was Godwin about to say something to Brad about charging him alone? Perhaps some kind of pressure—emotional or otherwise—which would force him to hand over control? Lilah bit her lip, waiting for the ax to fall.

"I'm so glad, son," the former justice said, a hitch in his voice. "If I knew what Steven was planning... once he told me about the

Iranians, I had no choice. We were lucky the military asked me to be present. Who knows what might have happened, otherwise? My God, what was Steven *thinking?*"

Godwin turned to Alex and drew him into a tight hug.

"So glad," the Kingsley patriarch repeated. Over Alex's shoulder, Godwin's gaze met Lilah's, bone-chilling in its blandness.

The former justice turned, hand gripping the back of a chair when he wobbled. Brad was instantly at his side, arm around his grandfather's shoulders. With a weary smile, Godwin waved away assistance. Brad murmured something, and the patriarch smiled fondly, gesturing at General Potts. Both men left the room with the general solicitously holding Godwin's elbow, neither sparing Steven or Armor a glance. Aaron followed Godwin and the general.

Lilah couldn't believe it. No way Godwin didn't remember the photograph. But he'd disarmed completely. What *was* in that note?

Steven Kingsley was watching the five brothers from his chair, eyes hot with fury. Major Richard Armor sat next to Steven, speculative gaze on Godwin's departing back.

Victor herded his brothers to the door, nodding deferentially at Lilah and signaling her to go along.

When she attempted to follow, Scott suddenly halted. She barely avoided a collision and caught his elbow to steady herself.

"Mrs. Kingsley, maybe you should sit for a couple of minutes," Armor said from the far end of the room. "Let me get you a chair."

She took in the smirk on his face. Before she could decline the offer, Steven ground out to his pal, "What the hell is wrong with you? She just beat the crap out of us *and* got Charlie into trouble. Offering her a chair! The only seat a woman like her deserves is some man's lap. Here..." Steven smacked his left thigh. "Come and sit on mine."

Lilah stilled for a moment. Gritting her teeth, she straightened and turned toward the door, toward escape.

"Someday," growled Victor, facing the criminal duo. "I swear... I'm going to break your damn leg, Steven. I'm not going to die until I do."

"Let's go," Lilah urged, but Victor didn't appear to hear.

"Victor..." chided Armor, laughing. "Steven was merely trying to congratulate Mrs. Kingsley."

"No, I wasn't," snapped Steven.

Armor said, voice now mild, "Nothing wrong with acknowledging the obvious. I thought for sure this would be the end of your cousins. I mean, they were up against the Army Intelligence and Security Command. Unfortunately, we underestimated the woman in their lives."

Ignoring the innuendo, Lilah tugged Victor by the elbow, and he finally obeyed her unspoken instruction.

"Look at him walking away," Steven sneered. "The traitor."

The accusation drew another growl from Victor, and the former boxer pivoted.

Alex murmured, "Later, dude. Let's just get out of here."

Please, Lilah thought. *Let us.*

Scott took one step out the door.

A chair clattered behind them. "Wait a second," Armor called.

The five brothers halted.

She turned to face the prosecutor, her body trembling in the effort to keep her desperation from showing. Other than the Kingsley brothers and Lilah, the only people in the courtroom were Steven and Armor.

"We need to leave," she snapped, voice shaking.

"Oh, not yet." Sauntering to the group, Armor said, "Let me congratulate Brad. Steven, you should, too."

"Why?" Steven asked, joining his friend. "Lilah saved their worthless asses. The boxer and the sniper sniveling behind a woman's skirts. There's a sight I never thought I'd see."

Malice in every word, Armor said, "It's not every day someone gets away with signing dirty deals with Iran."

"The perfect Kingsley grandson," said Steven. "He sold out his country, his employees, even his wife."

"Brad," said Lilah. "Let's go."

"Wait, Mrs. Kingsley," said Armor. "I want to talk to your husband." The prosecutor walked around them in a circle, coming to a stop three feet from Alex. "Isn't it lucky the court didn't consider charging only Brad? I wonder what his brothers would have done. Mrs. Kingsley, too."

Lilah clenched her fists, nails digging into her palms.

"What's that supposed to mean?" barked Victor.

"Just reminding you the contract Brad signed hasn't disappeared into thin air. We have those pictures of him with the nuclear traffickers even if he claims it was a coincidental meeting."

"What say, *Major* Armor?" Steven asked, his eyes glinting in understanding. "Is it enough to have *Brad* undergo a hearing all by himself?"

Armor was clearly relishing the moment. "You're absolutely right. After all, he hasn't been tried and acquitted. The colonel only said the military will be keeping an eye on things going forward, but what if we arrange an Article 32 hearing for the CEO of the Peter Kingsley Company? Without the innocent wife or helpless brothers to confuse the court, the case could go in the government's favor.

There's at least a fifty-fifty chance Brad will face court-martial. Remains to be seen what the rest of the family is willing to do about it."

"What do you want, Major?" asked Brad, sweat once again beading his lip.

Armor said, "You cannot be allowed to hold such a powerful position after creating a national security threat on this large a scale. Mrs. Kingsley and your brothers can leave. You stay to face a hearing."

Brad implored, "Major, I didn't know they were nuclear dealers. The court seems to have accepted the fact. Why can't you?"

Steven responded instead of his friend. "Because even if you genuinely made a mistake in meeting with the Sri Lankan, it means you failed to do due diligence before signing the original oil deal. You have a staff which includes some of the finest minds in the sector, and you neglected to use them. Your wife could have told you all was not right with the Iranian offer, yet you chose to act like an autocrat. You staked the livelihoods of all the people who work for you in one foolish move. You threw away everything your family achieved in one stupid gamble. For what? To prove yourself the master of everything within your reach? You may not be a criminal, but you *are* an incompetent imbecile and should not be allowed anywhere near the network."

Throughout the exchange, Brad's brothers stayed silent, realization dawning on their faces, followed by fear. Neil mumbled something incomprehensible. "What do you propose to do?" Brad asked, smoothing his hair back with a shaky hand.

Here it comes, Lilah thought, flinching.

Armor turned a half-circle toward the back door through which the colonel had left. "I'm going to call the colonel back right now. Unless—"

Jay Perin

"Unless what?" Alex snapped.

Armor continued as though he had not heard Alex. "—unless all of you—including Mrs. Kingsley—pack your bags and leave your home. You can never return to the United States. We'll even give you head start before I approach the court again. Forty-eight hours."

"Why would we do something so ridiculous?" asked Scott, bewildered. "If Brad runs, everyone will assume he's guilty. We will all look guilty."

"Precisely," the major said. "You can either stay and take your chances with Brad's life or run even if the rest of the world ends up thinking he's guilty."

Steven told them, voice gleeful, "*I* would prefer you return to your castle without Brad. Once he undergoes a hearing and court-martial, he'll get death penalty. Right, Rich?"

"Or at least life in prison," Armor said.

Mouth slightly open, Brad gulped. Behind the rounded glasses, his eyes were wide. "I trusted your uncle," he whispered. "It's all I did."

No, Lilah thought bitterly. *You trusted your grandfather. You trusted Temple. You trusted everyone except the one person who was telling you what you needed to hear.*

Victor hissed, "Steven, you're going to die for this."

Alex asked, "Why him, Victor? He's not the brains of this criminal outfit. *Mister* Armor is."

The prosecutor hissed, taking a threatening step toward the former sniper. "You will address me by my rank, *Captain.*" Eye to eye, they glared at each other.

Steven laughed tauntingly. "The only person here who deserves death is Brad. Our offer is generous when you think about what he did. This will give him a chance to escape the noose provided he's

518

not dumb enough to get caught. Are you brothers ready to fall on the sword for the eldest one more time?"

Scott asked, "And turn over control of the network to you?"

Steven raised an eyebrow. "Finally figured it out, did you?" He continued, "Yes. Once Brad runs, the military will immediately decide he is guilty. It will be enough for an Article 32 hearing for him alone. If Brad returns, he will be arrested. If any of the rest tries to return, if you try to regain control of the network from outside, the government will use the breach to track you down. Same result. Brad will hang."

Neither Steven nor Armor said anything about Harry still being chairman. Did they believe he was dead?

Brad and his brothers didn't mention Harry, either. In the brief silence, Lilah heard every hiss, every intake of breath, every angry mutter. In one sweep, she took in the expressions of Brad and his brothers. She saw the shock on their faces, the anger. The fear and the confusion.

"We agree," Brad said.

Steven took half a step back. "You didn't even ask them!"

Brad didn't look at his brothers. "They'll agree. They don't want to see me killed."

They wouldn't. Alex might have spoken up during the interrogation, but he wouldn't dream of tossing Brad to the wolves. None of the brothers would.

Steven's face twisted in loathing. "You selfish son of a bitch. What does your family see in you? What have you done for them? Call yourself the CEO? Your entire business was built by Sheppard and your little brothers. My God, you couldn't even manage to get yourself a wife." He pivoted to the brothers. "The four of you deserve every bit of what happens to you. Even after you saw what he did, you're willing to throw away your lives on the idiot." He flung his hands in the air. "Why am I complaining? Thanks to your stupidity, I can tell the world I won the network fair and square."

"Careful, Steven," Armor warned. "We can't have any ambiguity on this. We need to hear it from *them*. Who knows? They might have other ideas."

"Oh, I don't know," Steven objected, sneering. "Cousin Brad called them his arms and legs, right?"

"It's not the old days anymore," Armor said. "They all have their own lives now. Victor's got his new wife, his son..."

"True," Steven agreed. His tone changed. "Victor's not going to martyr himself, is he? Even if he did *nothing* to stop his brother from walking into the trap. Even if he sat on his hands and allowed Brad to skirt the rules of their own company."

Victor swallowed. Alex glared hard at the enemy, grinding his teeth.

"Victor was not the one photographed with an international criminal," Armor reminded. "He can return to his family and let Brad rot in jail."

"Or hang from a noose," Steven added. "All Victor would need to do is forget the part he played in Brad's death. What do you say, cousin?"

Victor swore. "I'll kill you—"

"Your answer," snapped Steven.

Shoulders bunched and shaking with the effort of holding himself back, Victor said, "I don't have a choice. I'll go with Brad. You just wait. I will break every damn bone in your body for what you did today."

Steven laughed. "Worry about your criminal brother for now. What about the rest of you?"

The twins eyed each other, then Brad. "We should've stopped him," Scott muttered.

"You didn't," Steven said.

Eyes tired, Neil nodded. "We'll go."

"The only one who hasn't said anything is the golden boy," Armor mocked.

Alex's face darkened.

Lilah bit her lip, thoughts ricocheting around her mind. If she refused to help save Brad, he and his brothers would refuse to work with her on any plan to take the network apart. And was she really ready to send a man to his death for his pettiness and insecurities?

Alex still hadn't agreed to Steven's demands. Tut-tutting, Armor said, "The Kingsley golden boy doesn't want to do it."

"Can't blame him," Steven said. "He has a wife and kid, too."

Armor laughed. "It could work out very well for Alex. Brad dead or in prison for life. The CFO ruling the network. Alex could have everything he's always wanted... a wife who's a Sheppard, their son, and the beautiful Mrs. Kingsley on the side."

"He was the only one to break ranks," Steven taunted. "The famed brotherly unity broken over a woman."

"Brad will always have my support," Alex said, nodding reassuringly at his brother. "As Victor said, wait your turn, Armor. You'll answer for what you did today. I'll make sure you do."

Lips pursed, Steven studied Lilah. "What about you?" he asked. "Are *you* going to follow them?"

She ignored the lead weight settling into her chest and shoved away every thought of family and friends, every longing for love and warmth. Brushing back the lock of hair clinging to her sweaty cheek, she said, "You haven't given me another option."

Steven tilted his head slightly to the side. "Oh, you always have options. Work for *me*, instead. The five idiots can leave, and I swear we won't go after Brad as long as he stays away."

Alex spat out a curse. "Don't trust him, Lilah. He wants support from Barrons and Gateway. Believe me, he's not offering out of the kindness of his heart. And remember what Charlie did. He'll try it again. Steven will do nothing to stop it. Son of a bitch offered you his *thigh.*"

"What the hell gives *you* the right to be angry, Captain Kingsley?" Armor asked derisively. "After what Brad did today, even if Mrs. Kingsley chooses to *marry* Steven, no one would blame her."

"Listen, you worthless bastard—" Alex shoved Armor back by his shoulders.

Roaring, Armor swung, only to be blocked by Victor's massive forearm. The three men shuffled back and forth in an awkward tussle.

Lilah made herself laugh, the sound pealing through the room. "Have you forgotten I'm already married to Brad?"

The brawl came to a clumsy stop. Steven said, "The one who forgot about your marriage was your husband. How many chances did he get to tell the court you weren't involved at all? Yet he didn't. Despite this, you're going to accompany him like a dutiful wife. Don't tell me you're doing this for true love! I don't think you're delusional enough to believe it."

"My motives are none of your concern," she told him.

Steven visibly seethed. "True. But I can and will judge you. When the investigation began, I had some qualms about including you. Not any longer. You enabled Brad, propping him up as the CEO. Even now, knowing the kind of man he is, you choose to stick by him. You deserve what you get."

Voice steady, she said, "Perhaps, but I still don't have to explain myself to you. Let's discuss terms."

"You have forty-eight hours to leave," Armor said. "The day after, I'll get the military to start a new Article 32 hearing for Brad. If any of you tries to return, if you try to take control of the network from outside, Brad will be back in front of the military court before you know it."

Steven added, "Before you step out of this room, Rich will write up a brief document for all of you to sign. You'll need to hand over complete control of the Peter Kingsley Company and the network. Transfer of actual stock to me would mean more government involvement than any of us would want under the circumstances. In any case, I don't particularly care about the shares. You can keep all of it, but the voting rights on it and the administrative control will be in my hands. There will be no cash dividends for you... only stock dividends. I don't want you using the money to attack me. The story we put about will be that Lilah advised Brad about the possibility of a hearing, and all of you chose to run. There will be some doubts about why you signed the legal rights over to me, but I'm not bothered by what people think."

"We're going to claim your cousins asked you to take over while they dealt with Brad's troubles," Armor said to Steven. "As far as the world is concerned, you didn't have a clue they were going to run instead of facing the law. Actually, the fact all shares remain in their name will give you protection from accusations."

"Victor and Alex have families to take care of," said Lilah. "There's also Patrice. What do you propose they do without cash dividends?"

"Come off it," Steven said. "As though they thought about their wives and kids when they followed big brother blindly. Besides, no one's going to starve. Alex's wife has her own money, and Victor's son and wife have access to all the millions he made off dismembering Sanders, Incorporated. Aunt Patrice can always come and stay with us. I mean, I have nothing against her. Also, since *you* were so eager to defend them, you can support the whole lot with your Barrons stock. Cash dividends! What kind of a fool do you think I am? You would use the money to attack me. No way it's going to happen."

"Fine," said Lilah. "I have one condition. The day the arrest warrant is recalled, we get the rights to our stock back."

"What?" exclaimed Richard Armor. "Steven, no. There's no guarantee the warrant *won't* be recalled."

Steven raised a hand, asking his friend for silence. "Lilah, unlike your precious husband, I'm not stupid. What makes you think I'll agree?"

She smiled faintly. "You're going to. Or you'll leave Harry with nothing to lose."

The expression of mild amusement was wiped clean from Steven's face. "Sheppard?" Steven exclaimed. "He's—"

Armor's hand shot out and pulled his friend back by the shoulder, stopping him from inadvertently disclosing their assumption Harry was dead. In the few seconds following, the major eyed the woman defiantly facing down her enemies and turned his head to look at the exit Godwin used. Lilah could almost tell the exact moment when Armor grasped her train of thought. There was a good chance the note which stopped Godwin came from Harry. Whatever message it carried, Harry was the one most likely to have sent it. Lilah had no other supporters... at least no one with enough power to force Godwin's surrender.

Armor dragged Steven to the back of the room. Indistinct murmurs and angry exclamations floated over as the two men conferred. Victor was straining to hear, but Lilah didn't bother. She already knew what the major was telling his friend.

The most lethal of all enemies was one with nothing left to lose. The power of the network lost forever to a criminal like Steven... no matter the cost to him, Harry would immediately switch to a scorched-earth policy, destroying the Kingsleys and the network with them. Unless of course he saw some hope of it eventually returning to Lilah. Steven didn't have a choice except to accede to Lilah's demand that he relinquish the throne once the arrest warrant was withdrawn. It was the only way to save himself from Harry's wrath.

If Steven wanted to keep his ill-gotten power, he would need to kill the exiles before the warrant could be recalled. And he'd never dare attempt another hit on them without first making sure Harry died. Lilah might have bought herself a chance, but she had also drawn a giant target on Harry's back.

Part XXI

Chapter 73

Before dawn

On board the USS Dwight D. Eisenhower

Two terror-filled nights passed in Cerro Azul, with Harry contacting the CIA, contacting everyone he could think of, but not a single person would admit to knowing what happened to Lilah. Then, Noah Andersen called Grayson Sheppard, informing him the former president managed to locate her through his connections.

Within minutes of the conversation, a terse message arrived from Southcom. Harry was to stay away from Gitmo. No explanations, no nothing. Just stay away or else. He was preparing to go rogue when Temple called in some favors to make arrangements with the captain of the closest aircraft carrier. Harry didn't trust Temple, but the politician still possessed enough clout to get the military to change its mind and let Harry into the naval base. So they were forced to tolerate each other's company while on this mission.

Harry followed the captain down the red-lit passage of the aircraft carrier, barely holding himself back from strangling Temple and Noah Andersen. The secret service officers—two in front and two behind—would've had something to say.

"The only thing predictable about North Atlantic weather is that it's unpredictable," the captain said, nodding at the crew members jogging along the cramped passageway. "This way, Mr. Temple." He gestured the former president and his companions toward the exit.

The moon was only partly visible, and dark clouds masked the stars. The vast flight deck was lit yellow, seamen in color-coded shirts swarming the place. Unmindful of the chill in the air, the sailors moved synchronously, checking the planes, wheeling them, readying them for assignments. The shouts of the crew and the crackling of radios mingled with the low-pitched hum of the ocean waves. To Harry's right, steam puffed out from one of the catapults which had just launched an aircraft on a humanitarian mission to Nicaragua.

Their group stopped next to a helicopter. "Petty Officer Sheppard," the captain called. "The Seahawk was deployed only after you left the service. How familiar are you with her systems?"

"I've been on test flights," Harry said.

"One pilot is all I can spare," the captain warned. "You'll be the co-pilot." If it were not for the direct order from the chief of naval operations, the captain might have refused the unusual request from the former commander in chief for transportation to Guantanamo Bay. Regardless, the captain was too well trained to betray curiosity.

Harry tossed inflatable vests at Temple and Noah Andersen. The older men were helped into the aircraft by the president's security detail.

"Thank you," Temple said, settling in. He waited until the pilot left to run a final check on the controls and the secret service officers were belted into their own seats. Pulling his vest on, Temple muttered, "I swear to you, Harry. I had no idea Godwin was going to do this."

Harry didn't trust himself to speak.

"Believe him, son," said Andersen, voice urgent. "We've been trying to corner Godwin on what happened at the board meeting, but he kept avoiding us. Temple and I were planning to talk to you and Lilah once you were out of the hospital."

"Helmets on, please," Harry said.

"Grayson called me after he talked to you," Temple said. "It was the first I heard of the situation. I sent a message to Godwin... let's see... I hope it got to him on time. I wish... if Lilah had mentioned something to me..."

Harry asked coldly, "What kind of an idiot do you think I am?" At the growl from Andersen, Harry added, "Forgive me, sir. Your concern for Lilah is touching, though... how shall I put it? Phony."

Temple said, "Can it, Harry. I'm trying to help here."

"I don't have another option worth a damn," Harry snarled. "Do I?"

Andersen said, "Hear him out, son. People do make mistakes."

Harry smiled unpleasantly. "Right now, I'm prepared to take help from the devil himself. Why wouldn't I hear you out?"

"Gloves off, huh?" The former president returned the smile with equal nastiness. "I suppose I deserve it, but take a look in the mirror. Your hands are as dirty as mine in what happened to her."

Andersen cinched the harness. "First, let's get them out. We'll figure out who's more at fault later."

In two more minutes, Harry was in the co-pilot's seat. "Prepare for takeoff—lean forward into the harness, chin to your chest, arms crossed," he instructed.

#

Later the same day

Destroy! screamed the voices in Harry's mind as the officer explained what happened at the naval base.

"Colonel," growled Temple. "How could the military let something like this happen? They were *civilians!*"

"I'm sorry, sir," said the officer. "It was only an interrogation."

"Only an interrogation?" shouted the former president. "How can you say so with a straight face? A woman was beaten up in front of her family, sexually assaulted while in custody, and dragged to the courtroom by her hair!"

"The army has initiated proceedings against Captain Charles Kingsley, Mr. Temple. Major Armor will be officially reprimanded. Beyond the sanctions, what can we do? We have already offered Mrs. Kingsley our apologies."

A knife twisted in Harry's chest, throwing his spirit back into the church in Libya where he and Lilah had hidden from the rapist. Harry held her through the long darkness, shed tears when she stared dry-eyed into nothingness, vowed vengeance on her behalf when she stayed silent. Yesterday, Lilah had been alone in the middle of a crowd. She battled the enemy on her own and won, but the people who should've helped her didn't, not even her husband.

Not Harry, either. He closed his eyes in guilt and misery.

Noah was perusing the report. "Says here her clothes were blood-stained when she got to the base. How badly did the bastards hurt her?"

An animal snarl escaped Harry's lips.

Flicking him a wary glance, the colonel said, "Probably not all from the injuries. She was... er... on her period, I believe."

"What?" snapped Temple.

The colonel grimaced. "The troops escorting them to Cuba said it was hard to miss. Unfortunately, she had to be—they *all* had to be—handcuffed for the trip, so there was no... er... privacy. There wasn't anything on hand to help her, anyway. Not even pain medicines, and I'm told she kept asking for some."

Holding a hand to his forehead, Temple asked, "You didn't let her clean up; you didn't give her anything for pain. Even murderers are treated better. What the hell were you thinking?"

Tone affronted, the colonel said, "*I* wasn't aware of it, sir. The decision was made by Major Armor."

Richard Armor, Harry murmured. The lawyer had mocked Lilah, finding amusement in her agony. He laughed and cheered while she was assaulted.

Andersen asked, "Isn't Major Armor a JAG Corps lawyer? How could he have allowed it?"

Regretfully nodding, the colonel said, "I agree... Armor should've known better. The United States Army will not let the major go unpunished." He looked toward the door, his relief palpable. "There is Mr. Aaron Kingsley."

Aaron nodded at the colonel and walked in. "I was talking to Brad when we heard you were on your way. They... uhh... couldn't wait, so I thought I would. We knew you'd want all the details."

#

Half hour later

Aaron's words wouldn't stop ricocheting around in Harry's mind. Lilah had to leave, to go into hiding.

"An exile," whispered Temple, walking with the rest to the waiting helicopter. "My God."

Aaron took a quick peek around. "The military doesn't know. Armor said they'll press charges once Brad and the rest leave."

Before the documents handing over power could be signed the previous evening, Private Prater arrived to let the Kingsley brothers know the military helicopter carrying the family back to Panama would arrive in a few hours. There was an offer of rooms in the staff quarters until then. As requested, the private waited outside the door while everyone concerned signed at the bottom of Armor's handwritten document. Aaron learned of the new developments later when he visited Brad. They were still talking when news of the former president's impending arrival reached the base, but the helicopter to return the Kingsleys to Panama showed up before Temple did. Brad and his brothers didn't dare wait even a minute and risk catastrophe.

"Of all the things!" Andersen exclaimed. "Brad just... I can't believe... he just let his brothers sacrifice themselves like this? Lilah... my God... how could he do this to her?"

"The deal says they'll get the rights back if the warrant is withdrawn," Aaron said, his voice hopeful. "We can arrange a presidential pardon for Brad, right?"

"For treason?" asked Andersen. "And after betraying the nation to *Iran?*"

"He didn't," Aaron cried, throwing his hands in the air.

"His intentions are beside the point," Andersen said. "No president will touch it with a ten-foot pole. The optics will be pure poison to even the best of politicians."

"What are our options?" asked Aaron.

Voice grim, the former attorney general said, "None at the moment. All they can do is leave as soon as possible and stay a step ahead of the authorities."

Aaron groaned. "And of Steven and company. I'm sure they're going to do their best to make sure the enemy never returns. Not Brad, not his brothers, not Lilah."

Abruptly, Harry asked, "Where are they now?"

"In Panama," Aaron said. "They have until tomorrow evening."

Less than thirty-six hours. "I've got to get there," Harry said, running to the chopper.

Chapter 74

A few hours later

Cerro Azul, Panama

Parking the vehicle outside Brad Kingsley's wing, Harry strode in, leaving Aaron and the secret service officers fussing around Temple and Andersen. There were people milling about, employees, perhaps. They scurried out of Harry's way. Grayson Sheppard said something before moving on to greet someone else, but Harry didn't hear any of the words.

Across the hall, he spotted Sabrina and her son. She didn't see him, but Michael's eyes widened. The boy's mouth opened, but no sounds came out. He tugged at his mother's arm, pointing silently.

"Harry," she called and came running, Michael stumbling behind.

"Where are they?" Harry asked.

"Alex is in there," she said, gesturing at the living room. "Harry, they have to—" Eyes puffy and red-rimmed, she swallowed.

"I know."

Marching to the living room, Harry homed in on Brad Kingsley. With a weak smile, Brad stood from the couch, hand outstretched.

Harry advanced with a roar, ready to squeeze the life out of Lilah's husband. A dark, disheveled form landed on him, blocking his view of Brad—Alex. Harry flung his brother-in-law aside.

"Get out of here, Brad," bellowed Alex, impeding Harry's way a second time. "Listen, Harry, please listen."

Shoving Alex to the carpet, Harry continued closing in on Brad.

"Victor," Alex yelled. "Get Brad *out of here.*" Alex scrambled up. Tossing aside a fallen chair, he slammed into Harry in a tackle.

They fell, Harry's head crashing into the side table. Something shattered. People screamed. Victor hustled his brothers out of the room.

Harry thrust his elbow back, hitting bone. Alex grunted; his hold loosened. Breaking free, Harry heaved Alex to the side and prepared to pound him to pulp. Alex kept his hands at his sides, not fighting back.

Patrice and Sabrina were tugging at Harry, imploring him to stop. "Harry, please," screamed Sabrina, "he's my husband."

"Hear me out, dude," Alex said. "Please... we didn't know."

"I asked you to do what *I* would for her," thundered Harry. "There was supposed to be no difference between you and me."

Alex fell silent, almost sinking into himself. Around them, the women continued to cry. Grayson Sheppard spoke in soothing tones to the agitated employees.

A sniffle broke through the tumult in the room. At the periphery of his vision, Harry saw Michael. The boy was staring at the scene, eyes dry, face strangely devoid of expression. He was mute except for the single sob that escaped his chest.

Taking a deep breath, Harry unclenched his fist. Moving away from Alex, Harry said to his nephew, "We'll make things all right, buddy. I promise."

Closing his eyes, Alex murmured, "I'm so *damn* sorry... it was a mistake... can't tell you how sorry..."

Harry ignored Alex and gestured at Michael. "Come over here."

The boy took two steps toward them and stood rigid as his father sat up, gathering him into a loose embrace.

"Your daddy will be back soon," swore Harry. "We'll see to it, won't we, Mike?"

After a second's hesitation, the boy nodded.

"Thank you," said Alex. "And I'll make up for everything... somehow."

#

In two minutes, Harry stood at the door to Lilah's home office. The need to take her in his arms was overwhelming. He wanted to spirit her away from the world. Far, far away.

She was on the couch, gaze resolutely pinned on the white orchids stuffed into the vase on the side table, studying them as though her next move depended on the flowers. A hot-water bottle lay discarded on the floor. Freshly washed hair clung to her scalp, dark ringlets caressing her ears.

Temple was seated next to her, Andersen and Aaron Kingsley in chairs. Lilah's brothers were leaning against her desk. Dan's face was a picture of helpless misery, and Shawn kept wary eyes on the confrontation going on between Lilah and the former president.

"Hear me out, Lilah," pleaded Temple. "No one told me what was going on. By the time I got wind of it, things had gone too far. I never meant this to happen."

Laughter—soft and bitter—escaped her lips. "Trying to have it both ways? As always, a politician."

"Lilah," chided Aaron.

Eyes softening, Lilah said, "I didn't thank you, Aaron."

"I didn't do anything," Aaron said, tone embarrassed. "I wish I could've. No one said anything to me, not even you, Lilah."

"I'd assumed..." she said. "Godwin's your father... you're close to Mr. Temple... I didn't know you weren't involved. Even if I did say something, would you have believed me?"

Aaron flushed. "Probably not. The first I heard anything was going on was when Steven hustled me into a helicopter with Father and brought me to Cuba. I wasn't needed, so I assume they were making sure I didn't get a chance to contact Mr. Temple."

"There *was* nothing you could've done," Lilah said gently. "But it's good to know there's at least one person in the family who doesn't want us dead. Just the fact you were present helped."

Temple paid no attention to the side conversation. "I swear I didn't expect Godwin to go after you. I had asked him not to."

She raised an eyebrow in mockery. "Oh? You mean to say you didn't deliberately arrange things so Brad would be the one I married? That you never attempted to have Harry killed? What you did in Argentina..."

Tone stoic, Temple quoted from the Bible, "'For unto whomsoever much is given, of him shall be much required.' You were blessed with many gifts, and humanity expected you to use those gifts. Harry was a SEAL. He pledged his life to the service of this country and its people even if it meant sacrificing himself. This, too, was a mission he was asked to complete. We did our best to avoid harming him in the beginning. When neither of you would concede, I thought, 'one man for a nation.'" Swallowing, the former president added, "'One tribe for the world.' Still, I never expected almost the entire village to... the calculation was we'd be able to keep causalities to a minimum. What occurred was not totally intentional, Lilah. It was a confluence of happenings no one saw coming. What's more, I never expected Godwin would unleash Steven on *you*."

"You believe I'm naïve enough to buy that," said Lilah. "Why does it matter, anyway? One man, one tribe, one woman. My name is simply the latest in the list of roadkills." Wincing slightly, she stood from the couch and walked to her brothers. "Suspected terrorists, huh?" she asked playfully. The fear on Dan's face didn't lessen an iota at her teasing. "I could have told the Belgians you're too darned fussy to be one, Dan. Shawn would have worried more about his necklace than his mission."

She didn't even glance toward the door where Harry and Sabrina stood. No one did. Temple went on trying to convince Lilah. "It matters because motive matters. All I wanted was someone reliable at the helm."

"Congratulations, then," she said, still with her back to the president. "Most people consider Godwin reliable."

Temple shook his head, expression profoundly regretful. "No. You sacrificed for a greater cause. What happened in Cuba was about power. Personal ambition at any cost. Moreover, the Kingsleys used *me* to get there. They abused the trust people placed in me to do what was good for the nation to the best of my ability. I swore an oath—"

Lilah pivoted. Spitting fury, she said, "Yes, you swore an oath. Where in the oath is it written power must be consolidated? Harry dreams of a world of peace and tranquility where a benevolent and capable few hold the reins, freeing the *hoi polloi* of their responsibilities. You claim to want the same. You both want to create this perfect world, this utopia where no criminals exist, nothing bad ever happens. Utopia is dangerous because it confers the illusion of omnipotence on those in power. Even under the best of circumstances, they become convinced of their own God-like superiority, and they take away the right of ordinary men and women to self-government. What was meant to be for the benefit of the common man results in him losing the right to his own choices, his own mistakes, his own ingenuity, his own growth. He loses his freedom. In some cases, his life. All for the greater good... it's what you and Harry insisted you wanted. When the circumstances are less than ideal... power corrupts, and the ruler becomes an unashamed tyrant. Like Sanders who didn't think twice before ordering an explosion in an oil refinery, which he *knew* would kill the children in the school next door. Like any number of despots around the world to whom millions of deaths are simply statistics."

"Brad wasn't—" Andersen started.

"Brad?" Lilah took a deep breath. "Your hand-picked emperor... he believed the livelihoods of his employees and the freedom of his family were his to wager on a dice roll. He completely lost sight of the fact that power is duty. Once the person—the CEO, the president, the king, or whoever—forgets his duty, the moment he starts ignoring his responsibilities, he should no longer have the power to command. Unfortunately, human nature makes it the nearly inevitable evolution of any empire, and the legal system makes it easy for rulers like Brad to continue in place. No, he didn't *intend* to do anything criminal, but how long before he got there? The existence of the network means what he did do will have far-reaching consequences, much more extensive than if he controlled a single company. Who knows how many businesses will fall, how many jobs will be lost, how many economies will crash, how many people will starve to death? That horrible power is now in the hands of actual criminals like Godwin and Steven. Thanks to *you*, Mr. Temple."

And thanks to Harry. He'd persuaded himself the puny safeguards were enough to deter would-be usurpers. He never imagined trouble would come from within. He swatted away every doubt which crept in about the massive reach of the empire, soothed by his belief Lilah and the network were safe with the Kingsley brothers. Guilt kept Harry's feet rooted at the door, his tongue mute. At his side, Sabrina was also silent.

Andersen tried again, "Lilah, we never expected—"

Ignoring him, she continued ripping into Temple. "Your duties as the president were to protect the nation and the people, to punish the criminals and reward the honest, to tax justly, and to be fair to all. But you thought you knew better than the citizens you served to the point you regarded them as pawns in your chess game. How is what you did any less harmful than what Sanders did? Or what Godwin and Steven did? Or what Brad did?"

For the third time, Andersen tried to intervene. "It was a mistake—"

Grimly, she said, "Brad's using the same excuse. It's been a day since we left that courtroom, and he still hasn't admitted to doing anything wrong. He claims his only mistake was trusting Steven's uncle. He is totally convinced his hands are otherwise clean. All these mistakes have cost us our freedom, our lives as we know them. Sons will now grow up without fathers. Wives will be separated from husbands. Your doing, Mr. Temple. Yours, Brad's, and Harry's. Each death which results from this saga can be laid at your feet."

The words drove a heavy fist into Harry's gut. At his side, Sabrina mewled before pivoting and leaving.

The former president spotted Harry at the door and nodded. "Ah, Harry... good. I need to talk to Brad. It will be difficult to get him and the rest to believe Godwin orchestrated everything... almost impossible. Godwin's always been shrewd. He left enough room for doubt in the military court." Temple shook his head. "It doesn't matter... we can't let the Kingsleys get away with this. Power-mad people *cannot* be left in charge of the network." Escorted by Andersen and Aaron Kingsley, Temple departed.

Shawn persuaded Lilah to the couch. "You haven't gotten any rest in a couple of days. At least sit for a while." He gestured at his brother. "Dan, let's go. Gray is waiting to talk to us about some financial arrangements."

Dan shoved off from the table he was leaning against. "We'll be back in fifteen, twenty minutes." With obvious reluctance, he followed Shawn out.

#

As soon as they disappeared, Harry strode to Lilah and went down on one knee. With a hand to her chin, he turned her face to the side. Her large, hazel eyes were red-rimmed but as fiercely bright as always. The broken skin on her cheekbone looked purplish and tender.

A beast roared inside him, threatening to tear limb from limb the men who did this to her. Throat painfully tight, Harry vowed, "They will pay. Every one of them."

Lilah laughed tremulously. "*Who* will pay, Harry? Small men like Steven and Armor who find it easy to attack someone they think cannot retaliate? Or the Kingsley brothers who placed their loyalty to Brad above their integrity? Or are you talking about Brad? Who are *you* to promise me vengeance on my husband?" With both her hands, she moved the fingers holding her chin to her lap. "Or perhaps you're talking about yourself."

Stricken, Harry said, "Lilah, I..."

Her thumb stroked the inside of his wrist, the gentle touch making her words more brutal in their honesty. "Why should *you* have to pay? The world is now in the hands of a powerful few. Granted, not quite the agent you had in mind to hold the reins, but why should it matter? Steven is just as competent, I'm certain. I'm sure he's equally willing to provide security to the oil companies, both big and small, and even to Gateway, given his affection for Hector. You know, Steven might've asked me to give him a lap dance, but he also offered marriage. It would've bought him support from Barrons and you. Passed from one Kingsley man to the other. Why should it matter to me, right? Why should *I* matter? So many others didn't."

"You do matter," Harry swore. "There's nothing in the world I wouldn't..." The heavens could fall, and the earth could splinter, but her happiness would still be more precious to him. Desperately, he called, "Habibti..."

"Don't you dare," Lilah whispered, flinging his hand from her lap. "You never meant it," she accused.

He shook his head in denial.

"Forget love, you didn't show even compassion for me," she insisted. "Or for yourself. What happened over last week was simply an extension of the sacrifice you demanded. So why would you want to make *anyone* pay?"

"I thought you'd be happy," Harry tried to explain, words feverishly tumbling over each other. "Not with me, but happy." Heaving himself next to her on the couch, he cupped her cheek. With shaking fingers, he soothed the skin under her bruise. "I will do anything to fix... gimme a chance, please... I swear I will make things right."

"Will you?" she asked. "And what about the others who're going to suffer because of what happened? Who will fix things for them?"

Others... there were so many others... flesh-and-blood beings whose lovers would shed tears for them. Parents, siblings, children grieved for the ones whose lives were cut short because of Harry.

His hand slipped from her cheek, and she caught it, once again holding it between cool palms. "This network should never have existed," Lilah continued. "Look at it now! It's a monster! And Brad..."

"Everyone said he's..." Memories, signs of trouble which went ignored, guilt... Harry couldn't think.

"A good man?" Lilah asked. "Someone who believed everything he said about wanting to run an ethical company? Of course he was good. Of course he meant every word of what he said. He will also give you plenty of excuses for what happened in

Cuba. I'm sure even Sanders didn't think of himself as a tyrant. I'm sure *he* found a way to justify everything he did... at least to himself. So what's the difference between him and Brad?"

"I never saw him coming," Harry said.

"Yeah, you swore over and over you'd never turn into Sanders. *I* was too busy worrying about Temple and Godwin. I was aware of Brad's problems, but I never saw this coming, either. He turned into his own version of Sanders. No, Brad never killed anyone, but it got to the point he was willing to see me killed. How long would it have been before he ordered a death to suit his purposes? Perhaps even mine?"

"The pre-nup," Harry said. "I thought it would... the changes you made to the power structure..."

"The pre-nup!" Lilah laughed bitterly. "Brad was so far gone in his insecurities, so *drunk* with power, he ignored everything our agreement gave me... my title, my voting rights, the corporate bylaws, everything. His brothers went along with what he did. Not one saw anything wrong with the behavior. Think of all the lives they wrecked with the foolish gamble. Not just those of the immediate family... our employees, our affiliates... what about those who will inevitably run afoul of Steven and company? We did this, Harry. We got rid of Sanders and ended up creating another tyranny. It's the inevitable end of any empire. Doesn't matter who's at the top."

"I get it now. The network was a bad idea." Lilah had voiced her doubts over and over, but Harry dismissed it all. He'd been wrong... so wrong. She'd had to bleed to show him how wrong.

"My God, *Steven* is in charge now! He is a *criminal.* So is Godwin. They, Brad, his brothers... I was treated like a... if they could do what they did to *me* with all my connections and power, what do you think will happen to the average Joe who goes up against them? The small business owner who dares to say no? The employee living paycheck to paycheck who dares to ask for a raise? To those who're mere pawns in the minds of their rulers?"

"We'll break up the network," Harry said, his body shaking.

"How?" she asked bluntly. "Godwin and Steven have complete control over it. The regular members... once you taste that kind of bargaining power, it's hard to let go. You're still the chairman, but they will eventually vote you out."

"I don't know... somehow..." If Harry needed to move mountains to make it happen, he would.

"It won't be easy," Lilah warned. "The one way out I see is through Brad. He will need a presidential pardon. Once he gets the network back, I want to dismantle it. The remaining control structure should function only in advisory capacity to democratically elected representatives of the people. It should have zero power to enforce."

"We won't be able to work through Brad. Even if he's allowed to return as the CEO, he ain't gonna take advice from an ex-wife to—" A flicker of something in her eyes... a hesitation... shock erupted in Harry's mind. *"You're staying with him?"*

"I don't have a choice. If I leave, he definitely won't cooperate. Do you think any of his brothers will? Even Alex? No, Harry. If I stay with Brad and go on the exile with him..." She detailed her plan... a pardon... an inevitable war. "...I want Brad desperate enough to agree to anything," Lilah finished.

How coldly logical she sounded. How could she when everything was falling apart? "Please, Lilah. Don't go. I'll make it up to you... everything I did... please give me another chance."

For a few moments, she simply looked at him, a hint of moisture on her blue-black lashes. "Then what?" she asked. "Leave the Kingsleys in charge of the entire oil sector?"

"We'll find a way," Harry promised.

"There *is* no way except through Brad."

"If you go..." Harry challenged frantically. "We can't tell how long things will take. Your life... my God! You could be on the run for years!"

"I'm hardly a victim of circumstances." Lilah laughed, mocking him and herself. "My destiny is the consequence of the choices I made, good and bad. Yes, Brad is responsible for what he did, but *I* put him in that position... within reach of enormous temptation. You, too, Harry. For what we did, we owe it to the nation—to the rest of the world—to try and stop the Kingsleys."

"Habibti, I..." Harry choked. "Please."

"You bought Temple's arguments about the network, and I didn't take any of the chances I got to call a halt to it." She waved her hand in the general direction of the room. "What happened was as much our fault as anyone else's. How can we move on? Every time Steven does something horrible, I'll think about my role in it. Harry, can you tell me you won't torture yourself with the same thought every moment of every day?"

The conscience, which already held his chest in an iron grip, squeezed hard. The guilt would only increase in pressure, eventually crushing him—and her.

"I kept telling myself Sanders's fall could not be allowed to create a power vacuum," continued Lilah. "Yes, there was a void, but we should've treated it as a short-term problem. Instead of the network, a very basic control structure would need to monitor the activities of member companies and make recommendations to governments. No more briberies masquerading as political donations. No back-and-forth movement between public and private sectors. Pollution laws need to be obeyed. So on and so forth. Eventually, new extracting technologies will become cheaper, and the U.S. might even become energy independent. The alternate sources of power you're always talking about... those, too. Free market needs to work the way it was intended but within the law and without centralizing decision-making to give a single individual or even a small group of people the power to bring down the whole world."

Harry looked at every feature of her familiar face, now steely with composure. She'd thought this through. She'd made up her mind and wouldn't relent. And she was right. Neither of them could truly move on without fixing the mistake—*his* mistake.

"There will be chaos," continued Lilah. "It happens in a genuinely free society. But out of that chaos will come creation, destruction, creation, again. It's the story of the universe itself."

"Is there no way to do it without—" he asked again, even knowing there wasn't.

Lilah held his gaze without blinking. "Tell me, Harry... would you desert your crew? Would you leave some victim somewhere to fend for himself?"

"No! I'm a SEAL—"

"You asked me to take on the responsibility for this network. You asked me to live for this cause. The moment I accepted the position and the power which came with it, I became bound by my promises. No matter how painful our war turns out to be, I cannot quit. I must see it through. *We* must see it through."

Chapter 75

Same evening

La Miel, Panama

Ignoring the buzzing mosquitoes in the clearing by the dense forest, Harry exchanged sweaty handshakes with each of the brothers, bidding goodbye.

The Kingsleys had asked one final favor of him before they left on their exile. They didn't dare hire an outsider to fly them to the Panama-Colombia border when there was a chance the enemy could track them through the pilot. Without filing a flight plan, Harry brought them to this place from where it was a short walk to the village of La Miel and the border crossing. But even *he* wasn't informed of their eventual hideout.

Once the network's executives disappeared, the government would go after every one of their friends and relatives to track them down. It was best no one knew.

Until they found a way to arrange a pardon for Brad, this would be the last time Harry saw any of them. This shadowed evening would be his last memory of Lilah, this image of her standing at the back of the group next to the helicopter.

"I'm worried," mumbled Brad. "Steven will definitely argue against us returning. Grandfather might be forced to go along because of Kingsley Corp exactly like it happened in court."

Harry managed to nod, reminding himself this petty schmuck who'd been willing to see his wife assaulted and put to death rather than admit he was wrong was crucial to their plans. "Whatever Steven does, it won't be long before you're back home. We'll make sure of it."

"I know I don't have to ask," Alex said, "but take care of Sabrina, please. And Mike."

Wrapping an arm around his brother-in-law's shoulder, Harry gave a silent promise with a couple of thumps.

"And watch your own back, Harry," said Alex. "Steven... he's gonna try to..."

"Yeah," said Harry. "Until the damn warrant is withdrawn, none of us can afford to relax."

"I swear," Alex continued, lowering his tone to a mutter. "Nothing will happen to Lilah as long as I'm alive. I know I haven't given you any reason to trust me, but you can."

"I do trust you," Harry said, letting go. "As far as mistakes go, mine were a lot bigger."

Finally, it was Lilah's turn. Like the men, she had on sneakers, cargo pants, and a long-sleeved shirt. Her hair was tied in a bun and tucked under a cap. The sky was fast turning into a deep purple, but there was enough light left for him to see the rivulet of sweat running down her cheek. He was looking his fill of her, but she had her eyes fixed on some faraway spot.

"Lilah?" Harry called, struggling to keep his tone even.

She glanced up, abject misery in her gaze.

"See you soon?" he asked. He begged in silence for a thread of hope to cling to.

"Soon," she agreed.

THE END of Book 3

For a sneak peek at the next book in the series, please head over to www.JayPerin.com

Want to know what happens next to Harry, Lilah, and Alex? Order *The Beijing Blunder* today to continue with this exciting tale!

Afterword

As mentioned in the afterword to *The Manhattan Swindle,* the One Hundred Years of War series is an adaptation of the *Mahabharata,* the Indian epic mythology.

A few comments (some are repeats from prior books):

1. My thanks to the writers whose works on *Mahabharata* I've enjoyed and learned from and to fellow myth enthusiasts from various discussion groups. Thanks to my friends who have patiently sat through my arguments on various plot points, especially Amrita Talukdar and Preeti Gopal.

2. For the purpose of this story, Temple was president from 1979 to 1986. Reagan-Bush (take your pick) from 1986 to 1992. Yes, I realize that doesn't make it eight years, but it can't be helped because I want to end the story the year I want it to end, so Temple's presidency had to come at this time. Also, I didn't want Temple identified with either a real president or with one of the political parties. Right now, he straddles Carter (D) and Reagan (R) administrations.

3. I did not use real characters except peripherally. That, too, only for things they were actually accused/guilty of doing. For example, Gaddafi did nationalize a lot of oil operations. Noriega is mentioned; he was imprisoned for drug trade and was supposed to have worked with Pablo Escobar.

4. I tried to stick to historical facts throughout the story, including the minor details, but some changes were inevitable.

5.   Citations for the maps of Asia/India are in footnotes.

6.   Article 32 of the UCM hearing in the military is similar to a preliminary hearing in civilian law. As I understand it, the exact procedure to be followed is not described in the Uniform Code of Military Justice or the *Manual for Court(s)-Martial.* Except for some rules of privilege, interrogation, and the rape-shield law, the military rules of evidence do not apply at an Article 32 hearing. This has allowed me some room to maneuver. This information is from that font of all knowledge, Wikipedia (via Google), and cannot be taken as gospel truth. And hey, if it isn't exact, this is just a story.

7.   From the supreme court ruling mentioned by Major Armor (*Ex parte* Quirin, 1942): 'The spy who secretly and without uniform passes the military lines of a belligerent in time of war, seeking to gather military information and communicate it to the enemy, or an enemy combatant who without uniform comes secretly through the lines for the purpose of waging war by destruction of life or property, are familiar examples of belligerents who are generally deemed not to be entitled to the status of prisoners of war, but to be offenders against the law of war subject to trial and punishment by military tribunals.' It's a stretch, but the Kingsleys, as military contractors, can be considered unlawful combatants for the crime they're alleged to have committed.

So that's it. See you again when *The Beijing Blunder* releases.

Sincerely,

Jay Perin

P.S. As always, if you liked the story, do tell others about it. Also, writers thrive on reviews. They help us figure out what worked and what fell flat. They help other readers make up their minds. Please do leave a comment on any of the sites.

Visit www.EastRiverBooks.com for a bunch of interesting stuff.

Made in the USA
Monee, IL
25 June 2022

98619782R00329